THE WITCH AND THE RECKONING

BOOK 3

Laura Detering

ISBN: 978-1-7351404-5-2 (ebook)
ISBN: 978-1-7351404-4-5 (paperback)
LCCN: 2022907486

Interior Formatting: Evenstar Books
Book cover Designer: Moor Books Design
Line and Copy Editor: Erin Darling
Proof Edits: Caitlin Miller

First printing edition 2023.

Visit the author's website at lauradetering.com

For Ang
You Know Why

To My Readers
I hope that I have done justice to the conclusion of this story.

Contents

Acknowledgments

About the Author

Pronunciation Guide

Abishai: *Ah-beh-shy*

Arbolias: *Are-bow-lee-us*

Bazin: *Bah-zahn*

Chaval: *Chah-bahl*

Coquina: *Ko-KEE-nuh*

Cristes Aventus: *Crease-tis Uh-ven-tis*

Eira: *i- Rah*

Hellebore Niger: *Hel-leh-bore Ny-jur*

Ines: *E-nez*

Mara: *Mar-uh*

Melchior: *Mel-key-or*

Melohym: *May-low-him*

Nicholas Klaus: *Knee-ko-lus Clow-ss*

Noorjove: *Nor-johv*

Raqs Rumba: *rack room-bah*

Roisin: *Roh-sheen*

Rumbiental: *room-bee-en-tul*

Valsanthe: *Val-san-thuh*

Vea: *Vay-uh*

Preface

SOFT HANDS CARESSED MY FACE. I snuggled into the warm palm and sighed with great relief. All that ugliness of the past few hours—painful neon blotches all over my skin, Nolan staying behind to give us time, our trip to Cristes—was all a bad dream. When I awoke, I'd be back in Illinois, in Shai's home. We would have another day to properly fix the globital device so we could portal safely to Cristes. No, I wouldn't open my eyes just yet. I was content to stay here next to Will.

The warm hands left my face and I frowned. Cold air froze the outer layer of my cheek. So. Cold. A tittering sound accompanied the stiffening of my body. Within seconds, a warm heaviness draped across me, but before I could snuggle in again, the hands gripped me and turned me onto my side before returning me to my back. Will probably lifted me and was taking me to bed. I arched against the hard, solid surface of his torso. His strong hands gripped my shoulders, helping me to sit, and then laid me down again. This time, I nestled into soft, feathery clouds. Yes. I definitely had fallen asleep on one of the couches in Shai's training room and Will just carried me to bed. Now I could finally get sound sleep so I could be useful on our journey to Cristes. All was right in the world.

Moments later, screams, full of bottomless sorrow, wailed in the distance. My eyebrows knit together at their intrusiveness. *Come on, brain! Everything's fine. Let me sleep!* Desperate cries pierced the air again, this time much closer. My heart thudded unrestrained within its cavity, understanding something my mind did not.

Boogey Man's Coming

A WAVE OF NAUSEA HIT ME HARD AND FAST. My eyes popped open as I turned my head, biting back bile, my throat burning. An endless view of flat, snow-covered land surrounded by a smattering of thick trees coated in snow and ice greeted me. Watchers I'd never seen before intercepted my view, and my gaze followed them as they ran between fur-lined sacks on their sleds to a small group crouched over a still body.

Shai!

Nick, Lana, and Brantley remained at his side. A blue and monstrous mountain in the distance with a few ice castles scattered at its base provided a stark contrast to the gruesome wreckage of Shai's body.

Panic flooded me as I searched for Will, relaxing slightly

as I found him only about a foot away from me. Though he still lay unconscious, he now rested on a golden sled. I traced the handsome features of his face, soaking him in. But then a small shadow clouded over me. My heart pumped harder, prepared to crack out of my chest as fear threatened to take hold of me. My connection to Will was barely tangible.

"Will," I croaked, my throat burning, as I reached for him. The ruddy beat of our bond was slow and faint. Will needed help. If I could just grasp his hand, I could...

In a flash, Nick was at my side, catching me before I fell from my own sled.

"What is it?" he asked, his eyes wild with concern.

"Will, he's... I can't feel..."

"Speak, girl!" Nick hollered and I flinched.

"He needs help!" I cried.

Nick whipped around on the balls of his feet. He took one step from his crouched position and laid his hand over Will's breastbone. A quick blue light lit up Nick's hand and Will's chest. Without a word, Nick stood. He flung his jacket tail and scooped me up, quickly situating me so that I lay on top of Will, my head on his chest, arms tucked into his side, and legs entwined with his. Nick turned, grabbed the fur blanket I'd been lying on in the sled, and draped it over us.

"He was beginning to freeze. Your body heat should help keep him warm enough until we reach the castle. In addition, your bond should help him greatly."

I wanted to ask more questions, but Nick turned his head and shouted, "Mother, we need to be leaving."

Immediately, a woman donning a silver laurel crown was at his side. I stared at her familiar gray eyes as they found mine, and words echoed in my mind, tugging at my recent memories.

"Welcome to Cristes, Lydia. We have been waiting a very long time for you."

So this was Queen Nicole. Though I hadn't met her in person, I felt as if I knew her thanks to Nick's and Mara's memories. Her appearance was much the same, except her hair was a little grayer, and a few wrinkles hugged her beautiful eyes.

She returned her gaze to Nick's. "We are working as fast as we can," she gestured to the twenty or so men and women clad in white. "We must stabilize Abishai before we can move him onto a sled." Nick leaned into his mother's ear. I couldn't hear what they said, so I watched his chin and throat move and bob. When he stepped back, his mother's eyes widened and gleamed silver.

Drums. Loud, beating drums assaulted my head. I clutched my ears to dampen the noise, but my body vibrated with the pounding. As if on cue, everyone's head snapped to the side, their lips all curved downward. I lifted the top of my body off of Will, hoping to glimpse what had everyone on alert and glowing like a string of soft Christmas lights.

Powdered snow as far as the eye could see billowed into the air, the colossal cloud concealing whatever was coming our way with unnatural speed.

"Ohanna!" Queen Nicole called out, keeping her attention fixed on the veiled threat.

A woman with tan skin and dark braids, aglow in green, was at her side in a split second. She crossed her right arm over her chest, her left arm bent, connecting the wrists over her heart, and bowed. "Yes, your grace."

"Is that who I think it is?" The queen's lips pursed.

"Yes, my queen. I was in the process of dispatching my captains and their legions to set up a perimeter."

"And my William is ready for us?"

Ohanna nodded once. "Yes, King Klaus and the rest of our forces, as well as the healers, are in position at the wall."

And then it dawned on me that Will was named after Nick's father, King William Klaus.

"Thank you," Queen Nicole replied. "I will do my best to get us out of here, but we will need more time. Can you provide a distraction?"

Ohanna smirked. The queen's brow quirked as she smiled in return. And then Ohanna was off barking orders to the captains.

"Mother, what is going on?" Nick demanded. I'd forgotten he was even there. It was unlike him to be so patient in a moment of crisis, stepping back and not taking the lead.

"That over there" —Queen Nicole pointed at the roiling storm cloud that grew louder and closer by the second— "is Melchior's army."

"Critosi!"

"Nicholas!" She gasped. "Watch your mouth. We have come prepared for this. Everyone here knew what they were getting into when you and Lana called for rescue."

I shuddered as I recalled an image of Melchior, leader of the Black Roses, from Nick's memories. *White hair and eyes so dark it appeared as if he had no pupils. Thin lips stretched in a wicked smile as he licked Mara's spit from his face.* I gagged at the grotesque image. Queen Nicole and Nick turned to me.

"What is it, dear?" The queen rushed over and stroked the hair out of my face.

"What's Melchior doing here?" I rasped.

She blinked, studied Nick, and pinched her brows.

"Do not fash." She smiled at me. "He is of no concern at the moment. There is a lot you do not yet know." Her eyes suddenly shifted to Will, who groaned.

"As I said, we need to get Prince William and Princess Lydia out of here—now!" Nick barked.

Queen Nicole's lids snapped shut. She loosed a long breath and then hustled over to the group surrounding Shai. I observed as she leaned into the center of the group. When she stood, she faced one of her guards, and her silver eyes flashed twice.

Immediately, an echo of "Bring the dogs!" chorused down the legions of Watchers. In seconds, four of them, tall and fearsome, led teams of large, high-trained dogs out from the small thicket of snow-covered trees. The dogs barked and yipped as they eagerly made their way toward us.

Instincts had me drawing my arm tightly across Will.

The queen turned to me. "Lydia, my mushers will hook your sled to a team. They are the fastest and most skilled in all of Cristes. However, the ride will still be difficult. They will strap you in, but I need you to make sure William's head stays as still as possible. Can you do that?"

My eyes were wide with fear, but I nodded at the queen in mock confidence anyway.

She smiled at me and patted my arm. "Good. Nicholas, you will follow Lydia and William out."

"And what about you, Mother?"

She cupped his cheek. "I will be right behind you. After I see to it that all of my people are taken care of."

"They are my people too," Nick argued.

"You have brought with you precious cargo. Ensuring their safety *is* for your people." Queen Nicole walked back to the crowd around Shai, disappearing as she knelt down.

I lifted my chin to Nick. He squinted in the distance at the turbulent cloud looming toward us.

The sled jostled and I steeled myself, holding onto Will and cradling his head.

Nick eyed me before turning to the two mushers who remained by us while the others busied themselves hooking up the other sled. They bowed the traditional Cristes salutation, taking their hats off when doing so. A long, red braid fell over the shorter one's shoulder.

Nick acknowledged them with a nod of his head. "Forgive my manners. I do not know your names."

"I am Tia, and this," the young woman said, gesturing to the tall, brawny man with the baby face at the helm of my sled, "is my brother Tannon."

"It is our pleasure to take you to the castle, Your Highness," Tannon said, placing his thick cap back over his cropped strawberry-blond hair.

Nick slid into his sled. "Ready when you are."

Tia readied herself to steer. One sharp whistle and all the dogs stood at attention. The air shifted and a surge of energy rippled through each dog as, one by one, like falling dominoes, they shook their coats. A melodic tune floated above my head. I peered up as Tannon released a little wooden object from his mouth. Each lead dog turned to look at their musher, and...

BOOM!

A blast of wind hit me and curled my hair out of my face. Snow and ice pelted the ground all around us.

"They've brought cannons!" someone shouted.

After scanning the people directly around me to ensure no one had been injured, my gaze landed on Nick in the sled next to mine. I sighed with relief when I saw he was fine.

His eyes narrowed at the group huddled around Shai, many of them people I'd grown to love, before his gaze snapped to me.

Tears stung my eyes, the frigid temperature freezing the liquid on my lashes before they could slip down my cheeks. "We can't leave without them," I pleaded.

Intensity burned behind his eyes, boring into mine before he tore his gaze away.

"Please," I repeated.

Nick growled through a clenched jaw. "Tia, we need to move...now."

"No!" I gasped.

"Yes, Your Highness," Tia answered him.

The thunder ramped up, crescendoing into another loud crack that shook the air.

"Take cover!" a male voice shouted. I flung the top half of my body over Will's as the ground rumbled with the explosion.

"Now, Tannon!" Tia yelled, her voice nearly snuffed out by the crashing chunks of snow and ice. He played his tiny, wooden flute but was cut off with an abrupt grunt.

"Critosi!" Nick bellowed. The dogs followed suit, crying and howling, jostling the sled as they thrashed.

I lifted my head, but Tannon had vanished. I found him on the ground, blood streaked across a nearby chunk of ice. Tia ran over and dropped to his side, her hands frantic over his lifeless frame.

Nick hovered over her. "Is he alright?"

"He took a hit straight to the back of his head," she faltered, removing her trembling hand, now slick with crimson.

Nick scooped Tannon up as if he were a feather and laid him on his sled.

"Your Highness, I was instructed—"

"You are the last of the fastest mushers. I cannot have you distracted whilst your brother is hurt." Nick placed Tannon into the sled and tossed a blanket on him. "I will drive the sled following you."

She slammed her hands onto her hips with an indignant huff at him, then drew her fingers to her lips. A shrill whistle pierced the air followed by two punctuated blasts. The other two mushers emerged from behind the nearby trees, hustling toward us. Their single sled was massive, and it took the two of them to control it, as well as the dogs.

"No offense, Your Highness, but you will not be driving any of my sleds. We planned for this." She held out the reins of my sled to the tall man with a dark beard and curls escaping from the sides of his cap. As she walked over to the sled her brother laid on, she handed the reins to the other musher with dark skin and amber eyes.

"They are nearly here!" an archer called in the distance.

"Ready the horses!" a voice I recognized as Ohanna's replied. "Archers ready!" she bellowed from atop a large boulder of ice.

At least two dozen bodies, so well hidden they were completely concealed by the snow-covered ground, sprang up and revealed themselves. They moved so quickly, I almost didn't see them reach behind their backs and knock their shimmering white bows. Gold sparks flickered at the tip of each arrow.

"For Cristes!" Ohanna screamed.

"For Cristes!" the guard echoed.

"Let it snow, archers!"

The arrows flew at Ohanna's command. One after another, the arrows burst into the air, a hailstorm driving hard and fast toward our enemy as they rained down. The ice melted as it gained speed, and as the water hit the ground, it shot upward and froze solid. A wall of ice erected itself before directly in front of me, creating a barrier to break up the enemy lines. Tia whirled around to face Nick. "Prince Nicholas, you will need to share this sled with my brother and help ensure that he does not fall out. Jack and Alpin are our next fastest mushers. They will deliver you behind the shield safely."

Nick pursed his lips and narrowed his gaze at Tia. "And how, pray tell, will the rest of my party be brought to safety? It appears that the remaining sled needs two mushers!" His hands landed on his hips as if his assessment were obvious.

Tia smirked. "I suggest you get into the sled, Your Highness." The winds picked up, flicking loosened pieces from her copper braid like embers of a fire. She turned without answering him, strode right up to the double sled and its dog team, and gripped all the reins in her small hands.

I sucked in my cheeks, shocked by her boldness, suppressing my body's desire to respond with a burst of laughter. But now wasn't the time for such things.

"Oi!" Alpin, the musher of Nick's sled, tossed something toward my sled. Jack caught the flute and blew into it.

The melody that sang in the air was overwhelmed by a sudden, deep rattle in the ice wall. Nick positioned himself in the sled behind Tannon. Jack wasted no time in playing the melody again, completing it this time. The dogs immediately heaved and pulled, panting and straining for traction, until they were in a full-on sprint toward the maze of ice castles.

Drums

WE'D BARELY BEEN PULLED A FEW FEET when little zips and zings echoed off the newly erected ice walls. Ohanna's eyes flashed with another order for her troops. In perfect unison, like a well-choreographed dance, the archers nocked their arrows. In a blink, tiny silver lines dotted the sky, forming a temporary constellation. The hexagonal shape unfurled and an iridescent film spread from each one, crawling across the sky and connecting them together.

KABOOM!

Dark gray wisps barreled directly into the barrier the archers had shot into the air. Little bubbles floated down from the parts of the shield where the Black Roses had breached. I tracked one as it floated lazily. Down, down, down it wafted, gaining speed as its shell began to freeze over. It emitted a soft tinkle when it crashed into the ground.

Jack blew a piercing whistle and the dogs gained speed.

More arrows shot into the air, but not fast enough. New wisps, red this time, pounded into the existing shield, some piercing through the holes. A few white horses and bodies tumbled into the air behind us. Ice exploded all around us, and I ducked my head next to Will's, protecting us both as best I could. I peered up at our musher, Jack. Blood poured down his face, seeping into his scarf.

"Jack!" I cried out.

"I'm—" His face contorted as he grunted with the effort of yanking the reins to the left, then swiftly to the right as we entered the maze of ice castles.

"Split up!" Jack yelled and Alpin obeyed, choosing a different path at the last second to run Nick and Tannon through.

Jack turned his gaze to me. "I'm fine, my lady. Do not fret. It's only a scratch. I'll live."

"Lid," a soft voice croaked out.

My attention snapped to Will, and I studied his face. Though bloodshot and glassy, his eyes were still the most beautiful things I'd ever seen. I made an ugly sound, something teetering between a cry and a laugh. The sight of him, conscious and calling my name... Relief washed over me, cleansing the bitter taste of fear that coated my tongue and gums. Fear that I'd been suppressing. He was OK. He would be OK.

One corner of his lip quirked. "Are we...are we sledding?" he asked.

"You can say that." I sniffled, wiping my nose with the cuff of my shirt. He made to sit up, but I pressed my upper body hard into his, forcing him to stay down. "Oh, no you don't. You are not supposed to be moving."

"I mean, don't get me wrong, I don't mind this position at all, but why am I not supposed to be moving?"

"Be on the ready!" Ohanna's voice bellowed from somewhere behind me, though not in my line of sight.

I pressed my lips to Will's for a quick kiss. "Don't freak out. Cover your face and try not to move your head." Now that he was awake, he could help keep himself still. So, I placed my head next to his and tried to shield the back of my neck as much as possible. A sizzling sound crackled from above demanding my attention, but I refused to look. Tiny, warm drops tickled my hands.

KABOOM!

The Black Roses landed another successful blow. We were now far enough away from the front lines so that no huge chunks of ice hit us this time, but the cries of others still punched me directly in the gut.

"What is going on?" Will tried to sit up again.

"Don't!" I yelled. "You were knocked out. This is hardly the time to explain it all to you, but you have a head injury. I was instructed to make sure you didn't move it."

Jack jerked the sled left, right, then right again through ice castles, and then a hard left that nearly threw me from the sled.

"Almost there, your majesties!" Jack called out. "Hang on tight, though. It's about to get bumpy!"

My eyes widened in disbelief. Had it not been bumpy

already? I'd barely been hanging on as it was. Will's arms wrapped tightly around me.

"I've got you," he murmured in my ear.

I picked my head up and peered over my shoulder past the dogs.

"What do you see?" Will asked.

"There are still plenty of ice castles, but they are thinning out."

Hopefully, that means less of a chance of crashing into the solid walls around us at high speed.

"The ground does look pretty bumpy." I conveniently left out that it reminded me of the kid-made moguls at the end of the sledding hill that gave Will those scars on his face. "But at least it's a straight shot to this gigantic wall up ahead."

"That's the entrance to Cristes," Jack shouted.

There, a few hundred yards directly in front of us, the immense wall loomed. Blended colors of white, yellow, pink, and mauve shimmered in the bold sunlight, and I had to squint against its beauty.

Jack blew into the wooden whistle, a short tune of four notes. The dogs lurched forward as if they'd just been given a shot of adrenaline. There it was, the end of the maze, a straight shot of maybe half a football field.

BOOM!... KABOOM! No warning this time. Shards and blocks of ice came crashing down just in front of us, missing our lead dog by inches. The dogs quickly dodged to the left, and the right side of our sled crashed into the pile of rubble that now blocked our path out of the maze of ice.

"Critosi!" Jack bellowed. "Everyone alright?"

"Just a little dizzy," Will answered, staring at me as

I frantically searched his face and palpated his head. He grabbed my wrists. "I'm fine, promise." He smiled, scanning me from head to toe, but then his lips turned down and his skin turned white as a snow-capped mountain.

"Oh, no. Will, are you—"

"Your leg!" Will shuddered, horrified. I followed his gaze and came to a gruesome discovery. My left leg was pinned between a slab of ice and the sled.

"Thundernation!" Jack exclaimed as he hopped down from the sled. He reached into his boot and whipped around, yielding a long dagger and some throwing knives.

"Neither of you move," he instructed. The ground vibrated beneath the pounding of hooves. My heart rate skyrocketed. "I will try to hold them off, but you both should be prepared to use your gifts. It will hurt, considering the state you're in, but they cannot have you, do you understand?" Jack's big body stood tall and rigid in front of us, prepared to fight.

A large horse and two soldiers came barreling around the corner, skidding to a halt.

"Oi! What happened?" I peeked around. Ohanna and her partner were there, cheeks pink from the cold. Their white stallion blew small clouds of smoke from its nose.

Jack relaxed his stance, sheathing his weapons. "Our path became blocked just as we were about to sail through it."

"Well, what the devil you waitin' for! Keep going, there are more—"

Jack cleared his throat, interrupting Ohanna. "The princess needs our assistance first, captain." He moved his body as Ohanna dismounted from her horse.

Ohanna's eyes flicked over me. She called over her

shoulder to her partner. "Brita, all hands on deck."

As the three of them spoke quickly, Will interrupted my eavesdropping. "How are you not writhing in pain? Why, *why* can't I feel your pain?" Will didn't yet know that I'd lost all feeling from the waist down, and I sensed panic begin to seize him.

"*Shhh.*" I stroked his cheek with the pad of my thumb. "Don't worry. Everything is fine."

"Everything is not fine!" Will bolted up, but quickly laid back down and closed his eyes.

"Right." Ohanna's voice startled me, along with the three bodies standing so close to us. She continued, "Prince William, we will remove your straps and adjust them to include the princess's body. Her leg will need to be braced." Brita propped her leg on the side of the sled with a thud and removed a white belt from her thigh. She quickly retrieved an arrow from her back, snapped off the tip, flung it over her shoulder, and handed the stick and belt to Ohanna.

Ohanna barked instructions as she removed the belts strapped to each of her thighs. "Jack, you and Brita will move the sled. When you do, I will be there to place the tourniquet and stabilize the leg."

KABOOM!

We all flinched, but at least this time, it was farther away from us.

"Liddy, what are you not telling me?" Will asked, his hands cupping my cheeks, his pupils wide with fear.

Concern marked his face as it scrunched in earnest. The truth was, I hadn't really had time to process my injury and what the lack of feeling meant for me and my future. Hot tears stung as I tried to blink them away. Dancing was not only a passion of mine, it was a gifting. Heck, what if I never walked again?

I opened my mouth to speak, but nothing came out, the tightness squeezing my throat too painful to speak through. After a moment, Will seemed to understand. Fighting his own tears, he brought his hand to the back of my neck and snuggled me close.

He continued to hug me as Jack rearranged us, and I relished the closeness to Will once the strap was tightened across my upper back, securing me to the one who was my perfect match in every way.

BOOM! Snow rained down on us.

"That was too close," Brita growled.

"Jack, Brita... on my command."

Jack gave Ohanna a curt nod, then blew three notes into his whistle. The dogs stood at attention. He positioned himself at the side of the sled opposite the wall of debris. Brita squatted a few feet from him and gripped the bottom rail of the sled. Ohanna nodded at Jack, who obediently played another short tune.

Ohanna held her forearm up and then...the drums started.

It Sounds Like the 4th of July

"**W**HAT WAS THAT?" Will asked, his heart fluttering hard enough that I could feel it against my chest.

"That would be the Black Roses," Ohanna answered.

Thud, thud...

"We have no time to spare." Ohanna raised her forearm again.

Doom, dum, dum... Closer this time.

Jack blew a few notes into his whistle and the dogs' ears all stood straight up, one paw off the ground, ready for their next instruction. A green light pulsed from Ohanna's armband, and Jack and Brita immediately pulled the sled toward themselves as the dogs began to pull it forward.

Da doom, da doom... Too close.

"Halt!" Ohanna yelled. She jumped into the narrow opening between the sled and debris and got to work on my leg. Judging by the expression on Will's face, I was glad I had no sensation.

When I tore my gaze from his face, I saw that Brita was already atop the horse, facing the way we'd just come. She had an arrow nocked and ready.

Jack was at the helm of the sled, one hand grasping the whistle, the other gripping the handle and reins.

A soft grunt at the side of the sled garnered my attention. "That should do it," Ohanna said, straightening her body to stand.

Doom...thud, thud. Da doom...thud, thud.

"Captain, we need to leave," Brita spoke over her shoulder, the light of her armband fading in and out. But Ohanna was already running toward her horse.

KABOOM!

The ground shook. The horse reared and the dogs howled, but Ohanna remained firm.

"What is *that*?" Will asked, pointing to the small path in which we had traveled to get to this point. I turned my head as an inky mist slithered over the ground toward us.

No one answered. Ohanna jumped onto the horse as Brita shot an arrow into the ground, and a clear glass wall blocked off the alcove we were in from the mist. Seconds later, a man with hair as white as freshly fallen snow and eyes as dark as a starless night came into view. A sinister smile quirked his lips.

"Peek-a-boo, I've found you." Melchior's inhuman voice grated against my ears. My blood ran cold. Clad in all black, his jacket billowing in the wind like tendrils of smoke, he was even more unearthly and horrifying in person.

Jack blew his whistle, one harsh note, and the dogs took off, the white stallion galloping close behind us. The detour only took a few moments, and then we were free from the shelter of the ice walls and dashing over the uneven ground.

Will scrunched his eyes and kept them closed with each bump that we hit. I tried to mute the bond between us, his pain so intense it seeped into me, becoming mine as well. Lying atop him, I still had my forearms pressed to each side of his head to try and stabilize it, but I moved my hands to try and offer some cushion. When his mouth twisted and small beads of sweat formed on his brow, I knew the pain the jostling caused him had become too much.

BOOM! BOOM! BOOM!

Explosions rocked the ground all around us as Jack deftly evaded each blast. Meanwhile, Brita knelt with her back to Ohanna as she loosed arrow after arrow at our enemies.

We were halfway to the entrance now. I scanned the edge of the ice castles, noticing the multitude of exits.

What I saw next had my heart sinking to my stomach.

Hundreds of people strode out from the maze of ice castles, walking in perfect sync with each other, as if all controlled by a puppet master. They were all clothed in black from head to toe, the tails of their scarves billowing in the wind. They carried black metal shields half their height in length. Each step they took resounded with a drum beat, in perfect rhythm with each other, their black leather fists pounding onto their armor.

I couldn't make sense of their movements. Though they appeared to be casually walking, they were gaining on us fast.

I stared harder, trying to make sense of it. My view of them glitched as they partially faded out and back in. Each time they did this, they gained double the ground.

Hundreds of red-tipped arrows sprang up from behind the first line, swirling with intent like a murmuration of blackbirds and heading straight for us.

"Thundernation!" Brita yelled as she launched at least twenty arrows, one after the other, her arm but a blur of motion.

KABOOM!

Brita managed to shield us from the worst of the attack, but we were not out of the woods yet. Tendrils of black smoke raced toward us from every possible direction. The drumming of the incoming army grew louder and louder, the tempo increasing.

Ohanna rode alongside us. "We need to go faster! We cannot lose the prince!"

"I have an idea, but we are too far from the wall yet!" Jack yelled back at her.

I angled my neck upward to peer at the wall, about a hundred yards away. Tia and the rest of our party were already disappearing into the metal gate.

"Can't you call for backup with that band thing?" Jack motioned to his forearm, where the previously glowing band lay dormant and white.

"I'm nearly out of arrows!" Brita called over her shoulder.

Ohanna bit down on her lower lip and held up her wrist. Colorful sparks of pink and green, like fireworks, shot high into the sky.

Peering down at Will, his face was smooth, and I realized

he was no longer conscious. I wouldn't let fear take hold just yet. I placed my cheek in front of his mouth and sighed with relief when his hot breath caressed my skin in slow, even breaths.

BOOM-DA-BOOM-BOOM...

BOOM-DA-BOOM-BOOM...

The Black Roses were only a few yards away from us now. The hairs on my arms stood on end as vibrations of the army's movement sang through the metal sled.

"I'm out!" Brita yelled.

"Jack, it's time!" Ohanna yelled.

"No! Not yet. We are not close enough!" he responded.

"We are too far out for the wall to help us...don't you get it? Help is not—"

A horn, deep and impressive, blew one long note. I didn't know what it meant. Was it a warning from Melchior that we should surrender? A celebration that they were close to capturing us?

Brita and Ohanna unleashed a war cry and pumped their fists in the air, their eyes bright green as they stared straight ahead.

I peeked over my shoulder and felt a whoosh of relief at the sight of the troops of Cristes, clad in white and silver, barreling out of the gate. Nearly ten groups of around five bodies each strained to get the colossal gray towers they were pushing to gain momentum on its wheels. Eventually, the Archers lined the top of the wall as far as I could see, their bows glinting like a chain link necklace: perfectly spaced, all working together as one unit.

The forms of the towers sharpened into recognizable

weapons as the troops rolled them closer—catapults and cannons. I returned my gaze down to Will. He was still out.

"We need to create more distance between us and the Black Roses," Ohanna yelled to Jack as we continued to race over the dimpled land that jostled aggressively.

"We can't run the horse any harder or she'll be finished," Brita remarked.

I lifted my head. "Don't you guys have some gifting that can supercharge you?" I asked, recalling the memory Nick shared of the time he saved Mara. His company, bathed in the light of blue gifting, whisked her away from her cottage and would-be captor, Melchior.

KABOOM!

Jack and Ohanna both swerved in unison with accurate precision.

"That was close," he grunted.

"Supercharge?" Ohanna cocked her brow.

"Yeah, you know. All the soldiers glow and move at sonic speed."

"No, we do not all have that gifting. In fact, very few of us do." She smirked. "You must be thinking of Prince Nicholas's ability. Unfortunately, he is not with us."

Ohanna and Brita's armbands pulsed, three times...two times...

"Brace yourselves," Brita yelled.

With what? I thought to myself. I literally could not move, even if I wanted to.

A sea of arrows hailed from the top of the outer ward, veiling us in shadow as they sailed past. They all buried themselves into the earth at the same exact time. The sound of a large crack rang out and echoed off the far mountain. Gold threads linked the ends of the arrows before knitting the spaces between and above them.

I gasped at the sight of the sparkling net. *Clever*.

"That will not hold them for long. We need to make the most of it," Ohanna urged.

A familiar roar, one of a starving hunter whose prey evaded their grasp, pierced the air and my gut. As the soldiers dressed in black hit the net, parts of them sizzled, the sounds crackling through the air.

"Ohanna, get your horse as close to the dogs as possible. It's time!" Jack yelled.

Ohanna's heels tapped the sides of the horse and within seconds, the white stallion was panting heavily, matching the last dog stride for stride. Jack blew into his whistle, a three-note melody, and the dogs yipped in response and increased their speed, suddenly glowing amber. Though not the sonic speed Nick's gifting offered, it was still impressive.

We moved so fast, it didn't feel real. Almost as if time around us had stopped, yet we were still moving. I had no idea how long this rush would last, but my nerves calmed the closer we came to the giant barrier wall. It almost appeared to be made from sand, but no...that couldn't be. A structure made of sand would not be very dependable.

Snip...snip...snip.

We all turned our attention to the golden net. Its fragments floated, momentarily carried by the wind before completely disappearing.

I saw the color drain from Brita's face before I registered the shift, and suddenly, we were no longer moving at warp speed. We were not moving forward at all. Instead, we were being dragged backward. Ohanna and Brita weren't affected as they continued on without us, though if their shouts were any indication, they definitely protested their inability to stop and turn around.

The dogs fought hard to heed their musher's command. The lead dog took the leash in his mouth, attempting to pull the sled and his comrades in the direction of safety. Ohanna flung herself from her horse, rolling as she hit the ground. She sprinted for us, but we were hurtling out of control toward Melchior and his band of evil mercenaries. Melchior struck a formidable presence at the front and center of his army, a wicked grin on his face as he pulled us in on his invisible rope. Bile stung my throat as I was reminded of the saccharine grin Mara wore as she reeled me in during one of my tortured dreams.

Seconds felt like minutes. All the while the space between us and the Black Roses that Jack had worked the dogs so hard to make grew smaller and smaller. There was no way the Cristes army would be able to use the catapults or cannons because we would soon be too close. We would be in the line of fire and Melchior knew it.

The Cristes army scrambled to help. Ohanna's face was nearly purple, but still she pressed on, pumping her arms and legs to their limit, never giving up trying to reach us. Brita had made it to one of the cannon groups, where she retrieved the arrows she was now sending at Melchior's army. In fact, all archers lined on the wall were sending the arrows of their own volition. Jack's brows were pinched together, sweat beading down his forehead. Everywhere I looked, chaos greeted me.

The familiar panic that my mother so often helped me settle upon waking from one of Mara's nightmares began to bubble.

Now is not the time, brain! Get a hold of yourself!

I glanced down at Will, who was still sound asleep. My choices were panic or ignorance, basking in his presence during the final minutes of my life. I closed my eyes, closed them against the destruction and pain that was sure to follow, finding solace that Will would not feel a thing.

Mists of colors swirled around me, different melodies accompanying different colors. Some colors harmonized with others when they came in close contact.

Well, this is new.

Normally, I'd have to desire my gifting to manifest. But here, amongst the chaos, it took charge on its own.

I wonder what would happen if I plucked two different colored droplets at the same time?

I extracted a drop of orange and blue from the mists surrounding me and placed them at my heart without further hesitation.

For a brief moment, my legs tingled, as did my arms, though the sensation in my arms was a hundred times more intense. I bore down against the strong cramping in my stomach, but the pain grew too severe and I was forced to release the giftings. I held my palms out and opened my eyes, but nothing happened.

The drums started again and my arms vibrated so hard with intense power that I thought they'd fall off. I opened my mouth to scream! Instead, I started singing a soft melody with a familiar chorus. The volume of my voice filled the expansive field of ice. I stared into Melchior's black eyes, directing the song to him and his minions.

The corner of his lip quirked and then fell. His brows pinched together in confusion, and he stumbled back as he shook his head, appearing drunk. He turned his head to the right and left down the line of his warriors. They too were stumbling, some already flat on their backs against the frozen ground.

"NOOO!" Melchior roared and slapped his hands over his ears.

I didn't know what was happening, but my body sure did. My hands went to Will's chest and pushed up as my chest pressed forward and head arched back. In the cobra position, my voice rang from me, thunderous and demanding, a command over Melchior's body. He stumbled to his knees as the notes hit him, and he dropped his rope.

The sled jerked forward like a slingshot, straight at Ohanna. With the agility of a cat, she jumped out of the way, snatched Jack's belt, and landed on her feet behind him. Loud cheering emanated from the great wall protecting Cristes.

A hand brushed my cheek. "You sang." Will smiled at me, and a drop of joy entered my nervous system at knowing he was awake.

"I... I guess I did. You OK?"

"Better than OK. I could listen to you sing for the rest of my life."

I rolled my eyes. "You're silly."

His palm slid behind my neck and pulled me in for a kiss. It lasted but a moment because the wretched ground shook and jerked our sleigh around.

When we broke apart, we'd covered enough distance to separate us and the Black Roses. The catapults launched what looked like large seeds, and the cannons fired right after. When the cannon balls hit their marks, the seeds exploded, and out came a substance that reminded me of yards and yards of tulle. It hovered and then shimmered as it moved in the air. A shape began to form and eventually presented as giant-sized knights waiting for a challenge.

The cannon and catapult teams hastened back through the lofty gate that glinted in the sun. We were almost there! A final roar blared from behind us, Melchior's warning that promised us this was far from over.

Jack and his team of dogs led us through the gates of Cristes, where Nick and his parents stood waiting for us, relief etching their faces. "Welcome home, Your Majesties."

A sob escaped from me. *We made it.*

It's All Too Much

THE GATES SLAMMED SHUT BEHIND US as our sled stopped at the feet of the king and queen of Cristes. The queen didn't seem to have a hair out of place, odd since she'd just dashed to safety herself. Though all around us was chaos, I imagine I stared at these rulers of Cristes with all the reverence of a groupie meeting their favorite celebrity. I found I couldn't muster up embarrassment for myself at this point.

Guards were changing shifts across the top of the wall. Others were securing the door with both thick bars and impressive giftings.

Queen Nicole walked to the side of our sled and bent over us. "You're awake," she commented, smiling down at Will.

He peered at me, and a vague question flitted through

my mind. I nuzzled into his neck and answered him, "Queen Nicole... Nick's *mom*."

"I am," Will answered her. "It is nice to finally meet you." He nodded his head in respect. "Where is everyone else?" he asked, turning his attention to Nick.

Nick's face turned ashen. I didn't need my gifting to tell me how my boyfriend responded to that. His heart fluttering against my chest was more than enough.

Will attempted to sit up, but he couldn't get far. Not with me tied to him and the both of us strapped to the body of the sled. Not to mention, a wave of dizziness hit me, alerting me that his condition was worse than he let on. He gently laid his head back down.

Before Will could interrogate Nick any further, Jack gave Queen Nicole and King Klaus the Cristes salute. "Permission to speak with you in private?" he asked.

"Of course, good lad," the king answered, opening his arm to usher his wife, Nick, and Jack over to the side.

I observed them as they all leaned into each other. Occasionally their attention flitted to me, their expressions unreadable, and my gut didn't like it.

The back of Will's hand brushed my cheek. "What is it, beautiful?"

"I wish I knew." I laid my head down in the crook of Will's neck. My upper back and shoulders ached from having held myself up for so long.

"They're coming back," Will whispered. I responded by snuggling in closer. Something told me I wasn't going to like what they had to say.

Someone cleared their throat and I reluctantly turned my

attention to them.

"Lydia, I understand you have faced some extensive injuries. We have some of the best healers this side of the realms." The king glanced to his wife before continuing. "We are awaiting another sled and will transfer you to that one and take you there."

"And what about Will?" I asked. "I mean, he was injured too."

"Of course," the queen responded. "He will see a healer as well. But you will not be seeing the same one. They do have their specialties."

Something felt off, but before I was able to answer, Will spoke. "I am not leaving Liddy. I can wait."

Nick shook his head, wearing an *I-told-you-so* grin. "As I said, Mother..."

She narrowed her gaze at him but then schooled her features. "Of course. Would you like your own sled, Lydia? It would be more comfortable for you."

Will tightened his grip on me. He didn't have to say anything. I knew he was asking me to stay. I shook my head, answering the queen without meeting her gaze.

"Very well, then. Jack, please direct your sled team to the healing sanctum." He bowed at the queen's order and took his post at the back of the sled.

"We shall travel at a leisurely pace this time. You need not worry about his head so much," Jack whispered down to me.

"How long will it take?" I asked.

"Less than ten minutes. It will be a great opportunity for you to see our capital, the heart of Cristes, Noorjove."

There was a shift here my gifting refused to ignore. Nick,

the queen, the king, and Jack...they all projected a strangled thought like a flag waving wildly in the winds of a hurricane. I briefly wondered if Will sensed it too. Though I wanted to scream, *Tell us what is going on!* I didn't. I figured I would ask them a short time later. For now, I wanted to see what the capital of Cristes looked like.

At first, we followed the great wall as we traveled. The pink, sandy color and texture were unique and unlike anything I'd seen before.

"Coquina," the king said, smiling at me as he walked alongside our sled.

"I'm sorry?" I asked, not quite sure I'd heard him correctly.

"The material of the wall. You appear to have taken an interest. This wall surrounds a majority of the capital and a few neighboring cities. There is a little ice and gifting mixed in there as well, but a majority is Coquina."

"It looks like a bunch of shells squished together," Will commented.

"Very astute." The king touched the tip of his nose. "Although you cannot see it now, under all this ice and snow is a tropical paradise with vast oceans. Coquina was exceptionally abundant here and we had to cultivate it in sizable quantities when we first noticed the temperatures significantly dropping." The king placed his hand on the wall.

I marveled at how much time and effort that must have taken to build the curtain wall. It had to be at least thirty feet tall and ten feet deep.

"Shells may seem fragile, but I promise you. These minerals are harder and stronger than any rock," the queen added.

Nick followed alongside the sled opposite his parents. My eyes traveled over him as he took this all in. How different Cristes must appear to him since the last time he was truly here, he was a young adult. How weird it must be to appear almost as old as your parents.

We veered right, and the crowded area around the gates began to decongest. This area did not resemble the Cristes in Nick's memories. Before, it was a bustling city center with parks, restaurants, and apartment buildings.

But now? Igloos and glass huts littered the entire landscape, some larger than others, and much of the aforementioned buildings were left dark, frozen in time. We ambled in solitude, and I appreciated the quiet, the only sounds from the sled slicing across ice and snow.

Jack broke the silence. "Just at the top of the hill." He pointed to a building the size of at least three of my high schools, painted light pink. "Only about another five minutes."

I craned my neck to peer at the building and returned my attention to Will, whose gaze was pinned on me.

"Would you like help holding your head to see?" I asked. He smirked, kissed me softly on my lips, and carefully nodded. I shifted my body to the left a little and cradled his head in my forearms, using the remaining strength I had to lift it.

"Why do I suddenly feel like a kid again entering camp?" Will joked, taking in the sight of all the small cabins dotting our path.

"Yeah, if that camp were held in Antarctica," I retorted and Will laughed.

"Seriously though, are you confident we are not in a remote Alaskan village?"

The king cocked an eyebrow at us and I almost giggled at how much Nick resembled his dad in that moment. "I don't know what Alaskan means, but we had little time to design and implement ways to survive our new climate."

"Alaska is a gorgeous state from Mortalia," I explained, my cheeks heating.

"We meant no offense. This is all just very different from what we were shown," Will explained.

"None taken. Your comments merely allow me to share some of our history. As I was saying, many citizens had to leave their homes to be closer to the castle." He gestured over his shoulder, and in the center of everything was indeed a castle. He returned his attention to the tiny homes in front of us. "Every home has a greenhouse where crops are grown. The castle grounds also grow some crops, and we have been somewhat successful in growing Christmas roses inside, thanks in large part to Nicholas's yearly deliveries." The king's eyes glistened with pride.

Nick gave his dad a tight-lipped smile and dropped his gaze, his cheeks flushed a deep pink.

"I do wish we were able to cultivate them on a grand enough scale necessary to wield enough power to fix all of this." The king gestured around him, indicating the climate and war outside the walls. "But alas, these roses do seem to only want to flourish in the soils of Mortalia."

The dogs grew more eager as we got closer to the healing sanctum. A new melody played from Jack's flute, and they begrudgingly slowed their pace again.

"Their barn is close to the sanctum. They get a little excited at the prospect of food, water, and rest," Jack offered.

"Who wouldn't?" I mumbled. Apparently, Will found this funny, laughing so hard he almost bounced me off the sled. I couldn't help but join in.

But our laughter ceased when the navy blue double doors burst open, Lana bolting through them. She didn't go far beyond the doors before she keeled over, her hands on her knees to steady her as she struggled for breath. Pain swallowed me, and I was dumped into an abyss of hopelessness.

"Mom?"

Her head popped up, her eyes glowing such a brilliant green, even her tears looked green. She locked them on Will.

"Mom, what's wrong?" Will tried to move, but for obvious reasons, he couldn't.

"Lana!" Brantley barreled through the doors after his wife. "It's not..." His voice trailed off as he took in the scene before him. Then he ran over to me and Will, flung himself on his knees, and wrapped us in a tight embrace. Relief flooded through me, and I knew Mr. Jamison was more than happy to know his son was alive and well, considering the last time he saw Will, he was unconscious.

"Thank Eira you're alright!" he said, withdrawing to examine his son more closely.

Seeming to have composed herself, Lana walked over to the both of us. She bent at the waist and caressed Will's face before kissing his forehead.

"Mom, what's wrong?" He inhaled sharply as if he'd just realized what he hadn't seen. More like, who he hadn't seen. "Where's Uncle Shai?"

Lana dropped to her knees and grabbed Will's hand. She opened and closed her mouth a few times, and I sympathized with how difficult this would be for her. Shai was her brother. This was the man Will had lived with for the past year.

More than that, I had seen Shai. I'd seen his broken body, crushed from the force of the fall, soaked in blood. So much blood. He'd sacrificed himself to save Will. This was something I couldn't stomach telling my boyfriend. At least not yet, not while he had healing to do. And I think his mom reckoned the same as I watched her pick over her words.

"He's with the healers now. Which is where the two of you need to be." She gave Will one last kiss on the forehead, kissed the top of my head, and stood.

Two Watchers exited the doors, each pushing beds that resembled gurneys—if gurneys were super fluffy and made of a mixture of woods and metals. The queen trailed behind them, though I hadn't seen her go inside.

"Lydia, correct?" A female watcher with a warm face and a streak of pink through her brown hair stooped down to address me.

"Yes, that's me."

"It is my pleasure to meet your acquaintance. I am Healer Ruth and this is Healer Leo. We understand you have a spinal injury, and as I have done a quick assessment, a leg injury as well."

An assessment? She'd barely glanced at me for all of ten seconds.

"Before we move you, I need to ensure that we do not further distress your injury." She spoke as she walked around the sled, studying our positions. I felt so silly, lying on top of Will, literally strapped to him and the sled, as she scrutinized us from every angle.

Leo joined her. He had dark hair that glinted navy in the sunlight. He stood tall and lean, quite a few inches taller than Will or King Klaus, though not as broad. "Moving you will be extremely difficult. But I believe I have a plan of execution. Do I have your permission to use my gifting on you?"

That was the first time this question had ever been asked of me. A nibbling of panic nipped at my chest, wanting in, but I shut it out. "I'm sorry. I don't know how to respond to that."

"Will it hurt her?" Will's voice had an edge to it, a protectiveness coating his words.

His tone was not lost on Leo. "It is customary, Your Highness, to ask permission to use a gifting on a patient in order to treat them after initial assessments."

"Yes, you have my permission," I answered Leo without further hesitation.

Ruth stepped forward. "And do I have your permission?" she asked. I nodded. "Thank you. Now, Leo and I will weave our gifting together. You may experience some sensations as it settles on you, but it should not be too uncomfortable. Think of it as a tight cast around your entire body."

Leo walked on the opposite side of the sled as Ruth raised her hands. "If this becomes uncomfortable for any reason, please let us know. We need to immobilize you in order to move you safely." Without warning, his hands began to move and glow in tandem with Ruth's.

Warmth started in my hands, spreading throughout the top half of my body, and I imagined it flowing through my lower half. It was so dang cold out here, but being close to Will helped keep much of the chill away. I shivered with pleasure as the sensation crawled up my neck. But the warmth turned to a feeling of stiffness. Unexpectedly, feelings of claustrophobia enveloped me, rapid and strong. My eyes widened as air seemed to elude me, becoming harder and harder to breathe.

Will stroked my cheek. "Hey, look at me."

I tried blinking away the rising panic. "I-I can't move," I stammered, the words catching in my throat. I didn't want anyone to overhear and think I was a coward.

"I am right here with you. You are safe. Breathe, Liddy. They are helping you. Just breathe." I glimpsed Will's face, full of love, and I followed his lead, watching him take long and deep breaths through his nose and slowly letting the air out of his mouth. A small hug seemed to wrap its way around all my vital organs and I calmed, knowing Will had sent that through our bond.

"Thank you," I whispered. "When we get out of here, I am going to kiss you *so* hard."

Will busted out a laugh.

"Your Highness! Please do not move her," Ruth shouted. "And for that matter, you should not be moving either."

Will bit back his bottom lip.

"So. Hard," I repeated in a whisper.

"You're killing me, Smalls," he responded.

More Watchers I didn't recognize circled around our sled. Soon, I was lifted off of Will and placed on the gurney. They positioned me on my back and I released a long sigh, my muscles uncoiling with relief at no longer having to hold myself up nor secure Will's head. My body relaxed so much I felt as if I were floating. Fatigue washed over me and I started to drift off.

"Stay with us, Lydia," Ruth commanded.

"What's happening?" Will asked, his voice strained with concern. I didn't know why he sounded like that; I was finally at peace. Surely he could feel that through our bond. "Whoa..." Will's eyes rolled, and he plopped back into the sled.

"Bring the prince over here please. Now!" Leo ordered two of the Watchers, who got Will onto a gurney, sidling our beds up against each other. "Thank you. Connect their hands, please." They did as instructed, and I immediately became alert, as did Will, who sighed with contentment.

Ruth and Leo exchanged worried glances and ushered us inside the facility.

"What is it?" Lana was not playing around, her words clipped and final as she marched after us.

Leo stopped and faced her. "Their injuries are more extensive than we were led to believe."

"As if we would try to sugarcoat things, healer," Lana sneered.

Ruth held her hands up and everyone halted. "I am not saying you were lying. I am saying their matching, the power they generate in each other's company, has masked our readings. We have never encountered—"

Leo huffed, throwing niceties out the window. "Lana, you are going to need to step aside and let us do our work. We must act quickly...for both their sakes."

To my dismay, Lana's bottom lip quivered. Brantley walked up behind her and wrapped his arms around her. She turned and buried her face in his chest.

"Team, we move fast, to bay three. Now!"

There was a whirlwind of activity after Ruth's order. With our beds side by side, Will and I were rushed down the shiny wood floors through the healing sanctum. My head lolled to the side and I witnessed Ruth jump onto Will's gurney and straddle him. Her head moved up and down robotically, her eyes igniting as she scanned him.

"What's happening?" I asked, yawning till the cows came home.

"Doing a more thorough scan of your injuries... Critosi!" Leo swore, and then his heavy weight landed on either side of me.

"Oh, no you don't!" His large, warm hands pressed on either side of my cheeks. "Stay awake, Lydia!"

Just a Kiss?

O NE AFTER THE OTHER, our beds were swung into a room, and I barely registered Leo jumping down from my bed. Voices spoke in hushed tones, though they didn't need to whisper. They spoke too fast and were far enough away that I couldn't make sense of their words, anyway.

A surge of energy jolted up my arm, and all the tiredness left my body. A young woman finished tying off the white silk strip of fabric around mine and Will's hands. Our beds had been shoved back together with the bars on the connecting side down and out of the way.

Will scrunched his nose at our hands. "I must say, I preferred our previous arrangement."

My cheeks heated. "Will," I chastised, "people are right

here." His shoulders popped up and down as if to say, *I don't care what they think.*

We were silent as the Watchers took our vitals. There were few differences between hospitals in Mortalia and this healing sanctum; they used familiar objects like stethoscopes to listen to our heartbeats and cuffs that squeezed our arms, although Ruth and Leo had no use for these gadgets.

"I would have loved a room like this," I commented absently. "A natural stone fireplace and bamboo flooring are so much better than puke green walls and yellowed tiles."

Will's jaw twitched, and I knew the images of me broken and battered in a cold hospital room after Winter Formal resurfaced in his memory. I gave his hand a little squeeze to bring him back to the here and now with me.

He returned it, and a smile played on his lips. "Really? I thought you loved green."

I giggled. "Eh, maybe not anymore?"

Will's face morphed into feigned horror, and I laughed some more. "You know I love any shade of green when it's on you."

Ruth and Leo both eyed us and their charts once more before stepping outside to greet Will's parents, the queen and king, and Nick, who were all waiting in full view outside the glass wall. My heart registered missing faces before my brain did. My chest tightened with the reminder that my own family and friends were not here. It hadn't even been forty-eight hours since Nick brought me to my house to say goodbye to them and then take their memories of me. It was better that they never knew I existed. I missed them something fierce and absently rubbed at the burning ache in my chest.

"What's wrong, Princess?" Will asked.

"It's nothing," I responded, turning away to blink back the tears that threatened to fall.

"Even if we did not have this connection where I could literally feel some percentage of what you do, actions don't lie," he said, arching his brow at my hand that rubbed circles over my chest.

I stilled my hand, pursed my lips, and let out a sigh. I opened my mouth, but movement caught the corner of my eye, and I turned my head.

King Klaus stood stock still, his arms crossed over his chest. Gone was the jovial face I'd just met. The queen's head drooped as she massaged her temples in slow circles. Lana's arms were expressive as she spoke with the healers, Brantley holding her across the waist as if he were holding her back. Lana's arms fell and so did her energy, as if what Leo told her stole the wind from her sails.

Nick caught me staring and pinched the bridge of his nose. He snuck away from the group and entered our room.

"Things seem intense out in the hall. What do we need to know?" Will asked, his grip on my hand tight as he sent calming waves through me.

Nick knew better than to lie to us at this point, but he still hesitated.

"It is not always easy to hear the things you share with us, but I have always appreciated your honesty," I said, even though his delivery was usually never softened.

His gaze connected with mine and quickly flitted to Will before finding the floor. Did he just blink back tears? Nick walked to the foot of Will's bed and cleared his throat. "Will, you have a small skull fracture, a concussion, and some bone contusions. You will need to take it easy for maybe a week, avoiding anything that could result in a possible head injury for another few weeks after that, but you should make a full recovery."

"Well, that's good news," I said, smiling at Will. But he and Nick did not return the gesture.

"And what is the bad news?" Will ground out.

"That *is* the bad news, right?" I asked, confused. "I mean, who leads with the good news first? You always lead with the bad."

Nick's coloring paled, and nerves threatened to twist my brain into a painful migraine.

"Say it," Will encouraged, channeling larger calming waves.

"Lydia, your spine injury is substantially more severe. Leo was able to scan you more clearly, but he was unable to determine if your injury was complete or near complete. There is too much inflammation to ascertain how many neural pathways were left intact."

"Near complete? Neural pathways?" I blinked. "Can you tell me what that all means like I'm five?"

Nick leveled me with glistening eyes, but his jaw twisted as if he were biting back words that would betray his innermost thoughts.

"Neural pathways are the connections between your brain and spine. In a near-complete injury, the healers assess those connections with the areas below the level of injury to see what is and what is not damaged. Leo sensed that not all pathways were destroyed, thus only a near-complete severing of your nerves. He knows at this point that there is a lot of swelling, impeding his total view. But he hypothesizes you have less than a ten percent chance of walking again...if they can save your leg."

A veil of gray clouded over Nick, and I tried to blink it away. But high-pitched ringing blocked my ears, ramping up in volume, and I could no longer hear what Nick was saying. Escape seemed like a fantastic option, but my legs refused to move, and I nearly slipped through the crack between my and Will's beds.

Strong hands held me. Suddenly the room shrunk...too small. It would suffocate me. My chest hurt as it heaved, trying to suck in air. The most gifted healers in all of Cristes said I would probably never walk again. That I might lose one of my legs.

Will's face appeared in front of me. I saw his lips moving, but nothing could break past the wailing in my head. Widened with fear, my eyes refused to blink. I was having a nightmare, but this time I was awake for the brutal reality of it.

Alarms blared to life around us, only drowning the ringing in my ears slightly. Leo and Ruth ran in and so did the rest of our party.

"Nicholas, you didn't!" His mother gasped.

"They had a right to know," he said curtly.

"The bond—"

"I haven't gotten to that part... yet," Nick chided Brantley.

Brantley's lips pressed into a line.

"We need to do the first procedure now," Ruth said.

Healers dashed in and ushered everyone out. One came over to wheel Will's bed away while another frantically untied our hands.

"No!" Will shouted as he was being carted away. "I will not leave her. She needs me!"

"Son, you do not have a choice," Brantley said, laying a hand on his shoulder as he walked alongside Will's moving bed.

"The heck I don't! Do you think I'm an idiot? I saw what happened when we lost contact outside not ten minutes ago. She does better with me right here and I with her!"

Leo raised his forehead. "Halt! The prince has a point, Ruth."

"You and I both know a fated match would not be able to withstand what we need to do," she responded.

"Whatever it is, I'll do it. I am not leaving. In fact, connect me to her right now. That's an order!" His growl, deep and feral, matched the flashing of his eyes.

It was as if I was watching this all happen to me from afar. All the voices were muffled, tinny. I could barely stay awake. And to be honest, I wasn't sure I even wanted to be present anymore.

When I awoke, the familiar sweet orange and woodsy scent of Will comforted me. He lay on his side, fingers caressing my cheeks and traveling up and down my arms.

Something about his face... I gasped, immediately regretting the pain it caused, as I took in how sallow his skin was.

I tried to swallow but couldn't, as if someone had jabbed

a hot poker down my throat and dried ashes of flesh now coated it. I tried to move, but my body felt as heavy as a large slab of cement. I strained to reach out to him with my gifting, trying to get a sense of what he was feeling, but couldn't even manage that.

"Would you like some water?" he asked. I nodded and he leaned back, grabbed a cup with a straw from a side table, and brought it to my lips. "Only a few sips at first, OK?"

I nodded as best I could, placed my lips over the straw, and pulled in some water.

The room was quiet. I remembered the talk of losing my leg and tore my gaze from Will.

"What?" he asked, sitting up and scanning me. "Are you hurting?"

"My leg," was all I could squeeze out. Will relaxed and gently lifted the blanket covering my lower half to the side. I sighed deeply with relief. I still had two. One was wrapped heavily in thick gauze-like material, which was soft and sticky to the touch.

"They were able to save your leg," Will shared, smiling. But I could see through that smile. Exhaustion hung in dark circles under his haunted eyes. I cupped his cheek.

"What's wrong?" I rasped.

Will dropped my gaze and I watched him open then close his mouth, swallowing down the words he wasn't quite sure how to say.

"He's been through quite the ordeal," Healer Leo answered for him as he strode into the room. Will laid back down next to me, but his gaze was far away, his skin clammy and pale. I turned to Leo for further explanation. "He insisted on being at your side while we worked on you. His bravery saved your life."

"My life was in jeopardy?" I asked, though I was surprised he could hear my whispers.

Leo gave me a quick scan and jotted down some notes on his clipboard. "You had internal bleeding and lost a lot of blood before you came to us. Then while we worked on you, some complications arose." Leo stared at Will and shook his head, his dark navy hair brushing against his forehead. "Regardless, thanks to this young man's insistence on staying with you, you survived. The power you two share is remarkable."

Will touched my throat. "The screaming..." he whispered. He started to shiver, and I leaned in and kissed him gently on the lips. I held them captive until the shivering stopped. Though it burned, I forced out, "I'm OK, Will. I'm right here."

"I do not normally have to use invasive measures to heal others, but every now and again, injuries are extensive." I turned back to Leo expectantly, hoping he'd read the unspoken questions on my face. "In your case, the added complication of a curse—as Will informed us and the likes I have not seen before—affected your entire body. As soon as we began, bright blotches covered your skin and melted into the tissues beneath. They dampened our abilities and thus slowed us down."

Leo came and laid a hand on Will's forehead. A soft pink light glowed bright, then slowly faded. "It was touch and go when we realized that nasty curse also reduced your healing. We had to open you up and proceed layer by layer. William witnessed *everything*. Not many people, exclusive of healing gifts, can stomach seeing that, especially on their fated match.

As you know, they can feel—"

I held my hand up, stopping his words in their tracks. Would I have been able to sit idly by while Will fought for his life? Watching him nearly die...watching others cut into him... I shivered and flung my arms around him.

"Thank you!" I croaked. "I don't think I could have done that for you." Shame heated my skin.

Will responded to me immediately, his arms comforting me as they held me tight. "Oh, I have no doubt you would have for me. Remember the sledding accident?"

"How could I forget," I whispered, thumbing the scar on his cheek.

"Then you remember how you were in full control and didn't hesitate to put those Christmas roses directly inside deep gashes. I'm sure after some time I will get over the 'Silence of the Lambs' procedure." He pulled away from me, just enough to hold my face, and caught his bottom lip with his teeth. "But you nearly dying? I don't think I'll ever recover from that. There have been too many close calls."

Leo cleared his throat. "Unfortunately, we were only able to stop the bleeding and tend to your leg. Your spinal injury will need treatment as soon as possible. Time is of the essence."

"So soon?" Will gritted out, the cords of his neck muscles straining under his palpable fear.

"I realize you are concerned, Your High—"

"It's Will."

"My apologies, William, may I be so bold as to remind you that you did not suffer for naught. Her leg is fixed, the curse drained from her body."

Will shuddered, and I knew he was recalling images I was very thankful to not have seen.

Leo flipped his chart and tapped a monitor. "I am getting much clearer readings on Lydia, and this needs to happen tonight if there is any hope to be had that she will walk again."

"Tonight? But can her body handle that? It hasn't even been forty-eight hours.

Leo met Will's fear-filled stare. "No, her body cannot, but—"

Will jolted, ready to fling himself out of the bed. Leo shot a gifting at Will, rooting him to the spot, and continued where he'd left off. "But with you at her side, she will be able to handle it. Now, rest up so you can be at full capacity tonight." Leo released Will from his hold and left the room.

I tapped Will's shoulder, and he redirected his attention towards me. I gestured to the pad of paper and pen on the side table. We needed to talk, but the little I did was too much, my throat raw and burning.

Will grabbed it and handed it to me. I struggled to sit up, but Will's strong hands maneuvered me into a comfortable position with the right amount of pillows behind me. I sighed in thanks and patted the space at my side. Will placed his arms over my shoulders, his side pressing firmly against mine.

I wrote, *U don't have 2.*

I stared at him, hoping he'd understand.

"I don't have to what?" Will asked.

I quickly scribbled my next message. *Stay w/ me during procedure 2nite.*

He shook his head. "Literally nothing could keep me from being there."

I huffed and started to write, *I can delay*

"But Leo said—"

I placed my finger over his mouth. "Let me finish," I rasped.

Will gave me an apologetic shrug. "Sorry, I'll be patient." He kissed the palm of my hand, and I gave him a closed-lipped smile that reached my eyes.

Then, I continued scribbling. *I can delay 'til I'm strong on my own. When I 1st woke, the look on ur face broke me. I've made u save me once. I won't make u do it again.*

Will waited to see if I would write more. When he was confident I was finished, he responded, "Liddy, you have never made me do anything. When your life was on the line..." Will shuddered. "Doing anything and everything in my power to save you was the only thing that mattered. I couldn't bear losing you. I just hate that I am not a trained healer."

I tilted my head, taking this in.

"I am forced to trust what Leo, Ruth, and all these other healers say, though I don't even know them, and I am not sure if putting you through another procedure so quickly is the right choice." He brought his forehead to mine, and I felt a surge of emotion, as if he were saying *I know you. I see all of you.* "And if we don't listen to them, and we are wrong, then we run the risk of you being paralyzed for life. I could never live with myself if I guided you to make a decision that ultimately stole your ability to dance, the one way you love to express yourself."

I pulled my head from his and scribbled on the pad, *Is that all?*

Will's lips parted in surprise, and then he laughed. After a moment, his smile turned upside down again. "What if I can't save you this time? What if—"

I silenced him by cupping his cheek with my hand, then slid it behind his head, bringing his ear to my mouth. "I trust you."

"Healer Ruth! She is waking up!"

"Consarn it! William, focus on me. Good! She cannot move, do you understand? If she moves, she dies."

"Healer Leo, she is losing too much blood."

"I told you she needed more time to heal between surgeries!"

"William, stay strong. She needs you to be strong for her. If you cannot do that, I will have you forcibly removed."

"It burns! Make it stop! I can't take it...it hurts so much. Please! Will, help me!"

"I'm right here, Princess. Just a little longer, I promise. Fight... fight for me."

My eyes fluttered open. I had the strangest feeling that I'd been in an alternate world, one full of darkness. I felt disorientated, vulnerable, trying to piece together where I was and how much time had passed. Slowly, a sense of clarity fought its way through the haze. Something warm was pressed against me. I tried to move to see what it was, but my body was numb, my brain's signals not reaching their destination. A wave of nausea hit me, and I was forced to breathe through it. The heating pad next to me moved.

"Liddy?" Will breathed out.

"I think I'm going to be sick," I whispered.

Cold air rushed against me and suddenly Will was stroking my hair, something firm pressed to my chin.

"We need a healer in here!" Will hollered over and over again, masking the sounds of my dry heaving.

Sneakers squeaked on the floor and bright lights ambushed me.

A cold hand pressed on my forehead and immediately the nausea was gone.

"Please bring her some broth and water." I opened my eyes to see Healer Ruth standing over me, Healer Leo near my feet and scanning me.

"I survived," I uttered weakly, trying to smile.

Ruth stared down at me. "That you did. A large part of that is thanks to William."

Will took up his spot next to me again, careful not to jostle me. I tried to give his hand a squeeze, though it was more like a frail pressure.

Lana came running into the room with Charlie at her heels. "Thank Eira we can finally see you. And you're awake!" Tears brimmed her eyes. She came over to greet me, but Will held his hand out.

"Gentle," he warned.

"Yes, sir," Lana said, smirking. "You know, if you weren't my son, I would take offense." She returned her attention to me. "He has spent his every waking and non-waking second by your side, only leaving to shower and use the bathroom."

Charlie came to stand by his brother, laying a hand on his shoulder. "You did it, bro." Will reached over his shoulder and gripped Charlie's hand.

Ruth stepped forward. "How are you feeling?"

"A little dazed. How long have I been out for?"

"A week," Will murmured, stroking my hair.

"A week?" I squeaked.

Leo and Ruth exchanged a telling glance.

"What is it?" I asked.

Ruth eyed the room. "Maybe you'd like some privacy as we talk and assess—"

"We are her family," Lana stated, coming to stand alongside her sons.

But Ruth did not seem to care what Lana said, her gaze holding mine.

I nodded once. "You can share."

Ruth flitted her gaze to Leo, then to Will, and back to me. "The good news is your leg was saved and is healing much more nicely than we anticipated. After it fully heals, you should only have a faint scar that runs down your shin."

"Why do Watchers not understand that you are supposed to start with the bad news?" Will gritted out.

Realization shocked me to my core. I stared at my feet and tried to wiggle my toes. *Nothing.* I tugged the blanket to the side. My leg was indeed saved, the swelling had gone down, and the oozing wound was now an angry red scar that ran the full length of my shin.

"I can't feel anything below my waist." Warm, salty tears

streamed down my face. So many emotions swirled within me, all of them grappling to be front and center. Yes, my leg was saved. I should be grateful, but what good was it if I'd never use it again?

"Please, no." Will's voice was strained. "All of this...for nothing!" Charlie pulled him from me and embraced his brother. Will stiffened at first, but as if a tidal wave of emotion broke the surface, Will sunk into his brother's arms and wept.

"No, Your Highness, not for nothing," Ruth tried to assure him. "We have no reason to believe she will not make a near-complete recovery."

Shame gripped me tight around the neck, and a sob wrenched free from the overwhelming guilt that came with it. Lana rushed over to me. I should be thankful for all the sacrifices everyone had made to save me. I was alive. Instead, I was secretly mourning everything I'd lost. Who was I without dance? Would I forever be a burden, only existing and not... living?

Leo averted his gaze, busying himself with his clipboard and the machines I was hooked up to, clearly uneasy with the heaviness that blanketed the room.

He cleared his throat. "Please know, it is far too early to tell how well the surgery worked in repairing the injury to your spine. In about a year, we should have a much clearer picture—"

"A year?" I sniffled.

"Why so long, Healer?" Lana asked, her grip on my hand strong and reassuring.

"Her injury was very severe. A year is generous, as most patients in her situation could expect it to take many years, *if* they make a full recovery at all. But Lydia is young and strong. Seeing the remarkable effects of her matching with William has on her healing gives us even more hope. But it may take us a while to determine how far her healing will go."

"Leave us," Will said flatly. I hadn't noticed him slip out of his brother's arms. Charlie was already standing by the door.

Lana walked to Will and wrapped him in an embrace. "Stay strong, son." She kissed his cheek and left the room.

"We would like to do a few tests—"

"I said, leave us," Will growled at Leo.

Ruth grabbed her colleague's elbow. "I know this is a lot to process, but we need to monitor her. We will return in the morning."

The door closed with a soft click and Will walked to it, locking the bolt and then closing the curtains to the wall of windows that overlooked the hall. He just stood there, with his back to me and shoulders slumped.

"I've failed you. You had complete trust in me, and—"

"Don't do this," I choked out through tears.

Will turned to me, his own eyes swimming with tears. I held my arms out and he crossed the room in two strides, bending over the side of the bed to hold me. We held each other for a long time.

Finally, the pain in my throat subsided enough to let me speak. "You didn't fail me. I am here, alive, because of you."

He held me tighter.

"Promise me you won't give up on me," I said.

"I could never."

Down But Not Defeated

THE NEXT FEW WEEKS WERE EXCRUCIATING. Each day that passed without any positive change made it harder and harder to keep my frustration and anger in check. Having no hope was a dangerous mindset to have, and I was straddling the edge of that cliff.

Will didn't understand why I didn't want him to be my nurse for every little thing. How could I explain how humiliating all of this was for me, to have to have someone help me use the bathroom? Luckily, I only needed a few days of manual massage on my abdomen to help me with regular bowel movements, as those nerves seemed to return from their vacation pretty quickly. Only yesterday was the semi-permanent catheter taken out and I was taught to self-cath.

"Day nineteen. How are you doing?" Ruth asked, a cheery

smile on her face that sadly did nothing to cheer me up.

"No change." My voice came out clipped.

Ruth's lips pressed into a hard line as she attempted to smile at me. "Lydia, I think it may help to get out of this room some." She turned her attention to Will, who sat staring out the window. "William, what do you think about that?"

Will glanced over his shoulder and shrugged.

Ruth left without a word. An hour later, a fist pounded on our door, and then it whipped open, startling me and Will, who had been in the process of helping me into my chair. Nick sprang into the room, his face pink.

"You almost made me drop her!" Will spat.

"You would fall on a sword before you'd let her fall. Now, what is this I hear? Since when do you both wallow in the pit of despair?"

"Save it," Will snapped. I placed my hand on his forearm.

My eyes locked with Nick's in a moment of unspoken communication. Then the tears began to flow.

"Balderdash," Nick breathed. He started toward me, but Will was in front of him in a flash, grabbing him by the collar of his shirt and pushing him backward.

"Will!" I called. But his anger was louder than my plea.

"You made her cry," Will growled. "Get out."

Nick latched onto Will's forearms and spun him around so that Nick was the one pushing Will. "We'll just be a minute," Nick called to me over his shoulder. "Will needs to take a little walk with me."

Nick grabbed for the door, but just before it closed completely, a little flash of blue sparked.

Loud voices were muffled by the door, and then, nothing.

I sat in my chair, trying to focus on Will's emotions to garner some insight into their discussion.

A few moments later, Will walked in with a new light in his eyes and a pep in his step. Nick was smiling. I blinked at them in confusion.

"Liddy, would you mind if I visited my family for a little while today?" Will asked, his hand raking through his hair. His nervous tick.

"Of course! You don't need to ask. You aren't chained to me." An uncomfortable heat churned in my chest as I thought of my family. Then, embarrassment washed over me, and I was ashamed that my boyfriend felt like he had to ask my permission to leave my side, like I was too weak to handle a day without him.

"Liddy, I didn't mean—"

"Will, I've got this," Nick said. "Go visit with your family. We will meet up with you later."

Will sighed and squatted down so we were at eye level. "I won't be gone long. I love you." He kissed me on the cheek and jogged out the door.

Of course he ran. He couldn't get away from me fast enough.

"Stop it," Nick said, his voice even.

Did I say that out loud? "Stop what?" I asked defensively.

"Part of healing is in here." Nick tapped his head with his index finger. "I have never known you to just give up."

I dropped my gaze to my lap. "What do you know?" I groused.

"Well, for starters, Ruth tells me that you have not left this room in the past ten days when you were cleared to do so."

I shrugged. "As you already know, I can't walk."

"And?" Nick shook his head. "What does that have to do with leaving your room?"

"It has everything to do with it! To have to be pushed around...to lose all sense of independence? To have everything stolen from me in the blink of an eye?" I snapped my fingers.

"No, Liddy. All hope is not lost. You have not lost everything...not even close." Nick took a step toward me, and I covered my face with my hands.

"I'm a burden. I can't expect Will to stay with me." I sobbed into my hands, sobs that wracked my body. After a moment, Nick laid a hand on my shoulder, his gifting pouring into me. I shrugged him off.

"We will face your fears together. But please know, even if you never walk again, which no one believes, you still have so much to offer this world. We need you. Will...needs you."

"This-is-so-unfair," I gasped between breaths, my chest cleaving in two.

Tentatively, Nick placed his hand on my shoulder again, his healing a tender embrace to my soul. "I cannot imagine your pain. But I do know that your story is not over yet. This too shall pass."

I cried until the tears would no longer fall. Nick had pulled up a chair, keeping his hand on my shoulder, continually encouraging me through the breakdown.

When I finally lifted my chin, Nick gave me a tight smile that showcased his few crow's feet. He stood and went to the sink, returning with a wet washcloth which he held out to me.

"Thank you." I sniffled, taking the washcloth and pressing it against my face.

"How about we go for that walk now and meet back up with Will?"

I bit my lip. "I don't think I should intrude on his family time."

Nick blew a raspberry. "Rubbish. I had to practically punt him down the hallway to get away from you. Both of you were a sorry lot, and he needed to get out. Just like you need to get out. But, if we do not meet him soon, I'm afraid he will come racing back here in a panic."

I wiped my eyes once more. "OK."

The hall was empty as Nick wheeled me past the desk that a young healer-in-training manned, stopping at a fork in the hallway. We followed the gradual curve on the left, where a mosaic of plants covered most of the bamboo walls.

Nick pushed me slowly, letting me admire the plants that were every shade of green imaginable. A familiar floral scent filled the air as I rolled past. My senses heightened and I held my hand out. Nick stopped.

"I know that scent," I whispered. I was immediately brought back to the morning I woke and discovered the Jamisons had fled Cherrywood Drive.

"Ah, yes. I imagine you do. Valsanthe is a rare flower, but its petals are used in many tinctures." He walked over to the wall of plants and started gently moving leaves and vines. "I had to use some in a tincture the morning after Charlie was taken to help Will's family move swiftly."

A few white petals poked out from a sea of foliage. Nick brushed away the two big leaves that blocked the flower and it sprang out, the blossom larger than my outstretched hand. Its long slender petals came to a point at the end, and a large mass of small, bell-shaped petals dotted its center.

Nick stretched the flower to me. I rubbed a petal between my thumb and index finger, then leaned in and inhaled, the scent so overwhelming, I almost fell from my chair.

"Damfino!" Nick helped me to sit up and a blue light danced from his palm and up into my nose. "I apologize for not telling you before I handed the Valsanthe to you." Nick guided the flower back to her hiding place. "You are not supposed to inhale it in raw form. It won't hurt you, but it can sure make you dizzy. Are you able to continue?"

I nodded. "Where are we headed to anyway?"

"To visit Shai."

We traveled down a few more halls and came to a hall with a single door. A soft pink glow pulsed from the bottom of it.

"We are here," Nick said. He rolled me up closer to the door and knocked three times.

A healer with a blond bun at the top of his head and shaved on the sides answered the door.

"Come in, come in. I am Wallace. We have been expecting you."

Wallace wore an aqua long-sleeve top with a mock turtleneck and jogger bottoms. Its design was in much the same fashion as the training gear Will and I wore at Shai's when we had first learned to wield our giftings. It must have been some sort of uniform here in Cristes, or at least a popular design choice. I wondered if it, too, held magic that protected him from unwarranted gifting attacks, though I couldn't fathom why it would.

When I saw Shai, I nearly burst into tears. Nearly every

inch of him was wrapped in bright white, scarf-like dressings, the same type of bandages that encased my leg after surgery. It was hard to assess how Shai was doing as only his eyes, a bit of his nose, and his mouth remained uncovered.

"His eyes fluttered a little today," Wallace said, breaking the silence. "Which is excellent news. It means he is still with us and one day may wake."

Magenta seeped into the white bandage that wrapped around Shai's head.

"What's happening to him?" I squeaked.

Nick laid a hand on my shoulder, a wave of calm washing through me.

"That is a medicinal salve for the brain. Lord Abishai sustained numerous skull fractures resulting in extensive swelling. We needed to remove a portion of the skull to help his brain heal. Once the tissues restore fully, we will be able to take a portion of bone from his ribs and close his skull."

"But he will fully heal?" Will asked from a corner of the room. I hadn't even noticed he was there.

"We choose to remain hopeful," Wallace responded, but he didn't meet Will's eyes.

I relaxed some, but knowing Shai may not make a full recovery was unsettling. More unpleasant and uninvited thoughts crept into my mind: a portion of his skull missing, with parts of his brain matter exposed. Suddenly, I didn't feel so well.

I expected Will to come and help me through the nausea, or even Nick, but was surprised when Charlie appeared before me.

"I've got you," he said.

"Thanks...have you been here long?" I stopped talking to focus on my breathing as he placed his hands on my shoulders, bringing his face into full view of mine.

"Will has been here a little longer than me." Charlie dropped his gaze. "I wanted to give him some time alone with Uncle Shai. I just came back a few minutes before you got here."

Nick was talking quietly with Wallace just outside the hall. Charlie led me to the foot of Shai's bed.

Will was seated at the edge of the bed, his back to me. From his profile, I observed him at his uncle's side, his hand resting gently on Shai's. Will's face was soft and thoughtful. Though he appeared at peace, a gentle tugging pulled all my attention to my match, letting the background noise fade into nothingness.

I expected my heart to squeeze painfully in conjunction with Will's. I expected my chest to tighten, making it hard to breathe. Heck, I even expected to feel tiny pricks of fire behind my eyes as tears threatened to spill over. But what I didn't expect was the black hole of guilt that Will was being sucked into with absolutely no resistance.

Focusing on Will's face, I followed a single tear as it slid down his sullen cheek. I would not let him disappear into despair. Not when we had already struggled so much over these past few weeks. Not when we were just starting to work on our mindsets, not letting our circumstances break us.

"I crushed him," Will croaked. I winced, recalling Shai's broken body. "He's hanging on by a thread because of *me*... he protected *me*, and now he might die because of *me*." Will ran his hands through his hair, yanking so hard I thought he'd scalp himself.

His torment crashed into me over and over again, hard and fast like waves in a tsunami. Not being able to get up, walk over to him and embrace him so I could take some of his pain was beyond frustrating.

Charlie shrank back into the shadowed corner of the room. Suffering was something he was all too familiar with, and I couldn't help but frown as the light in his eyes that had only recently returned to him dimmed a little.

With my hand pressed against Will's back, I thought of a hundred reasons why he was blameless and worthy of his uncle's love—all the things that made him unique and amazing—and then poured all of that into him.

He arched his back slightly, and I sighed when his hands gripped mine.

"There is nothing I've done to deserve you, Princess," Will whispered. He strained his neck to kiss my cheek.

"What is Lydia doing out of bed?" a woman's voice I would recognize anywhere scolded from the doorway.

Will shot off the bed and ran over to Lana. "Hey, Mom! The Healers felt it was time for her and I to explore the sanctum a little." He picked his mom up and twirled her around. She laughed as Brantley and Nick walked into the room.

"Put me down," she said, joy shining in the fine lines near her eyes. She walked over to Charlie, who waited quietly in a corner, and hugged him hello. When Lana spotted the reason she was here—her brother, Shai, unresponsive and broken in the healer's bed—her face fell.

"So, now you and Liddy are up to date," Brantley said, resting a hand on his son's shoulder. Will only nodded, his happy mood souring. "All is not lost, son."

"Shai is strong." Charlie came to stand beside the rest of his family. "He will make it through this."

Lana blotted the corners of her eyes with her fingertips. "Yes, he is out of the woods regarding the chance of death. However, we have not been able to determine if he will ever return to us."

"Wallace said his eyes fluttered today," Nick offered. "He told us that's a good sign."

Lana whipped her head to Brantley, who had a wide smile on his face. "I mean, I really want to tell you I told you so, but—"

Lana swatted his shoulder as a short giggle erupted from her, and then we were all laughing in celebration.

With no warning, exhaustion sunk its claws in greedily and tried to pull my eyelids shut. Will's attention snapped to me for a brief moment before he addressed his parents. "I need to take Liddy back to our room so she can rest."

I made to protest, but his lips silenced me with a swift kiss.

"No fair," I whispered, scrunching my nose and narrowing my eyes at him. His chuckle, warm and deep, reverberated through me, and I shivered.

"William, can you please come back here for a short time when you get her situated? I have something I would like to discuss with you," Lana said.

"Of course, Mom."

"You are welcome to stay, Liddy, but we understand and agree with our son that you need rest. We do not want you to push yourself and hinder your healing. Will can fill you in when you wake."

"Thank you, Lana."

Nick patted me on the shoulder. "If you ever need anything, just call for me."

I nodded. "Thank you," I said quietly. "For today." Nick gave me a solemn nod in return.

Will walked me back to our room. With one swift motion, I was in his strong arms. His eyes lit up to a bright teal before he gently placed me on the bed.

"What are you smiling about?" he asked coyly.

"Oh, I don't know, probably anticipating the delicious kiss you are about to give me," I said, suddenly awake. It had been longer than I cared to count since Will last kissed me... really kissed me.

"You think you are so smart, acting like you *know* what I am going to do before I do it." He brushed the hair from my forehead and slid it behind my ear as he drew his face closer to mine, his eyes smoldering. All I had to do was pucker my lips and they'd be touching his. At the last second, he ducked his head into the crook of my neck and blew a raspberry.

I shrieked with laughter. His playfulness turned to soft kisses that trailed up my neck and to my jaw and...

The abrupt loss of his touch sent my body into a spiral of longing.

Will's bottom lip was pinned beneath his teeth as he stood next to the bed. His eyes were aglow to nearly sixty watts, but his face had sobered.

"Rest, now, alright?" he said, his voice husky. "I'll be back soon."

I wished I could have curled onto my side, hugged my knees to my chest, and cried. *Why won't he kiss me?*

Stronger Together

"AND HOW ARE YOU FEELING TODAY, WILLIAM?" Healer Ruth asked upon first entering the room.

Will and I had been playing cards, and he stiffened. He hated this question. We were asked at least twice a day and since he was fine and I had not improved much, he didn't like to share his good fortune in front of me. He argued that it only added salt to the wound.

He let out an exasperated sigh as he eyed a Watcher who'd come into the room. "I'm fine, thanks."

Ruth gave him a smile, but he just continued to concentrate on his cards. "I know you must be so tired of my questioning. But you too had severe injuries, and you overextended yourself in those first few days. I have to make sure you are trending toward full recovery."

Will got up to face her. "I'm sorry. Can we talk outside?"

"Of course, after I am done introducing Harvey."

Another healer followed at her heels. His cropped light-brown hair swept freely over his forehead.

"William, Lydia...this is Healer Harvey. He will be taking Lydia to the training room to help her begin her rehabilitation program."

He bowed to us in the Cristes salutation. "It is nice to meet you both," he said, his voice deep and rich.

Will's bicep flexed. "Isn't it a little too soon for this?"

Now it was Ruth's turn to huff out a breath of irritation. "No, it is not. We discussed this. I respected your wishes to hold off last week, and again three days ago. I have spoken with Lydia, and she wants to begin."

Will turned his gaze on me, a pang of hurt registering in our bond.

I couldn't bring myself to lie to him. "I'm not getting better, Will. But I'd like to try," I admitted.

As he dropped his chin, a heavy weight of fear pressed on my chest, making it hard to breathe. I wheeled over to him and nudged him behind the knee.

"Ruth, Harvey...can you please give me and Will a minute?" I asked, my eyes locked with Will's in a wordless exchange.

"What are you so scared of?" I asked as soon as I heard the door close.

"Nothing." Will tried to smile but couldn't fool me.

Crossing my arms, I asked, "Since when do we lie to each other?

Will blew out a long breath, wheeled me back to the small

round table where we'd been playing cards, and sat in the chair opposite me.

"Fine, you got me. I'm...scared."

I reached out to take his hand. "Of what? Therapy is meant to help me, not harm me."

"But what if it does? What if their best intentions ruin the little that remains intact in your spine?" His face was so earnest, begging me to agree with him. But I couldn't.

"Is that why you won't kiss me?"

Will's eyes widened in shock. "What? I kiss you all the time."

"Yeah, like I'm just some good friend."

"That's not true," he retorted, dropping my hand in favor of running his own through his hair.

"Please, Will. If you're not in love with me anymore, if this is all too much, just tell—"

Will shot from his chair, and I flinched as it crashed to the ground. "How could you think so little of me?"

Tears streamed down my face. "Because I know I'm no longer what you signed up for. I see how hard this all is, a burden for you, and I can imagine someone as young as you would not want to be saddled to—"

"Enough!" Will's eyes flashed with a passion and possessiveness I'd never witnessed before. His emotions were so ramped up it felt as if I were being struck by miniature lightning bolts. Overwhelmed, I dropped my face into my hands.

It was quiet for a few moments when a knock sounded at the door. "One minute!" Will yelled.

Careful as if I were a newborn babe, Will lifted me from

my chair, laid me in bed, and snuggled up close, wrapping his arm around my waist.

"Sweet Liddy. I'm at a loss for words." And then I felt it... the moment he'd finally realized I was not accusing him of anything, rather I was letting him off the hook. He hugged me tighter. "It would be my pleasure to take care of you for the rest of my life. Literally, nothing short of death could separate us...maybe not even then."

"But I don't want you to love me out of obligation." I sniffled through sobs.

Will got on his knees and carefully turned me on my side, laying back down to face me. "Nothing could be further from the truth."

"But you aren't attracted to me anymore, I know it."

"Who is telling you these lies so I can kill them?" Will deadpanned. But then he cracked a smile. "I have to admit, I've been too stressed to think of anything else but your health, but that doesn't mean—"

"Don't you think connection with you would be good for my healing?"

Will scrunched his eyes, wrestling with his thoughts as if they pained him.

I reached out and stroked his hair, offering reassurance. "Please, Will. Just try it. I won't break...it's just kissing."

Will tried to keep a smirk off his face as we both recalled Nick letting Pree know, *It is anything but just a kiss.*

"Seriously, Will. I need you. We're more powerful together."

Will groaned, then ran a hand through his hair. "I'm worried I won't be able to stop."

"Oh." I blushed. "Well, we have two healers who are waiting patiently outside this door. Can we try and see?"

His jaw clenched and ticked as he searched my eyes.

And then, a cunning grin spread across his face, setting my body to *aye carumba* hot. He turned to sit and straddled my hips, careful not to place any of his weight on me. He leaned forward, his chiseled body moving into my space, forcing me to lay back into the pillows.

"Wait, is the door locked? What if Ruth and—"

"Let them see. Their fault if they don't know how to listen to a simple request."

I gaped up at him. What had gotten into him? He'd been too afraid to touch me in Mortalia, so as not to put us in danger with Mara, and too afraid here with all my injuries.

His mouth swallowed my gasp. His slow kiss left me desperate, demanding more, as his hands ran down my arms and entangled themselves with mine, stilling me. The kiss deepened, and I sighed with pleasure. One of his hands slid behind my back, capturing the nape of my neck. He took his time with his massage. Every vertebra he caressed, his touch feather-light, tingled as he moved from my neck, to my mid-back, then slowly lower, and...

ZAP!

"Will!" I squeaked.

He pulled back, his body aglow in teal and pink, and I momentarily forgot how to speak. Would I ever get used to how breathtaking he was?

"Do you want me to stop?" His lips and breath tickled my ear, then jaw, then neck.

No, I don't want you to stop. "I... I..."

He stilled his lips, which had been trailing kisses along my collarbone. "Did I hurt you?"

"No. There was a little zing down my legs. When you, ummm, when you were..." I bit the inside of my cheek.

He moved so fast I barely registered his movements until he was at the door ushering in Ruth and Harvey, who had to shield their eyes from the bright light Will emanated.

"What happened?" Ruth asked.

"Ummm, Will was massaging my back and a little zing ran down my legs." I dropped my gaze, slightly embarrassed by my glow. "I mean, it lasted maybe half a second. It was probably my imagination."

"Lydia, your foot," Harvey said, pointing to it.

Sure enough, my foot twitched a few times.

"Harvey, please call Healer Leo," Ruth instructed, and Harvey bolted from the room. "Now, Will, can you please show me exactly what you were doing to her back?"

Kill. Me. Now. My eyes beseeched Will in a silent plea.

He came and sat on the side of the bed and began to touch each vertebra. "Well, Liddy reminded me that our connection helps us heal."

"Understandable," Ruth said, her clipboard in hand, ready to take some riveting notes. This was all data to her.

Will refused to look at me. He was going to tell her, *actually* tell her. Now my body heated to scalding, but for completely different reasons.

"In the past, our connection has been more intense when we are connected in ways beyond holding hands...if you catch what I'm throwing, which you probably do by the way we were...*are* still glowing."

An audible smack resounded in the room. Will tried but wasn't fast enough to stop me from slapping my hand over my face.

Ruth shifted her weight from one foot to the other, curling the stripe of pink hair around her finger. "Are you talking about intercourse, Your Majesty? Because that could be very dangerous for her right now."

"No! I'm not an idiot."

"I was not suggesting—"

"All we did was kiss, and while we were kissing, I attempted to push the energy it gave me back into her," he explained, gesturing wildly. "Specifically, into her spine."

Ruth's brows raised high on her forehead. "And what gave you the idea to do that?"

Will shrugged. "My Uncle Shai once told me he thinks one of my lesser giftings is healing. And the idea just came to me."

"And you glowed that brightly from a kiss?" Ruth narrowed her eyes and pursed her lips.

"You don't have to believe me, but that's what happened," Will huffed.

"I believe you, it's just... I am going to check on Leo." Ruth tucked the pink strip of hair back into its clip. "I shall return promptly."

When the door closed behind her, Will turned to me and a slow, flirtatious smile slid into place.

"What are *you* so happy about?" I asked. "I'm mortified. You know how much I hate that everyone literally knew we were doing something intimate!"

"We will learn to control that. But you are missing the point."

"And what is that?" I asked, my voice about three octaves higher than normal.

His smile widened to a full-watt grin. "You got feeling back in your legs. If I have to kiss and massage you twenty-four hours a day, seven days a week, then sign me up. My princess is going to walk again!"

Straight-Up Chaos

"GOOD MORNING, PRINCESS. Ready for therapy?" Harvey asked me as I sat at the table in front of the fire, eating breakfast with Will.

Ruth and Leo were so excited with yesterday's developments that instead of having me do physical therapy, they decided to run some tests...make that a lot of tests.

"How long will this take?" Will winked at me, shuffling cards. "I was about to beat Liddy in a round of Speed."

Harvey straightened, not sensing Will's playfulness. "For the first day, not long, Your Highness. We—"

Will held up a hand. "I must stop you right there. My name is Will—just Will—please."

Harvey nodded. "Will, we will start with only one or two small exercises as she builds endurance. With your permission,

Liddy, I will use my gifting to scan your body and make sure everything is working as it should as we attempt each new movement. If everything checks out, we will continue those exercises until they are no longer a bother or are no longer challenging."

Ruth walked in. Will waved to her but then asked Harvey, "What do you mean until they are no longer a bother?"

Harvey pressed his lips into a tight line and turned to Ruth. She nodded her permission for him to continue. "Well, at first, each new exercise we teach Liddy will be challenging. It may also be painful at first, but my team and I will be making sure that every step of the way, she is safe."

Will bristled. "No. Figure out a different way."

I laid my hand on his forearm and plastered on a big smile. "No pain, no gain."

Harvey's eyes flicked between us and Ruth, Will's protectiveness making him uneasy.

Ruth shook her head. "Lydia will need to prove the results for at least five consecutive days before she can advance to the next step," she explained while tying her chestnut hair into a ponytail. "William, maybe it would be best if you visited your uncle or spent the day with your brother?"

He shook his head. "I won't leave Liddy when—"

"I think that is a great idea." I smiled warmly at him.

Will eyed me incredulously. "You do?"

I could feel the hurt rolling off of him. I placed my hand over his. "What I mean is... Well, you and I are so connected that I worry about...well, I don't worry, but I do take your feelings..." I trailed off, sinking back into my chair, unsure of how to turn my thoughts into words that wouldn't further hurt him.

Harvey interjected, "What she means is, because you can feel her pain, you may try to stop the session. Because, of course, it would be extremely hard for you to just sit and let her experience pain." He crossed his thick arms. "I assure you, however, that if you do join us and stop our therapies, you will delay her healing."

"Is this true?" Will blinked at me, his thumb now rubbing lazy circles on my palm.

I sighed and dropped my gaze. "I just know how difficult it would be for me if our places were reversed, and I know my instinct would be to rescue you from the situation."

"A time estimate, please," Will requested, his gaze never leaving mine. When no one answered him, he twisted his neck to glance over at Harvey. "About what time will you return? I'd like to be here when she gets back."

I awoke to hushed voices. I cracked an eye open to witness Will tiptoeing into the room and closing the door on whoever was in the hall.

"Hi," I said, my voice weak with sleep.

He turned around. "I didn't mean to wake you. How did your first day go?"

I sat up and peered out the window. The day had slipped away, and blue and golds painted the sky as night began to make an appearance.

"It was...better than I expected, but also frustrating." My stomach growled.

Will smiled. "I see you worked up an appetite?"

"I could eat. I only meant to take a quick nap until you returned. What have you been up to?"

Will walked over to the fire and stoked it. "I hung out with Mom, Dad, and Charlie at the castle for a little bit." He popped his head out the door to call for some dinner. Then he snuggled onto his side in the bed and slid me to him until my back was pressed against his chest. One hand lazily stroked my arm. "I know everything has happened so quickly since we've been here."

"Straight-up chaos," I agreed.

Will continued his rhythmic caress. "I inquired about Alex."

My stomach tightened. Will and Alex never got along and, at best, tolerated each other. Yet, Will still had the foresight to check in on him.

"Well, I feel like a terrible person," I huffed.

"Why?"

"Because I haven't even thought about Alex these past few weeks."

Will squeezed me into him. "Listen, we crash-landed here, and you have literally been fighting for your life since." He nuzzled his nose into my neck. "Don't give me too much credit. Me asking about Alex was more for me than any concern for him."

I gazed over my shoulder and knitted my brow.

Will chuckled and kissed the tip of my nose. "I don't trust him, and I don't know if I'll ever be capable of doing so. Not after he put your life in jeopardy so many times."

I understood where Will was coming from, but I also

understood Alex's motivations. Desperate people make desperate choices. "So, what did you learn?"

The anger that coursed through me was not my own, and I braced myself as Will prepared to speak. "He is being held with a foster family here, on guard all day and night. Charlie believes that he is not a threat and that he is truly sorry."

"Well, we should trust Charlie, right?"

"Of course. It's just...difficult."

A knock at the door interrupted us, and Will hopped up to open it. He thanked the staff who delivered my dinner, and as he came toward the bed holding my food tray, I sat up and fluffed my pillows.

"What else did you talk about with your parents?" I asked, sensing he had more to tell me.

Will set my tray down in my lap. "My parents have a theory they would like us to try out." A pregnant pause lingered, but I gave him the time he needed to gather his thoughts and join me back on the bed. He let out a heavy sigh. "They want us to use our combined giftings to heal Shai."

I dropped the forkful of mashed potatoes onto my plate. "Why do they...what makes them think—"

"I know, right? I felt just as confused as you. But then they brought up things about Watchers and provided some new information, and, well, I'd like to share them with you. Then we can decide together what to do."

"Ooooo-kay." I picked my fork back up and took a bite.

"We've been hearing for a while now that we show promise of having white-lighter powers, right?"

I nodded, but Nick's words still hung heavy around my neck. They knew for sure Will held white-lighter gifting, but me? *You, dear, are a strong theory.*

"White-lighter pairings combined are able to wield all of the giftings. For example, with us, we know my giftings are green and pink. Yours are purple and blue. So—"

"I'm a blue?" I paused, a strawberry inches from my mouth.

"Well, my parents think so. And they reminded me of your eye color as a child."

He was right—my eyes were blue before they changed to violet junior year. "And what about the other colors?" I asked, curious about the gold and brown factions.

Will plucked a strawberry from my bowl and downed it before continuing. "We're not sure yet, and probably won't know until after we get married and our giftings merge."

My cheeks must have turned pink as Will waggled his brows at me. I threw a grape at him, which he deftly caught in his mouth.

"Let's say we want to heal someone. The partner without the gifting—you—can provide the partner with the gifting—me—a power boost, so to speak. In other words, I can draw from your power to strengthen mine."

"And they think I can give you this power boost?" Once again, Nick's words that I was a theory haunted me.

"Yes, they do. Once you are strong enough, of course. You have a near-complete spinal injury, correct?" I nodded, but my face pinched in curiosity at the change of direction in conversation. "Well," he continued, "what Leo and Ruth didn't tell you is that initially, it was a complete injury. But my parents hypothesize that I must have subconsciously tried my healing on you, as a fated pairing would."

"Yeah, but how do they *know* that?"

Will grabbed my hand and locked eyes with mine. "Because of what happened when I was purposely putting healing into your spine and you got that zap of feeling. My parents were intrigued that I was able to help heal such an extensive injury without any training."

I cupped his cheek. "I love you, and I do believe you helped me to heal. I'll forever be grateful to you for giving my body a fighting chance."

Will hugged me tighter. "That is not all that gives them hope for our potential in helping heal Uncle Shai. The other day, when we kissed and you got that little spark of feeling back? They recognized that not only was I untrained, but also weak due to my injuries. And if I was weak and could do what I did, imagine the potential when I'm healthy again."

I took a long swig of juice, processing what Will had shared.

"So, are you willing to try and heal Shai with me?" Will asked.

"Of course!" I blurted out. Then, I laughed at my passionate outburst. Will's expression was so hopeful I didn't want to lay on him the downer thoughts I was having about my own abilities.

But Will didn't laugh. He squeezed me tighter. "I was afraid you'd say yes, without thinking what that might mean for you."

"I don't understand."

"Well, for starters, you are modest and like to keep things private."

My stomach flipped at the realization of what he implied.

He was right. I definitely hadn't thought of *that*. When I got some feeling back, we had been sharing a passionate kiss. We knew our powers were heightened when we were *close*.

"Which wouldn't be a problem," he continued. "Because we don't have to have an audience. But..." Will trailed off, worrying his lip.

Now I was thoroughly confused. I turned my body and held my head back to gaze up at him. "We don't have to have an audience, but..." I prodded. I was all ears if Will could think of a way that we could call on our power that didn't include PDA.

Will flopped onto his back and draped his forearm over his face, shielding himself from my gaze. "They think we should get married."

"Married?" I tried the word, and was pleasantly surprised when excitement rather than panic set in.

Will's neck turned pink, the color traveling up the thick column of his throat. "Yes. When we consummate the marriage, our bond will snap into place both fully and permanently. We will gain access to our giftings that have currently only partially awakened."

I was quiet for a moment. This was huge, but if I was honest with myself...

"I told them no," he said at the exact moment I replied, "I'll do it."

He dropped his arm and lifted himself onto his elbow. Now it was his turn to furrow his brow, and I reached up and massaged the crease that formed between them just as he'd done for me a minute ago.

"Will, I love you. You and I both know where this

relationship is heading. There is no one else for me. Ever. If us getting hitched sooner than later can help save Uncle Shai, I am all for it."

Will tried to hide a smile, but did a terrible job at it considering his dimple still creased. "Getting hitched?"

I smacked him playfully on the shoulder and rolled my eyes. "You know what I mean."

"I told you before. When we marry, it will be our choice. I do not want it to be because of any other reason than what we want."

"Do you not want to marry me?" My voice quivered on purpose, and I had to press my lips into a thin line to hide the giggle that wanted to escape. I already knew the true answer.

"What? How could you ask that? Of course I want to marry you. Liddy, you're—"

Laughter escaped me in a burst, and my head dropped onto his chest.

"That's not nice," he said, giving me a soft noogie.

I lifted my head and planted a kiss on his lips. Playful at first, my hands slid behind his head and through his hair, my kiss deepening with the movement. He returned my advances, matching my passion.

Zap, Zap, ZAP!

I gasped at the sensation in my feet and behind my knees. I think Will mistook that sound as something else and deepened the kiss. I didn't mind in the slightest. After a few more minutes, I pulled away before a beacon could shine from us like a lighthouse guiding a ship home.

"Everything alright?" he whispered.

"Yes, more than alright. I had feeling for a second in both

feet and behind my knees this time." I pressed my forehead to Will's as our smiles lit up the room. "Listen, I'm aware I freaked out at Christmas, thinking you were proposing to me. But, well, a lot has happened since then, and—"

Will placed a finger over my lips, silencing my words. "How about this—we spend a heck of a lot of time making out. If we can't muster strong enough giftings, then we consider marriage."

I laughed. "Deal."

"Alright, we should get some sleep. We can start tomorrow."

"You're kidding, right?" I scoffed. "I was literally just sleeping for hours. I'm not tired."

Will dragged his hand down his face. "I am so sorry. I have my very own Sleeping Beauty right here and I forgot she spent all day in bed. I'll go freshen up, and we can get back to..." He waggled his brows at me, and I laid my hand on his chest to still him.

I tilted my head and studied his strong jaw and rumpled shirt. Tonight wasn't it. There was no hiding the shadows under his kind eyes, not to mention, through our bond, his fatigue threatened to pull me back asleep right along with him.

"No. I need to get out of this room, and you need to rest. You've clearly depleted yourself, and I have no problem exploring the halls on my own for a little while." When apprehension entered his features, I quickly added, "I won't be gone long. Promise."

Though my arms were getting stronger, when Will offered to help me into my chair, I obliged. As I rolled out of our room, I scanned the amber-lit hallway until the door closed behind me with a soft click. Then I proceeded in the direction of Shai's room.

When I'd made it to the hallway with the Valsanthe flower, a familiar red braid caught my eye.

"Tia, right?"

She uncurled her arms from across her chest and pushed off the wall she had been leaning against.

"Good memory." She smiled and walked over to me.

"What are you doing here, especially so late?" I asked her. She quirked her brow at me. "If you don't mind my asking," I added quickly.

"Visiting my brother Tannon. Poor lad's bored out of his mind. I brought him his favorite treat, honey sticks." She reached into her back pocket and procured five slender straws. She fanned them out, an ombre rainbow made of various shades of gold.

"Honey sticks?" I asked, having never heard of such a thing.

She stepped forward and handed me the darkest one from the end. She took the lightest one with the purple hue on the opposite end and tore the tip open with her teeth. I followed her lead and sucked from the straw.

"Well, I'm an idiot." I laughed at myself. "It quite literally is honey in a stick."

A laugh escaped Tia, and a little bit of honey flew from her mouth hitting the tire of my chair. "Dog water!" She smacked her forehead as her neck turned beet red and she attempted to clean up the splat with the cuff of her sleeve.

I couldn't hold it in any longer, and I busted with a deep

belly laugh. At first, Tia joined me, but I continued long after she stopped. She regarded me as if I'd cracked.

"Sorry...sorry," I said, wiping a tear from my eye. "I legitimately needed that."

"I am relieved you did not send me away for practically spitting on you," Tia said.

"Never. It was hilarious and so something I would have done. I think we will be fast friends."

Suddenly, I felt like the biggest jerk in the world. Did I truly not care what happened to everyone else, especially those who risked their lives to get me and my friends to safety?

"So, he's still here? Is he going to be OK?"

"Tannon's healing has been on the slower side, but the healers believe it had something to do with the elemental magic the Black Roses used. They assure me that he can come home tomorrow or the day after."

I sighed with relief.

"Can I see him tomorrow? I'd love to thank him for his sacrifice."

The side of Tia's mouth quirked up. "Sure! He'd love that. Tomorrow, then. Have a peaceful night, Princess."

I nodded my head and she turned away, both her pockets filled to the brim with sticks of honey in every color and shade of the rainbow.

I continued on my journey to Shai's room, having taken a wrong turn only once, and wound up at the door with the pink pulsing light. I paused just outside the doorway, knocking before I entered.

"One moment!" A familiar male's voice called out, followed by a rustling noise. A moment later the door opened.

"Charlie!" I whisper-yelled. "So glad to see you."

Charlie opened the door wider. I took my cue and rolled myself into the room, appreciating its warmth after roaming the chilly halls.

He bent low to hug me and then stepped back, rubbing his hand on the back of his neck. I took a moment to study him. In less than a month of being in Cristes, Charlie changed a heck of a lot from when he first landed. Gone were the bags under his eyes. Though still pale, his skin was livelier, not the sickly ashen color it was when he stumbled from Mara's portal. He'd put on a few pounds of muscle as well.

"Your eyes," I whispered behind my hand.

"I'm sorry? I couldn't understand that."

I removed my hand and cleared my throat, trying to stop the giggles of happiness at having the real Charlie back. "Your eyes. They're very blue again."

"Are they? I...uh, I haven't really noticed," Charlie said sheepishly, looking back at something over his shoulder. As he turned away, I swore I saw a glint of orange spark in his irises.

I clamped down on the visceral reaction that quickly came to a boil. It had to be residual from his time with Mara. Heck, I didn't expect him to look this well so quickly. Not after being imprisoned and tortured for eight years in Beldam. His body needed some time.

"I suppose I'm not surprised, though," Charlie said, turning back to face me. "Healers have been with me since I arrived, and I'm sure they used at least fifty Christmas roses on me these past few weeks."

"Will you stay while I visit Shai?" I asked.

"I've been here long enough. If I don't return to the castle, Mom might organize a search party."

"No, we definitely don't want to worry her. It was nice bumping into you. Please come and visit anytime you'd like."

Charlie nodded and gave me a tight-lipped smile before walking out. I turned my gaze to Shai as he lay in the bed. His body was still wrapped in the tacky, gauze-like bandages. I watched for a long time, his body still, the only signs of life the weak rise and fall of his chest.

I winced when the machine made a soft tinkling chime, and then the magenta liquid seeped into his white bandages. Shai sighed heavily and the tincture disappeared, leaving white bandages again.

Once again, shame over spending so much of my time being angry that I couldn't walk while he was fighting for his life seized me. I wiped away a tear that slipped out before I could even muster the energy to stop it.

Warm hands rested on my shoulders. Had I not known it was Will, I may have been scared, but my body was no stranger to his when he was near.

"I'll never not be thankful for his sacrifice." I sniffled as I patted his hand over my shoulder.

When Will still hadn't said anything, I peered up at him over my shoulder. I could see the pulsing in his jaw as he clenched it.

I pulled at my bottom lip with my thumb and forefinger. "Are you OK? Do you want to leave?"

"I'll be alright," he answered, grabbing a chair and placing it next to mine. "I just wish he'd never had to be put in this position in the first place." He studied his hands, and I felt his love for his uncle wash through me. "I wish there was something more we could do that would help him right now."

I didn't want to make him promises I couldn't keep, but I desperately wanted to help Shai while also making Will feel better.

I turned and smiled at him, biting down on my lip to keep myself from glowing at the sight of him. I sighed wistfully at his delicious profile. His white t-shirt stretched tightly across his sculpted shoulders. As if he could feel my gaze, he fidgeted and adjusted his position. Will quirked his head, his expression turning pensive. But he shook himself out of it and cleared his throat.

"What got my handsome boyfriend out of bed?" I asked.

"I couldn't sleep, and when you said you would only be gone for a short while, I kind of got worried."

I raised my eyebrows at him, a smirk playing at my lips, knowing full well that he knew I was alright. Our bond would have alerted him otherwise. Plus, it had only been like thirty minutes.

"Alright, so I got a little curious as to where you went off to." He leaned into my side and whispered in my ear, "And I was a little worried, too. We don't know how far our abilities stretch." He righted himself.

"I ran into Tia on my way here," I explained. Will turned more fully to me. "You were mostly unconscious, but she and her brother were part of the musher team that helped get everyone back behind the wall when we got here."

Will rubbed my knee. "Yes, I remember you mentioning her once or twice. What was she doing here so late?"

I told him what Tia said and how we'd made plans to

greet her brother tomorrow. "I couldn't believe he was here for so long."

"My mother told me that usually non-life-threatening injuries heal rapidly here in Cristes, but the Black Roses' magic has made healing those with injuries difficult," Will responded.

"Tia mentioned that about the Black Roses. Maybe we could help him and the others?"

"Maybe we can one day," Will replied.

"No, I mean, like right now." I grabbed his hand, suddenly excited with the plan forming in my mind.

"Here, right now?" Will motioned around the room.

"I mean, I do really want to kiss you. It would be a shame to let that charged energy go to waste," I responded coyly, even though my heart was hammering faster than a hummingbird's wings.

"I really want to kiss you, too—"

"But?"

Will ran his hand through his hair. "But, just kiss. I think we should talk with Leo and Ruth, possibly Harvey, too, to make sure you are well enough for that."

"Will, I'm not asking you to push it tonight. All I am asking is for you to kiss me, really kiss me, and then we can just try to channel some of that power into Shai." I stilled my hand just above his knee. Will had been studying the floor, his foot bouncing up and down. "I'm not asking you to try and draw any power out of me besides what I give you."

Will leaned back and crossed his arms, looking at the ceiling. He sighed heavily, a low whistle sounding from the air being pushed through his teeth, and I thought he was about to deny me. Then all of a sudden he was kneeling before me, squeezing between my footrests. And then his lips were on mine.

I kissed him with everything I had, slow and teasing at first. I shocked myself when I nipped, then soothed his bottom lip. A pleasing growl rumbled from him, and I captured his mouth yet again. His tongue danced with my own as his hands caressed the sides of my body.

I broke away from him, only long enough to ask, between pants, "Are you...sure you don't...want to...get married tomorrow?"

Will chuckled, the sound reverberating in his chest, and my toes curled in response. I should have been jumping for joy, but I was too enraptured by the taste of him. He leaned into me, his hands now in my hair while my hands were free to roam his chiseled chest. My hands traced every ridge of muscle over his t-shirt as they traveled down his abdomen, and for the first time, he did not stop my exploration. One finger, then two, slipped under the hem of his shirt as I brushed his stomach. His skin was hot, like he'd been at the beach under the full sun for hours.

He stilled, and before I could process the loss of his lips on mine, my left hand was laced with his, my free hand being guided to Shai's chest. It took a second of mental gymnastics, but I quickly pictured all of Shai's injuries. I imagined my gifting, swirls of pink this time, entering his body and healing the parts of his injured brain, careful not to close his skull quite yet.

When I began to shake with the effort, Will reached over and removed my hand, keeping one hand on me, one on Shai.

I was spent. If I were able to walk, I'm sure I would have collapsed. Will and I finally dimmed to a modest glow, and I watched in fascination as silver swirls ran up from his chest, through his neck, and faded into Shai's head. Then Will was hugging me, strengthening me.

I'm not sure how long we embraced, but between the warmth of his body and how much energy I'd just spent, I immediately fell asleep.

"I've found you!" a familiar voice sneered gleefully. "You cannot escape me."

"No!" I woke up screaming the word over and over again as Will gently shook my shoulders, calling my name.

His face was so close to mine. And just when I didn't think I'd be able to take a deep breath or stop screaming, his eyes flashed pink, and I was snapped out of my panic.

Will held me in his arms in a thickly-padded rocking chair in the corner of Shai's room, cradling me, stroking my hair until my heart rate returned to a normal rhythm. "You haven't had a nightmare in a while. What were you dreaming about?"

A tremor of fear coursed through me, and Will squeezed me more tightly against him.

"It was Mara...her voice, anyway." My lip quivered, but I forced myself to continue. "She said she found me and that I'd never be able to escape her."

Will was quiet for a few long minutes. Then he tucked his finger under my chin and raised my face to his. "We are safe here. I hate that she has hurt you so much, but there's no way for her to get through the wall without notice. Not with all the Watchers manning it and the gifted enchantments on it."

I blew out a long breath through pinched lips. "You're

right." Suddenly, I was self-conscious that Will was holding my sweaty body so close to his. I pushed away from him. "I need a shower. Can we go back to our room?"

The skin on my neck prickled as I could not shake the feeling Mara really had found me. The gentle squeeze of Will's hand on my knee stopped the loop of negative thoughts.

Will stood with me cradled in his arms and sat me back in my chair. I released the brake, ready to roll out of there, but found myself frozen in place instead.

My back muscles pinched, erupting in spikes of pain that stole my breath. My pulse thrummed in my ears, my heart threatening to break open my chest. Waves of nausea rocked my stomach, and I grabbed it as if that could keep me from spewing what little contents remained of my dinner. Will was at my side in a flash.

"Is it your back? I can help..." I shook my head, uncoiled myself, and pointed to the crisp white corner of an envelope as it lay on Shai's bed.

"It can't be," Will breathed out. He reached for it, but I slapped his hand away.

"It's probably nothing." I tried to smile, but in truth, even my face muscles were paralyzed with fear. My head swam.

Will whirled, his head moving side to side.

"What do we do?" I asked, shaking.

"First, I just want to make sure it is what we think it is." Will searched the small wardrobe and found a pressed pillowcase. He shook it out and shoved his hands in the white linen pocket. Then grabbed once more for the envelope. He flipped it over and dropped it onto the floor, taking a giant step away from it.

Shai's eyes fluttered open for a split second and then they closed. Will and I both exhaled sharply after a minute.

"Did he just—" Will's words simply stopped. I nodded my head vigorously.

"We need to call someone," I whispered.

"Would someone mind telling me what in thundernation is going on right now?" Nick's voice boomed from the doorway, Ruth at his side, and Will and I both jumped.

Nick's assessing eyes cut through the room, finally landing on the envelope on the floor.

"Ruth, please call Lana and Brantley. Probably the king and queen as well."

Ruth bowed to Nick. "I will see to it immediately." Then she hustled from the room.

Nick glowered at us. "Do either of you care to inform me what is happening here, especially so late at night?"

"Me first," Will addressed him. "How did you know Liddy and I were in here?"

Nick slammed his hands on his hips and leaned forward. Practically snarling, he answered, "I am a first alert if anything were to change in Shai's vitals." His brow ticked high on his forehead. "Now, answer my question."

While Will explained everything to Nick, I could only sit there, staring at the envelope. I could swear that the longer I stared at it, the more its white seal glowed orange. I continued to breathe through the fear, the dark thoughts pestering me, taunting me that it would open on its own. Worse, who would have delivered this for her? Only two people came to mind— Charlie and Alex. I couldn't even fathom the former when the latter seemed more likely. But *how*?

Nick began to pace around the room as Will came to sit next to me.

"What's going on in that beautiful head of yours?" he asked, gently tugging on a strand of my hair.

"My dream..." I shuddered. "Doesn't this prove she has access to me again?"

"Not necessarily," Will whispered to me. "You only *heard* her, right? Because you didn't see her, I believe this is more like how Nick placed that fail-safe with the envelopes in Arbolias Sang." I closed my eyes against the reminder of a half-dead Will at the base of that tree at Nick's place. "In other words, she was only messing with your head."

I bit my lip. *Only messing with me?*

Will tapped the side of his fist against his forehead. "I didn't mean to make that sound trivial. Of course, messing with your head is not OK." He sighed and dropped his arm. "My mom will know what to do."

Lana whisked through the door as if we'd summoned her. She glided right over to Will and hugged him tightly.

"Where is it?" she asked hurriedly. He pointed to where the envelope lay on the floor beside Shai's bed. Seconds later, Ruth, Leo, Brantly, and the queen and king all rushed into the room.

"Lana, do *not* touch it," Nick growled.

"Why not? I need to inspect it for charms."

"Because Mara is clever and if the right person touches it, it will open, and then we will be in a whole lot of—"

"Understood," Brantley cut him off, coming up alongside his wife. He nodded at Will, who seemed to understand what his father wanted and moved to wrap his arm around his mother's shoulders. Brantley kneeled over the portal disguised as an envelope, careful to inspect it with his eyes only.

"Mrs. Jamison," I whispered. She made no indication she'd heard me, so I cleared my throat and tried again. "Mrs. Jamison?"

Her head snapped to me. "Call me Lana, dear."

I forced a response from my tight throat. "What does it mean if I heard Mara in my dreams?"

Like the eye of the storm, the room went still and silent, even the humming and chirping of the healing equipment. "You heard Mara and you did not think to say anything?" Nick bit out.

"Easy, Nick. That's my girl you're growling at," Will warned, his jaw clenching.

Nick's eyes flared. "With her dream history with Mara, telling someone should have been the first thing she did."

"Well, we weren't really given a chance, were we!" Will snapped. "It literally just happened, and then we saw the envelope." Will dropped his head with a heavy sigh and placed his hands on his hips. "I was just leaving to call for help, but you were already here."

Queen Nicole moved to stand in front of her son. "Nicholas, breathe. They are but children. Not one of us has clear direction on how to approach matters with Mara. Otherwise, she would have already been dealt with."

"I told you..." Nick bent down until he was eye to eye with his mother. After giving her a hard stare, he turned his head and leveled his gaze at each one of us. The power in his ice-blue irises flickered, but he kept it tethered. "I told you," he added more quietly, "getting these two together would put a target on their backs, putting us all in jeopardy."

"Yes, but they are safe within our walls," King Klaus said, tipping his chin upward.

Nick raked his hands through his hair. "Clearly, you misunderstand. Take you and Mother..." He lowered his hands and gestured toward them. "You are two of the most powerful Watchers to ever exist. Now, multiply your giftings at least tenfold, and you have William and Lydia. And that's *before* they finish the mating ceremony and are bound together."

Gasps filled the room, and all eyes flicked to me and Will.

"Is this true?" the queen asked as she took us in.

Ruth bowed toward the queen. "We have not officially run any tests, Your Majesty, but Will's secondary gifting is much stronger than most of the gifted of Watchers within the same colored faction...well, to put it bluntly, we have never seen it before," Ruth added. "We can only assume he will be the strongest healer in our history once fully bonded. And Lydia? Well, there has been talk of her power through song when freeing herself from Melchior's clutches."

Flames crept up my neck and into the apples of my cheeks. "Are we in trouble?"

"No one is in trouble," Ruth said, though Leo's scrutinizing gaze directed at me and Will begged to differ.

"Ruth and I believe someone tried to help heal your uncle tonight." Leo's gaze cut to Will. "And based on everything we have seen, we have a pretty clear idea who."

I heaved a sigh. "Well, we aren't trying to hide the truth. I told Nick it was me and Liddy."

"So, you tried it, then?" Brantley's question rang in earnest, the scientist in him buzzing to see if his and his wife's hypothesis worked.

"Maybe?" Will caught my gaze and grabbed my hand. "We both thought we saw Shai partially open his eyes, but—"

Lana gasped and nearly collapsed, save for Brantley catching her around the waist. Leo scratched feverishly on his clipboard.

"Go on, son," Brantley urged.

Will rubbed the back of his neck. "But he closed his eyes immediately. It was such a small movement I thought I imagined it, except Liddy saw it, too."

Nick's jaw clicked as he stroked his beard. "I will secure the envelope." He turned to Ruth. "Do whatever tests are necessary, but I need you to ensure that Liddy can join me at the castle tomorrow."

"I-I am not sure she is quite ready," Ruth stammered.

"That was not a request." He turned his scowl on Lana. "Let me guess, this was your encouragement?"

She bristled. "You know they can do this."

Nick shook his head. "Right now, Cristes is soaked in kerosene, and you just struck a match."

Lana's eyes flared. "They are protected here! Mara cannot—"

"I assure you she can!" Nick took a sharp inhale through his nose and slowly let it out. He dropped his voice. "I do not think Mara was able to bring the envelope here, but that is a mystery for another day. However, she was successful in infiltrating Liddy's dreams again."

Brantley's forehead shot up, but Lana shoved him away. "Just a week. Give them a week to try and heal Abishai, please," she pleaded.

"We do not have a week," Nick groused. He whirled and started toward the door before stopping short, his shoes squeaking on the tiled floor. "Everyone," he said briskly, once again making eye contact with everyone in the room. "Meet me in my chambers for dinner tomorrow night, five-thirty sharp." His eyes narrowed. "We need to discuss how we are going to move forward now that the witch knows exactly where Liddy is."

War Plans

A T FIVE-THIRTY ON THE NOSE, Will wheeled me into Nick's chambers at the north end of the castle. It was the first time I'd been in the castle, and I couldn't help but gawk. I was in a freakin' castle! The door swung open and a butler who looked an awful lot like Nolan ushered us in.

"Welcome," he said. "You are the first to arrive."

"Hello. I'm Will, and this is Liddy." Will held his hand out, but instead, the butler gave us a practiced bow.

"My name is Duncan. I can see by the expression you wear that you have surmised I am related to Nolan."

It was true. He had the same twinkle in his eye, and I had to swallow the thick lump of emotion that threatened to make me cry.

"Fear not." He patted my shoulder. "Nolan is a lot stronger

and more resourceful than he appears. May I lead you to your seats?"

I nodded, then nearly fell out of my chair as we exited the receiving area into the quarters. It was beautiful. Will pushed me and followed Duncan to a long, white-washed table that seated at least sixteen.

"Here you are," he said, pulling out the center seats closest to the fireplace. "Do you prefer to stay seated in your chair, Madam, or would you like assistance?" He gestured to the tufted parson chair.

"No, thank you. That is my honor," Will responded, resting a hand on my shoulder.

Duncan smiled and nodded once. "Of course." But he lingered still.

I darted a quick glance to Will and back to the butler. "Thank you for the offer. If you wouldn't mind putting my chair nearby, I would really appreciate it," I added.

"At your service." Duncan swept into a bow. And then he was gone, walking briskly to the door, which he flung open before giving another low bow. Will, who had been cradling me, peered into the receiving area before placing me in my seat. Lana and Brantley wore equal looks of surprise, her finger hovering above the doorbell.

Duncan returned promptly and pulled out the two chairs directly in front of me and Will, then came around the table and took my chair to the side of the fireplace, folding and tucking it into the corner.

Duncan's every movement reminded me so much of Nolan it made my heart sink. *Nolan.* Was he OK? If so, where was he? I blinked rapidly. I would not start crying all over again.

The doorbell rang, and the rest of the party was escorted to the table; the king and queen each at a head, Tia next to me, and Tannon next to Will. There was one more table setting arranged next to Lana, which I assumed was Nick's.

"Your host will be with you momentarily," Duncan said. "In the meantime, do let me know if the room is warm enough for you. Drinks and appetizers will arrive in a jiffy." He gave the Cristes salute, clicked his heels, and disappeared through a swinging door, his coattails flapping out behind him.

"Son, you are staring." Brantley leaned toward Will across the table.

"I am sorry, but he reminds me so much of Nolan. It's uncanny."

His parents nodded in understanding, Lana's eyes glistening in the candlelight.

While Will chatted with his parents, I took a moment to observe my surroundings. The sun was setting, casting the room in a deep orange glow. A wide spiral staircase led to a small second floor, and the glimpses I saw of the upper level revealed a large bed on the back wall and what appeared to be an extensive library lining every wall.

A stark contrast to the dark, thickly-woven fabrics and colors Nick favored in his home under the hill in Illinois, the decor in this room was light and airy. I wondered if this stylistic choice had much to do with the balmy climate he was accustomed to, so unlike the deep chill that now tormented Cristes. However, there were also some heavy draperies, along with thick carpets and heavy blankets, strewn on the furniture helping to ward off the cold.

Duncan came back into the room with two female servers

behind him, each balancing a tray over their shoulder. I wish I could have helped them. Though I hadn't served at The Continental in quite a while, it still felt awkward to be the one being served. Nolan hadn't succeeded in breaking me of those habits before he... I couldn't finish that thought.

Duncan took glasses off the trays and set them on the table. When the first tray was emptied, one of the servers left and returned with a large glass pitcher in hand filled with a pink frothy liquid that was an identical twin to what Nolan made us for Valentine's Day. My stomach dropped again.

Will leaned into me. "What's wrong?"

"I can't help but worry for Nolan. I really hope he is OK." Will nodded in understanding and rubbed my back in slow, steady circles as the servers poured our drinks.

I took a sip and my tongue danced. *Yep, just like Nolan's.*

"Did you say something?" Will whispered to me. I shook my head.

The servers disappeared together behind the swinging door as Will's parents were chatting with the king and queen. I turned to make conversation with Tia but noticed Nick descending the spiral staircase. Exhaustion was evident in his slumped posture, his hair unruly and extra curly. And his beard needed a good combing.

Everyone but the king and queen and myself stood when he reached the table and sat when he sat. He shook his head. "You do not need to keep up pretenses for my sake."

"You know what they say—when in Cristes," Brantley teased.

"Nicholas, do you have a plan?" Nicole addressed her son, her forehead creased with worry.

"Patience, Mother." Nick gestured around the table. "I want us to fellowship and fill our bellies first. We have a long night ahead of us."

As if on cue, Duncan returned with plates covered in silver domes. I lifted the cover and a puff of steam escaped, the scent of truffle mashed potatoes and steak drizzled in garlic butter wafting into the air. Warm buttered bread, fresh from the oven, sat in wicker baskets on either end of the table. Immediately, my salivary glands cranked into high gear and nearly growled out loud, desperate to dive in. I sank back into my chair, practically pouting when I realized not everyone had been served yet.

Will chuckled, and my eyes snapped to him. He held his hands up and laughed even harder, his amusement infectious.

"Is something the matter with your food, Your Highness?" Duncan asked, concern etched on his face.

Will cleared his throat and gave his head a little shake. "No, sir. It smells delicious."

Duncan smiled, and I nearly rejoiced when he set the last tray down.

"Saludic," Nick said as he raised his glass of pink froth. We all returned his toast and dug in. The room fell into a comfortable silence, other than the subtle clanging of silverware against plates.

After we finished our main course and our settings cleared, silver goblets filled with chocolate fudge cake drizzled with warm caramel sauce were set before us.

"Alright, my son. My belly is full. Can we please begin the discussion?" King Klaus was the first to speak. I froze with a spoonful of chocolate heaven a few inches from my eager mouth.

Nick nodded curtly and took the linen napkin from his lap, wiping the corners of his mouth. "It is no secret that Mara was able to breach your defenses, Mother."

"We do not know—" Queen Nicole attempted to defend herself, but Nick held up his hand.

"But we must assume. That envelope is her weapon of choice, so to speak, and it appeared *after* Will and Liddy decided to push their giftings..." He paused, his eyes narrowing. "Even though I have warned them time and time again."

"We were trying to help," Will argued, his body rigid and voice deep.

"That is my fault," Lana piped up. "I took a calculated risk."

"I am not judging anyone's actions, just stating facts," Nick responded, barely glancing her way. "There are a few things we need to discuss. One, someone delivered that envelope to Shai's room. We need to know who and how. And two, Will and Liddy's giftings combined produce a power so great, they can be seen and felt in other realms."

The queen steepled her fingers and leaned forward, resting her elbows on the hard wooden surface of the table. "You make an interesting point. What shall we do with the traitor who delivered this foul envelope to my country once we find them?"

"*If* we find them," Nick amended.

Will drummed his fingers on the table impatiently. "There is literally only one person it could be."

Nick frowned at him. "Alex is under guard round the clock. It would be foolish to only put our efforts on him. In the meantime, I have a temporary solution."

When he didn't continue, Lana sighed heavily. "You are literally killing me. Out with it."

Nick let out a deep sigh and gritted his teeth. "I assure you, I am not trying to frustrate you on purpose. I am fully aware of how this news will be received." Nick turned his full attention to me.

A shadow was cast over the evening as I sensed something I wasn't going to like coming my way. I pushed my half-eaten dessert away and grabbed Will's hand under the table, twining our fingers together.

"When Will and Liddy use their gifting, Mara can pinpoint where they are. But what they, and many others" —he frowned at Lana and then at the table— "fail to comprehend is the strength of their bond. When they are merely in the same room as one another, the energy between them is noted by all, whether you realize it or not. You are drawn to them."

Everyone assessed us and a collective realization dawned.

"The second they combine their giftings, their powers then amplify each other..." Nick looked pointedly at us. "It acts as a tracking system for Mara. Not only as bright as the moon, they *are* the moon, exerting a gravitational pull that draws Mara straight to them."

Lana tried to give me a smile, but it didn't reach her eyes.

Nick massaged this forehead. "Unfortunately, their gravitational pull has consequences of great magnitude. They are sitting ducks, and everyone around them—collateral damage."

"What do you propose, Nicholas?" Queen Nicole asked, resting her hand on her husband's shoulder.

"We are not prepared for a war on two fronts. Not yet, anyway. I had no idea what to expect when arriving home for the first time in nearly fifty years. The fact that you have been battling the Black Roses on and off during that time was not something I was prepared to see." Nick paused, shaking his head. "We need time to develop a solid strategy." He turned his attention to Will and me. "But first, we need to rescue our friends Mara kidnapped—*if* they are still alive—before we can even think of engaging her in a battle."

"Engaging her?" Tannon asked. Clearly, he was not up to speed on the history Mara had with Nick and his mother.

Nick quirked a brow at him but continued on as if he hadn't spoken. "We need to configure a plan so thorough it is infallible in defeating the Black Roses and Mara. I cannot say why, but my instincts are clawing at me. Somehow, Mara and the Black Roses are connected, and therein lies a huge problem."

"Well, we did inform you about the soil," the king responded.

"There is more to it than that," Nick answered.

"So my William is too powerful when he and Liddy are together, thus putting them and everyone else in harm's way." Brantley rubbed his chin, his expression pensive.

And suddenly the reason for this dinner, where Nick wanted us to all fellowship and have a good time, became crystal clear to me. My gaze shot to Nick, and I swore I saw him flinch a little.

"No." The word came out before I could stop it.

Everyone stopped their side chats and musings to stare at me. Nick just stared at me like I was someone to be pitied.

I slammed my fist on the table. Suddenly Will was out of his chair, searching for a threat.

"Come out and say it. You promised not to hide anything from us anymore," I said, my fist gripping the linen placemat.

Will stood behind me, wrapping both of his large hands over my shoulders. I could feel the confusion of his thoughts as wisps of hesitancy flickered through my head.

Nick ticked his chin but quickly dropped it. He knew what he was about to say would hurt us, and acting indifferent would only make matters worse. "Your bond is too strong and growing every day. We cannot risk you coming into your full powers."

"And that means...?" Will let the question hang in the air.

Nick pinched the bridge of his nose. "You and Liddy must separate."

"Whoa, what do you mean, separate?" Will's muscles filled with adrenaline, veining out.

"Separate. To divide, move apart." Nick rose from his seat and began pacing. "You cannot be near each other until we are ready to face our adversaries."

"And how long do you think that will be?" I asked, my dinner souring in my gut.

"A year," Nick said flatly.

"A whole year!" Tia, who I'd forgotten was sitting next to me, blurted as she bolted up. "Do you have any idea—"

"I am aware!" Nick snapped. The flare of his nostrils and ring of blue fire in his eyes screamed that we were trying his patience.

"No, no. Wait a minute. What were you going to say?" Will asked Tia, who wore the pinched expression of someone clearly miffed she'd been interrupted but was also holding her tongue because the person who'd cut her off was a prince.

"Tia, maybe you should sit down." Tannon tugged at her elbow, but she shrugged him off.

"How could you do that to them? To Cristes?" Tia briefly scanned the faces of everyone at the table, searching for an ally. "Besides the fact that you are denying our people their gifting for a year—"

"I am not denying Cristes anything. I am saving her!" Nick shot back.

Tia splayed her hands on the table and leaned forward. "Have more faith in us than that, Your Highness."

The anger emitting from Nick's body had me truly worried for her. I tugged at her arm. "Sit down, please."

She dropped her chin toward me, her neck scarlet, and plopped in her seat.

Will clasped my hand while turning toward Nick. "What did Tia mean when she asked how you could do this to us? I feel like Liddy and I aren't being given the full picture."

Tia didn't wait for permission to speak as she leaned over the table to face Will. "I heard it is nearly physically impossible for a couple to stay away once the bond forms. The amount of pain alone—"

"They have not bonded yet," Nick ground out.

Will's face paled, and then his eyes turned to a cold, boreal forest.

"Has it been done before?" the king asked, his voice quiet, his gaze far away as if he were thinking about what might have been if he and his wife had been forced apart.

"No." This time, Lana responded, her golden skin pale

with worry. "Not for a year, anyway."

"Can it harm them?" Brantley asked.

Nick stopped his pacing. "Harm them?"

"You must know," Brantley said, "that this will be painful for them. But do we know if it will harm their fated bond?"

"I do not see why it would," Nick replied, confusion marring his features.

The queen stood and grabbed Nick's hands. "I know you never got the chance to meet your match, but once the bond has formed, maybe even after it has only started forming, left unnourished, it could die. In the very least, it will weaken. And will we not need them at full strength when we go to defend and restore Cristes?"

Nick moved out of his mother's reach and sank heavily into his chair. "That is a risk we are going to have to take. Weakened powers are better than none, and we are woefully unprepared to meet a war on two fronts."

Will's hands shook with both fear and fury. "No, we will not comply."

Lana tried to hide her smirk behind her hand.

"Come again?" Nick seethed, his irises igniting.

"Liddy has spent the last month fighting for her life," Will said. "Only now are we just seeing some progress in her recovery to even be able to walk again."

The fire in Nick's eyes died immediately as Will's words sunk in.

"She needs me to heal," Will continued. "Separating us risks her recovery. You can't ask me to leave her like this when I know I can help."

The queen suppressed her surprise by covering her mouth

with the back of her hand. The king leaned into his hand, his fingers pressing and massaging his temples. Only Nick met my gaze.

Suddenly his voice was in my head. *I'm sorry.*

I shouldn't have been upset. When we visited Florida, I was willing to fall on my sword if it meant freeing all the children Mara had stolen away to Beldam. One life for many.

I closed my eyes, tears falling freely, pressing my lips together and accepting my fate.

Will must have felt my resignation. He pulled my chair out from the table and turned it to face him, then kneeled down in front of me. "Liddy, look at me." He cupped both my cheeks.

My eyes popped open and were met with his earnest expression.

"I told you, we get to make these decisions. Together." Will kissed me softly on the mouth. "I will not let them sacrifice you for others. I cannot—"

I placed my forefinger against his lips. "And I can't be selfish enough to risk the lives of so many. We will be together again before you know it."

"But what about—" Will mumbled against my finger.

"I'll still have Ruth and Leo...and Harvey. They will help me walk again." I tried to smile but couldn't make it past a tight quirk.

"I know you well enough to know I can't change your mind." Will leaned in and kissed my forehead. "Mom, Dad, follow me, please."

Lana and Brantley arose with no questions asked, following their son through the swinging door. I could only stare at the small crack in the saucer in front of me that had been filled in with silver. My heart ached as it pounded in my chest, but I didn't try to calm it. For the first time in a long while, I let myself feel the grief, letting the muscle beat so hard it threatened to cleave in two.

A warm hand touched one shoulder. A moment later, a smaller hand rested on my other side. But I didn't care to see who they belonged to. I wouldn't be able to regard them through the haze of tears that blurred my vision, anyway. Over and over, my vision would clear a little as tears streamed down my cheeks, only to blur again.

Even the soft squeak of the swinging door didn't motivate me to lift my head. The warm hands were gone, and familiar, strong ones took my hands, securing them in theirs. A finger placed gently under my chin brought my face up to his. Using the heels of his hands, Will wiped my tears, and I threw my arms around his neck, clinging to him.

He stroked my hair and rubbed my back for several long minutes. When my sobs quieted, he spoke over my shoulder, addressing the room. "Liddy and I agree to what you are asking us, but I require three things, and these are non-negotiable."

His words were quiet but so full of strength no one would dare cross him. When no one spoke, he continued. "First, I get tonight with Liddy. No interruptions. No tests. Just me and her. This was sprung on us and I want the chance to say goodbye properly. Two..." Will nodded behind him, and his mom and dad each took one of my arms, placing them over their shoulders, helping me to stand. Then he got down on one knee. From his pocket, he produced a small, shimmery box.

A collective gasp echoed throughout the room. I smiled brightly as a swarm of bees drunk on honey buzzed in my stomach. This time, I wasn't scared. This time, I couldn't care less that I hadn't graduated college, that I was only months away from being eighteen. The man before me was it. There would never be anyone else, and I knew I was lucky to be given such a gift. I made a noise that was something between a laugh and a sob.

Will smirked at me. "Like I said, you would know when I was actually proposing. I've had this in my pocket for the last three months, just waiting for the right time." He flipped the pearl-white top open, but inside were a pair of opal and diamond earrings.

I cocked my head in confusion and he laughed.

"To go with the engagement ring you already own and wear every day."

Lana shifted her arm around my waist so Will could take my hand, and he helped me uncurl my fingers from their tight fist. He tried to remove the promise ring he'd given me last year, but it wouldn't budge. Will took his mouth and opened it over my finger, his tongue circling the ring, and with his teeth, he slid it off. Lana averted her gaze. Brantley, too, appeared to find the ceiling mesmerizing.

Oh, my! If I were a snowman, I would've been a puddle on the floor. Someone cleared their throat, but I didn't dare take my eyes off of Will's, entranced by their cerulean glow.

"I wish you could see yourself right now," Will breathed. "You are so beautiful." I knew he was referring to the fact that I too was glowing, because I could see lavender cast on his face and clothes.

He held the ring at the tip of my finger.

"I have always known that you would be mine forever. Even when I freaked you out, back when I first came for you in Illinois, and again on your porch at Christmas when I first presented this ring to you." Lana and Brantley chuckled. "The idea of having you as my forever has always felt perfect to me. Now we know why."

"Here, here!" the king cheered.

Will chuckled. "But even if it wasn't for Watcher giftings and pairings, I would still love you, for *you*. Your wonderful mind, your kind heart, and your gentle soul. There is no one like you. It is my absolute joy to do life with you now, to be yours forever and always."

My hand shook with anticipation as I felt his energy boosting him for his next words. "Lydia Andra Erickson, would you make me the most blessed man in all the realms and honor me by choosing me to be your husband?"

My throat bobbed with so much emotion I couldn't speak, so I nodded enthusiastically.

"I'm sorry, I couldn't hear you," Will teased.

I scoffed and playfully hit him on the shoulder. I cleared away the lump in my throat. "As you wish! Yes! An infinite amount of yesses!"

Will slid the ring down my finger to the celebratory whoops and shouts of joy from the rest of the dinner guests. He jumped up and wrapped me in a big bear hug, though his pressure remained gentle.

"I love you," I whispered.

"I love you more," he said, his lips tickling my ear.

"Well, that is enough of that," Nick grunted, though I

thought I saw him quickly brush away a tear before everyone quieted.

Will struggled to hold on to me as he lowered himself into a chair. Tannon rose from his seat and moved to Will's side, helping him to cradle me in his lap.

"What is the third demand?" Nick's arms were crossed as if bracing for something that asked too much of him.

"That would actually be *my* demand," Lana said.

Nick let out a drawn-out sigh as he dropped his arms and faced his cousin. His lips curled into a half-hearted smirk. "Yes?"

Lana tilted her chin up. "Will and Liddy will use their gifting once more to help heal Shai."

Nick shuttered his eyes so tightly, deep crow's feet fanned around their outer edges. "You ask too much." His fingers pinched the bridge of his nose.

"We need him, and you know it," Lana spat, her body already humming with energy, her gifting igniting.

Nick opened his eyes and held up his hands. "You would risk the lives of all of Cristes...of Liddy...your son? Because that is what you are asking."

Lana dimmed some. "I am not asking. And I am not risking anything. Tomorrow morning, they will do this, and then they will immediately separate. No one will know of this, except for those in this room tonight, so no one can deliver another one of Mara's envelopes."

"It is still risky," Nick countered.

"I can shield them," Brantley piped up. "We all can."

"What do you mean?" Tia asked him.

"I can form a short-term shield with a little bit of

chemistry and my gifting." Brantley steepled his fingers. "It doesn't last long, but if we do this together, we can surround Will and Liddy with a barrier that can mute the energy of their combined gifting long enough to treat Shai."

"And you have done this before?" The king arched a brow.

Brantley scratched his chin, frowning. "In theory, yes. Just not with the degree of power Will and Liddy need to mask their gifting."

"Sorry," Tannon interjected softly, clearly nervous to interrupt. "But I am still unclear as to why me and my sister are here."

Nick turned to acknowledge the other man. "Tannon, you will become Will's chaval—his new best friend. Wherever he goes, you go."

Tannon blinked. "I am sorry for my ignorance, but wouldn't his brother be a better fit?"

Nick shook his head. "Charlie is too close to all of this. Being so connected with Will, he may give in."

"Give in?" Tannon quirked a brow.

"You work with animals, yes?" Nick bypassed the question.

"Yes, sir," Tannon replied, puffing his chest.

"Good," Nick continued, "because there will be times when your prince will act more animal than human as he tries to get back to his mate. Your job is to make sure that he does not get to her. Tia, the same goes for you with Liddy."

Tia and Tannon both stood tall and gave the Cristes salute.

Nick dipped his chin. "Very well. Everyone is free to go. We meet in Shai's room at seven a.m. sharp. See to it that you are not followed, and tell no one."

Saving Uncle Shai

THAT NIGHT WILL AND I HELD EACH OTHER. We cried, we kissed, we talked, and we cried some more. We decided on a plan to write a letter to each other every week so we could feel somewhat connected. Eventually, Will coaxed me to sleep so we could be well-rested to try and help Shai.

I awoke with my head on Will's chest, his hands stroking my hair. "Good morning, princess."

"What time is it?" I yawned.

I felt Will shift slightly. "A little after six."

"Already?" I whispered, squeezing him a little tighter.

Will rolled over me, careful to keep his weight off of me. I brushed his hair off his forehead. "You need a haircut." I smiled at him.

"I'd like to kiss you," he replied, his expression serious.

"You never have to ask."

Will didn't hesitate, his kiss both desperate and slow, commanding. Within seconds we were shining bright, and his hand slipped under my low back. Little tingles and shivers danced down both legs.

I paused my kisses, and Will moved his head back an inch.

"Please don't ask me to stop, not just yet. I want to give all I can to you now, to give you the best chance at making a full recovery, before..." He trailed off, the corners of his lips turning downward.

"*Shhh.*" I couldn't bear to see him sad. I slid my hand around his neck and pulled him to me once more.

Will finally broke the kiss and rested his forehead against mine, sliding his hand from my back and lying by my side.

"We have to leave soon. Breakfast should be here any minute," he said, his voice flat.

I wanted to scream, to cry, to throw something. This wasn't fair; I wasn't ready. But I needed to be strong, not just for Will, but for myself.

A healer knocked on the door to help me get ready, and Will excused himself to use the shower in the next room—which was supposed to be his room for a week, but he had refused to leave my side.

When he joined me again, I was already at the small round table, taking a bite of my breakfast. We sat in silence, and I don't think I tasted any of my food.

Though our door was open, a knock on the frame had me picking up my head.

Lana was dressed in a forest green sweater with white

pants. "Hey, you two."

Will looked over his shoulder as he clasped my hand. "Hey, Mom. We were just getting ready to head over."

"Mind if we walk with you?" She took a step into the room, freeing up the doorway, and in came Brantley and Charlie.

"Not at all." Will stood and walked behind my chair, releasing the brakes, and began pushing me. We strolled down the halls, Lana trying to fill the silence with her thanks for helping Shai. Charlie kept catching my gaze, but then, as if my sadness was crushing him, he set his jaw and stared straight ahead.

"Right on time," Nick said from just outside Shai's room. Tia and Tannon lingered off to the side. Based on what Nick said last night, I knew why they were there. They were going to be the ones to rein in Will and I when we were torn from each other, in case we lost control over our actions.

"Shall we go in?" The queen walked up to our group, clutching the king's arm.

Nick held the door open and swept us into the room. Will walked me up to the side of the bed. Once Nick came in, the others made a half circle behind us. The weight of everyone's emotions furled in the air, the atmosphere heavy and oppressive.

I tugged at my bottom lip with my teeth. Will, sensing my unease, tilted my head back and laid a heavy kiss on my forehead. "I love you so much, you know that?"

"I love you more," I teased, trying to lighten the mood.

Will moved to kiss the tip of my nose and then lower, pausing just before our lips met.

"Ewww, get a room," Charlie needled us, and the room

erupted in laughter. His cheeks turned light pink, and suddenly the heaviness in the room lightened.

Will straightened, beaming a wide grin at his brother. "Sorry to disappoint you, little bro, but we have to kiss if we are going to try and combine our giftings."

Charlie clapped Will on the shoulder. "I'm just messing with you. How about we all close our eyes to give them some privacy?"

Brantley tousled Charlie's hair. "Always thinking of others."

Nick cleared his throat. "Yes, of course. But first, some ground rules."

"We aren't children," Lana scoffed.

"No, you are not. So, when I give you an order, you will heed it. Understood?"

If looks could kill, Nick would be dead—twice.

"We have one chance at this," Nick barreled ahead. "I will not risk another attempt."

Lana's gifting smoldered an angry green. "But what if—"

Nick held his hand up to halt her. "Lana, you act as if I am not considering the man who is like a brother to me. But there is a lot at stake here."

Lana's giftings fell away from the surface, and she hung her head. Brantley wrapped his arms around her, and she rested her head on his shoulder.

"When Will and Liddy are finished, Liddy is to be immediately brought back to her room, and Will is to be taken to the castle," Nick instructed.

Everyone's eyes bore into me and Will with so much pity. Or was it empathy? Either way, their sorrowful expressions weren't making this any easier.

King Klaus nodded solemnly. "Well, then, let us not prolong this any further. Best to get on with it so we can reunite these love birds sooner than later," he bellowed.

Everyone behind us grabbed hands to close their circle, then closed their eyes. Soon, a wave of comfortable heat infiltrated the space around us, and a semi-translucent globe encased us.

Will came around to kneel in front of me so we were eye level. He peered briefly at his uncle. Then, his hands were on either side of my face, his lips on mine. I grabbed on to his wrists for purchase, pulling him in closer as his arms wrapped around me and I sank into him.

I pushed all thoughts of Will leaving me aside and instead focused on being present with him. The feel of him, the way he knew when to be gentle or more assertive. Then, all too quickly, Will broke off the kiss, guiding my hand to Shai's heart while placing his hand on Shai's head.

A low hum reverberated in the room as the protective globe surrounding us began to shake. The faces of our friends and family on the other side of the barrier grew strained, their muscles tense with exertion as sparks started to fly.

"We need more time!" Will cried out.

The king and queen began to glow, feeding their white-lighter power into the shield. The globe stabilized, but I was losing steam, and fast.

"Will?" I croaked, the edges of my vision darkening.

"Stay with me...just another minute," he pleaded with me.

I watched as silver and pink tendrils of gifting marked Will's skin, then traveled into Shai. Just before I broke off,

Shai let out a loud gasp. I slumped over in my chair, and Will was immediately at my side, holding my head against his chest.

The shield fell and disappeared. Lana ran up to her brother, gently laying her hand on his chest. "Shai, can you hear me?"

His mouth moved, and I was scared I wouldn't be able to hear his brittle voice over the loud thumping of my heart.

Shai smiled as he opened his eyes. "Hi," he breathed before his eyes rolled back into his head, and he lost consciousness again.

Without warning or time to protest, Tannon and Nick swooped in, each grabbing Will by the arm.

Will tried to plant his feet. "Wait, I didn't get to say goodbye!"

"No time!" Nick yelled.

"Nick, please! Let my brother say goodbye!" Charlie's eyes were wet with unshed tears, as if he could feel the pain Will and I felt.

I tried to wheel myself over to Will, but Tia held the chair back. I slid to the floor, attempting to army-crawl to him while Will bucked and kicked against the two men.

Lana joined me on the floor and held me against her chest as sobs wrenched free from me.

"Father!" Nick yelled. "I need your help over here."

The king strode right up to Will and placed his index and middle finger on the pulse point at Will's throat. Immediately, Will's head slumped forward and he stilled.

"This young man is a fighter, so he will not be out long." The king gestured to his wife to follow him. "Tannon, you get the sleigh ready. Nick, carry him outside."

And then the room was still and quiet, the only sound my shattering heart.

Dear Will,

My gosh, I never thought I would make it to two months. Did you? The first month was beyond difficult, but your mom, the queen, and Tia have been really great.

You asked me how my recovery was going, and I have put off answering you (which I know you called me out about in your last letter). To be honest, for 2-3 weeks, I was lucky if I ate and showered. It's like my body thought you were dead even though my brain knew you weren't. But then your mom and I had a really great talk and, well, let's just say she helped me to see how cool it could be if I gave myself a fighting chance to walk down the aisle next April. I know it's not guaranteed, but it is something to hope for.

Last week, we focused mainly on range of motion exercises as I was pretty stiff. They have also been working on my upper body strength and endurance so that I can get around more on my own and be more independent. This week we started to add some balance training. I promise to be open and honest with you in all of my letters regarding the healing journey, no matter how difficult. So, I'm not going to lie. Sometimes the pain has been unbearable, but my team in the sanctum is really great at helping me to alleviate it (even though they are not as good as you, I am not suffering). If all goes well, in a month or 2, I will start training to stand!

What have you been doing to occupy your time? The ladies are going to start dance parties with me once a week, which Tia kindly arranged. We've been talking a lot lately after she realized how much I missed dancing. Though I may move differently, I'm hoping a little activity and music will help lift my spirits, even if I'm just watching others having fun. I'm also getting to spend a lot of time reading.

Well, I am off to the barn to play with the dogs and then to book club. Say hi to everyone up at the castle for me!

Always and forever,

Liddy xoxoxo

P.S. I cannot wait to call you my husband.

Dear Liddy,

My beautiful fiancée. Sometimes, if I distract myself enough, I can get through the day. Recently, Nick and King Klaus have taken to leading me through rigorous strength training. Tannon takes me outside to run with the dogs.

Even though we are separated, my love for you only grows stronger every day. I am so proud of you. You are the strongest person I know, and everyone at the castle is marveling at the progress you have been making! Normally I don't listen to gossip, but Mom came back from visiting you yesterday and she could barely contain her joy...you took a step! I wish I could have been there to celebrate with you. But for now, I will dream of it, reimagining it with me there. Speaking of dreams, you are my dream come true. I still pray sweet dreams over you every night.

Tannon got me into this really intense card game. Charlie joins us for our weekly card game. When I am not working out or playing cards, the king has taken me under his wing to start my tutelage, learning the ways of diplomacy and statecraft. I guess I should know these things if I am expected to reign over Cristes one day, right? Sometimes it is a little overwhelming to think that I will be responsible for so many people, but then I remember I will not be doing it alone.

Well, it's late and I need to get to bed if I am going to wake at dawn to train some more.

Sweet dreams, Princess.

Love always,
Will

Dear Will,

Do you ever miss Mortalia? I guess with Christmas right around the corner, it has me really missing my family and friends. I know that Nick took their memories, so they don't even know I exist. I am glad for that. I am. But it still hurts.

And then I think about Pree and Justin and Nolan. I wish we could move this faster along. I just fear that something has happened to them or will soon if we don't get to them, and it's frustrating that I am stuck here. And what if they lost all their hope? I have been there, and there is nothing darker than feelings of despair and hopelessness. Have you been privy to any meetings regarding how they plan to try and get them out of Beldam?

I know you keep reminding me that I am not responsible for the fact that Mara snatched them, but I can't help but feel responsible. I won't say more on this, as it will only bore you, but please let me know if you've heard anything.

Miss you every second of every day,
Xoxoxo
Liddy

Dearest Liddy,

Mom and Dad tell me that Shai has started sitting up on his own and is talking more and more. I am so jealous that you get to see him every day. Please tell him I said hi and that I wish I could see him.

I know Charlie wants to come visit you. He refuses to go, though. I think he believes it will send me over the edge if he gets to see you and I don't. Or maybe it's that he doesn't trust Tannon to keep me away from you on his own. Neither is the case, but I can't convince him either way.

The Black Roses seem to have taken a break from their twice-a-week attacks. Mom is concerned that they are planning something bigger, something that would force our hand into an offensive position instead of playing defense. I just think they probably tuckered out. As I am sure Mom has informed you, they have been attacking since Cristes' shield was compromised back when Mara broke it.

I am studying longer and harder than ever before to be a good king for Cristes. Has the queen started training you yet?

Love you more,
Will

Dear Will,

There are less than 45 days until I get to marry you! I thought this day would never come. The queen is having a blast overseeing the wedding planning with her staff. She asked if I wanted to help, but I told her I trusted her. Honestly, there seems to be so much work that it would just stress me out. In any case, giving her full reign (she did give me veto powers) seemed to lighten her spirits. She said it has been a while since Cristes had something to celebrate.

I am trying not to be bummed, but my therapy has kind of reached a standstill. I should be happier to report that I am able to walk again. However and here is the part that is hard to accept I need a lot of assistance to do so. And I am only sharing my feelings on this because you asked me to. Please don't beat yourself up about my healing. So I walk a little differently. So, my dance moves are small and rooted to a single spot. I am alive and soon, I will get to be in your arms again.

Until then, my love, keep sending me all your healing vibes.

Miss you so much it hurts,

Xoxoxo

Liddy

The First Dance

I SAT IN THE DANCE STUDIO, waiting for the choreographer. Although I was excited to finally be seeing Will soon, my confidence was shattered. I had only been walking for about a month now, thanks to Ruth, Leo, the queen, and the king all trying to combine their giftings to give me a healing boost. However, I still worried if I would have the strength and coordination to dance.

The door swung wide, and in strode a familiar face. "Are you ready?" Gene asked as he made his way to me.

I couldn't believe Gene stood in front of me— the legend that was Queen Nicole's favorite choreographer. A man I'd only previously seen in Nick's memories. Watching him set the Argentang piece on Nick and Mara made me feel as if I knew him already. And yet, technically, I'd never met the man. It was...weird.

Gene quirked his brow and wiped the corners of his mouth. "Do I have something on my face?"

"No, nothing like that. I'm sorry, this is a little...strange," I replied, somewhat embarrassed for staring at him.

"Ah, yes. Nicholas informed me you were privy to some memories involving me, which I do not mind. It should make things easier for us. You know how I work and what my expectations are." He smiled reassuringly at me.

"Did Nick also happen to mention where I'm at in terms of recovery?" I asked. Nervous bubbles flitted in my stomach.

He held his hand out, and I took it. "Yes, and not to worry. You will do beautifully," he said, helping me to stand.

Gene would be teaching me one of the dances for the wedding. My freakin' *wedding*. I still couldn't get over it. It had been just over a year since Will proposed to me. A little over a year since I'd last seen the boy who had my whole heart.

Will knew that I'd worked my butt off in therapy, but what he didn't know is that I would be walking down the aisle.

He also didn't know that I would be dancing with him.

"The Rumbiental is a traditional wedding dance all royals perform for all attendees at your wedding celebration," Gene explained as he led me to the center of the dance floor. "Within the dance, the woman represents Cristes, and the man her protector. Combined, it signifies your commitment and love to the kingdom of Cristes."

I nodded and shifted my feet. "Um, so Will doesn't really know that I will be dancing with him. Will that be a problem since I know the bride and groom practice together for many months beforehand?" My nails bit into my palms.

Gene glanced at me sidelong. "Of course not. His great-aunt is practicing with him. She, my dear, is talented, but I have heard of your giftings as well. Queen Nicole will have him ready–and I, you. Do not entertain thoughts of fear, Princess."

I dropped my gaze from him and relaxed my fists, but a moment later Gene lifted my chin with the back of his hand.

"I commend you for trying this. It shows your strength and love for your match and Cristes." He dropped his hand. "I have confidence that you will be great. But if you feel as if this is all too much, the queen would be honored to take your place."

I nodded. This was true. The queen mentioned this once before when I was seriously stressed but has since refused to discuss it as an option until the moment before I would be tasked with performing it.

Gene beckoned me to the center of the room. "It is far from ideal that the first time you perform this dance with His Royal Highness, it will be in front of your wedding guests. Nevertheless, my choreography is catered to you." Gene's eyes twinkled a soft lilac. "Trust the prince, trust yourself. You have danced together before, yes?"

I nodded, my heart aching. I understood why Will and I had to be separated, but my heart couldn't care less. Some days, the pain of his absence threatened to overwhelm me.

"Lydia, it will be fine," Gene said, rolling his feet and doing side stretches. "These traditions are centered around a Watcher's gifting, and since you are a purple..." He studied my face. "...dance and song are how you honor yourself and your beloved. Breathe, darling." Then he patted my back, and

I let out a desperate breath.

"Thanks. I guess I'm just nervous."

"Perfectly natural to be feeling this way. Anyone else would be, especially with the circumstances surrounding this wedding. But, again, we will not cater to negative thoughts. We have work to do." He gestured for me to follow him in his stretching routine. "Right, so we only have five days to set this piece, but lucky for us, your gifting is purple, and a strong purple at that. Though, do you mind me asking, is purple your secondary gifting?"

I knew where his question was stemming from. About six months into my separation from Will, my purple irises began a metamorphosis back to their original blue color. No one—not Ruth, or Leo, Lana, not the queen—knew why. But I could feel the fear behind their pacifying words, *Not to worry. It means nothing.*

"Umm, we actually aren't sure. Did you say five days?" My stomach tightened with trepidation. One hundred and twenty hours. Seven thousand, two hundred minutes. Not nearly enough time to master a dance to be performed in front of everyone who mattered in Cristes, especially considering I only learned to walk again last month. I took another breath.

"Queen Nicole informed you of costume fittings during our break times?" Gene was asking. I nodded. "Great! Let us see how far we get with the choreography before lunch when we break for costuming."

Dancing with Gene was a challenge at first, and not just because of my previous injuries but because I'd never really done ballroom before. He was patient with me, not as intense as I remembered him being with Nick and Mara. Soon, I was able to force my brain to see reason by recalling something Gene had said to Nick. *Dancing is about feeling the music. It requires acting.*

So I pretended not to be bothered by my back pain or by the fact that my foot would sometimes get lazy and flop instead of point. Once I conquered my nerves, my body relaxed and started working with me instead of against.

Gene clapped his hands together twice, and his eyes glinted violet for a brief second. The melohym in the corner glowed, humming to life, and started playing the track that was to be Will's and my first dance.

Hours passed, and my hair was damp with sweat, my legs, hips, and back all screaming and quivering from the effort. During our final run-through, a silver-haired butler came into view, and for a moment, my heart leaped with joy thinking it might be Nolan. My hopes sank when I realized it was Duncan, and I stumbled.

Dang it. I should be used to him by now.

Gene caught me, flipped me into a dip, and helped me complete the rest of the dance steps.

"Princess." Duncan bowed. "The queen and her seamstress are waiting for you in the lounge. I have taken the liberty of having your lunch brought there."

"Sorry," I said to Gene, wiping beads of sweat from my temples with the backs of my hands.

"For what, dear?"

"For messing up in the middle of—"

Gene held up his index finger, silencing me. "Only I knew of the mistake because it is my choreography, but no one else would have because we kept dancing. Now, go take that break. We will add another thirty seconds to the dance in the afternoon session, which puts us at the halfway mark."

I smiled at him and went to the settee to grab my pink sweater. I started walking–more like limping–to the door. Gene took my hand and guided me to the studio's exit. "On second thought, take the rest of the day. See Harvey and Healer Ruth to aid in your sore muscles." He gave me the Cristes salute and closed the door.

Duncan waited patiently a few feet ahead of me with his hands behind his back and a warm smile on his face. He had long ago stopped trying to make small talk with me or help me walk in any way. Something told me he was just as discerning as Nolan. Though I tried to stop the ache in my chest every time I saw him, the guilt of Nolan's sacrifice pierced straight through my gut, and talking to Duncan only dug the knife in deeper.

My dance heels clicked and clacked as we strode down the hall with its arched ceilings and shiny wood floors. Eventually, soft music and feminine voices greeted my ears. Duncan stopped in front of a door and knocked three times.

"Come in, Duncan," Queen Nicole's voice called from behind the door.

He opened it and turned. With a flourish of his arm, he waved me in. "Enjoy your lunch, Princess. Shall I ring for Harvey?" I shook my head. "Very well, if there is anything else you need, do not hesitate to ring for me."

"Thank you," I replied before stepping into the lounge. The door closed behind me with a soft click. I'd not been to this part of the castle before. The faces in the room were familiar, though, and I grinned.

I'd expected castles and their many rooms to be dark and dreary, based on what I'd learned about medieval history in school. But here, I was greeted by a glass wall that offered a picturesque view of a private courtyard. Queen Nicole and her seamstress, Cynthia, along with Lana and Tia, sat in the circular conversation pit that surrounded a robust fire, its shoot extending all the way through the wood-beamed ceiling. Ohanna stood guard in the corner.

"Lydia! Come sit, sweetheart," Lana said, patting the velvet sofa cushion next to her, her smile comforting. As I sat, Tia slid the food tray over to me.

"What are you waiting for? You must be starving after working with Gene all morning," Queen Nicole said.

I flushed. "I didn't want to be rude. No one else was eating."

"Nonsense." The queen waved a hand. "We have all eaten. It would be rude not to eat, thus making all of us wait longer to have a peek of you in your dresses!" Everyone laughed at the queen's cheekiness.

I gratefully tucked into the hearty soup and sandwich while Lana shared memories from her wedding, and I listened fondly as the others asked her many questions.

"Well, things in Cristes were a little chaotic, if you all remember. Brantley and I did not have the traditional wedding."

"Ah, yes. If I remember correctly, it was my William and I, Brantley's parents, and your family," the queen interjected.

"Yes, and Nolan hosted the ceremonies," Lana added. We all grew silent for a brief moment. Lana sighed deeply but continued. "I am actually thankful for the intimate union. I still had a fabulous dress, thanks to the two of you." She gave Cynthia and the queen a meaningful look.

"You were sacrificing so much to bring my Nicholas back to me and save Cristes. It was the least I could do." Queen Nicole placed her hand atop Lana's and gave it a gentle squeeze.

"Speaking of dresses, are you ready to start the fittings?" The seamstress, Cynthia, stood and walked over to the corner of the room to a tall chest.

I leaned forward to place the tray back on the hearth and caught a whiff of myself. I wrinkled my nose. "Actually, is there somewhere I can shower first? I worked up quite the sweat with Gene, and I do not wish to subject Cynthia or any of her creations to my B.O."

"B.O.?" The queen furrowed her brow.

Tia giggled. "Body odor."

Queen Nicole smacked her forehead with the heel of her palm. "Good gracious! Of course you would want to freshen up before trying on gowns. Through the curtains is a full bath, dear. I shall have Duncan grab you some—"

"Please don't!" I interrupted.

"I can collect your things for you," Tia chimed in, and I mouthed 'thank you.' After being my right arm day and night for a year, she knew how modest I was.

"I will try to clean up as fast as I can," I called over my shoulder as I stepped through the thick white curtains. "Oh!" I exclaimed as I was seemingly transported to a secluded lagoon back in the rainforest.

"Everything alright, Your Highness?" Ohanna asked.

The women in the room all giggled, but I didn't care. I

popped my head out. "Uhh, yeah! More than good. It's like heaven in here!" I went back into the bath, scratch that, the luxurious spa.

At the far end sat a jacuzzi made entirely of smooth black rock, striking against the white and natural wood. Not a faucet or spout could be detected, and yet, the water was filled to the brim. Heat vapors danced over the surface. To my left stood a shower stall big enough for six grown adults or more. Three of the walls were made of natural stone and different types of moss. I counted seven shower heads, three from the ceiling and two on each wall. Suddenly I was a little jealous of Will for having access to this room all year.

A fluffy white towel, robe, and slippers were arranged plumb in the middle of a teak bench near the shower's glass door. I reached my hand in and turned the water on. Within seconds, the water reached the perfect temperature. *This would have been nice to have in Mortalia,* I laughed to myself.

I quickly stripped and got into the shower. As the door closed behind me, a lock revealed itself, and when I slid it, the entire glass wall turned black, blocking anyone's ability to see inside or out.

Less than ten minutes later, I was standing next to Cynthia, dressed and smelling like hibiscus flowers. She opened the chest, and it was like watching someone undoing Origami. She'd unlatch, unfold, bend, and snap. In less than a minute, she stood back, revealing a three-way mirror, a small podium, shelving with fabrics of all colors and textures, a little closet, and an area to sew, complete with a sewing machine.

"First up, we need to decide on your wedding dress," Cynthia said, motioning to the podium. She opened the closet and pulled out a rack holding five wedding dresses and the same number of dance costumes. All were different shades of white, but the fabrics were vastly different. Shimmering organza and silky charmeuse, soft velvet and stretchy tricot... I wanted to run my hands over all of them.

"They are all gorgeous!" I exclaimed as I scanned the intricate beading patterns, each one more beautiful than the last.

"Thank you, but these are simply prototypes. I took the liberty of selecting a few silhouettes I believe will complement your figure. But you do not have to choose any of them if you have something else in mind."

"Are you kidding? Having to choose only one is going to be the death of me!" Cynthia gave me a disconcerted look. "In other words, an impossible task."

"And that is what we are all here for." Lana came up next to me and squeezed my hand.

"I am flattered, Princess," Cynthia responded. "You are not limited to choosing one dress. We can take things you like about one dress and combine it with another. Or, you are welcome to change from the ceremony's gown into another for the reception."

"Isn't that more work for you?"

"Not at all. As I said, these are just prototypes."

"You don't have to—"

"Lydia, this is her gifting. Let her use it." Queen Nicole came up beside me, laying a hand on my shoulder. I immediately relaxed against her touch.

Cynthia held out a dress. "Let's try this one first."

Bachelorette Party - Raqs Style

ODAY WAS MY LAST DAY AS "LYDIA ERICKSON." Tomorrow, the new Mrs. Jamison would be showcasing all of her dancing skills, albeit a fraction of what I was once capable of.

Sitting at the vanity that overlooked what once were lush gardens, I twisted my wet hair into a top bun and swiped my lips with some honey-lavender lip oil Tia had gifted to me.

I flopped back onto my plush bed. I'd done it. I had exceeded my own expectations and conquered my fears. Yes, my leg still hurt a little where it had been mangled in the ice castle maze as we fled from Melchior and his army. As the healers said, the scar was only a pale faint line down my shin. Cynthia offered me tights, but I wanted to wear my battle scar proudly.

I shifted in bed, my lower back stiff and achy. I had been worried I might not be able to dance at all. But Gene was as kind as he was a creative genius, and he choreographed a dance that played to all of my strengths, putting a lot of the work on Will. I smiled remembering the kind words he spoke to me at the end of our rehearsal last night.

If I hadn't seen you dance with my own eyes, I would not believe it. You are a beautiful dancer, and Cristes is blessed to have such a strong up-and-coming ruler.

I had the Rumbiental memorized to a 't'. Rehearsing with the live band went better than I'd anticipated. Cynthia would be delivering the dresses for the final fitting tonight. I could not wait for Will to see me walk down the aisle.

Soft knocks sounded at the door. *That must be Cynthia.* I rose to my elbows. "Come in!" I called out.

The door opened a crack. "I am sorry to intrude, Madam. I have—"

"Oh! Duncan. I'm so sorry." I ungracefully rolled out of bed to greet him. "I thought you were someone else. Come in, come in."

He inclined his head and then held out a covered silver platter. When he raised his head, he lifted the cover. Sitting on the tray in front of me was a green envelope with my name scrawled in Will's handwriting.

"One sec!" I left the door open and ran to my side table to grab the purple envelope I'd prepared for Will. "Here you go. Have a good night and stay safe," I said to him before closing the door, beyond excited to open the contents of my newest letter.

The fire crackled in the corner, casting my room in a soft

glow. I tucked my legs underneath me as I sat on the large chaise in front of the fireplace. Sprawled all around me were the numerous letters Will and I had written to each other over the past year. And in my hands, the final letter:

Liddy,

I realize I've said it over a thousand times, but I find I need to say this once more. I miss you so darn much! I will be more than thankful when you return to me, for I have not been whole without you.

Tomorrow, I get to finally see your beautiful smile outside of my dreams.

Tomorrow, I get to touch you and watch your gorgeous eyes light up.

Tomorrow, I get the privilege of being your husband and calling you my wife!

Tomorrow, even with all the ceremonial customs attached to it, you and I become one and our giftings will join. I know this is something we both have wanted. No, wanted isn't strong enough...desired every day since they separated us. You cannot possibly know how many times I almost caved. Nick was right to appoint Tannon my accountability partner. He has stopped me more than once! Everything about you is so very tempting and brings me so much joy. That being said, the circumstances surrounding this marriage...if this is not what you want, then we will not go through with this. I made a promise to you that this would be our decision. I do not want the start of our marriage to be tainted by obligation and masking what it should really be about: Love. Commitment. Choice.

If we decide against this, my parents will help us figure out a new path. What I unequivocally know to be true, despite all we have been through, is nothing could ever diminish, let alone break, the love I have for you. In fact, I believe one day, our love story will be known as one of heroic endurance and taught in every school across Cristes. Maybe they will even make a movie about it.

Sweet Dreams,
Your Will
P.S. Flip over.

An excited giggle erupted from me, and I hastily flipped the page.

I have one final question for you. Do you still want to marry me tomorrow? Circle YES or NO

Happy tears clouded my vision and I swiped my eyes with the cuffs of my cream-colored sweatshirt. Tomorrow, I would become Mrs. Jamison. This sweet man, my best friend in the whole world, would commit himself to me, and me to him, forever. I leaned over and grabbed some of my stationary off the gold side table. The pen glided over the parchment as I scrawled a big fat yes as large as I could, then I rang for Duncan and waited.

Only seconds later, rapid knocking sounded on the door. Duncan might have been fast, but not that fast. A series of loud knocks rapped again, so I got up from the chaise and padded over to the door. As I got closer, I could hear a gaggle of excited voices. Another step, and a single voice rose above the rest, shushing all the others.

I opened the door, and wide-eyed stares greeted me.

In delayed unison, a chorus of women's voices sang, "Surprise!" One by one, Queen Nicole, Tia, Lana, and Ohanna walked into my suite, their arms full and Cynthia behind them pushing a cart.

I peeked my head out into the hall expecting Duncan, but he was nowhere to be seen. So I left the note for Will on the shelf next to my door, where I usually left my letters. I knew Duncan wouldn't be much longer, but curiosity seized me, and I had to discover what these ladies were up to.

When I turned around, my visitors were bustling about the room. Lana and Cynthia were hanging garment bags on a clothing rack, unzipping them to release their contents. Tia and Ohanna were setting out snacks and drinks on the table. Meanwhile, Queen Nicole was using her gifting on the melohym in the corner, until drum beats filled the room, tempting my hips to move to their rhythm.

"Not that I don't love you all, but what is happening right now?" I asked when no one seemed to notice my staring.

They all blinked at me a few times, then laughed.

"In Mortalia, you would recognize this as something akin to a bachelorette party," Lana answered, pulling forth another gown. "Traditionally, all the women gather together before the wedding and celebrate. Matrons and single ladies alike dance the Raqs Rumba together."

"That...that is so nice of you all," I said. Lana came up to me and wrapped her arms around me, my next words muffled into her shoulder. "But Gene should be here soon to do a final run-through, so I don't think I can really—"

"About that." Queen Nicole stepped toward me as Lana released me. "Gene will not be coming tonight. Surprise!"

"But I need to rehearse. I don't think I'm ready."

Lana chuckled. "I, too, was worried about not being ready enough when I was marrying Brantley. But you need not be. Tonight, is a celebration of you and your impending marriage, and I am so happy and excited for you."

The queen was setting up glasses. "Not to mention, I have checked in with Gene and he says you are more than ready."

Lana grabbed my hands. "It is an honor to be here and welcome you into my family officially, even though you have always been like a daughter to me, from the first moment I met you riding your pink Schwinn bicycle outside our house on Cherrywood."

I blinked back the tears and the sting that accompanied them. "Thank you," I whispered. I let out a deep breath, letting some tension go with it. "So what's first?"

"First, we eat and toast," Tia chimed in.

Ohanna stood stock still near the door, apparently here on duty.

"Will you be joining us?" I asked her.

"I already am," she answered with a nod of her head.

"No, I mean, I would like you to come hang with us."

"Hang?" She tilted her head slightly, looking genuinely confused.

"Sorry, more Mortalia lingo. What I mean is, I would like it very much if you would actually join us and partake in the festivities," I clarified. "I'm perfectly safe, and have been since I crossed the wall a year ago."

Ohanna appeared conflicted as she bit her lip and dropped her gaze, then looked at the group, then dropped her gaze again.

"Ohanna, you must join us. That is an order," Queen Nicole stated.

Ohanna's jaw dropped. "But—"

"Ah-ah...no butts," the queen continued. "Do not disobey me, or I will have to invoke consequences." She winked back at all of us, covering her face so Ohanna couldn't see. "Lydia is right, she is safe whether you are standing guard or celebrating with us."

Ohanna's stance relaxed, and she unburdened herself of half of her weapons, careful to leave them all within arm's reach. While we were busy convincing Ohanna to join us, Tia poured what looked like champagne into frosted crystal flutes, then handed them out until we each held a glass in our hand.

"Here in Cristes, it is customary to offer a blessing or words of advice to the bride-to-be. We toast and take a sip after each person speaks," Tia explained. "I will start. Since I am not married, I have no advice to offer. However, I wish your marriage to be one solidified in respect, love, peace, and protection."

"*Saludic*," everyone chanted. I, of course, had no idea what the salutation was. And so I stood there, silent, with my glass, rushing to take a sip as they did. The sweet bubbles danced over my tongue and I wanted to giggle. I was glad I was self-restricting to one sip at a time; otherwise, I could have probably chugged the entire bottle.

"I fear I might have too much of this drink and forget to share some important lessons I have learned. So, before

I forget, I will share now." She unwrapped the shawl that covered her shoulders. "I have been married a very long time and understand the pressures of leading a kingdom as you shall soon discover. One piece of advice I will offer is this: There will be good times and hard times, mountains of joy and valleys of pain. You will make it through them, as long as you work together."

Queen Nicole laid her hand on my shoulder and gave it a little squeeze. She continued, "Spending time each day making each other a priority, even for five minutes, will help you learn to communicate through it all. But most importantly, your relationship comes first over your subjects." She held her hand out and Lana placed a champagne flute in it. "Your cup needs filling before you can fill others." Queen Nicole raised her glass.

This time I joined them in toasting "Saludic." Then I took another sip.

Cynthia and Ohanna both took turns sharing their blessings, and our flutes were nearly drained when Lana cleared her throat. "Saving the best for last, of course," she teased, laughing lightly. "Lydia, marriage can be a beautiful blessing. But, it is not easy. When you live as long as Watchers do, you quickly learn how emotions can run hot, cold, and everywhere in between. Yes, we have fated matches, if we are lucky enough to find them. But fate alone is not enough. *Choose* William every day, as I know he will do the same for you. Choosing love is always worth it."

I started to cry; I couldn't help it. Memories of sitting with my mom at my kitchen table resurfaced at her words.

Lana's eyes widened as she gasped. "I am so sorry, Lydia. I

did not mean to offend. I am only sharing what I have learned, but please do not feel you need to—"

"No, it's not that," I cut in, wiping my nose with the cuff of my soft white pajamas. "Your words reminded me..." I took a steadying breath. "Your words sounded like something my mom said once."

The room fell silent, even the melohym. The quiet stretched, my ears uncomfortable with the loudness of it.

At last, Queen Nicole spoke softly. "Your sacrifices have not gone unnoticed. When it becomes safe again, we will host a second ceremony in Mortalia, and of course your mother, friends...they will all be in attendance."

I nodded. I knew this. But it still hurt. We raised our glasses and took our final dregs of the liquid. This time, I did giggle. "Well, I'm apparently on an emotional rollercoaster."

"Perfectly natural," the queen responded.

"So, what's next?" I asked.

"Your dress and costume fittings," Cynthia chirped. I think everyone—well, maybe not Ohanna—squealed with excitement.

Cynthia ushered me behind the privacy screen. "We shall start with the most important gown, then the Rumbiental, and, finally, the Raqs."

Adrenaline coursed through my entire body, and my chin chattered as if I'd been out in the cold for too long.

Cynthia popped her head out from behind the bamboo screen. "Someone has the excited jitters! We need some more bubbly back here!"

"On it!" Tia responded, and in less than a minute, Cynthia was offering me another champagne flute, but this time the sparkling liquid was slightly pink instead of gold. I gulped half of it, and immediately my body calmed.

I attempted to hand the glass back to Cynthia, but she pressed it back toward me. "Drink all of it. It will help even you out." She winked. "I'll be right back with your dress."

I don't know how long I waited in my strapless bra, undies, and heels, feeling ridiculous. Cynthia, Lana, and Queen Nicole all had parts of the dress draped over their arms as they walked the dress back to me. I had no words. None. My hand covered the gasp that so badly wanted to escape my mouth. The dress was exquisite, beyond anything I could have imagined. At first glance, the dress was a traditional white. But as it moved, it shimmered in colors of purple and teal, the colors of Will's and my gifting.

"Please kneel and raise your arms."

I did as Cynthia instructed, and together the three women guided the dress over my head and arms.

"Stand please," Cynthia directed me, and Lana and the queen helped me to stand before disappearing on the other side of the screen. Cynthia flitted about the hem of my dress, making sure it laid just so. She circled me, tilting her head to and fro, occasionally marking the dress with peach-colored chalk or adding a pin. "Alright, let's go show them before they have my head for taking too long."

I giggled. Cynthia showed me where to hold the dress in the front so as not to trip, and I followed her out. Collective gasps and hands over chests and mouths left me blushing.

"Exactly the reaction I was hoping for," Cynthia beamed. "Someone get the lights, please."

With a flick of her hand, Queen Nicole dimmed the

fireplace and all of the candles. As soon as the lights died down, my dress began to glow. Sparkles, like little fireflies in shades of purple and teal, twinkled as if my dress were alive.

"You have outdone yourself!" Tia gushed.

"Darling, I think you are the most beautiful bride I have ever seen," the queen said, her eyes glittering.

"Let us hope my son does not pass out at the sight of her! If she stole our breaths, I can only imagine how her match, who has not seen her in a year, will take it."

My pupils dilated in disbelief. That is the last thing I'd want to happen.

"Everything will be perfect," the queen assured me. "Alright, the hour is getting late and we still have much to do and celebrate." She clapped her hands twice as if snapping us back to attention. The lights went up and my dress went out.

Back behind the screen, I was instructed to put on the white dance costume for the Rumbiental while Cynthia carefully tucked my wedding gown back into its protective garment bag.

The costume took a minute for me to figure out how to get on; there was only one long sleeve, bedazzled with crystals that glistened like icicles in the sun. The other side was sleeveless, save for a single sparkly strap that started at my shoulder and snaked around my waist. It had the most subtle ombre in shades of ivory and white. The ensemble was complete with beautiful Christmas rose embroidery and beading that sparkled and shimmered from every angle.

I stepped out from the screen and was greeted with applause and more excitement.

"Gene is going to love it!" Queen Nicole beamed, fingering

the flowing skirt that left my front open but dramatically flowed out in the back.

"If we thought your husband was going to pass out before, this might actually send him over the edge." Tia laughed, gesturing to the bodice, which was cut in a deep 'v' nearly to my belly button, and we all joined her. The front would have left me exposed, except for a stretchy flesh-colored fabric filling in the cutout.

Cynthia circled me once again, nodding her approval. "It is perfect," she declared. "No alterations needed."

"Time for the party to get started!" Lana announced. She was met with trills and whoops of joy.

"Wait! I haven't tried on the last costume or even learned the last dance!" Panic seized me.

The women all traded smirks.

"Am I missing something?" I asked.

"Your final fitting will be private with Cynthia. After you finish with her, we shall dance," the queen assured me.

I sucked my bottom lip in and held it with my teeth as I walked behind the privacy screen.

I changed for the final time, understanding immediately why this was a private fitting. Though all my lady bits were covered, I was pretty much wearing lingerie crossed with the carnival-style costumes I saw in Nick's memories. There was skin showing— a *lot* of it. My entire abdomen, for one thing, and I was sporting some major cleavage; not to mention the high slits on either side of the plum skirt.

Cynthia fitted a second lavender skirt, a coin skirt with lots of dangling charms, around my waist. They sounded almost exactly like Nick's melody when he walked, only louder. I laughed, remembering how I used to fear the sound.

"Is something funny?" Cynthia asked.

"No, sorry. Just overjoyed."

She smiled regarding the armbands on my biceps and cuffs at the wrist. She also placed a sheer veil over my face, leaving only my eyes revealed. She circled me a few times. "We are all finished. I apologize I cannot stay for the dancing, but I have work to complete and I am on a deadline." She winked.

"Thank you again. For everything. You all have spoiled me."

"Of course. It has been my greatest pleasure! Now, get dressed in your pajamas and tie this around your waist before you join the ladies again." She handed me a teal coin skirt.

I stepped out from behind the privacy screen. The women were wearing coin skirts of their own and had not only cleared the table but pushed it aside to make room for dancing.

They swarmed me and brought me to the center of the makeshift dance floor.

"Raqs Rumba is one of the oldest styles of dance. It is as natural to you as your own bones and muscles," the queen began. "So, my dear, there is no set choreography. Your gifting will guide you, your body moving how it desires. Over the past few months, you have been instructed on how to use your torso rather than just your legs and feet for the movements, so use it."

I smiled remembering the many dance parties we had this year, especially on days when missing Will was especially difficult. Though I sat for most of them, my friends always found ways to include me.

"You've also been introduced to isolation movements, the

focus on moving specific parts of the body while everything else stays still." The queen demonstrated with a quick hip shimmy. "But you are a purple and a fated white lighter." Her gaze darted to Lana briefly and then back to me.

"In other words, I'm supposed to improv this whole thing?" I nearly choked on the fear as it crept its way into my thoughts.

"Improv?" Ohanna questioned.

"Make it up as I go along," I translated.

"No," Queen Nicole said, "what I am saying is, there is no need to fear. No movement you make, literally none, could mess this up. Your gifting will take over for you. Trust it."

"But for now, we are going to have a dance party for ourselves as women to celebrate your union," Lana chimed in.

"You can choose whatever moves you like, but the point is to have fun," Tia said.

Queen Nicole turned the melohym on, adjusting the volume until the bass hit as if a live drummer were performing for us. And then we danced.

Confirmation

WE DANCED FOR OVER AN HOUR that night and laughed even more. I thought I'd have trouble sleeping, the excitement of finally seeing Will keeping me up. But I actually slept deep and sound. I would have to remember to thank whoever made the bubbly concoction; its promise to calm and lull me to sleep, not to mention numb any pain, worked.

I turned on my side and peered at the two costumes hanging from my vanity. Soon, a team would be here to help me prepare for my wedding. I swung my legs over the side of the bed and took in a deep, steadying breath. Today was for celebrating. I would not think about tomorrow and how our union would mean the start of a war with Mara. No, today I would focus on my love for Will.

I sat down at the vanity to write Will one more letter, wanting to document my feelings on this day. Just as the ink of the first letter stroke dried, a soft knock sounded on the door.

I padded across the lush carpet and answered it, surprised to see Tia.

"Good morning!" I greeted her, arching a suspicious brow at her anxious expression. "You're early," I added.

She flashed a smile before glancing around her. "Can I come in?"

"Of course, please do." I stepped back, holding the door open.

"So, last night was fun, wasn't it?" Tia asked casually, crossing the room and sitting on the chair next to the fireplace. She gave me another sheepish smile that had the back of my neck tingling.

"It really was," I agreed, shutting the door and making my way to the chair opposite her. "I'm very thankful for you all." I sat and waited for her to speak. When she just smiled strangely again, and her neck began to redden, I let out an exasperated sigh. "What's going on?"

She started fidgeting with her braid. "So, I'm not technically supposed to talk to you about this until later in the reception. However, if I were you, I would want to be informed sooner so I could prepare."

My stomach dropped. "Is something wrong? Should I be worried?"

"Nothing like that. I am hesitant only because I'm not sure how you will react." She bit her lip. "Alright, that's not true. I have a pretty good idea of how you will react, and that has me on edge."

I threw up my hands in exasperation. "Oh, Tia...spit it out already!"

Her cheeks matched the scarlet of her neck. "Well...you see, we have this custom with Watcher royals. On your wedding night, elders of the court will be present to verify the..." She dropped her gaze. "...consummation of the marriage."

I stared at her, unblinking. Slowly, my body leaned forward of its own accord, and I had to place my hands on my knees to steady myself. But it wasn't enough. I let my body fall forward until my head was between my knees. I was going to puke. The room swayed.

"Dog water!" Tia muttered, and immediately her hand was on my back, rubbing circles. "It's not as bad as you think, I promise. I am only telling you now because I knew you would be a worrywart, and I didn't want you to make yourself sick at your wedding."

I whipped my head up and nearly clocked Tia in the face. "Not as bad as you think? I'm sorry, but where I come from, watching a royal couple consummate their marriage is a medieval practice, and it was abolished for a reason! No one should have the right to watch you...you know...make love with your spouse!" I lowered my voice to a whisper. "It's already awkward enough that we don't even know what we're doing!"

Tia started giggling. I stared at her, opened-mouthed. *She's seriously laughing at me?*

"Well, I am *sooo* glad my humiliation is so dang funny." I sneered and stood up, turning my back to her.

Tia was laughing so hard she was crying, a combination

of snorts and high-pitched squeals. Finally, she caught her breath. "Liddy, no one will be in the room with you. No one will observe any of your body, well, except for Will." She chuckled. "Nor anything the two of you do together. You are right, that is no one's business but your own."

I whipped back around to face her, confused as all get out. "But you just said—"

"I said the consummation will be *verified*."

"Where are we getting our signals crossed? Where I come from, there is only one way consummation can be verified," I argued.

"Well, not here. Do you remember how you and Will would light up when you were near each other? Especially after you kissed?"

I crinkled my brow. "Yeah?"

"Well, royal matches have the potential to become white-lighters—something Cristes values a great deal."

I tensed, and she patted my hand. Tia knew the stress I was under. Months ago, I confided in her that I was worried I wasn't Will's fated match. She held me during my panic attack the day the last of the violet disappeared from my irises, and I'd been convinced my separation from Will broke whatever bond we'd had.

"Elders will be watching for your colors, to determine if your union will be a blend of your giftings, devoid of any enhanced giftings," she explained, "or if your joining will be white as a giant star."

"How will they know, though, if they aren't in the room with us?"

"The wedding suite is located at the top of a tower, and the ceiling has a special glass panel in it. It cannot be broken and no one can see through it, except it allows your gifting light out. Elders are in a different tower, watching and waiting."

Though the need to throw up subsided somewhat, this custom still nauseated me.

"So what you're telling me is that strangers are going to realize the exact moment Will and I..." I trailed off, too embarrassed to continue.

She shook her head briskly. "I promise, they are not thinking about that. They only care about the color of the light. I tried to fight it for you, though. I knew how hard this would be to come to terms with, and I tried to get them to agree to simply take your word for it. But, with so much riding on this union, I was vetoed."

I took a moment to process her words. "Thank you. You tried to change tradition for me, and that means a great deal." But I was devastated. This was not how I imagined my first time with Will.

"Well, I wasn't totally unsuccessful." A large smile inched across her face. "Instead of all the elders bearing witness, they agreed to having only one person present, and *you* get to pick who it is."

I let out a stark laugh. "I don't know if I should be happy with their concession or not." Then I dropped my face into my hands and groaned. "*Ugh.* It's still weird!"

"I get it!" Tia splayed her hands. "But again, they won't be verifying whether or not you've had *relations*..." She used air quotes. "But rather how your gifting has changed."

I sighed. "Can't the changes be verified some other time? Like the next morning?"

"No." Tia shook her head and sighed. "You have an entire nation that's been awaiting the savior to come and fix what Mara and the Black Roses broke. Besides," she added, "coupled giftings do not present the same physical manifestations from one couple to the next."

I nodded, slowly resigning myself to my fate. "Does Will know?"

She shrugged. "If he does, it is news to me." Then she leaned forward in her seat, clasping her hands together. "So, who will you choose to sit in the tower? I am supposed to report to the queen."

I sat back down, my knees were shaking so badly they nearly knocked together. I would have chosen Nolan, had he been there. He was a loyal soldier, had discretion down to a 't'. But he was gone, because of me. I sighed and tried to refocus my thoughts on the task at hand.

Choosing someone to "verify" the consummation of my marriage.

Obviously, Will's parents were a 'no' because, well, eww. The king and queen probably had a million duties to attend to, and I didn't want to complicate their lives even more. Only Nick, Tannon, and Tia remained. Because of their assigned duties to me and my fiancé, Tia and Tannon had barely seen each other over the past year. I didn't want to disrupt the siblings' reunion and fun at the reception.

"Nick," I decided. And as I said his name aloud, a peaceful confirmation washed over me. After all, he was the one to counteract Mara's spell when she cursed everyone to Mortalia and set this union into motion. Nick helped find me. And he protected me all these years. I could trust him with this.

Tia nodded, looking more relaxed. "I will inform the queen and return after to get ready with you."

As Tia exited, Lana stood in the doorway, trailed by two female watchers in all black. Lana caught Tia as she passed, and the two women had a brief exchange before Tia sauntered off to fulfill her errand. Lana then introduced me to Ines and Vea, my hair and makeup artists for the day. But we barely exchanged two words before Lana was grabbing my hand and whisking me out of the room.

"Where are we going?" I asked.

"The bathing chamber," Lana answered, although we were headed in the opposite direction of the master bathroom.

We took a right turn, and after a short walk down the hall, Lana stopped in front of a painting of Azure Mountain. I'd never noticed the faint outline of a Christmas rose carved into the wall before until Lana placed her palm over it and the outline of a door appeared. She gave it a gentle push and I stepped in after her. As we passed the threshold, little candles flickered to life, and the door closed behind us on its own.

There must have been hundreds of candles tucked into the little ledges and crevices of the earthen walls. They illuminated what appeared to be a cave, with lush moss all along the ground. Following Lana's lead, I removed my slippers and let the moss squish between my toes. It glowed with each step I took, shades of purple, green, and blue.

At the back of the cave, water trickled down the wall and into a deep pool, carving the stony earth beneath it. Black, smooth stone cradled the water.

Lana turned to me. "Though it doesn't look very big, this lagoon is deep and tunnels long, eventually connecting with

Azure Mountain," she explained. "Legend has it that deep inside the mountain, waters with healing properties flow abundantly."

She gestured to the wall behind her, where pegs had been drilled in. Some were empty, but one held a pristine white towel, another a white robe. Lana picked up a jar from the floor, opened it, and sprinkled Christmas rose petals into the water. They burned gold as they floated, then melted into silver as they disappeared beneath the surface. Staring into the pool reminded me of gazing at the wintry night sky dusted with bright stars, brilliant against the dark backdrop.

"Undress and use the stairs carved into the stone to enter," Lana said. "I will wait outside the door and knock three times to signal when it is time for you to get dressed."

I nodded, and when the door closed behind her, I quickly undressed and hung my fleece pajamas on the empty hook. Dipping my toe in the water first, I wasn't surprised to find the temperature perfect—not too hot, not too cold.

I lowered myself into the pool and breathed deeply, detecting the faintest scent of coconut and hibiscus. *Holy cow, this is amazing.* The waters were thicker, more luxurious, and nourishing than anything I'd ever experienced before. All the tension in my muscles from earlier evaporated. Tingles traveled up and down my arms, legs, and torso as if they were growing stronger, any weak spots shoring up. I gasped. I hadn't felt that since... since the last time I saw Will.

"Will?" I called out into the empty chamber. No answer. *Weird.*

I laid my head back on the edge of the pool and stared at the smooth ceiling.

"Liddy?"

I started and searched the cavern. That was definitely Will's voice.

Will? I tried again, but this time I didn't call his name out loud. Rather, I searched within myself, feeling for the bond between us, and called to it.

The water started to glow, and I realized it was me who was shining. Three sharp knocks wrenched my attention away, and I sighed. Besides being relaxing, the time in the pool reminded me of how badly I missed Will; so much so, I'd just imagined talking with him telepathically.

I slipped out of the water, careful to hold onto the wall in case my legs gave out. After drying myself off with the plush towel, I pulled on my clothes and slippers just in time to meet Lana at the door as she opened it.

"You look radiant." She smiled warmly.

"Thank you. That was so special, and I feel wonderful." Together, we made the short walk back to my room.

Ines and Vea were fully set up at a large vanity. On one side of the white styling chair was a makeup display that would rival any Clinique counter. On the other side stood a trolly with drawers full of hair accessories and tools. Cynthia had also arrived, and she was setting up a podium, my dress and dancing costume hung on a clothing rack behind her. Noticeably missing was my Raqs Rumba costume, but Cynthia had already promised to deliver it to the wedding suite for me.

I slid into the white chair with gold metal accents and stared at myself in the round mirror. My skin was luminescent, not the same glow I achieved from my gifting, but one more human. One I'd noticed from time to time in moments full of joy and anticipation.

As Ines curled my hair, her gifting making swift work of it as the styling wand glowed purple, Vea buffed my fingernails and painted my toes a champagne pink with small floral designs in crystal. Ines pinned a piece of hair here and sprayed a section there, while Vea painted a whimsical, white lace design over my blush-colored fingernails, complementing my toes.

"Your Highness, I am finished with your hair." Ines turned my chair around and handed me a mirror so I could see the back. My dark hair cascaded down my shoulders in thick waves. "I will leave to set up now in the reception location and return to adorn your circlet," she told me.

"Thank you, Ines. I love it!" She smiled and took the mirror from me. When she spun me back around, Vea was waiting with a makeup brush, ready to start my face.

Then I glimpsed red hair curled in perfect ringlets bounce by. Most of Tia's curls sat atop her head, but a few loose pieces softened the look. Her light makeup only enhanced her natural beauty and made her hazel eyes pop.

"Tia, you are stunning!" I exclaimed.

She paused mid-stride and struck a pose. "Oh, this?" She framed her face with her hands and batted her lashes. "This is my 'just rolled out of bed' look. What can I say? I am blessed."

We both erupted into a fit of giggles.

"Truthfully, I'm used to smelling like dog and plucking hay out of my hair, not all this fuss," Tia confessed. "Are you sure it isn't too much?"

"Nonsense." Queen Nicole came up to her, the stylists flitting around her parted like the Red Sea to allow her to pass.

"You are perfect, and I am proud to have you as an esteemed member of this wedding party."

Tia's chest puffed a little at the high praise and she smiled, her shoulders relaxing.

Vea turned me away from the mirror so I couldn't peek at myself until the end. "You need to eat something, and when you are done, I will finish with your lips," she instructed.

"No, thanks. I'm not—"

But Lana was already shoving a plate into my hands. "My dear, the excitement doesn't leave a whole lot of room in your stomach, true. But we can't have the bride passing out at the altar, now can we?" She quirked her brow at me.

"I guess not," I said, taking the plate full of fruit, warm, syrupy bacon, and bread caked in egg and sprinkled with powdered sugar. "Is this French toast?"

"Will requested it for you," Lana replied, her grin lighting up her whole face. I returned the smile... Will knew me so well.

I slid from the chair and joined Tia in the sitting room, where she, too, ate her brunch.

I held a piece of toast on my fork, covering my mouth, and quietly asked her, "So, did Nick agree?"

Tia didn't miss a beat. "He sure did," she whispered back.

This little confirmation, along with the fact that Will had my favorite food sent to me, calmed me enough that I was able to eat my fill of breakfast. After breakfast, I returned to Vea so she could finish my transformation. "Can I look now?" I asked impatiently, butterflies flitting wildly. After seeing how gorgeously Vea had styled Tia, I knew I could trust her, but nerves still reared their ugly little heads.

"Not yet." She *tsked* at me. "Cynthia would like you to

put on the dress first. Next, the portraitist will commit this moment to our history."

Lana walked up beside me and linked her elbow in mine. "I will be helping you dress, if you don't mind."

"Of course!" If my own mother couldn't be there, Lana was an excellent substitute.

We strolled over to the large partition, offering me privacy from the hustling bodies around the room. She stopped me before we disappeared behind it.

"I realize in Mortalia, wedding customs are slightly different. You typically wear something old, something new, something borrowed, and something blue." Her eyes ignited with her gifting as she reached for and held the inside of my wrists. "Here in Cristes, the parents of the bride and groom offer a mark of their gifting onto the person joining their family, and vice versa."

She stared so deeply at me, so sincerely, I felt like she could see into my soul. She closed her eyes, and a tingling sensation, prickly but not unpleasant, bubbled over my skin. Then the bubbles burst, oozing quickly like a cooling gel. Lana released my wrists. I held them up and watched as what looked like twin tattoos of the Jamison family crest gradually dissolved into my skin.

"You cannot see them, but these markings bond you to us," Lana explained. "It's more of a formality than anything, but if you find yourself in trouble, we can get to you more easily." I held my wrists over my heart and bowed to her. I'm not sure why I did it, only that I felt like I wanted to.

Lana cupped my cheek, dropping her head slightly to meet my gaze. With wet eyes, she said, "You have always been like a daughter. But I am privileged to be the first to officially welcome you into the family."

"Thank you," I rasped, my own tears brimming, threatening to ruin Vea's artwork.

Lana laughed and gestured to my stylist.

"Oh dear, none of that," Vea said as she flicked her fingers in front of my face. The tears were gone. *"Humph!"* she resounded with satisfaction before returning to her post.

Lana laughed and winked at me. "Come on, let's get you into your spectacular gown."

I grinned back at her. "Let's do this."

I Do

STOOD IN THE BACK OF THE CHURCH, my nerves flitting in my stomach like frenzied moths fighting to reach the flame. My breathing exercises only helped so much.

"Liddy, what is wrong with you? Get a hold of yourself, girl. Your anxiousness is messing with me, so much so, I actually think I may puke," Tia said, rubbing my arms vigorously.

"I hate being the center of attention. Not to mention, I haven't seen Will in over a year, and everyone will be privy to that private moment. What if I mess up the vows? What if my legs give out and I trip and fall flat on my face? What if I—"

"We won't let you," Shai said as he and Nick stepped out from an alcove.

My knees buckled, and I would have fallen if Tia hadn't caught me.

"What would you do without me," she said jokingly, grabbing my bouquet after I was standing with sure footing.

Shai... Shai was up and *here*.

I ran and flung my arms around his neck. He gave me a strong hug in return.

"How?" My voice was quiet, muffled against his shoulder. Though Will and I had created the spark that helped him to heal, like me, his recovery was arduous.

"Well, while you have been at the castle this week, my nephew has been visiting me at the sanctum, pushing me in therapy and offering to try his healing giftings on me."

"He has much improved over this year," Nick added.

"I'll say. I obliged him of course because here I am. I would not have dared miss this for the world."

I stepped out of his embrace and stared up at him.

"I am so glad you could be here." Tears began to collect in the corners of my eyes.

"So am I," Shai responded.

"Tsk, tsk, tsk." Vea cantered over and again flicked her fingers at my face. She gave the men a hard stare and walked away.

Guilty, strained smiles adorned the men's faces. I laughed. "She means no harm. She worked very hard to make me presentable and wants to keep me that way."

"Even if she had done nothing, you would still rival any Watcher royal." Nick smiled, his eyes crinkling at the corners.

"Yeah, she would," Tia agreed.

"Thanks," I replied sheepishly.

"What is that face for?" Shai tilted his head.

The plan had been that Nick would walk me down the

aisle. But now that Shai was here too...

"So, does this mean both of you will escort me down the long, scary aisle?" Hope sprung wild and free in my heart. Two escorts meant even less of a chance I'd fall on my face.

The men smirked.

"Mostly. We only walk you to the end of the pews, but you must walk the remaining six or so feet on your own," Shai replied.

"Think you can handle that?" Nick asked with a wink.

Tia linked her elbow in mine. "Of course she can."

"Lydia, it's time to line up," Lana said as she strode in from the back doors. Her ivory and olive dress billowed around her feet, and just like the first time I met her, she walked with such grace, it gave the illusion that she floated with each step. "Are you ready to greet your husband?"

I grinned, excitement vibrating through me. "I'm ready." I couldn't wait to show him that I could walk on my own.

Tia kissed my cheek. "You are going to do wonderfully." She handed me back my bouquet, then she took her place as second in line, holding a Christmas rose over her heart.

Vea and Ines were at my side, touching up my hair and makeup. Cynthia fluffed my gown, whispering, "I hope you like the surprise." She opened the door a crack to slip in and find her seat to watch the ceremony, Ines and Vea following after her.

Moments later, a choir of ethereal voices echoed from within the cathedral. The chorus was so beautiful, tears pricked my eyes as their voices plucked at my heartstrings.

"That is our cue," Nick said as he sidled up to my right and presented his arm, Shai doing the same on my left. I laced my arms through theirs, readying myself. Suddenly, the large wooden doors in front of me were opened and the warmth of the music and the curious gazes of all the guests greeted me.

I nearly stumbled, but the two men on either side of me held me firm and led me through the doors.

Queen Nicole and King were in their private box near the front, their view completely unobstructed. Lana reached the end of the aisle first, where Brantley met her halfway and escorted her to their seat in the front row.

My attention was hyper-focused on the pulpit, where an elder waited. Tannon came down the steps as Tia approached and guided her to stand on the steps. He returned to his place next to Charlie, who stood tall and proud at Will's side. *Will.* An electrical pulse was rapid-firing in my chest, and I was confident that if my heart were being monitored at that moment, doctors would rush in, worried about its erratic beat.

But Will was too far from me, and I couldn't make out the details of his face. As soon as I passed the threshold, the choir dropped out, save for one ethereal voice cascading over the room. Flower petals, white and fresh, floated through the air like a snow shower in spring. With the sunlight streaming in from the high windows, they sparkled like falling stars.

But I was immediately distracted by the thousands of Watchers in attendance, watching me. It was intimidating, and I tried to avoid eye contact as they all dropped to one knee as I passed by each row.

"You're doing beautifully," Shai whispered.

I squeezed his hand, but in truth, it took everything I had not to run because we were not walking fast enough. I wanted to be down the aisle standing next to the man I would soon call my husband. As if on the same brain wave, Shai and Nick placed their warm, strong hands over mine in sync, helping me to slow back down.

As promised, we reached the end of the pews, and the protectors who I'd held onto stopped their procession. They each kissed my cheeks and headed to their seats in the front row. Lana stood and pinned a diamond pendant onto the wrapped stems of my bouquet. She, too, kissed me on both cheeks, then returned to her seat next to Brantley.

The music changed once more, and harmonies joined the solo voice. I lifted my chin up from my flowers and found Will's face. His glorious face. He'd just finished wiping tears from his eyes. And when those gorgeous eyes met mine, they immediately ignited. What he was feeling slammed into me. Joy. Love. Passion. Desire. Need. We both faltered at the rush of it all. I'd been so worried our bond would dampen with absence. Maybe it had, but now? I was certain it was back; our affinity for each other was stronger than ever.

A collective gasp buzzed throughout the church, echoing to the ceiling that seemed to touch the sky. Their exclamations didn't worry me, but they did pique my curiosity. Flickering light coming from below forced me to look down. Cynthia's surprise was in full force. My gown glowed, but not from my giftings— bright white, like a northern star, a promise of what our union would mean for Cristes.

I found Cynthia and mouthed, "Thank you." Turning back to Will, I took a few slow steps to close the gap and nearly skipped to him. My legs were suddenly strong, like before the accident strong. I giggled when Will's patience ran out and he tried to come to me, but Charlie latched onto him by the collar of his tux.

"You look so beautiful," Charlie whispered quickly before tugging Will back.

Finally, after a few more agonizing seconds, I was next to Will. My body vibrated with the knowledge we were moments away from being whole again, as he truly was my other half. Our bond heaved, and Will took a shuddering breath. Our bond, relentless in its demand for us to touch, nearly knocked me over.

Will grabbed my hand and placed my arm in his, turning us to face the elder, and I almost sagged with relief upon the skin-to-skin contact.

Will leaned in and whispered, "Finally, I get to peer into those beautiful violet eyes. I thought you'd never reach me. That aisle is ridiculously long."

"*You* didn't have to walk it." Wait, did he say violet?

The elder cleared his throat and began.

I don't remember much of the ceremony. Everyone and everything faded except for my sole focus, like the blur setting on a camera, leaving only Will and me. It'd been so long since I'd last seen him. I studied his face, my eyes tracing the scars from our sledding adventure that marked him, which only made him more beautiful. I reached out to caress them, and he snuggled his cheek into my palm, inhaling the skin at my wrist.

His eyes glowed brighter. I dropped my hand when Tia gave me a little pinch in the back of my arm, and I yelped, snapping me back to the present.

"Sorry," I whispered to the silver-haired elder, but he just smiled wide and continued on as if nothing had happened.

We were instructed to clasp our left hands and intertwine our fingers. The elder bound them with a silken white ribbon and led us to a black-stoned basin, the water filled with Christmas roses.

"William and Lydia will dip their conjoined hands into the waters, signifying the death of their individual selves." The elder used his golden gifting to gently push our hands into the water. He sang some words I could not understand in a monotone fashion.

"Let them raise their hands from the depths of the water to signify the birth of their perfect union," he said loud enough for the congregation to hear. We raised our hands, and Tia and Tannon were there with small towels to dry them off. We returned to the front of the pulpit.

"William Lucas Jamison, of the Royal lineage of Klaus, do you promise to cherish your bride for all the days of your life?"

"I do," he replied, his eyes never leaving mine.

"Do you, Lydia Andra Erickson, of the royal lineage of Summervale, promise to honor your groom for all the days of your life?"

"I do."

"William and Lydia, do you promise to be united in your duties to Cristes, to use your combined giftings for good and not evil, for service and protection to your people no matter the cost?"

Answering in unison, we replied, "We do."

A trill-like cheer rose up from the crowd and quickly faded.

"By the powers that be, may Eria bless your union with everlasting love, wealth in health, and the strength and wisdom needed to lead your people. You may now seal your fate."

Will had been inching closer to me with each word the elder spoke. All I had to do was lift my chin mere centimeters and our lips would be touching. Will didn't wait for that little movement. Confident as if no time had passed at all, his mouth was on mine, and my lips parted some from the force. A low growl rippled in Will's throat, and his arms wrapped around me, pressing my torso into his, deepening the kiss. Warm zings and zaps soared through my body.

Cheers, boisterous and numerous, erupted within the church walls. Flashes of color appeared behind my closed eyes as all the Watchers shot off spurts of their giftings into the air, our own personal fireworks show.

Will pulled away from me, but only slightly. "You're walking." He sighed and touched his forehead to mine. "Thank you for marrying me. There were so many days I thought I would lose my mind not getting to see you."

"Thank *you* for marrying me, for being the best part of me." My lips met his again.

The kiss was gentle, tender, and when we broke apart, he whispered, "You taste exactly how I remember."

The elder turned us to face the citizens of Cristes. We held up our conjoined hands and more jubilation erupted from the guests. We made our way down the aisle, this time moving much more quickly. I no longer feared tripping or making a fool of myself. Will was here, and I knew I would never fall again.

We broke through the doors, and Will frantically searched the hallway.

"What are you looking for?" I asked.

Will responded by racing down the corridor and I was pleasantly surprised that I had no problems keeping up with him. He found an alcove that appeared to be used for prayer, with a kneeling bench and candles, and pulled the coral curtain closed behind him.

And then he was kissing me, his hands in my hair, on my waist, up and down my arms. His lips trailed along my jaw and down my neck, across my clavicle, and up the other side of my neck.

"You smell heavenly," he groaned.

Swoosh! Clink! The curtain was whipped open. "Oh no, you don't," Tia said, reaching into the alcove and yanking me back.

"Will! Come on, man, you avoided temptation for three hundred and sixty-seven days. Do not let me fail my duties now," Tannon complained.

Will whipped his head at Tannon, his eyes blazing a dark green. Tannon stepped back, his hands up in surrender. "Easy now. I have my duties to perform, as assigned by the king and queen."

Will shook his head and dug the heels of his hands into his eyes, snuffing out his gifting. "Sorry. I don't know what's come over me."

"Sure you do, mate, and I do not blame you. So, the quicker we get you two to the reception, the faster you both can, well...you get the idea." Tannon's cheeks flamed red.

"Can I please hug him one more time?" I asked, scared they would separate us again.

"He can come with you," a familiar, velvety voice spoke

from behind us.

Queen Nicole stood there, on King Klaus's arm, smiling at us. Both pairs of eyes were lit with silver joy.

"Let us promenade to the reception together," the king suggested. Tia and Tannon sighed with relief.

Gene, Cynthia, Ines, and Vea all waited outside a door to our right as we walked into the receiving area just outside the castle's large ballroom.

"Lydia, this way," Cynthia said, gesturing to the door behind her.

I continued holding Will's hand and held it up to show that we were still attached. Gene walked up to us and with a quick tug, the ribbon slinked over our wrists. Will snatched it before it touched the ground and placed it in his suit jacket pocket.

"William, you are going directly across the hall to change," Cynthia added, where one of her assistants stood waiting.

"I don't want to leave her," Will said matter-of-factly.

"You both need to change. Besides, it will be but a few moments." Tia attempted to placate Will, who clutched me to his side.

"As soon as you are dressed, you can come back to your wife," Tannon assured my husband. "You will both be announced as one when you enter the ballroom."

Will maintained his ground, letting us know he would not move from my side. Tia audibly groaned. "All the guests need time to arrive and find their seats. How about we give you five minutes of alone time before you are announced in the ballroom?"

"You can do that?" I asked. She shrugged.

"Enough of these dramatics," Cynthia mumbled under her breath. She grabbed my hand and pulled me toward the dressing room. "I'll bring her right back, I promise," she said over her shoulder in a sing-song voice before closing the door.

Though I was sad I only got to wear the most gorgeous gown ever for such a short time, I never changed so quickly in my life. Will was waiting. As I sat in the makeup chair, my new lovely dance costume reflecting off the lights of the mirror, Cynthia caught me eyeing the wedding dress.

"You can put her back on after the Rumbiental if you would like."

"I can?"

"Of course, you can. It is your wedding day. You do as you like." Cynthia winked at me.

I tried with every ounce of my being to be patient and still for Ines as she transformed my hair. Eria bless her, she never huffed or rolled her eyes at me once. Her skilled hands were swift with their work, and before I could protest being away from Will any longer, my hair was done in the most beautifully classic updo I'd ever had.

Vea bent to add more makeup to my face but paused with the shadow brush millimeters from my eyelid. Then she stood, her tongue in her cheek. "Well, that's... I'll be right back." She smiled as she turned to her kit. Speaking over her shoulder, she explained, "It seems your irises have changed back to purple after being near your match, so now I need to change shadow colors."

My heart sped up. "Really?"

"Really." Vea laughed as she returned with another palette. "Now, please hold still."

I squeezed my eyes shut and stayed still as possible as Vea dusted more makeup on my face. She handed me a mirror moments later, and I gasped.

Between the extra-long lashes, smokey eyeshadow, and bold, glossy red lips, I scarcely recognized myself. It was a much more dramatic look compared to the more natural makeup I'd had for the ceremony.

"Well?" Vea asked as she caught my reflection in the mirror. "Do you not like it?"

"I do! I really do." My cheeks flamed. "I guess I'm worried I'll get this lipstick all over my..."

"Husband?" she finished with a knowing smile.

"Right. My husband." That word was going to take some getting used to.

Vea laughed again, the sound like a soft melody of outdoor chimes.

I thanked her and slipped on my dance heels, every space on their shell encrusted with crystals. For the first time since my injury, I felt confident about dancing with Will.

I exited the room and there he was, pacing the hall in front of my door. He stopped dead in his tracks and turned to take me in fully.

His eyes gave him away, turning a light cerulean and immediately firing up. "You look... I mean...you are..."

I walked right up to him and kissed him softly on the lips. "Thank you. You look rather smashing yourself."

I stood back and checked him out from head to toe. Taking in the hypnotic scent of him, my eyes followed the trail of buttons down from the side of his neck and across his broad chest, ending at the side of his waist. I circled him, touching his bare biceps, which were even larger and more defined than they were a year ago, admiring the fit of his black pants.

He grabbed my wrist and pulled me to him. "Are you nervous?"

"I feel better than ever. Last week I wasn't sure I could even dance, but now that I'm with you, it's like I'm complete again...every part of me healed and put back together. Plus, I get to dance with my *husband*, and I know he won't let me fall."

Will stiffened as if I'd shocked him.

"Did I say something wrong?"

Slowly, the corner of his mouth hitched upward, transforming into a devastatingly handsome smirk. Then the other corner lifted, and he practically beamed. He shifted his hands on me and dipped me back, never once taking his eyes from mine.

"I have waited an entire year to hear you call me that. Say it again."

"Say what again? That being near you makes me feel stronger? Like I was never paralyzed?"

"I mean, that is great and all. But, no. The name you called me after that." He nipped my bottom lip. "Please?"

"*Husband*?" I whispered.

Will's eyes brightened another ten watts, and then he was fully kissing me.

"Ah, ah, ah! You will mess up our masterpiece before she has had the chance to present herself to the public," Cynthia scolded, though there was no gusto behind her warning.

Will growled his annoyance, sighed, and straightened me to standing.

"Aw, there you two are!" Lana exclaimed as she walked in on the arm of Brantley, Charlie right behind them, and we all exchanged hugs.

"Are we ready, dear?" the king asked.

"Lydia, are you ready?" And I knew what the queen was asking.

"Yes. I cannot wait to dance with my husband."

The queen's eyes brightened ever so slightly. "Glad to hear it. Well then, if we are all ready—"

"Almost!" Gene swaggered into the receiving hall. "Will, Liddy...knock 'em dead. I will be front and center to see the best Argentang ever to grace these halls...no offense, Your Majesty."

"None taken," the queen replied with a smile.

"Everyone line up, Will and Liddy in the back," Lana ordered.

The king and queen set the pace. Charlie and Tannon both escorted Tia into the reception hall. Brantley and Lana were next, and then... Will and I were alone.

"It seems like only yesterday we were dancing together," I whispered.

"Only yesterday? I'm so happy the time apart went quickly for you, because for me, it felt like ten years." Will winked a sassy twinkle in his eye, and I playfully nudged his shoulder.

Our names were announced, thwarting my rebuttal.

"And now, presenting Their Royal Highnesses, William and Lydia Jamison!" Gene's voice rang out. "May their giftings bring the promise of the greatest blessings Cristes has ever known to fruition!"

"No pressure," Will whispered in my ear before offering

his arm. I slipped mine into his, and then the doors swung open once more. We stepped into the ballroom that seemed to go on for miles.

A blast of humid air hit me as if we had stepped off a plane and right into a tropical rainforest. The walls were covered in greenery, the ground sand, save for the dance floor and the paths winding to it, which were magically pristine.

Will leaned in and murmured, "This is the ballroom? Feels more like paradise."

Lush tropical flowers in vibrant colors adorned the all-white, wood-slatted ceiling. Birds flew from perch to perch. And I realized that this is what Cristes was supposed to look like, what it was supposed to be before Mara came in and ruined it all.

"Yes, the tropical paradise that is Cristes," I breathed. "It's beautiful."

"It really is," Will said. I tilted my head back to find him staring at me. My cheeks heated under his steamy gaze.

Will led me to the dance floor to the wild cheers of the crowd, and we took our positions.

Rumbiental

SILENCE WASHED OVER THE ROOM IN ONE FELL SWOOP. Will and I stood front and center on the dance floor that had been shined so hard it appeared as if we'd be dancing on glass.

The band began to play. Their rhythmic music started slow and reverberated deep within. And then we danced. I don't know if it was due to the time apart and our bond now basking in connection after so long, but the amount of energy flowing between our bodies was a catalyst, demanding we not stop moving or touching. We fit together perfectly, anticipating each other's bodies with each movement of the choreography.

Gene was right. The ease with which we danced was as if no time had passed at all. I no longer had to act, as I did when rehearsing with Gene. I poured every ounce of what I was feeling for Will and my new family into the Argentang.

In the final sequence, with my leg outstretched and Will standing behind me, his palm connected to the outside of my knee, tracing my leg up, over my hip, to my waist. Then, at the last second, he changed the choreography on me.

My hand was supposed to find his. He'd twirl me out, in, then out again, ending with me inches from the floor in a dip with him standing over me. Instead, his hands continued up, caressing my ribs, gentle pressure moving up my arm as he slowly pulled me to standing.

He turned me around and dipped me, transporting me back to our high school's Winter Wonderland dance. His face was so close to mine my heart raced and blood sang. Once again, I couldn't help but stare at his perfect lips and wish they were on mine.

"As you wish," he said.

A few scattered whoops and hollers of encouragement echoed in the room as my husband kissed me. Instead of fake snowflakes fluttering down on us like they did at the winter dance, a mist filled the air and sparkled in the light like little flecks of stardust. When he led me to standing, he encouraged my body to roll, first my hips making contact with his, then my abdomen, my chest, and finally my head to rest on his shoulder.

The music ended and the guests went wild.

"You could have warned me you were going to change the choreo," I whispered in his ear.

"And rob us of this moment? You are beyond talented. I had zero doubt you'd be able to follow my lead." Will winked, twirled me away from him, and we both bowed.

The music changed to a waltz. Will's parents, along with the king and queen, joined us on the floor. Tia asked Charlie to dance and he obliged, though I tried to suppress my giggle when he slipped a little on the floor and his cheeks pinked. After a few sets of eight, someone tapped me on the shoulder.

"May I cut in?" Nick asked.

"Of course." I curtsied and joined Nick in hold. We floated around the perimeter of the dance floor while everyone else stayed near the center.

"Are you ready for what tomorrow brings, Princess?"

I stiffened. Did we have to discuss this now... at my wedding? "I guess I am as ready as I'll ever be."

"I know. This is not a great time. But I thought it might help to share what to expect. Tomorrow, the council will introduce you and Will to the plans we have worked on diligently over this year. This will not be an easy feat. You and Will, more than any of us, will be challenged beyond your limits."

"I'm not sure about that. I think war, any way you look at it, will have negative effects on us all."

He nodded his head in agreement. "Of course. I only meant that there will be a lot of pressure on you and Will to save us all. I want you to fully comprehend how many of us are in your corner. You are not doing this alone, and we'll stop at nothing to help you both be successful."

"In other words, you have our backs." I smiled. "Thank you, Nick. For everything. You have given up so much of your life for Cristes...for Will and me. Always putting yourself last. I pray that one day, you get to choose you."

Nick stopped abruptly mid-step. "Was I too forward? Did

I speak out of turn?" I asked bashfully. He did not answer, his gaze severe and fixated on a point over my shoulder. I turned and saw a familiar stranger only a few feet away.

I whipped back around to face Nick. "Is that who I think it is?" Nick only nodded in response as he continued to stare straight ahead, then flared when someone gently tapped my shoulder. I tensed but plastered on a smile and turned to face the man I knew had a hand in breaking Cristes.

"Wow!" Gavin breathed even as his face fell and his eyes swam with tears. "You are practically her twin."

I blinked up at him. "I'm sorry?"

"My Ellasyn. Your grandmother, or maybe your great-grandmother. I do not have the acumen to determine how many generations have passed in Mortalia compared to here."

I held my hands up and Gavin stepped in, taking over for Nick and moving me across the dance floor with ease and grace. Even after all these years, Gavin remained handsome, seemingly untouched by time, whereas his two best friends had aged more noticeably due to their time in Mortalia.

"I am sorry," he murmured. "More sorry than you could ever know."

I furrowed my brow. "Why are you apologizing to me?"

"It is because of me that you are even here, sacrificing everything. Having to face something that I inadvertently caused."

My heart sank as I took in Gavin. By all outward appearances, he was strong and healthy. His hair was still a rich brown and the whites of his eyes were bright against his vivid green irises. But his face still bore the long, silvery scar on his cheek where Mara had sliced him with her red talons while swiping his tears away.

The cocky boy from Nick's memories was no more. Gavin wore his guilt and pain for all to see.

He shook his head as if coming out of a daze. "But enough of that." The music ended, and I felt the familiar ripple of Will's presence wash over me. Gavin dropped his hands. "Listen, I would appreciate your ear, as soon as possible. There is much I would like to share."

"There's my bride," Will cut in, grabbing me around the waist and pulling me toward him. I saw the moment Will registered who I'd been dancing with.

"Gavin?"

"Hello, William." His eyes widened. "Thundernation, you are nearly the spitting image of our king. I am eager for the opportunity to speak with you and your bride in the coming days." He gave us the Cristes bow and disappeared into the crowd.

"It never gets old, does it? Seeing someone you've met before but technically never met?" Will asked.

I shuddered. "But it's extra weird with Gavin." I peered over my shoulder and lowered my voice to a whisper. "I guess I hold him somewhat responsible for what happened here in Cristes. His actions caused a domino effect that hurt so many people."

Will leaned in and feathered a soft kiss to my lips, his thumb caressing my cheek, trailing my jaw, landing under my chin. He tugged it up gently so that he was all I could focus on.

"We can worry about him later. Tonight is all about you and me."

A hand tapped Will on the shoulder. "Your Highnesses, if

you would follow me to your head table. The guests would like to pay their respects." Duncan swept his arm toward the gold and teal thrones on the other side of the dance floor.

As Duncan helped us into our seats, lines of Watchers appeared on either side of us. They walked forward two at a time, converging in the middle and turning to face us. Most bowed and wished us well. Some left bouquets of flowers or other trinkets at the foot of our table. This procession lasted nearly an hour, and my neck grew stiff with each nod of thanks.

Finally, the last person to pay their respects, with Shai and Nick flanking him, was Alex. My breath hitched. I hadn't seen him since we'd landed in Cristes.

"You look well, Liddy," he said, bowing to me.

"Thank you. So do you."

Gone was the overly confident jock. He smiled sheepishly at my compliment.

"Congratulations. It is nice to see you both happy. Thank you for bringing me here."

Will grabbed my hand and gave it a little squeeze. "You are welcome, Alex. I hope your time here has been the sanctuary you've been needing."

"Oh, it has. Though, I do miss my family." He dropped his chin, rubbing at the back of his neck. "I...uh, sorry. I didn't mean to be a downer right now."

"I totally understand," I said, and I meant it. "I too miss my family. Hopefully, we can return to Mortalia soon."

Alex blinked at me, then shook his head, plastering on a smile. "So, I'm starved. Guess I'll head back to my table." He swiftly bowed again and hustled away.

I looked at Will and grasped his arm just above the elbow.

"Thank you."

"For what?"

"For how you treated Alex just now."

"Ah, that." Will played with his wedding band. "I've had a lot of time to think this past year. I've even visited with him a few times. Knowing you were safe allowed me a clearer head and perspective. I understand his 'why' now. I think he too realizes his errors and is working on forgiving himself."

Will's stomach growled. As if on cue, Duncan and his two helpers, who served us dinner in Nick's quarters, placed a giant plate in front of us. It stretched over both our place settings.

"It is customary for the bride and groom to feed the first bite to their partner," Duncan said, handing each of us a fork. "It symbolizes putting the other before yourself. In the end, when both partners do this, you will never be unfulfilled."

I speared a juicy cut of meat and Will forked a piece of cheesy potato. We looked at each other, awkwardly at first, not sure if we were supposed to do this at the same time.

I clinked Will's fork with mine. "Saludic! Now open up." Will laughed.

Will laughed. "Only if you open at the same time."

We fed each other and had no idea we were being watched so intently. A pop of confetti burst, the surprise nearly sending me sprawling out of my chair, and Will righted me reflexively.

"I don't think anyone noticed," he said, gesturing to the crowd as they clinked their glasses or clapped in appreciation of the honored tradition.

Guests trickled onto the dance floor, and I enjoyed watching them. All of Cristes had been through so much it was nice to see its citizens having fun. Though it was freezing outside, many wore attire fit for a summer wedding. Bright-colored gowns and suits that matched the array of flowers in the ceiling bedazzled the dance floor.

"Liddy, may I have this dance?" I turned to see Charlie standing tall, his hands behind his back.

"You may," I responded.

Will helped me out of my chair, and I took Charlie's proffered hand. He helped me down the few steps and guided me through the sea of people, who quickly parted for us.

"So, do all Watchers just know how to dance?" I asked, genuinely curious. He didn't guide us all over the floor as Nick and Gavin had led me. Instead, we stayed within our own small circle, guests giving us a perimeter of at least five feet.

Charlie studied me. "Mara taught me...when the black rose's magic allowed her a good day. They were rare, but we'd have dance—" He abruptly shut his mouth and dropped his gaze.

"You can tell me anything, you know that right?"

But he only worried his bottom lip some more.

"If you keep doing that, you're going to bite a hole in them," I warned.

"I have a confession to make, and I am not sure how you will take it." His cheeks flushed a light pink, and for a second, he was the little boy again that I loved so much.

I released a breath, and with it, some of my nerves that had started to creep up. "Sometimes it can help if you say the hard things at, like, super-sonic speed."

"Like ripping off a band-aid?" he asked sheepishly.

"Yes, just like that."

He quirked his brow, giving me a faint smile as if to say *yeah, right.* "I used to have the biggest crush on you. When I was little," he added, his cheeks going from salmon to maroon.

A giggle erupted from me. Charlie's cheeks drained, and now he was nearly as white as a fresh Christmas rose.

"Wow, OK. I didn't expect you to return the feelings, but—"

"No, no." I swiped under my eyes and regained my hold of him. "With how serious and nervous you were, I thought you were going to say you left the envelope for me last year or something equally as awful like you still work for Mara. But Charlie, thank you for telling me that. I've always loved you, just maybe not in that way. You have always been a brother to me."

My rambling prevented me from noticing that although I still swayed with the music, Charlie had frozen, rooted to the spot. Sweat dotted his forehead.

"Charlie, are you OK?"

A static shock zapped me in every place I was connected to Charlie.

"Ouch!" I immediately dropped my arms.

"Sorry!" Charlie raked his hands through his hair.

"What the heck was that?" I demanded, my hands still tingling from the unwelcome sensation.

Wordlessly, Charlie snatched me by the wrist and hastily led me back out to the hallway and into my dressing room, quickly shutting the door.

Trust Issues

"CHARLIE," I HUFFED. "What-the-heck?"

He gently pushed me onto the plush, champagne-colored sofa and paced the room, his hair standing on end. "Why did you have to say that?"

"Say what?" I asked, baffled.

Charlie paused in front of me, his wide eyes holding me in their intensity. "The envelope in Shai's room. You think I did that?"

"No." I shook my head. "I was comparing the statement to your body language, which made it seem like what you had to share was a lot worse than it was. Like what you were sharing would be something horrible like that. Not that you'd actually done it."

He went back to walking the room in measured steps, his

hands rubbing the back of his neck. "What if I did do that, or at least something like it?"

My stomach dropped, and that small orange glint in his eye, the one I'd noticed only once when he first came to see me in the healing sanctum—the glint that I'd reasoned was no big deal—was suddenly a big freaking deal. I leaned away from him, my body recoiling at the thought that Mara could be possessing his body. Feeling for my connection to Will, I tugged on it, hard.

"Damfino! Don't alert Will." He splayed both his hands. "Please. Let me explain."

"He will be here in less than two minutes. Talk fast," I said, crossing my arms over my chest so tightly I was giving myself a bear hug.

He plopped in the chair adjacent to me and tugged on his ear, avoiding my scrutinizing gaze. "That night at the park... It wasn't an accident."

I stared at him, unblinking. "What wasn't an accident?"

"Tripping out of the portal." He bit his lip as he stared down at his feet. "I staged it."

I uncrossed my arms and leaned forward. "Go on," I prodded him.

"You see, I snuck a few envelopes from Mara. They were never meant for you." His knee bounced so quickly I could feel the vibrations in the floor. "I always kept an extra one on me in case an opportunity like the park ever happened. So that I could return one day and save those kids."

I let out a sound of disbelief. "She just let you have one?"

His knee stilled. "No. I stole it. I really wanted to return home to my family." His knee started its up-and-down dance again.

I was going to be sick. Right here, on my white dress, on the couch. Little stars began to pop into my vision and blinking did nothing to remove them.

"Breathe, Liddy." Charlie sat next to me and rubbed my back. "I do not expect you to understand. You've only seen the part of her she wanted you to see, the part of her the black rose forged. But it's not the real her." He removed his hand and stood, his features pleading for me to comprehend. "I do not want Mara to die. I... I've grown to care for her, despite her faults, and I think we can save her and save Cristes."

Knock, knock, knock. "Liddy, are you in there?" Will's voice boomed from the other side of the door.

Charlie's eyes flashed to me, glistening and ready to spill over. "Hear me out, please, before you meet with the council tomorrow."

I didn't like what I was hearing, but this was Charlie, and I needed to grant him a chance to explain himself.

"Of course, I'll listen, but your brother gets to hear it, too. He and I are a team now... and I won't keep secrets from him."

"Can you just—"

"This isn't a negotiation." I stood and opened the door, ushering Will in and locking it behind him.

Will's eyes were already lit up, the color of protection. "You alright?" he rasped.

I hugged him. "I'm safe," I murmured into his neck.

"You had me freaked out when you screamed down our bond like that."

"I'm sorry. I did overreact slightly, but I ask you not to follow in my footsteps when Charlie tells you something. Keep in mind, I am fine." I stepped back from Will and nodded to his brother. "Charlie, do it quickly. Our absence will be noticed soon."

Charlie launched into what he'd revealed to me while he paced the room, careful to leave a few feet between him and his brother. Will's hands were fisted, the veins popping and pulsating.

I grasped Will's hand as I felt his frustration rise. The move didn't go unnoticed by Charlie, and his words sped up.

"And then you interrupted when I was in the middle of telling Liddy the most hopeful part. We can use these envelopes to meet Mara on her turf, not risking the lives of more Watchers than necessary." Charlie sat down again on the seat but continued to hold Will's intense gaze. "Best of all, we can rescue all those kids and, Liddy...that means your friends, too."

Five seconds. Twenty seconds. A full minute. No matter how the time ticked by, his words did not squelch my anger.

"You've had a way to save my friends this entire time and are only now telling me?"

Charlie held his hands up in surrender. "You know it is not as simple as that."

"So how did one of your envelopes get into Shai's room?" Will asked, his teeth clenched. "Do you have any idea what finding that envelope—"

"It was an accident!" His hands flung in the air.

Will raised his eyes in exasperation and turned his back on his brother. Charlie ran around him, demanding his attention.

"I swear. I always carry an envelope on me, just in case. Liddy, if you remember, I was visiting our uncle that night you came to visit him."

"I remember."

Charlie turned and sat in the chair. "Shai was unconscious as usual, but with Wallace saying his eyes fluttered earlier in the week, I wanted to see if he would do it again. I had been leaning over him for quite some time." Charlie bent over, his head in his hands. "I didn't even realize it had slipped out, and by the time it was discovered, based on everyone's reactions and assumptions—"

"You didn't feel as though you could tell us," I finished for him.

Will stared up at the ceiling and let out a loud sigh. "You really should have told us sooner, little brother," Will chided him. "Mom, Dad, Nick...everyone, they have already made plans for dealing with Mara. That does not leave us much time to—"

"Don't you think I know that?" Charlie's chin snapped up and his eyes flashed sky blue. "It was now or never. We can rescue those kids and your friends and Mara." Charlie softened his voice, "Will you please trust me?"

"What if we can't trust you?" I asked. Charlie seemed to shrink, slumping low in the chair again.

"Liddy," Will said softly, a hint of surprise in his voice and a whisper of pain down our pairing.

"I'm sorry, but I need to know she doesn't have a hold on him...that this is really all him talking."

"I understand, but this is all me." Charlie got to his knees before me, pressing his hand to his chest. "Look at my eyes. She is gone, her tinctures completely out of my system."

I leaned in, studying him as Will leaned over my shoulder

from behind.

Charlie was still as a statue, but his words had the power to shake me. "If you choose not to trust me, then bringing Mara into this conflict blind will turn very ugly very quickly. Are you prepared to use your giftings in ways you may not agree with?"

The door handle started rattling. "Liddy? Will?" a woman's voice called.

"Tia," I breathed. We all stilled.

"Do not play me for a fool," Tia bellowed. "I know you are both in there! Do not make me bust this door down and whoop you."

"Yeah, I will drag you out if I have to," a male voice chimed in, followed by pounding on the door. "Do not think for one second that I won't, or do I need to remind you?"

"Tannon?" I guessed.

Will nodded. "He may have had to do it a time or two."

"Or twenty," Charlie deadpanned.

Will shook his head, a little grin lighting his perfect face as he walked over to Charlie and laid a hand on his shoulder. "You should have told me sooner. Something tells me Nick would have been more than amicable to listen to your plea. For now, do not tell anyone else. You were never in here with us, so go hide."

Charlie glanced around the small space. "Where?"

"Behind my wedding dress," I suggested, motioning toward the clothing rack. "It's poofy enough." Charlie nodded and ducked behind it.

The knocks turned to pounds. "You two better—"

Will flung the door open, arching back and narrowly

avoiding a knock on the kisser.

"I knew it, I knew—hey, why are you not glowing? Weren't you both..." Tia trailed off, her neck scarlet.

"No, we were just talking," I said innocently. I leaned in and whispered, "I was filling him in on the little elder situation that you and I discussed earlier today."

Tia touched the tip of her nose. "Oh my goodness, I feel so silly. I am sorry." Then her eyes narrowed and arms crossed. "What am I apologizing for? If you'd have told me, I would have had time to make up an excuse for all the people noticing the absence of the newlyweds."

I placed a tentative hand at her elbow. "I am sorry for putting you out."

Tia uncrossed her arms. "I forgive you. Now, you two need to do one more trip around the dance floor before you retire for the evening."

"It is tradition to dance with your guests as a farewell. Plus, they like to send the couple off in true Watcher fashion," Tannon added.

"I'm scared to discover what that means," I said.

"It's more of those ceremonial fireworks. Nothing to be wary of," Tia replied, elbowing her brother.

"We are right behind you," Will said, gesturing to Tia and Tannon to lead the way back to the ballroom.

When the twins were far enough ahead of us, Will leaned in. "What did you mean about the elder business?"

"I'll tell you later," I whispered.

"Promise?"

"I promise."

Under Pressure

WILL AND I LEFT THE RECEPTION as Tannon promised, in true Cristes fashion. With Watchers creating a human tunnel, standing in sand on either side of an imaginary aisle that extended the entire length of the ballroom. With their gifting sparking overhead in glittering clouds, Will and I walked through and had the pleasure of thanking every guest in attendance.

We reached the hall and when the doors shut with a satisfying click, I nearly collapsed from exhaustion.

"Does your jaw hurt?" I asked, massaging my mandible's joint on either side.

"A little," Will chuckled. "That was a lot of smiling and 'thank you's."

Duncan appeared out of a small alcove. "Your Highnesses,

if you would follow me, I am to take you to your new living quarters and to the honeymoon suite for the night."

"The honeymoon suite will not be necessary," Will said eagerly. "We will be more than fine right here in our own place."

Duncan sucked in his cheek, attempting to suppress a laugh, whereas I wanted to disappear.

"What am I missing?" Will asked innocently.

Duncan gestured to us to follow him, and we did. "Your Highness, the honeymoon suite is necessary for royal unions. It is how consummation is confirmed."

Will halted in his tracks. "What?" The word echoed off the walls, and Duncan flinched.

"Sir? Did you not—"

"I've got this," I interrupted. "Will, let's get to the room, and then I'll fill you in. It's not as bad as you think."

"No, it's probably worse!" His now pallor skin adopted a green hue.

Duncan turned his back to us and continued walking. However, Will stayed rooted to the spot.

"This is the only way to verify our combined gifting's light without being invasive," I whispered.

"Why are you not more upset about this?" Will asked, his brows furrowing. Then his face smoothed out. "You knew, and I was left in the dark."

"I promise, the plan was always to tell you when we got to the suite. And I only found out about it myself this morning. Tia did me a solid."

"Tannon should have done the same," Will growled.

I glanced pointedly at Duncan, who was just about to turn

the corner. I had no clue how to get where we were going.

Will sighed but resumed walking. "Fine, but don't leave anything out."

Duncan led us through a series of halls, and I was certain I would get lost trying to navigate this on my own. He stopped at a door with fresh flowers decorating its frame.

"Here we are, your wing. Please take a minute to tour your new home. I shall remain out here and guide you to the suite."

Will ushered me in quickly, giving Duncan a tight smile, then shut the door. In front of us was a main living space, hallways on either side with more doorways leading to who knows what. "OK, *now* can you please fill me in?"

"Wow! We get to live here?" Tingles of excitement danced up my legs. I had to move, to check out our new place. *Our place.* The view through the large bay windows, an endless sea of ice castles and frozen tundra with Azure Mountain in the distance, captivated me.

"Liddy, you promised," Will stated, his arms folded across his chest.

I sat on the couch and patted the cushion next to me. He sat, looking at me expectantly. "So, Cristes has this little tradition when it comes to royal weddings..."

I launched into what Tia had shared with me this morning and the lengths she'd gone through to help me and therefore Will.

"So you see, it won't be that bad. At least it isn't anything like what we learned in medieval history."

"Yeah." He grimaced. "That's kind of gross. Not to mention, how awkward. Can you even imagine?"

I shivered. "Honestly, I would not have made it down the

aisle. I would have figured out a way to get you to meet me somewhere secret, like the hidden bath chamber your mom brought me to this morning."

Will opened his mouth to speak, but a knock came from the door. I stood and opened it.

"Princess, do you and His Highness need any assistance?" Duncan checked his watch.

Very subtle, sir.

"We do not. But we do wish for five more minutes. This place is massive and we haven't finished touring it."

"Of course," Duncan said, nodding. "Though, I will need to wait inside the door."

"Sure," I said, stepping aside.

Will still sat, his elbows on his thighs, his hands clasped in front of his lips. His jaw worked, and I understood he was processing what I shared. Tonight, our first time...we'd have an audience of sorts.

"Actually, Duncan. Can you please take us to the suite now?"

Duncan nodded once and left the room. I didn't want Will so in his head that it tainted our night. The sooner we got to our suite, the sooner we could do what we'd been denying ourselves for so long.

"Will?" When he didn't answer, I approached him, placing my palm on his cheek. He peered up at me through his thick, dark lashes. "We need to leave for the suite."

Will rubbed his hands on his pants and stood. Before he could move, I moved into his path, waiting for eye contact.

"Tonight is something I've been dreaming about for a very long time and nothing else matters. This part...it is just for us."

Will pressed a soft kiss to my lips and smiled, but he couldn't fool me. He was still worried. I could see it in the way his smile didn't reach his eyes, though he masked the sensation in our bond.

At the end of the third hall, a stone wall appeared to be a dead end. The large woven tapestry depicting a single Christmas rose hung undisturbed. Duncan tugged on the bottom of it and slowly, the tapestry rolled up on its own. A Christmas rose the size of a small plate that matched the tapestry stood out to me, etched into one of the bricks.

"Prince, your hand, please?" Will stepped up to the wall and placed his palm over the rose. When he dropped his hand, emerald green light traced the rose.

"Princess?"

I followed Will's actions. When I removed my hand, violet traced the rose. For a moment, nothing happened. Then the rose glowed a brilliant white, vines extending from it. The outline of a door appeared, and with a soft grinding noise of rock sliding over stone, the door opened.

"Everything you could possibly need is already in the suite," Duncan said. "If for some reason you desire something else, there is a service bell with directions on how to utilize its services."

Duncan closed the door behind us. As soon as it clicked shut, amber lights glowed all the way up the tower.

"A winding staircase...kind of like home, right?" Will smirked.

"Yeah, if your spiral staircase was bigger and about thirty more stairs. How do they not have an elevator?" I asked rhetorically, taking my heels off and dangling them on my pointer fingers as I started up the stairs.

I sensed some heat behind me and turned to see Will's gifting aflame all over his body.

"Like what you see?" I laughed, continuing my journey up the tower.

Will coughed and ran a hand through his hair. "I...uh... the walls in here are nice."

I only laughed more.

The landing at the top was an ivory carpet with accents of navy and gold. The door had an exact copy of the Christmas rose from downstairs painted gold on the wooden door. I reached for the handle and gave it a turn.

"Wait!"

I started at Will's outburst.

"Oops! I didn't mean to startle you," he said, rubbing my arm. "I was a little distracted downstairs when entering our new living quarters and didn't do what I was supposed to. So, if you do not mind, I would like to make sure I do it now."

I leaned my head to the side, one eyebrow raised in confusion. The corner of his heart-shaped lips quirked, and he came in close to me. Then he bent and lifted me into his arms, carrying me over the threshold, kicking the door shut behind him.

"Well, then." I smiled at him, my eyes never leaving his face.

He chuckled.

"You can set me down now."

He shook his head and proceeded to carry me across the room, stopping short in front of the bed. He worried his bottom lip. "Liddy, can we talk a little before we..."

I palmed his cheek. "Of course."

He visibly relaxed. We studied each other on the sage couch that practically touched the ground. I hugged one of the burnt orange, circular pillows to my chest.

"Is this room awesome or what?" I asked, taking it all in. "Like, my mind knows we're in a tower in a castle on land that has frozen over, but my eyes are like, are we not in a tree house right now?"

Will belly laughed, deep and free. "I thought the same thing when we walked in."

I grinned at him. "What's your favorite part?"

"Hmmm...it would be the river of sand that tracks all around the perimeter of the room. I especially love the inground tub." His brows waggled as he pointed toward the large tub with sand snaking around it.

"That is cool. My favorite part is the bed," I said, pointing to the four posters attached to the wicker ceiling like vies of a tree.

Will's cheeks reddened.

"It looks like it's floating! Ohhh, and the tiny lights all around it? They remind me of fireflies."

Will dropped his head, avoiding my gaze, his cheeks still burning.

"Is the fact that Nick is waiting to see what color we shine bothering you that much?" I asked.

"Not really. I mean, in part... yes. But what if...what if we are not what they expect us to be? What if we aren't the saviors of Cristes? That is a lot of pressure."

"I feel the same way. I was a theory, remember? You have

always had the markings. But no one knows for sure if I bore them."

"I'm sorry." He rested a hand on my knee and squeezed it gently.

"What are you sorry for?" I tilted my head, trying to read him.

"I should have tried to understand more from your perspective. That is a lot of weight to carry on your shoulders, and yet, you went along with everything. Risked everything."

"Well, don't give me too much credit. Mara was a big factor in all of this. She sees me as a threat and therefore, I had no choice. But..." I trailed all off, wanting to get the words right.

"But?" The hand that was on my knee now slid higher onto my thigh.

"Even if Mara wasn't targeting me or forcing my hand, I would still choose you."

Will's eyes ignited a bright aqua. "Same." He smiled. "So, I was informed that in keeping with tradition, the wife shares her gifting with her husband."

"I was informed that the husband does the same for the wife," I countered playfully.

Will angled his head, a quizzical grin tugging at his lips. "I, uh, I have not heard of that."

"Are you serious?" I asked, miffed that it was up to the woman to present herself to the man.

"You don't...you do not have to do anything you don't want to," Will stammered. "It is a Cristes tradition and, well, you and I didn't grow up here. We can do things the way we want."

We fell silent for a moment, contemplating our next moves. Then Will grabbed my hand and gave it a little squeeze. "So, would you like to talk more or—

I pounced on him, my lips locking with his. I broke away quickly. "Of course, I want to talk. I want you to tell me everything about this past year without me, and I want to share as well. But tonight, I'm ready. If you need time—"

This time, Will silenced me by pressing a soft kiss to my neck, and I let out a happy sigh.

"I—" I said breathlessly. "I need a minute to freshen up, and then I *want* to share my gifting with you."

Will stilled as he stared at me, his eyes smoldering. "Of course. I should as well. Meet you over there in a few?" He nodded his head toward the area of the suite where the bed hung.

"Yes, but first, can you please undo the top buttons?" I turned my back to him and lifted my hair from my neck.

Slowly, Will's nimble fingers worked the small buttons of my costume, and I couldn't help but remember when he helped detach my sweater when it was stuck to my earrings on my first visit to his house.

"All done." His voice had lowered, seductive and tempting.

"Thanks!" I squeaked before rushing into the bathroom and closing the door. Any toiletry I could need was neatly placed on the vanity, but spotty washing up would not be enough. I needed a full shower to ready and relax my body. I was nervous as heck. Before stepping into the shower, something sparkled off the light. Hung up on the back of the door was my Raqs Rumba outfit.

I gulped. Dancing for Will had never been a problem

before and, maybe, just maybe, it would distract me enough from the nerves that were running wild.

I was in and out of the water in less than five minutes. I clipped my wet hair up and brushed my teeth. Then I took the costume off the hanger and slipped it on. The fabric caressed my skin, a perfect fit.

I inhaled deeply, held my breath for a few seconds, then slowly released it.

You can do this, Lydia. Nick doesn't matter. The color of our combined gifting doesn't matter. What happens after doesn't matter. Enjoy this. Enjoy him.

I strode out of the bathroom, but the room was dark, and I couldn't really see.

"Will?" I called out.

"I'm here, on the bed." He must have opened his eyes because I could make out a faint aqua glow. "I found this note."

"A note? From who?"

"I don't know, but it told me to sit tight and to press this button when you were ready to share your gifting," he responded. "Are you ready?"

Eira be with me. "I think so. Go ahead, press it."

"As you wish."

Dim lights winked awake in the bedroom, lighting my path to him. A drum solo started, slow and seductive. It sounded as if the skin-covered instrument was actually here in this room, coming from all around me, and instantly my body responded.

Will's eyes tracked me predatorily. It was almost as if we were back at Nick's, sharing our first kiss, one that I'd thought quenched my thirst for him. But we'd soon learned it was only the beginning, which set in motion this moment. No, it didn't satiate our hunger. It only made us more ravenous.

Every move I made was an invitation, one only for him, and I loved seeing his enjoyment, loved watching him glow a little brighter with each hip shimmy and shoulder roll. The drums died down, and I stopped a few feet away from the bed, directly in front of Will. Our chests heaved in unison, his pupils blown wide, darkening his eyes.

We stared at each other, neither of us moving. Will wet his bottom lip and came to me.

"You are amazing. I don't know what I have done to deserve you, but I plan on showing you now and every day after how much I appreciate and love you." And then he lovingly kissed me, carefully directing my body down on the bed.

Tomorrow we would face the reality of what our union would set in motion. But tonight, in this moment, we would snuff out the dark as only light can. Not only would we embrace the light, but be the light...for each other and all of Cristes.

The Morning After

WINDOWS I HADN'T NOTICED LAST NIGHT let in the first glowing colors of sunrise. The filtered rays warmed my face, and I snuggled in deeper to Will's side. His arm tightened around me, and he brought his face into my neck, inhaling deeply, giving me a kiss and sending chills all down my body.

His voice, rough with sleep, whispered, "Good morning, beautiful. How do you feel?"

I took a quick assessment of my body. He'd been concerned about my first time being enjoyable, and he took great care to try and make it so. "Wonderful. Amazing. Perfect. I think you lied about the whole men-don't-share-a-gifting on their wedding night."

Will rolled onto his back laughing, but then he scooped

me into him once again, and I snuggled in.

"Seriously, thank you," I said.

"I only have one more question."

"Shoot."

"Can we do that again?"

I giggled and turned to face him when I let out a gasp.

"What's the matter?" he asked, his hand stilling where he'd been lazily stroking my hip.

I studied his face. "Your eyes..."

He frowned. "We expected them to change, right? What do they look like?"

"Well, they used to be all green, but now..." I leaned in closely, examining his eyes. "Now, they have a ring of purple around the irises."

"Do you hate it?" he asked, his muscles tense.

I laid my hand on his chest. "No, just...different."

Will smirked. "Yours have changed too, only the opposite...yours have a green ring."

"Weren't they supposed to change totally, like King Klaus's and Queen Nicole's? Shouldn't our eyes be the same color as theirs now...gray or something?"

Panic seized me.

"Breathe, Princess." Will stroked my hair and held me to his chest.

"Does this mean we don't have white lighter gifting? How can I face everyone, knowing I've let them down?"

"OK, one thing at a time. What do you remember from last night?"

I buried my face in the nook between his chest and shoulder, the heat of my body rising, and I began to glow.

Will growled, deep in his chest, his voice low and

seductive. "Please don't do that. I'm trying to help, but you are very distracting at the moment." His hand tightened on my hip.

"Sorry. I-I remember lots from last night."

"Don't be sorry. What I'm getting at, and it's why I am not stressing, is do you remember what color we glowed at the end?"

My mind raced, replaying every glorious detail, and then, I gasped again.

"White! Like a star!"

"Exactly. The eyes must be an anomaly, but they do not seem to have a bearing on our shared power." Will hugged me, his confidence leaking into me, shoring me up.

"I guess I was more anxious about the results than I thought," I sighed.

"I'd be happy to calm your parasympathetic nervous system," Will said, cheekily.

"My para-what?"

Will bit his lower lip. "Your parasympathetic nervous system. Normally, your body takes a little while for the endorphins to kick in. But since what your body perceives as a potential emergency is not really an issue, I can help you feel better, more relaxed, much more quickly." He rolled on top of me, bracing his weight on his forearms, then kissed me on the nose.

"Oh yeah? You would do that for me?"

"All you have to do is ask."

"Will, would you please help me?" I batted my lashes at him.

"As you wish."

We'd fallen back asleep. Tapping on the window woke me, and I groaned.

"*Ughhh*, go awaaay."

Will didn't even flinch. His arm was heavy across my abdomen.

The tapping continued, repetitive and growing more incessant. I groaned again and tried to slide out from under Will's arm without waking him. My first attempt was unsuccessful. I tried again. Using all my might, I lifted his arm a few inches and maneuvered my body out from under it.

At the window was a pretty bird, mostly white in color with a little black on his tail. A teeny-tiny note was tied to his equally tiny foot. I opened the window, and he held his foot out to me. I untied the pink ribbon and patted him on his head. He blinked a few times and flew away.

I opened the note.

Congratulations on your union. Undoubtedly you are hungry. Please be advised that breakfast is waiting for you. All you need to do is drop the covered basket outside the window. When you hear the bell chime, give the rope a tug and the bucket will return.

Enjoy.

-Duncan-

On cue, my stomach rumbled, and Will stirred rubbing his hands down his face.

"Why are you out of bed? It's cold without you in it."

"One sec, I'm grabbing breakfast." I stuck my head out the window, and there on the left was the large basket. I untied the knot and the brown canister slid through the pulley with ease. I ducked back into the room, assuming I would have a few minutes before it reached the bottom and someone filled it. Not to mention, the air was freezing and my nose had gone numb. But as soon as I turned to face an expectant Will, a tiny bell chimed.

I bolted back to the window. The basket had a blanket over its now-full contents. I attempted to bring it into the room but couldn't lift it. Will was behind me in a flash, unlatching the metal brace that held the basket, allowing it to swing into our room.

He unhooked the wicker basket and handed it to me. I carried it into our sitting room, removing its contents and setting the table.

I glanced over just as Will reached outside to set the brace back and shut the window, admiring the expanse of his torso as his joggers hung low around his waist, his white robe open.

"Bon appetite," I said, lifting the silver domes off of the large plates.

My salivary glands worked over time as I took in the array of breakfast meats, potatoes, eggs, and fruit. Bread that was still warm filled the air with its yeasty goodness. I sliced off a piece and slathered it with butter, taking a large bite, nearly moaning in delight.

Will lifted the dome off a small plate in the corner, the last one to reveal its contents. Underneath it was a piece of parchment with handwriting I recognized.

"What does Nick have to say?" I asked, taking another large bite.

Will picked up the parchment and read it aloud.

Will and Liddy,

Thank you for trusting me to document something so intimate and important. I was more than happy to share the wonderful news with the royal family and your parents. Liddy, my dear, we now have actual proof that you are no longer a theory but a fact. There is hope for Cristes yet, thanks to both of you. Enjoy another full day of rest. The entire village will be celebrating my prophecy coming true. We shall start the battle strategy tomorrow.

Congratulations,

Nick

"They postponed our duties?" I asked around a mouthful of bacon.

"You know what this means? We get the whole day together. Hmmm, I wonder what we can do with all that time?"

I playfully smacked him on the shoulder.

"I'm kidding, I'm kidding. Well, mostly kidding." He waggled his brows at me.

"We can go down to our wing and get settled into the new place," I suggested.

"We could. Or, there is this hidden room with a pool full of water from Azure Mountain. It's amaz—"

"You've been in it? I mentioned it yesterday, but you didn't say anything."

"You did? Sorry, I was a little distracted by the whole confirmation-of-consummation thing," Will said.

"Want to know something crazy?"

"Shoot," Will said as he scraped a second large helping of potatoes and eggs onto his plate.

"I could have sworn I heard you when I was submerged in the water."

Will stilled and put his fork down. "No way. I totally thought I heard you too, but when you didn't answer, I chalked it up to just being really eager to finally see you after so long."

"What does that mean? Were we actually hearing each other? Maybe through the walls?" I suggested.

Will shook his head slowly. "I heard you...in here." He tapped his temple.

I gaped at him. "So, you could actually make out words?"

Will nodded. I sunk back against the couch. Was it the magical waters of the pool? Or, what if it was more like how Nick spoke into my mind when Will and I rescued him from the spiraled ceiling of his place in Illinois?

Will quietly chewed his food, squinting in concentration.

"Well, we obviously should try to talk to each other like that again," Will stated, breaking the silence.

I nearly choked on the bite I'd been in the process of swallowing. I grabbed the pitcher of O.J. and chugged it.

"Telepathy could be really useful," he continued, patting me on the back.

I shrugged him off. "Right. You think now is a good time?"

"I'm gonna go out on a limb here and say, judging by your reaction and the vibes you're sending me, that, no...now is not the time?"

I tilted my head, "Very funny." It had been trying enough to get used to someone knowing how I was feeling and the general location of where I was all the time. But someone being able to ascertain my true thoughts? Could he intrude and hear what I was thinking whenever he wanted? Maybe I was getting ahead of myself.

I dropped my face in my hands. "I'm sorry."

"What was that?" Will asked, pulling my hands away from my face.

Turning to face Will, I wrapped my arms around his neck. "I said, I'm sorry. The past twenty-four hours have been a lot. I'm not sure I want to tackle that today. Could we just go back to our new place? Settle in for a minute?" I asked, examining his countenance. "Tomorrow is going to bring more chaos, especially when we drop Charlie's bomb on them."

Will rubbed my shoulders and I relaxed into his touch. "You don't need to apologize for that. I understand. But, in light of what tomorrow means, the start of actually attacking the Black Roses and not just defending, of bringing Mara into it all" —Will tucked some of my hair behind my ear— "it may be a good skill to have, don't you think?"

My eyes popped open and I pouted. "You're probably right, but—"

"How about this? We settle into our new place. I run you a bath, give you a massage, and when you feel more settled, we can try it a couple of times. Can you give me ten minutes to see if we can speak telepathically?"

"Only ten minutes?"

Will shook his head.

"Promise?"

"I promise." He grinned. "Now, how the heck do we get out of here?"

It took us a few tries to find the hidden rose in the wall by the door, but we made it to our new home within the castle with only a few wrong turns.

Since we'd essentially arrived in Cristes with nothing but the clothes on our backs, everything we'd needed had since been provided for us. I was relieved to see that everything we now owned had been moved from our separate quarters to our new home and unpacked for us.

I sat on the bench, appreciating the magnificent sunset through the bay window. Though the stillness of the frozen landscape was beautiful in its own right, I tried to picture the lush tropical climate that Cristes once was and smiled.

"I love it when you smile like that," Will said, picking himself up off the floor, where he'd been doing push-ups. He had put on a good amount of muscle over the past year and explained he'd worked out every time he missed me. Judging by his physique, he must have missed me a lot.

"You know how I hated the cold in Illinois, always saying how I was going to move somewhere warmer?"

Will chuckled. "I remember clearly."

"My body knew I was called here, even when I didn't. Cristes was a tropical climate. I hope we can restore her."

Will stood behind me, his hands on his hips, his chest glistening as he peered out the window with me. "I truly believe we will be successful."

I inclined my neck to gaze up at him. "Even if we're not, our wedding reception was something I will never forget. Everyone seriously went above and beyond to make our day so special." Tears of joy streamed down my face.

Will palmed my cheeks and kissed my forehead. "It really was special. I'm going to hop into the shower."

I'd been lost in thought when Will called from the bathroom door. "Your bath is ready, Your Highness." Leaning against the door jamb in nothing but a towel wrapped low on his waist, Will's rosy cheeks and the clouds of heat that billowed all around him sent my heart fluttering.

"I don't recall asking for a bath," I teased as I padded along the lush, cream carpet in the opposite direction.

"Suit yourself." Will winked, turned, and dropped his towel. I gaped at both his cheekiness and, well, his cheeks. A second later, the sound of Will splashing in the water set me on a path to join my husband.

I entered the bathroom—or rather, the sauna. The air was thick with steam, so much so that I could barely see Will as his head lay back against the tub's rim, his eyes closed and arms splayed out.

Though we'd seen each other fully naked last night, I still felt shy about being exposed. I stripped as fast as I could and quickly got into the bubble bath, covering myself with the soapy foam.

Will quirked open an eye. "I knew you couldn't resist."

I splashed him in response. Without warning, he pranced, and I let out a yelp. I turned to escape, but he snatched me up, his hands firm on my hips as he pressed my back to his chest.

"Now, you just lay back and relax. Think of me as your pillow."

I did as my husband suggested and closed my eyes, breathing in deeply the essential oils that perfumed the waters with tranquility, inviting me to rest. Will's hands stroked my arms, up and down, up and down, eliciting tiny goosebumps on my flesh.

Liddy, can you hear me?

"Yes...your mouth is literally right next to my ear." I giggled.

I wasn't using my mouth.

My eyes flung open, and I whirled to face Will. His irises glimmered green and purple.

Now you try, Will said, tilting his head towards me. Again, his lips didn't move.

I wrung my hands and closed my eyes once again. I didn't think I could make eye contact with Will while trying this.

Will?

There was no answer. I squinched my face harder.

Can you hear me? I tried again. When there was no answer, I cracked one eye open to peek.

Will sat there, studying me, and quirked a brow. *I'm waiting.*

I huffed, and the strand of hair that had slipped out of my top knot blew up and out of my face.

I pursed my lips to the side, my brain working out this puzzle. And then it hit me—our bond, the sensation that already connected us through feeling. I found it luminescent and constant, a steady rhythm of light pulses.

Will?

Again, no response. I shouted with internal frustration. *Of course, Will would get this so easily. He's basically perfect.*

Will's face started to morph; his soft smile grew tense and crooked, his cheeks sucking in, the veins in his neck bulging. And then, he busted out laughing.

"What is so funny?"

"I heard you the first time." More laughter erupted, and my jaw dropped. "But you decided so quickly that it didn't work, that..." Tears, actual tears, were streaming down his face. "You look so dang cute when you are determined. So easily frustrated." He chuckled.

He wasn't wrong, and I couldn't help but join in. Laughing at myself felt good.

"OK, mister, turn around. I'm getting out," I said to him.

He scoffed. "You don't have to hide from me." A tiny light flashed in his eyes.

Dude, did you just sparkle?

Did I? Well, with a wife as hot as you, can you blame me when I see you in your birthday suit?

"OK, this is getting weird," I said aloud. "Please turn around. You know I'm shy."

Will quirked his brow and smirked, threw his hands up, and obliged me. With his chiseled back turned to me, I slipped out of the tub and into my towel.

On my way out of the bathroom, I called over my shoulder, "You can turn around now," and then I zipped out of there, threw on thermal pajamas, and hopped in bed before he came out of the bathroom.

Will laughed. "Are you the Flash now?"

"Maybe. Hurry up. I'm exhausted and won't be able to sleep without you snuggled next to me."

Within a minute, Will joined me under the covers, dressed

in joggers and a t-shirt.

"Sweet dreams, Princess. I love you."

"Love you more." And then I passed out.

Boom bum boom boom.

Boom bum BOOM BOOM!

I jolted upright, startling Will.

"What's wrong? Is it another nightmare?"

Flashes of colored lights lit up the sky and my stomach sank.

An incessant buzzing sounded from the main room.

"What is that?" I whispered, fear beginning its chokehold.

"I think it's just the door. Hang tight." Will flung the covers off and raced to the door. No way in heck was I going to stay here alone. I sprinted after him through the main room.

BANG, BANG, BANG. The door shook with the force of the knocking.

"Will, Liddy, open up! We are under attack!"

To Beldam We Go

W ILL FLUNG THE DOOR OPEN. Nick was braced against the doorframe, breathing heavily.

"We need to get you both into the safe room." Nick pushed past us into the entryway. "Every wing is equipped with an access tunnel, but I do not believe you've been instructed on how to enter yours yet."

"What is going on?" Will asked, grabbing my hand and holding tight as we followed Nick down the hall to the right, back to our room.

"We are under attack. The Black Roses have breached the perimeter. Our forces are confident they will not reach the wall, but we need to take precautions nonetheless."

Nick pulled on the wall sconce above my nightstand. The white-washed brick wall folded in on itself, revealing a small alcove with a door. He knocked three times and a small hole appeared in the upper middle section of the door. Nick put his eye up to it. With a soft click, the door opened a few inches, allowing Nick to thrust the door all the way open. The wall pieced itself, accompanied by a series of gentle clunking sounds.

Will and I rushed through the door, Nick following close behind. Once inside the narrow passageway, we pressed against the wall, letting him lead the way. Nick held his palm up, conjuring a blue ball of flame that swirled hypnotically in his grasp. With a quick flick of his wrist, he flung the orb forward. I gaped, mesmerized as the ball of light ricocheted off the walls, igniting a cascade of hundreds of small, floating bulbs that cast the entire hall in a warm, beryl glow.

His deep blue robes billowed around his ankles, his curls bouncing as he sped through the tunnel ahead of us. As we journeyed through the tunnels, Nick would periodically launch a new light orb, providing safe passage through three more doors.

In each new hallway we entered, the blue glow grew progressively darker than the next, and the temperature felt like it dropped with every step. As my teeth chattered, I was thankful I'd dressed in thermal pajamas, though I worried Will would freeze to death.

"I'm fine," he said gruffly, though his hands were pressed firmly in his armpits, his shoulders shrugged to his ears.

"Did you just—"

"No, but I can sense your worry for me."

Nick glanced back at us over his shoulder. "The safe room is equipped with enough resources to host the entire royal family for ten days. One more hall, and we can all warm up."

The final door, infused with coquina shells, was the largest of them all. It flickered to life as we stood before it, changing colors as if it had a fiber optic unit built within. Each color took a turn, etching its unique design into the steel door.

Nick addressed us over his shoulder, "The door has been warded with a gifting from each color faction."

I assumed we'd have to wait in this freezing hallway for a long time while Nick disabled each gifting that had enforced it, but he simply knocked a practiced pattern and rhythm followed by the smooth slick of a bolt sliding, then another, and another, and finally, the door opened.

Duncan guided us in. I jolted to a stop and peered up at Will.

"Deja vu, right?" he said.

We stepped into a dome-shaped room reminiscent of a log cabin. It had a spiraled ceiling with hardwood clad in between each piece of rounded timber. "You could say that." This was a near replica of Nick's place back under the sledding hill at Huskey Park.

"William, Lydia, welcome." The queen greeted us with an embrace. "Come sit by the fire."

Another knock at the door, the cadence the same as Nick's, and Duncan opened it. Brantley and Charlie strode into the room.

"Hey, Dad," Will called from the hearth, but then his brow furrowed. "Where's Mom?"

Brantley stifled a yawn. "On the front lines."

"What?" Will rocketed up, and the blanket I'd placed over his shoulders puddled at his feet.

"Son, she is one of our top warriors. It is her gifting."

Will just stood there, his jaw working, as he stared at his dad.

Charlie came to sit next to me at the fire, grabbing a blanket from the basket on the floor. He leaned close to me. "Did you tell them yet?"

I shook my head subtly. Since the war council was delayed, Will and I hadn't gotten to share with them about Charlie and his envelopes yet. We could have called for Nick, but truthfully, I'd wanted one chill day with Will before we dove headfirst into chaos.

Another patterned knock at the door and seconds later, Shai entered the room, along with a few others I did not recognize.

"Is that everyone?" the king asked him.

"Yes, Your Majesty," Shai responded.

"Uncle, you know you can call me 'Uncle,'" he corrected Shai before giving him a hug.

"Can someone please tell me what my mother is facing on the front lines?" Will cut in.

The queen stood, and King Klaus grasped her hand, holding tight. "She is shoring the protection sphere. The Black Roses are hitting it incessantly, hoping we'll break before they do."

"What do they want?" I asked. "I mean, I understand everything with Mara. But how do the Black Roses fit into all this?"

Nick quirked a brow at his parents. Queen Nicole clicked her tongue and waved her hand. "Might as well tell them now."

Nick cleared his throat. "Have a seat," he said, gesturing

to the hearth. Then he turned a chair backward, straddling it to face us.

"I showed you what Mara did with that black rose she had hidden in her cabin."

"Yes, she...ate it," Will chimed in, sitting next to me. Charlie steepled his fingers, listening intently.

Sorrow was a heavy yoke on my shoulders. I didn't want to see the images that so freely invaded my head space. Gavin's dad. Mara eating the black rose. Her baby suffering the consequences.

"Well, the Black Roses do not believe their final rose is gone. They believe we are holding it hostage, manipulating it for our own gains."

"Why not just invite Melchior in so he can see for himself?" I asked.

Laughter and chuckles surrounded me. That is, from everyone but Nick and Will.

"That makes a lot of sense, right? We invited him and he obviously refused." Nick grimaced at his steepled hands, then held up his index finger. "For one, he rightly believes a well-placed trap would be waiting for him" —he held up a second finger— "Secondly, he and his leadership say they can feel the magic of the black rose calling to them."

"But it's gone," Will stated, though his words were sprinkled with uncertainty. The queen dropped her gaze, seemingly transfixed with addressing the comfort of all her guests in the safe room.

"Precisely," Nick nodded.

"As you can see," Shai cut in, "we are at an impasse. We do not have the rose, and yet no matter the lengths we go to prove this fact, the Black Roses do not believe us."

"I wonder if the magic of the rose somehow seeped into the ecosystem that day when everything...broke," I contemplated out loud.

"It wouldn't matter," Shai replied.

"Why not?" Will asked.

Nick cleared his throat. "Now, if you remember, the Black Roses also wish to rule Cristes, gain what they believe is justice for a history hundreds of years old in which none of us had a hand—Noorjove, the capital of Cristes, whose very essence may be steeped in the magic of the black rose, is what drives them harder to conquer it."

My stomach tightened with the dark reality. "So no matter what we do, they will never stop coming."

Will draped his arm over my shoulder. *Don't lose hope, Princess.* His voice entered my mind, his face carefully poised, betraying nothing. I glanced around the room to make sure no one noticed anything, but Nick's eyes bore into mine, like he could see directly to my soul...and knew exactly what Will and I were able to do.

"Not necessarily." Charlie's voice was quiet, so small that I was surprised Shai heard him.

"Come again, Charlie?"

"Not necessarily," Charlie repeated, more confident this time.

Brantley came to stand next to him. "What do you know, son?"

Charlie took a deep breath and stood. I took his hand and held it, hoping to offer him my support and love.

"Mara can help us put an end to this."

The room went utterly still at Charlie's words. The only hint of movement was the way shadows flickered, cast by the glow of every Watcher's now-burning eyes. By now, every royal member sat at the round table in the center of the sparsely furnished room, and their brightening faces indicated their interest was piqued by this development.

Shai shifted in his seat, glancing sidelong at Nick. "I know you spent many awful years in Beldam with her, but—"

"I lived it. I do not need your pity or reminders," Charlie snapped. For the first time, his eyes glowed, but not with the poison of Mara's influence. They were bright blue and smart, like his father's.

"If the magic of the black rose is what they seek, then they need to know that it still lives inside Mara," Charlie continued. "We set our sights on her, we can negotiate with the Black Roses for peace."

Someone laughed, followed by a few others. I gave these strangers a withering look of disapproval.

"You dare laugh at my brother?" Will growled, his irises changing to that deep green I had come to recognize as a threat, a warning to those in his sights that he was moments away from throwing down.

A slender female spoke after reining in her laugh. "I am sorry, but you make it sound as if Mara is easy to retrieve, as if summoning her is a realistic move."

"Easy, Blanche. May I remind you that Charlie is a prince? Your sarcasm is not appropriate," Brantley scolded.

She huffed in exasperation. "Well, excuse me for bringing him back to reality."

Shai stood. "You will respect him. He has sacrificed much

and yet he is here with first-hand knowledge of our greatest enemy."

Nick had sat silent, his hand stroking his beard as he studied the face of the boy—now a young man—who'd been to hell and back.

"Charlie, please continue. And no one—" Nick caught the eye of every Watcher in the room, his power rippling over each of their bodies. "No one will interrupt you again."

Charlie bit his lip, and I squeezed his hand to remind him I was still there. Will was at his other side, Brantley behind them both, one hand on each of their shoulders.

"The rose's dark magic still resides within Mara, a toxin infecting her blood," Charlie explained. "What she siphons from the children not only makes her temporarily more powerful, but their pure light also keeps the infection from spreading. She may be interested in speaking with us if we offer a way for her to rid herself of it. And I never said we would just invite her to Cristes and she would come," he added. "We go to her. Make her listen."

"You may be on to something," Shai said. "There is just one problem. The last known globital we had broken upon entering the realm of Cristes. Our top experts, your father... no one has yet been able to produce another one. Our Christmas rose supply is seriously lacking, considering routine trips to Mortalia have been disrupted for far too long. And the protective dome over all of Cristes, the one that maintains the ecosystem, is fractured. A giant hole in the barrier that kept us separate from the frozen lands surrounding us has depleted our environment." He hung his head. "Cristes is weak, her power fading."

"I have another way," Charlie said, dropping his head.

I know you know what it is.

Nick's voice in my head startled me, and all heads whipped to me. I smiled apologetically and he chuckled softly.

You might as well put him out of his misery, Nick prodded me.

I stood and Charlie watched me, his brows furrowed.

I needed to choose my words carefully. What we didn't need right now was more of these sticks in the mud dismissing Charlie any further.

"Charlie was so smart in how he planned his escape from Mara's clutches. You see, she uses these envelopes to portal her victims from Mortalia to Beldam and vice versa," I said, explaining to those in the room who weren't privy to that information. "They are a direct link to her residence. And Charlie, bless him, made sure to take some of these envelopes with him to help us should we need them."

Collective gasps echoed in the room. Some Watcher's lights blinked out while some burned brighter.

Well done, Liddy. Nick nodded and smiled at me. Slowly, he stood, his wide shoulders seeming to take up most of the space in this small room.

"Well, friends, colleagues, family...tonight, we shall try to get some sleep. For tomorrow, we no longer discuss battle plans but a coup."

"You cannot be serious!" A middle-aged gentleman with salt and pepper hair at his temples pounded his fist into the table. "That would be a death sentence, and I will not send anyone to meet Eira before their time."

The king tipped his head toward the man. "Edmund, I

have no doubt infiltrating Beldam would be a risky move. But with all things considered, we cannot ignore that this gives us the element of surprise."

"And the possibility to see the fruition of peace on these lands once again," Queen Nicole chimed in, her eyes glimmering. "If Mara can be negotiated with, we may be able to finally appease the Black Roses." The queen moved to stand beside her son, placing a hand on his shoulder.

Nick laid his hand on top of hers and addressed the room. "As I was saying, rest up, folks. Tomorrow, we plan how we will access Beldam and put an end to this war before it smashes past our wall and taints our soil."

Will and I were shown a room to spend the night in. Although it was small with only a bed and nightstand, we would be cozy and warm and safe. Which was more than I could say about the Watchers outside in the below-freezing temps, risking their lives for a battle we had just learned would never stop coming. Not without a lot of sacrifice, anyway.

We lay on our sides, my body pressed into Will's, as we held each other tight.

Will? I reached out with my mind.

"Yeah?" he responded out loud, his voice gruff and quiet with sleep.

"If they decide to invade Beldam, I'm going with them," I said fiercely, my heart pounding. "I'm bringing my friends home."

Second Chances

ILL WENT STILL, the tension of his thoughts pressing into me as heavy as an anvil on my chest. He reached over and turned the small lamp on. A soft amber glow filled the small room.

He returned to holding me. "What do you mean you're going to Beldam?"

I turned to face my husband. "Why does this surprise you? They're my friends, and you, more so than anyone else, should understand why I feel responsible. If it wasn't for me, they wouldn't be there."

"No." Will's voice was calm, his eyes dark, which unnerved me.

"Excuse me?" *Did he just say no, as if that settled it?*

"They aren't going to let you go."

"And?" I pressed.

"And..." He searched my face. When I gave him nothing, he exclaimed, "Damfino, Liddy. I do not want you to go. I don't think it's smart for you to go."

"Did you just say 'damfino'?"

"Focus, Lid."

I narrowed my eyes at him. "Listen," I snapped, "we may be married now, but I am my own person. You, nor anyone else, get to tell me what to do."

Will winced as if I'd hit him. He shook his head, his jaw tensing. "Wrong. I am definitely not your keeper, and I wasn't trying to tell you what to do. But Liddy, you have to realize—"

"But you just said—"

"The fact that you think I am trying to tell you what to do tears at my heart." Will dragged his hand down his face. "We are connected as one. You're right about how I can't tell you what to do, but I do respect you. However, deciding this on your own, without talking through it with me first, is not only rash but also disrespectful."

"I don't see it that way."

Will chuckled humorlessly, moving away from me. He lay on his back, staring up at the ceiling. "Fine. Let's see what the team who is planning this coup has to say about it."

When I didn't respond, he moved to get out of bed. "I'm going to go sleep on the couch."

I grabbed his arm before he was out of reach. Maybe Will had a point. We were partners, after all, and even though I didn't need his permission, I still owed him the respect of a conversation.

"I'm sorry," I huffed out, guiding him back to his place

next to me. "I should have spoken with you first. But please understand how badly I want to be in Beldam to liberate my friends and the multitude of kids imprisoned. You weren't there," I added softly. "You didn't hear the way they pleaded for my help. I can still see their eyes, hear their voices."

Will stroked my hair, placing his palm on my cheek. "And what if plans fail? What if it is one big trap?"

"You think Charlie would do that?" I asked, flabbergasted at the insinuation.

"No, of course not. But Mara has always been a step ahead of us. It is reasonable to expect the worst. If everything goes south, why would Cristes want their most valuable asset in harm's way? It would end the war, and not in our favor, before it even started."

"We can plan for a way out. Plus, you would be here, safe," I reasoned.

Will shook his head and pressed his forehead to mine. "I am nothing without you."

"That's not—"

Will's desperate kiss broke off my words. He pulled back slightly, his breath tickling my face.

"You don't fight fair," I grumbled.

Will chuckled. "I cannot live without you. Besides, my gifting is strengthened by you. Without you, I am nothing special, the same as every other Watcher. In other words, we doom Cristes. So either we both go or we both stay here."

"I don't want you to come," I pleaded.

Will smirked. "There is only one reason you do not wish for me to join you." He squeezed me tighter, and little butterflies began to awaken low in my belly. "If you keep looking at me like that, we are going to have to postpone this conversation."

Heat rushed up my neck, and I bit my lip. Will continued, "If you don't want me to go because the risk is too great, then why, my wife, my better half, would I want *you* to go?"

"Someone has to!" My voice rose unexpectedly, surprising me, and tears pricked behind my eyes.

Will grappled my shaking form in his arms, his strength swaddling me in a secure but gentle hug.

"Liddy, my love, you're right. Someone has to, but you are not alone. *We* are not alone. And some decisions we should seek counsel on. Now, let's get some sleep. We will join the council in planning this trip to Beldam. Let's hear all options first before running into something that can have far greater consequences than anyone is willing to bear."

He massaged the base of my skull and neck, calming me further. "Fine," I sighed. "But it will take a lot of convincing to keep me here," I added coyly.

Will laughed once again. "I have no doubt." He turned out the light on the end table. "Sweet dreams, Princess."

"But I'm not tired now."

Though I couldn't see him, I could practically feel his brows raise and the corner of his lip hitch, based on the amorous vibes he sent my way.

"I think I know what may tire you out a little..." And then he was kissing me, and I sunk into bliss.

Loud knocking at our door had us stirring. Buried deep under the castle, the room was pitch black.

Will turned on the light after nearly knocking it down. He looked me over up and down, his pupils dilating slightly, and brought the comforter up over my chest and shoulders.

"What are you, the modesty police?" I teased.

"No, but I know that you wouldn't like it if others saw you...plus I don't want others to see what's mine."

"What was that last part?" I asked.

"Nothing. Come in!" Will called to whoever was at the door. It opened, and in stepped a sheepish Duncan. He bowed low, averting his gaze.

"Their Majesties have said it is safe to return to your rooms now. Breakfast has been prepared and will be served upon your arrival. You will have a meeting in the king and queen's council room late this afternoon and are to wait for the call to join them," Duncan said.

"Understood. Will you be leading us back then?" Will asked.

Duncan gave a quick bow of his head. "As soon as you are ready." He swiftly closed the door behind him.

I couldn't wait to get out of there and scrambled to get dressed.

We traveled back through the secret passageways to our corridor of the castle, the trip looking the exact same as it did on the way down last night. Duncan took great measures in making sure we knew how to access each door.

"Ah, here we are," Duncan said as he pushed open the final door leading into our master bedroom. "I will come for you when it is time for the meeting."

Around four in the afternoon, Duncan came to our room and escorted us to the council room.

"Oh, my, gosh!" I whispered to Will as we were led through the alder wood doors. "It's a round table!"

He looked at me, his face scrunched in confusion as to why I'd be so excited about a table. But then, his face brightened, and we said in unison, "King Arthur!"

Eight faces of those already seated at the wooden table with resin inlay swiveled to us, some with their faces pinched like we'd interrupted something.

"William, Lydia, please come sit by me," Queen Nicole greeted us. We bowed with our forearms over our hearts and followed her to the table.

Will held out a wicker peacock chair for me, and I slid right in. The high curvature of its back made me feel as if I were in my own cocoon.

We need some of these chairs in our quarters, I said to Will via our mind link.

As you wish, he responded.

Will's parents entered the room, Lana appearing in great health, if a little tired. Will shot from his chair and beelined to his mother. She held her arms open and he slammed into her, Lana returning the embrace before I'd had the chance to even get out of my chair.

Charlie snuck into the room behind his parents. He peered around and when his gaze caught mine, his body uncoiled. I gave a little wave as I made my way over to my in-laws.

"Mom! I was worried about you all night." Will's voice was muffled against her shoulder.

"It is alright, son." She patted his back, attempting to reassure him. "I was never in any real danger. I mainly helped to organize the troops."

"But still, you were on the front lines," I interjected as I finally reached her. "Thank you for helping."

Lana's eyes ignited a little. "Of course. It's my pleasure to serve and protect those I love."

Charlie came to sit by me while Lana and Brantley sat directly across from us.

"Your Majesty." One of the gentlemen I recalled seeing in the safe room last night addressed the queen. "How much longer must we be expected to wait on Prince Nicholas?"

"Yes, Colden makes a valid point," said Edmond, the royal with the salt and pepper hair at his temples we'd met in the safe room the previous night. "We need to act now, while we still have the element of surprise on our hands, especially if we are to risk the lives of Watchers."

The queen rose to her feet. "Now, Lord Edmond, Lord Colden, we must be patient. There is—"

Nick and Shai appeared, but from where I have no idea, as he wasn't visible when I came in, and he sure as heck hadn't come through the front door. Shai followed in his wake.

Nick's eyes locked on mine. *Apologies for the slight delay, although I have been here the entire time.*

Here the entire time? Where?

Nick winked at me and continued, "I was tying up loose ends with Lord Abishai."

My thoughts must have been betrayed by my face, for

Nick quickly looked away from me, suppressing a snicker.

A hidden door floated into my mind and I sucked in my cheeks, attempting not to respond to the vision Nick was sending me. Will squeezed my thigh under the table, acknowledging he, too, was in on the secret.

"We are awaiting final persons to join us," Nick addressed the council. "Which is my fault, for Abishai and I decided to include them only moments ago."

As if summoned, someone knocked at the door.

Duncan grabbed the handle and gestured into the room. I pressed my lips into a flat line when I saw who entered first.

Gavin looked as uncomfortable as I felt, but Shai arrived at the door and hugged his old friend. At first Gavin stood, unmoving. Tia and Tannon followed him and shared awkward glances. When the twins spotted Will and me, their shoulders dropped a few inches, and I waved them over.

"So, are we really telling anyone and everyone?" a snarky woman commented under her breath, though conveniently loud enough for all to hear, as her eyes narrowed in disapproval at the twins.

I remembered that difficult woman from last night.

Nick turned his gaze on the slender woman, coming to stand by me, his eyes flashing in warning. "Blanche, unless you consider yourself 'anyone and everyone'," he bit off, "then I would suggest respecting my authority in regards to whom I have chosen to be in this room today."

Uncle Shai had returned to stand next to Nick, and his scoff had me turning my head to see him better. He mumbled under his breath, "She's lucky royal customs did not afford us the option to choose *every* person in here today."

I clapped my hand over my mouth to stifle the giggle that so badly wanted to escape. Blanche's cold blue eyes snapped to me, and I immediately sobered, looking around the table to avoid her gaze.

Another woman—a little familiar, I noted—sat by herself. Ohanna and Duncan stood off to the sides, their faces stoic, and I wasn't sure they were technically part of this meeting.

The king stood, his arms relaxed and hands clasped. "Now that we are all seated, I am officially calling this meeting to order."

Duncan sealed the door with his gifting and took a seat off to the side of the queen.

"Nicholas, the table is yours, son," King Klaus stated as he sat.

Nick pressed his outstretched fingers on the table, taking a sharp inhale through his nose. He released it in a huff and stood.

"Edmond was correct. Time is of the essence. We need to act quickly if we are to salvage what remaining element of surprise we have left."

"What do you mean?" Lana asked outright, not waiting for permission to speak.

Nick looked to Charlie, who nodded and drew his mother's attention. "Last night, I confessed to having envelopes in my possession. In full transparency, I've had them for over a year now. Though I was very discreet in my acquisition of them, no doubt Mara realizes some of her enchanted envelopes are missing by now."

My stomach tightened at the idea that she may have known we had access to her. Will again squeezed the top of my knee, sending a rush of calming, confident energy coursing through me.

"And would she suspect you, son?" Brantley asked.

Charlie rubbed the back of his neck. "I don't think so. She may assume Alex has them, but then again, he really didn't spend any time in Beldam for months leading up to his detainment by Nick. She may also assume she miscalculated or that one of her prisoners got into them." He visibly paled, and I grabbed his hand for support. His eyes were locked on Alex, who looked as if he'd just seen a ghost. Charlie gulped and turned to face me, his eyes dull, sweat beading along his forehead.

I opened my mouth to call for help, but Shai was already at his side, his hands on Charlie's shoulders, speaking quietly in his ear. Duncan was at Alex's side doing the same. Within seconds, the color returned to them.

Charlie shook his head. "It would be best if Mara believed either me or Alex had these envelopes. Otherwise, the punishment..." He cleared his throat. "The punishment these kids would face would be..."

"Worse than your worst nightmare," Alex finished for him.

A quick glance around the table at the wide eyes mixed amongst grave faces made it obvious I wasn't the only one shaken to the core by this revelation.

"But I thought you said—"

"It doesn't matter what I said," Charlie cut me off with a severity that took me aback.

I shook my head. How could he love someone who would hurt people, let alone children?

The queen looked from me to Charlie. "Right. So either way, it is in everyone's best interest that we get to Beldam as quickly as we can."

A loud thud sounded, and I flinched, then gasped when I saw that one of the women, the older one who'd been by herself when I'd first entered the council room, had fainted, landing face first onto the table. Gavin sprang into action.

"Mother?" He shook her shoulders gently.

I thought I remembered her, although she looked so frail now, I couldn't believe she was the same person. This shell of a woman had appeared so confident—smug, even—in Nick's memories of the Carnival night.

"Mother!" Gavin shook her more forcefully this time, and her face lolled to the side. Blood—lots of it—streamed from her nose.

Will pulled me into his lap and wrapped his arms around me, snuggling me to his chest.

"Don't look. Think of the first day we danced together," he murmured, smoothing my hair.

I buried my head into his solid chest, focusing on his heartbeat, the dance in my mind playing out to its own rhythm.

I heard the door open and close. "She's gone," Will whispered.

I lifted my head as Nick returned to his position at the table, wiping some blood from his hand with his pocket square.

"Father, I understand there are traditions and formalities you are honoring, but someone's station does not mean they are equipped to handle the nature of what needs to be done," Nick barked, agitation seething through his clenched teeth.

The king nodded and addressed the room.

"I understand that for some of us, the nature of our work here may be hard to accept or deal with. Therefore, is there anyone who does not wish to be here?" He paused, his measured gaze landed on each individual at the table before continuing. "If so, you are welcome to leave, no questions asked."

Hushed voices from across the table turned more anxious as the woman seated by Colden rose from her seat with her head held high and swept out of the room without a word. Colden addressed the table.

"Zoey, would like to be with Mrs. Frosters when she wakes in the healing clinic?"

Gavin sat staring at his shaking hands, now coated in his mother's blood. His face was gray, eyes glossy and beseeching. "Have I not been punished long enough?" The table remained silent, as if no one dared interrupt. "She has taken everything, *everything* from me!" His fists slammed the table, and I jumped. I would have fallen out of Will's lap if his arms weren't securing me.

"Gavin, brother, I sympathize with how hard this is—" Shai started, cautiously approaching his once-best friend.

"You know nothing! She murdered my father, my daughter...took my match from me!" Now Gavin was standing, restlessly marching up and down the length of the room, his eyes wild with pain. "I became the nation's pariah for following what Eria himself ordained, what he put in my heart. And I was blamed for the fall of Cristes into this barely-inhabitable landscape, why? Because I had the misfortune of falling in love twice?" Gavin dropped to his knees.

"Quit feeling sorry for yourself," Nick growled. "You aren't the only one who lost everything in this."

"Nick, we talked about this," Shai warned.

But I could see by the silver light of his eyes that Nick was too far gone, his anger simmering to a boil.

"Balderdash!" Nick rounded on Gavin, dropping into a crouch so he was at eye level with him. "You know as well as I that much of this is your fault just as it is hers. No one can blame you for choosing your mate over Mara. But it was the way you did it—the coward's way."

Gavin slumped forward, his head in his hands, as he let out loud, gut-wrenching sobs that burrowed into my heart. Warm tears streamed down my own face, and I stood. Will grabbed my hand, stilling me, but I shook my head. He cocked his head and let go of my hand. I walked to the group of broken men who once were the best of friends— practically brothers.

"You both need to forgive," I said.

Nick and Gavin looked up at the sound of my voice. And at the sight of me, both men's jaws dropped, and I sensed I was glowing not just from my eyes but from my whole being. Sparks of green and purple flickered in their eyes and in the resin portion of the table.

"Gavin, you made some poor choices, but you were young and also deceived by your father. Nick, more could have been done before that day at the park instead of waiting to talk with Mara. Swift action may have prevented all of this. But you too were young...and in love."

Gavin's eyes flitted to Nick, searching his face, but Nick avoided his gaze.

"Gavin's parents, heck, most of Watcher society who

viewed Mara as less-than, are responsible. The fact is, no one is perfect. No one. We can live in the past hurt and let it continue to taint everything good that enters our lives, or we can forgive and move forward. What do you say?" I had no idea where this bravado was coming from, a wisdom beyond my experience and years, and yet, my gut told me they were the right words.

"You look so much like her," Gavin whispered, staring at me in disbelief. "My Ellasyn Lydia. Your demeanor, your voice, they, too, remind me of her." He broke down again, and I kneeled before him, encircling him in a hug. He leaned his forehead on my shoulder, and I rubbed his back while his grief gushed out.

I stared up at Nick, challenging him to do the right thing.

You're a stubborn lass, you know that, right? He spoke directly into my mind, ensuring only I heard him.

I replied without missing a beat. *You're welcome. Also, you are an even more stubborn jerk face for not fixing this between the two of you sooner.*

Nick rolled his eyes and Shai looked between the two of us, his lips puckered in concentration.

I continued, my eyes trained on Nick, all the while not saying anything aloud and not caring if Shai knew. *Can't you see that the guilt is literally killing him? Help him to redeem himself, to regain his honor and manhood. Let him be a part of helping to correct his mistakes.*

Nick placed his hands on his hips and arched his back, looking to the ceiling and muttering something under his breath. Then he looked at me with narrowed eyes, shaking his head in disbelief.

You win, Princess.

Best-Laid Plans

NICK DROPPED TO HIS KNEES AT MY SIDE, then pulled Gavin to his shoulder. Shai knelt down next to them, wrapping an arm around each of their shoulders.

I realized someone had placed a privacy screen around our little group. When I came out from behind it, everyone else was gathered at the far end of the room, sipping on drinks and eating hors d'oeuvres as if we were back at my wedding.

While scanning the group for Will, Lana came into view and embraced me.

"Thank you," she whispered.

"I didn't—"

"Oh, but you did, and with the confidence of a true leader." Lana pulled back, her eyes shining with emotion.

My friends were standing in a corner, all chatting. I joined

Will, Tia, and Tannon, trying to engage in the conversation, but the room was heavy, the conversation stilted, until Nick cleared his throat.

When he spoke, his voice came out raspy and tired, his eyes puffy from tears shed. "Sorry for the delay. If we could all return to our seats, we can complete the planning of our mission."

Will held my chair for me, and I tried to be discreet when glancing at Gavin. Though he looked spent, his countenance was lighter.

Where Nick stood, both Gavin and Shai flanked him. The room quieted, and only the faint howling of the wind registered.

"We leave at dawn. Charlie has allowed me access into his memories, and it appears Mara is most active in the evening hours. By leaving at dawn, we give her the element of surprise as she will probably be exhausted from a busy night."

He didn't have to explain what he meant by a busy night. Hundreds of eyes staring at me in my nightmares were explanation enough. She'd be kidnapping more kids, imprisoning them in her lair.

I shivered involuntarily. Will gave my hand a squeeze, and warmth flooded through me.

"Who is 'we'?" Ohanna challenged, leaning her forearm on the table.

I'd forgotten she was with us. She'd been so still, so quiet, she practically blended into the walls.

"Nick, Lana, and myself," Shai answered.

"Only the three of you?" Queen Nicole's voice shook but still carried across the room. Her hands clenched into fists against the table, knuckles white with strain.

Lana reached over and placed her hand over the queen's. "Auntie, I know this must be hard for you with all of us having been gone for so long..." She turned to address the table. "But all three of us have history with Mara. We are the least threatening to her should things turn south."

"Exactly," Nick said, swiping his forehead with the sleeve of his shirt. "We do not wish to come in with large numbers and inadvertently start something, putting more of our citizens at risk."

"Not to mention, we can hide more easily," Shai said.

"Are you quite certain that is such a good idea?" Blanche asked. "Much time has passed since you have had a relationship with Mara. If she becomes aware of your trespassing, she may not hesitate to retaliate immediately, and you may need reinforcements."

My jaw nearly hit the table. Was Blanche being reasonable right now?

At the pregnant pause, I decided to shoot my shot.

"I'm going too," I announced.

Every head snapped in my direction. Nick crossed his arms, sighed, and rolled his eyes to the heavens. Shai just kept shaking his head, as if that might change the trajectory of my plans.

"You must be joking?" Edmond nearly laughed.

I glowered at him. "I assure you, sir, I am serious. Dead serious."

"Sir?" Then he laughed so hard he nearly fell from his chair before he was able to wheeze out, "And dead you will be if you go."

My body heated as my magic awoke, ready to play teacher and give this man a lesson.

Cooling waves crashed over my cells, chilling each one, and I glared at Will, annoyed he wasn't letting me feel this. His eyes widened and he shook his head.

That was not me. He spoke without moving his lips.

Shai was staring at me. I tilted my head in question, and he brought his pointer finger to the tip of his nose.

I wanted to protest, but the screeching of a chair stopped me.

"You can't go!" Alex shouted. His reaction elicited a surprised gasp from me. Tia laid a hand on his elbow, but he shook her off, his eyes blazing at me. "She'll kill you on the spot!"

"Not necessarily," Charlie said, his voice quiet and hesitant.

Alex slammed his hands on the table, then brought them to his head. Gone were the golden blond spikes he used to style his hair in; now it lay flat, kissing his forehead and the tops of his ears.

"I have to agree with the young man, Lydia," the king asserted. "If something were to happen to you, it may doom us all. We cannot risk it."

I opened my mouth to retort, but Charlie beat me to the punch.

"Mara once negotiated with me," he said. "All the children would be released in exchange for handing Liddy over to her. I honestly do not believe she will expect to see Liddy. In that split second, while shock seizes her body, I'd be able to sneak Liddy out to safety."

It took a moment for my brain to register the fact that Charlie was putting in his bid to go under the guise of supporting me.

"No!" I screamed. Apparently, I was not alone in my opinion, as a chorus of voices rose up with mine. Charlie could not return to Beldam. Never.

Charlie gave me a sad smile. "If you truly want to go, then I am going, too. I'm the only one with firsthand knowledge on how to get you out of there quickly."

People spoke over each other, arguments waged with fierce tongue lashes, but I couldn't make out what they were saying. Everything around me went fuzzy, and I could only see Charlie. He had endured so much; way worse than what I had, and yet he was offering to go back—for me. Not just for me but for them—the kids he felt responsible for.

A war broke out within the confines of my body. My brain had no idea what to do, but my heart knew what it wanted. My friends needed me, and I needed to make sure they got out no matter what. But was I being rational? Could I jeopardize Charlie and Cristes while playing the hero?

Charlie looked at me for a long moment but was the first to break eye contact.

Ohanna stood. "Shut it!"

I was snapped back to the surrounding chaos. All the voices hushed at once.

Ohanna unsheathed her sword and pounded its pommel against the table twice. "Since no one deemed it wise to ask the leader of your armies her opinion, I will offer it on my own accord."

"Careful," Nick warned, his eyes narrowing.

Ohanna's quirked brow and pursed lips seemed to dare anyone to challenge her. She stomped her foot on the chair, laid her sword across the top of her thigh, and stroked the blade, clearly sending a message: *Mess with me and we've got problems I'd gladly deal with.*

"Ohanna, out with it," the king spoke through clenched teeth.

She gave a swift nod in obedience. "Now, Charlie is right in ascertaining how Mara would never expect us to bring one of our greatest assets. You must realize this is not only a mission to capture her and effectively end this conflict before it begins. My understanding is that this is also a rescue mission. Altogether there are too many moving parts for only three of you to go." She glanced quickly at Lana. "No offense, seeing as you are the most gifted warrior Cristes has ever known."

Lana inclined her head, hiding a smirk. "None taken."

Ohanna turned her gaze back to the king. "I suggest we strategize a more sizable team and divide them into three groups." She began ticking off her fingers. "One to assist in obtaining our target, and one to free the children and bring them here safely."

"And what is the third?" Tia asked the head guard, her brows furrowed.

"Well, the princess is our most valued asset—not that you are an object," Ohanna amended. "I am speaking as a combat strategist."

"Oh, so she is the bait," Tannon blurted.

Will growled. "No way."

Ohanna sent Tannon a look that would have any man shivering in his boots, but he remained oblivious. She schooled her features and turned her attention to Will. "Your Highness, we wouldn't let anything happen to her."

Will leveled a hard stare in the commander's direction. "You have absolutely no idea what Mara is like," he said. "No offense. Don't take it personally that I do not trust my wife within arm's reach of the woman who has been trying to kill her since we were children, no matter who her guard is."

Colden cleared his throat. "Going in, trying to be unseen, with so many moving parts, it can turn messy, and fast. If we pretend to offer the princess in exchange for all the captives, we control the situation." His words shocked me. I figured he was there solely because of his blue gifting, not that he had any opinion of substance.

Nick paced the room, his hands clasped behind his back.

Shai looked to me and then to Charlie. "Charlie, are you confident you can make sure Liddy escapes—as well as yourself—should our plans go awry?"

"Did you hear a word I said?" Will asked incredulously. The anger coursing through our bond made me want to get up and punch something. I placed a calming hand on my husband.

Shai kept his gaze on Charlie. "Answer the question, Charlie."

"Yes, Uncle."

"I mean it," he said sternly. "No matter who else may be left behind, your priority is Liddy and yourself. Do you understand?"

Charlie chewed on his bottom lip, glancing nervously at his big brother. He'd confided in all of us at his parents' house in Florida how he tried to capture me and deliver me to Mara, all to save those kids. And now Shai presented an ultimatum in clear terms. Me or the kids.

I can't believe this. Fine, keep ignoring me, just so you know... "I am going, too." Will blurted the last part aloud with conviction.

Nick threw his hands up in the air. "Critosi!"

"Nicholas!" Queen Nicole admonished him, and Tannon snickered behind his hand.

"I am sorry, Mother, but what in the actual tinsel and berries is going on here? Have you all lost your ever-loving fopdoodles?"

"Absolutely not," Lana exclaimed. "You *and* Liddy cannot go. If we lose you both, the war is over before it even begins."

"But Mom, I cannot—"

Brantley placed a hand on his chest. "Son, I will not survive it if my entire family leaves me here. You are connected to Liddy. You will be able to at least feel what is going on. You will know if they are safe. I need you..." There was a long pause. When Brantley spoke again, his voice was pinched as if this pained him. "I need you to stay and report to me what is happening to the other half of our family."

Will sat back in his chair. I'd never even considered using our bond to keep tabs on each other before. I mean, it made perfect sense considering he always knew how I felt and I him.

"Liddy and I are fully bonded now. Our gifting ensures Mara would be no match for us. You may need me to help defeat her, and if you refuse me, then what?" Will tried to reason. His eyes pleaded with me to have his back.

But I couldn't let him do it. My friends were down in Beldam because of me. Mara wanted me, not Will, so I would be the one to go. Not to mention, if things went poorly, I had to make sure Charlie saved the kids this time, and I knew Will wouldn't allow it, couldn't allow it. Going to Beldam already risked enough for all of us, but I could not risk losing any and all hope the people of Cristes managed to carve out from the thick cavernous ice when Will and I entered their borders.

And so, using our mind link, I explained to Will how necessary it was that he stay in Cristes with his dad. How we would need him on that side of the wall when we returned with the threat.

His eyes glazed over for a brief moment. "Dad?"

"Yes, son?" Brantley paled, gripping the arm of his chair.

"You got your wish. I am staying here with you."

Brantley and Lana embraced and sunk into each other with relief.

Ohanna struck her sword's pommel against the table again. "Alright, so I will lead the rescue mission. Prince Nicholas, you will head up the extraction, facing off with Mara, accompanied by Princess Lydia. Charlie—" Her eyes practically pierced him smack in the middle of his forehead. "You will wait in the shadows with a few guards as life insurance for the princess."

Her last words hung in the air, hinting at a deeper meaning. Did Ohanna not trust Charlie?

"And what will the rest of us be doing?" Tia asked, gesturing around the room at everyone who wasn't going to Beldam.

"Yeah, why am I here?" Alex asked, a nervous giggle accompanying his words.

Nick stopped pacing and turned to face him. "Well, our

initial plan was turned on its head, but luckily your role has not changed."

Tia's eyes tracked Nick as he walked back to his seat.

"Tia and Tannon, since we are unable to portal everyone in and out of Cristes behind the wall, we will need you both waiting in a designated spot to quickly fill the sleds. Once we portal in, we face the wrath of the Black Roses and need our best mushers to transport those kids to safety."

Tia and Tannon each nodded solemnly.

"Mother, we need a portal to open as close to the wall as possible. We barely made it last time."

"Your father and I are on it," the queen responded with a hand over her heart.

"The entire city will be placed at risk," Blanche scoffed.

Up till that moment, I'd never seen Queen Nicole look intimidating in the least. But the look she gave Blanche rivaled the frozen tundra outside.

"Blanche, trust when I say the wards will keep us protected. Travel through the portal will be well orchestrated by my competent military leaders, only opening long enough to let me people pass back through. You would do well to remember..." Her eyes flitted to everyone in the room, narrowing back at Blanche. "My authority or my loyalty when it comes to protecting my people being questioned does not sit well with me."

Blanche sucked in her cheeks, as if fighting the urge to retort but realizing it would not be in her best interest.

Edmond spoke. "I agree, we need to allow the portal to open closer to the wall. However, I suggest we move all residents five miles inland away from the wall, evacuate them to the countryside, and allow only essential citizens to remain."

"Noted," the king spoke thickly, clearly miffed at the slight his wife just handled. "You and I will make those arrangements and see to it they are heeded before nightfall. We do not wish to have families roaming so late at night."

"Um, hello. I still don't know what my role is in all of this." Alex gestured wildly.

Shai turned to look at him. "You will be at the wall, waiting and ready. We are going to need someone on the ground here ready to receive the children. It may help them trust us, seeing as they would know you and observe you in good health."

"I... I will be at the wall?" His Adam's apple bobbed with effort.

"Not guarding it," I clarified for Alex. "Helping the kids feel safe, answer their questions, provide them comfort."

Alex rubbed the back of his neck. "I don't think I'll be very good at that. I'm not the nurturing type."

Charlie rolled his eyes. "You weren't in the past, but you were in survival mode."

"So were you," Alex grumbled, "but I didn't see that stopping you from helping them."

"Now is the time to change that," Charlie urged. Alex stared at him for a few long seconds, his jaw muscles working, and then gave a sharp nod.

"Tia and Tannon, you will guide your sleds to the healing sanctum. I have already spoken with healers Leo and Ruth regarding setting up temporary housing behind the main building." Nick pointed out the window in a general direction. "Deliver the children there. They will all need attention."

"I will ensure that every available healer, both with first and second giftings, be ready and waiting," the queen promised.

"And what can I do?" Gavin asked, his voice scratchy, almost too quiet to make out.

Both Shai and Nick turned to him in unison.

"You cannot come with us. We do not know how she will respond upon seeing you," Shai said gently.

"I understand," Gavin sighed. "But here, what can I do to help?"

"Well, Gavin," the king interjected. "What would you like to do?"

Gavin played with the hair on the chin of his beard. "I would like to be wherever you bring Mara to. There are some things I would like to say to her that are long overdue."

Arbolias Sang - Part 2

"I STILL CANNOT BELIEVE you convinced me to let you go alone," Will said once we were back in our quarters.

The meeting had finally wrapped and everyone rushed out to prepare for the early morning departure. Will and I waited in our rooms, contemplating all the ways this coup would pan out.

"I won't be alone." I laid my hand on his chest, offering reassurance.

His jaw clenched. "We've never tested our gifting limits since we've been married. What if once you walk through that portal I can no longer sense you?"

"You can still talk to me, in here," I said, resting two fingers on each of his temples.

He closed his eyes at the touch and held onto my wrists.

"And what if too much distance breaks that connection?"

"Then you'll just have to believe that I am fine. I trust Charlie and Nick, Shai, your mom...they are not going to let anything happen to me."

"Yeah, but what—" I cut off his words by capturing his mouth with mine. "What if she..." His mumbled words moved against my lips, then swiftly ceased as he joined me in the kiss.

"Better?" I asked after pulling away.

"Not fair." Will smirked, his eyes heavy-lidded. "I'm aware I shouldn't go into this with the attitude that things will end badly, but I can't help it. Too many of the people I love are going straight to the threat, on her turf, and I will be sitting in the safe room, twiddling my thumbs."

"You will not be twiddling your thumbs," I countered. "You are going to be the one person who can communicate with someone on the inside, providing important information so that everyone here in Cristes can be ready. Not to mention the comfort you'll be offering your dad."

Will sighed and wrapped his hands around my waist, resigned to the fact that I was going and he was staying and there was nothing he could do about it.

"Fine, but I'm not letting anyone take you away from me for the next twelve hours. I plan on taking full advantage of every second I have with you until you depart for Beldam."

Duncan woke us a little before dawn. He presented me with the clothing I was to wear on this mission. It was just like the gear I wore in Shai's basement, only deep purple, the color of my gifting. This time, I wasn't surprised by the fabric's weight; I knew it would be enchanted to act as armor. It comforted me to remember Nolan's words: *"No gifting can truly affect your body when wearing this."*

My heart sank a little once again remembering all that Nolan sacrificed for us. I donned the form-fitting long-sleeved shirt and leggings. I brushed my long locks and swept them up into a high messy bun, then walked out of the bathroom to meet Will.

He laced his fingers with mine, and we proceeded to the arboretum located deep in the South Wing of the castle. Though I'd never been there, Will had visited once before.

Guards greeted us at the doors. "Everyone else is just inside," the taller guard relayed.

Bright beams of morning light shone through the high windows on the wooden doors, their gold inlays glittering in the rays. Will grabbed the long handle and guided me inside. The warm, moist air and lush plants with vibrant colors transported me to a tropical rainforest. Everyone was milling about the room.

A small room at the far end, enclosed in all glass, demanded my attention. "Is it snowing in there?" I whispered to Will, pointing to it.

"Yes! Isn't it cool? Come see what's inside," he responded as we walked toward a small stage flanked by a few rows of bookcases and desks.

He led me right to it, and I understood immediately why this little piece of the rainforest arboretum was separated from the rest.

"Christmas roses!" I gasped with joy, bringing my hand to my mouth.

Will's hands came around my waist, and he pressed my back into his chest. "I thought you'd like them. I asked if I could go in and grab one for you but was denied for obvious reasons."

Christmas roses were extremely difficult to grow in Cristes. Previously, the climate was too warm, and now it was far too cold. With Watchers unable to make deliveries, and the roses necessary for so many tinctures and elements in the society, no part of the roses went to waste.

"Just you thinking of me is enough."

We held each other for a little while longer, watching the roses as they twinkled under the lights. Every now and again one would glow brighter than the rest.

"Lydia, William, we are ready," Ohanna said, stepping out of the shadows.

We turned and realized everyone else had gone. As Ohanna walked toward the back of the room, I saw it—a little door handle that blended in with the earthen wall behind her.

Ohanna pressed open the door and ushered me through, holding her arm out to barricade Will from entering.

"I am sorry, Your Highness, but you cannot come in. We do not want to risk you falling into the portal." She gave Will a pointed look as if she could foresee the future.

Will looked affronted. "Relax. I won't make myself a stow-a-way. I know I have to remain here." When Ohanna still didn't move her arm, he continued, "Well, can I at least say goodbye to my wife?"

Ohanna rolled her eyes. "Is that not what you were doing

for the last ten minutes?"

"Ten minutes is not nearly long enough." Mischief twinkled in his eyes, and I giggled.

I ducked under Ohanna's arm and wrapped my arms around Will's neck. "Kiss me."

"As you wish."

We kissed good and hard until Ohanna coughed loudly. "Alright, you two. I am now practically blind, and we cannot have the princess traveling through Beldam with a big spotlight on her."

Will pulled away, worry flooding his face. "Crud."

I closed my eyes and focused. When I opened them again, I knew I was no longer lit up to one hundred and fifty watts.

Will sighed with relief, and I stroked his cheek. "I'll be back before you can spell 'supercalifragilisticexpialidocious'." We hugged one last time, and Ohanna closed the door. For a brief moment, I had a flicker of fear that it would be the last time I'd see my fated match.

Ohanna and I walked along the soft, earthen path, which transitioned from dirt to sand as we traveled. A dim amber glow filled the space, and it felt as if I were under the earth's warm crust.

We reached a large opening, and I shrunk back. This room was almost an exact replica of Arbolias Sang in Nick's place, though thankfully, there were no floating envelopes with Mara's voice emanating from them.

"What is it?" Ohanna asked.

Nick walked up and answered for me. "Yes, these trees are siblings. With a complete and functional globital, we can use their connection to travel between Cristes and Mortalia."

"But we don't have a globital," I pointed out.

"No, we do not." He shook his head. "But we do have an enchanted envelope that shall allow us the energy we need to travel."

"But I thought we had to portal in and out of Cristes outside of the wall?" I scrunched my brows, confused.

"We can portal out of Cristes within the limits of the walls. The wards prevent us from portaling back in. We do not have to worry so much about who is leaving versus who is coming in. So we will use this room," he said, gesturing to the space, "which was designed for these travels long ago, much like we used Arbolias Sang in my home. Do you remember what I shared about Watcher history and how often we used to travel?"

I nodded. "Mostly around Christmas, though some were given permissions to visit Mortalia more regularly for research purposes."

"Exactly." He walked over to Shai and addressed the rest of the group. As I made my way over to Lana and Charlie, I noticed how crowded the room was. Ohanna had a group of almost twenty troops with her, all clad in charcoal gray and holding heaps of arrows on their backs.

I smiled at Brita, the trooper who'd assisted Ohanna in getting me and Will within the walls of Cristes. She didn't smile back. *OK, then.*

Liddy? How's it going? Will's voice popping into my head startled me, and Lana grabbed my shoulder to steady me. I forced a smile and hastily apologized, blaming the sand.

Are you OK? What's going on? he pressed.

I'm fine. You startled me, that's all. We haven't left yet.

OK, cool. I'll check in again in five.

No! Please don't. I need to focus on the mission. I will call out to you if anything changes.

My mind went quiet as I tuned in to Nick's voice.

"Does everyone understand the plan?" he was asking.

Dang it. I hadn't heard a word.

Nick walked straight up to me and pulled me by the arm over to the side. "Your life is on the line, and you spend this time talking to William?"

"I didn't, well I did, but I told him—"

Nick pinched the bridge of his nose and sighed. "I get it. He is nervous. But he needs to understand that you need to concentrate. He could be a major distraction."

"I told him that. I said not to contact me that way, and I would contact him."

"Good, Liddy. Just one more thing," he said, placing his hand on my shoulder. "Please leave all the talking to me. I do not want you speaking with Mara. Understood?"

I nodded. *I don't want to talk to her anyway.* That wasn't totally true. I actually had a lot I wanted to say.

Nick offered me his arm and leaned in so he was at eye level.

"Let's go end this, shall we?"

I wrapped my arm around his offered one and proceeded to the front.

Shai turned to Charlie. "Can you please remind us what we can expect when we travel using Mara's portal system?"

Charlie came to stand next to Nick, who nodded at the young boy, encouraging him to answer.

"I have never used a globital before, and I've learned

neither have most of you. This could be a good thing as we have nothing to compare it to. Understand that with Mara's portal system, it is as easy as walking through the old location and into the new one. You may be disorientated at first, but that is your body adjusting to the sudden changes in temperature, altitude, and time and space. Your body will adjust."

Using my gifting, I spoke to Nick. *Well, that would have been nice to have when traveling here instead of a broken globital.*

He chuckled. *Definitely. Remind me to ask her how she does it.*

"Once I open the envelope and place it in its position, we will have but a few minutes to enter before it closes and the envelope dies. It cannot be used a second time."

"How many of us can go through at a time?" Ohanna inquired.

Charlie appeared to think on that for a moment. "About four people shoulder to shoulder."

Ohanna went to work arranging her troops. She had two rows in the back of me and my group and placed herself with Charlie and two others that would lead us in. Another two would flank me.

When we were all lined up, Charlie stepped in front of us and placed the envelope on the ground. He broke the wax seal, opened the top flap, and promptly stepped back into position.

We all collectively held our breaths while we waited for something to happen. I sent the message *I love you* to Will and felt a little hug on my heart.

Sparks of orange flared and popped, transforming into shades of pale pink, blue, purple, and green. They cloaked the orange and formed a tight spiral. After a breath, the spiral began to expand, and expand, and expand until a sound like shattering glass crackled through the air. And then, we were looking into a very dark tunnel.

Beldam

Y BREATH HITCHED AS FLASHBACKS of my very real nightmares pricked at me. Dark tunnels. The feeling of desperate eyes on me. The faint echo of my name by a sickly-sweet voice.

Lana and Shai each held onto my arms to steady me as they guided me through the portal.

I followed after them blindly and about fainted when a cold dread dropped heavier than a pregnant elephant into my stomach.

What is it, Liddy? Nick spoke into my mind.

"Something isn't right," I managed to breathe out.

The portal closed seconds behind the last of us, and we were left in pitch blackness.

Where was the guiding light that always led me to

Mara's throne room when I was brought here against my will?

"Where to, Charlie?" I heard Shai ask.

Blue light softly lit the immediate area around us, and I realized it came from Nick's hand. Shai and Lana still held on to me, but I shook them off. I closed my eyes and reached for my gifting currently swimming in my chest. I let it seep out in its own electric current, lighting my hands. Many troops followed suit, illuminating our entire path.

The light we created, though dim, shone off the black walls of the large circular room, the reflection making them appear wet. The darkness above us seemed to go on forever. Between no visible ceiling and the illusion of wet walls, my lungs constricted with the feeling of being stuck underwater.

Charlie stood stock still and pale-faced, like he'd be sick at any moment.

"Charlie, where to?" Nick asked again, a little more stern.

"This-this is not where her portals typically bring me," he answered shakily.

"What do you mean?" Ohanna asked. "Tell me now, for if this is a trap, it is urgent we abort the mission."

"Like I said, this isn't the room I normally portaled in and out of when I was under her dominion," Charlie rasped, his voice on the verge of breaking.

His fear was palpable. A protective instinct hummed through me, dousing my own flames of fear.

"I think I remember this path," I said quietly. Everyone but Lana appeared confused, for she alone knew what had haunted my dreams for so many years.

"This way," I ordered, holding my light up to mark the

path through the tunnel before us. I touched the smooth walls as I walked, ignoring their frigid bite as everyone followed behind me.

The tunnel was short, and soon, we were in a small, circular room with five passages tunneling from it like the spokes of a wheel. I closed my eyes, recalling images from my nightmares as Mara's amber light guided me.

"There." I lifted my hand at the left-most tunnel, washing it in a violet hue.

Ohanna whipped around to face Nick. "How is it she recognizes where to go, but Charlie cannot?"

Lana stepped forward. "Because she does." Her tone left no room for questions.

Ohanna turned around but nocked one of her arrows before forging ahead. After a few wordless minutes, we came to a fork; but instead of saying anything, I simply guided them with my light to the left again into a shorter passage, followed by a sharp right.

This tunnel was colder than the rest and seemed to drag on forever; so much so, I almost panicked second-guessing myself. But before the negative emotions could overcome me, we arrived at another circular room. In front of me were the familiar large double doors encrusted with marcasite jewels, though their sparkle seemed to be hiding.

"We're here," Charlie whispered.

I looked around for the small orbs that greeted me out here once before, but they were nowhere to be found. Everything was quiet—too quiet.

Tension filled the air, and my gifting tingled just beneath the surface of my skin.

"Positions, everyone," Ohanna ordered. Her eyes ignited for a brief flash, and her troops swiftly formed two rows on either side of the doors.

Charlie came up behind me with his two guards. He stood close enough to my back so that only I could hear him.

"Something isn't right," he whispered. "The air has become too thick. Be prepared to leave with me at once. She knows. I know she knows." He moved back, not far, but far enough that I could no longer feel the heat of his body. Still the back of my neck tingled as if I were being stalked.

Nick stood at the seam of where the two doors met, readying himself to grab the knob with the 'M' on it that burned my hand once before.

Wait! I called out to him, and he froze. *Check the handle for heat first.*

I stood directly behind him, willing my heart to slow so as not to worry Will. Lana and Shai stood on either side of me, just a pace behind, at the ready for anything.

Nick held his palm close to the knob for a brief moment. Then, using the back of his hand, he tapped the knob once. He turned his head over his shoulder and gave me a curt nod. Without any further hesitation, Nick grabbed for the handle, flung open the heavy door, and entered Mara's throne room.

It looked exactly the same as I remembered it from my dreams, though this time it was empty, or at least it appeared to be. I couldn't ignore my body's readiness nor Charlie's warning. I watched as Ohanna's troops filed in one after the other so quickly and silently they were but a blur. Had I not walked in with them, I'm not sure I'd be able to tell they were even there.

I turned my attention to the dais, where the throne sat, dark and lifeless. Christmas roses were still carved into the throne's silver-leafed frame, but missing was the living canopy, like the roses were nothing but a mere carving.

What now? I asked Nick, not daring to speak aloud. The room was heavy with anticipation, everyone curled to strike.

Gold dust began to float about the room, just a fleck here and there, one caressing Nick's cheek as it made its way to the dais. Then thousands of specks lit up the space rushing to the throne, organizing themselves until a recognizable shape emerged.

I think you know what, Nick responded to me. *Be ready.*

Slow laughter echoed off the walls, gaining in speed and volume as the gold shape continued to form and display more details.

Ohanna's eyes ignited, and within a heartbeat, her warriors followed her lead. A green glow encircled the room.

Nick tensed and stood straight. Lana's grip on my arm was near painful. I followed both their gazes and nearly collapsed in fear at the sight of Mara, now fully formed and seated on her throne.

Her champagne-colored lips curled up at the ends, revealing perfectly white teeth. "It's about time you paid me a visit."

Deal or No Deal

THE MARA THAT SAT ON THE THRONE was unlike any version she'd presented to me in my nightmares before. But I had seen this Mara before—the Mara from Nick's memories. The innocent young girl that he first met on the beach all those years ago. She sat there with her hair a light blond in tousled waves, blown by an imaginary wind as if she stood by the sea. She even wore the faded white dress with a dirty smock and her feet bare.

"Hello, Nicholas." Her smile was sweet and warm, her voice almost...shy. She turned her kaleidoscope eyes of beautiful pastels on Shai and Lana. "Hello friends, it has been a long time. Tell me, what present have you brought and are hiding so fiercely from me?" Orange sparks flashed in her eyes, and I immediately tried to make myself shrink, to become invisible behind the solid wall that was Nick.

Nick, who stood so tall and strong, was shaking. I don't think anyone else would have noticed except me, since his back was pressed into me. Despite his body threatening to betray him, Nick responded with a strong and steady voice. "Hello, Mara. It has been a long time. How are you?"

"Oh, perfectly well, thank you for asking," she responded airily, her voice equally calm. "Do you like the home you sent me to all those years ago?" She gestured in a sweeping motion to the room.

Swirls of purple and gold dust flitted about the room and after a few minutes, bits and bobbles of handmade jewelry and random household accessories filled the small tables and shelves.

I placed my hand in the center of Nick's back as I directed my thoughts toward him. *She's trying to distract you. To make you forget what she truly is now.*

The tick in Nick's jaw told me he'd heard me, but he didn't respond.

As if Ohanna somehow tapped into our mind link, a subtle green flicker emitted from her, and her warriors responded in kind.

"Your friends aren't very nice," Mara said, her eyes narrowing in on them. She stuck her tongue out as if she were in a grade school playground fight.

Still, we just stood there. What was the game plan here? We needed to advance and capture her, especially while she was toying with us. She always liked to play with her prey.

"I asked you a question, Nicholas. Who do you have with us today? I can hardly contain my excitement, for I think I know. And oh, what a sweet gift she will be." Mara cocked her head and took a step down from the dais, pausing on the topmost stair. "Although, it makes me wonder what I would need to give you in return."

Nick perked up a little, as if this was the 'in' he was waiting for. "Can you please reveal yourself as you are now? It is a bit unnerving to see you as you were back when you were a weak, naive girl."

I wanted to pinch him right in that back part of the upper tricep that hurts the worst. Was he crazy? Did he want to anger the monster?

Her lips quirked to the side. "As you wish." I peeked out from behind Nick just as Mara made large sweeping motions of her arms, and the Mara I remembered from my nightmares appeared. Flames now rippled along the ends of her platinum hair, ash floating on a nonexistent breeze. She licked her marcasite-encrusted lips like a serpent ready to strike. Thankfully her eyes remained orange and not the bottomless pits of despair. I tucked myself firmly behind Nick. If it wasn't for Lana and Shai, I'd be racing out of here.

"I've made a few improvements. Do you like?" she asked, her voice giddy with pride as she swayed side to side, showing off her figure. The flowers on her throne awoke to their master and reached toward her, arching into a live canopy above the throne.

I watched as Nick's head bent low and traveled up achingly slow. I could only assume he assessed her from her toes to her head. But he stood strong, and I prayed his features mimicked Shai and Lana's, stoic and almost bored. The black, form-fitting gown sparkled, though I couldn't understand what light source made it do so. She did a slow swirl, and the back of her dress sunk so low, if it were any lower, we'd see a crack. A few strands of pearls were scalloped across her exposed back.

A cold mist began to work its way up my legs to my torso, continuing to my chest and out to my arms. Shai did a double take but quickly schooled his features. I opened my mouth to ask him what the heck he was staring at, but then the heavy weight of a crown and the pain of it digging into my scalp registered. I glanced down at my body and discovered I was now bedecked in a purple gown. So much for the gear that was supposed to protect me from enchantments.

Unperturbed, Nick continued. "We have a mutual enemy. We need your help in defeating them. After we are successful, you can be on your merry way back here to Beldam."

Mara turned and sat on her throne, her red nails clicking against its silver frame as she studied him.

"And what if I'm not interested in working for Cristes?"

"Simple. We leave like we were never here," Nick replied, his arms extended wide in a display of peace.

"Liar," she hissed. Her orange eyes flickered as she smirked. "You are not one for lying. You've never been very good at it."

"I am not—"

"Do not dare contradict me!" she snapped, effectively silencing Nick, though my guess was he was only humoring her.

"I have a better idea. Bring them in," she ordered, but to whom, I had no idea.

I turned my head to and fro, waiting for something to

happen, while everyone else's bodies vibrated with tension. And then...movement. Tiny pairs of orbs blinked to life and filled the wall space behind Ohanna's troops, who were spread around the perimeter of the throne room. The soldiers all took two long strides toward us, creating distance between them and the children.

Two green flashes from Ohanna, and every other soldier turned to face their new threat while the soldiers in between remained facing us.

"Tell Ohanna to stand down. Those are the children!" I whispered. I know Nick had asked me not to talk at all, but I could not let the kids be put at risk.

Mara sniffed, her eyes rolling in ecstasy. "Hello, *Princessssss,*" she hissed, her smile as serpentine as her voice. "*Missss* me?"

Nick took a step back toward me while Shai and Lana pressed into my sides.

Nick scoffed. "Well, this is a side of you I never want to see again. It is beyond ugly." His voice was ice.

Mara looked affronted but quickly wiped any emotion from her features. She feigned a lunge at me and hissed.

Nick moved back into me until I was fully pressed against him once again.

"Oh please. You three cannot stop me from taking her." She steepled her fingers. "I will tell you what we are going to do."

"Mara, this is a negotiation. I believe we can come up with a plan that is mutually beneficial." Nick turned to face me, his eyes widening at the change in my attire. Though he didn't look at me, he spoke directly to me in the way only we could. *Remember, I am playing a part. Do not speak.*

Nick grabbed me by the shoulders, jerking me out of Shai and Lana's hands, and roughly pushed me forward to stand in front of him.

Mara hissed more loudly upon seeing me and jerked forward. Her nails scraped against the metal of the chair, and I cringed as she struggled to keep the animal that wanted to tear me to shreds—her inner monster—at bay.

"You help us, and we give you the princess," Nick deadpanned.

"Nick, what do you think you're doing?" Shai growled.

"Saving Cristes," he shot back.

Mara took a minute to study each of us, her face shrewd and cunning. She licked her red lips, and where her tongue passed, tiny red jewels decorated the thin skin. "How can I trust you to hand her over?"

"Have I ever led you astray?" Nick asked. There was a challenge in his question.

But Mara didn't take the bait. "Yes. You should have let me take William that night."

Nick shook his head. "Think harder. *Before* the fall even and after. When I pulled you from that cave, when I took you from that cottage away from Melchior's wrath and when I..." Nick trailed off, and I felt his body stiffen. He cleared his throat. "I have always done what is right, and you know it."

She crossed her arms and tilted her head in annoyance.

"You said so yourself. I cannot lie. I will hand over Lydia personally when this is all over," Nick finished.

"But in doing that, would you keep up your do-gooder image of always doing the right thing?" she challenged, her pencil-thin eyebrows arched high.

Nick's jaw flexed. "One life for thousands. There is no right choice here, only the lesser of two evils."

I tried to pull away from Nick, his words cutting deep. I know he told me he was only pretending, but to use my own words against me? Words I'd used in Florida when I begged everyone to turn me in. I already knew it was the right thing and wished Charlie had done so. But I'd stupidly let them convince me that there was another way, that I, too, was valuable.

A quiet sob ripped from me and I clamped it down. It simmered, burning my throat and stinging my eyes. Nick gave me a gentle squeeze, but I tore myself from him. I know he meant to reassure me, but was it enough?

Mara sat back in her chair, wrapping one arm around her stomach and cupping her chin with the other. She snapped her fingers. "Bring them in!" she summoned no one in particular. "You know," she continued, her dangling foot swinging circles, "one might think that it would be utterly lonely living in Beldam by myself. Especially after you stole Alex and Jaime from me."

When Lana flinched, Mara laughed, a tinkling sound that grated on my nerves.

"Oops, I mean Charlie. I mean, I did raise him, so it's only fair that I get to change his name."

Lana lunged, but Shai was at the ready, wrapping his arms around her, pulling her back. She fought him, trying to free herself, but Shai just squeezed harder. "Not worth it," he ground out. "Not worth it."

"Someone is touchy." Mara smirked.

A door opened, and a beam of green light flooded through. I'd never noticed the door before in any of my dreams, nor had I paid it any attention until now. And that was probably because it was hidden in the wall itself.

And then three figures emerged, trailed by two larger ones.

Little sparks of stars entered my vision and swirled all around, increasing in number and velocity.

No! You will not faint! My body tried to ignore Nick's commands. *Liddy, you are a princess, a gifted warrior...act like it!*

Slowly, the stars started to clear.

That's it, lass. Breathe. You trained for this!

Nolan, Pree, and Justin were led into the room by two large men. Though I couldn't see a chain or rope, judging from the way my friends held their hands and shuffled their feet, they were tied up and strung together.

Breathe, Liddy, Nick commanded me again. *Just breathe.*

Thinking became increasingly difficult as I watched my friends being directed like puppets on strings by this witch.

"They are alive," Nick commented aloud, his expression blank.

I caught a trace of emotion flitting across Mara's face, as if she was hurt by his comment. Then she schooled her features.

"I figured they may come in handy at some point." She shrugged. "And would you look at that? They did."

In a blur, Nick was helping Lana keep Shai upright. Nick gruffly wrenched Shai by the shirt and tugged him close, then whispered in his ear. Nick pulled back far enough to level his gaze at Shai who nodded. Nick took a cleansing breath and was back at my side.

Justin looked dazed, like he had no idea if he was asleep or awake. Pree, though she had dark circles under her eyes, and was thinner than I'd last seen her, still looked ready to give someone the verbal smackdown of their life.

Nolan just stared at me, then at Shai and Nick, and back to me. I'd never before seen a hair out of place on his head. And now, his clothing was askew, hanging off his frame.

Pree strained to open her mouth but failed. Her body wriggled and her face reddened with the effort to speak, the veins in her neck popping, but no sound left her lips.

Mara cocked her head and smiled in Pree's direction. "This one really has something to say, doesn't she? She's a bit of a pain, but I admit this little parakeet has been quite entertaining."

Mara flicked her wrist and Pree fell forward, landing on her knees and catching herself with her hands before she could faceplant on the floor.

Pree raised her head to meet my gaze. "Don't believe anything you see. This is a tr—"

"Enough!" Mara screeched and without warning, we were all sightless. Panic seized me as I remembered the sledding hill with Will when we were younger, losing my sight and causing us to crash.

Ohanna's orders came both verbally and in flashes of brilliant green. "Protect the princess and fall back!"

I reached within and ignited my gifting, letting it flow freely from my heart and through my veins. Nick was doing the same, but Lana and Shai shone so brightly they were barely visible behind their shared brilliance. In response, all the warriors held green orbs of flame in their hands.

Mara advanced on me. The warriors shot their green balls of flame into the air. Once the orbs reached the ceiling, they burned bright white.

All of a sudden, Lana was in front of me, unleashing her gifting. It ricocheted off the white spheres floating above us and blasted a shield down around us. Mara slammed into it, mere inches from my face.

Up close, I could see every detail of her perfect face. Not a blemish, fine line, or freckle in sight. Unfazed by the barrier, she seemed to enjoy bearing down on me, goading me into action. Her eyes bore into mine as her nails screeched down the invisible barrier, the sounds raking down my spine.

"Charlie, now!" Lana ordered. I was over someone's shoulder in seconds, racing away from the witch.

Mara cackled and waved her arms in big sweeping gestures.

"Stop!" I yelled. But the body that carried me kept moving. "Stop!" I screamed again, letting my gifting come in a short burst until the person carrying me stopped— just in time to avoid being crushed by the doors that slammed shut in front of the soldier's face. The momentum from the abrupt stop sent me flying up and over his back. My side slammed into the closed doors and I landed on my butt with a loud thud. *Dang it!* That would hurt tomorrow.

"Are you alright, princess?" the kind soldier asked.

But I couldn't respond. Panic was an uninvited guest vying for my attention. *Not now, Will!* I screamed down our connection and it disappeared.

Mara cackled. "Do you all think I am stupid? I know when

parts of my magic are missing. I have been preparing for your return for a long time." Mara pierced Nick with her glare. "Give me the girl, and I will let you live."

Ohanna's warriors fanned out around the room, some trying to open the doors and guard me, the rest attempting to release Pree, Nolan, and Justin.

"Mara, stop this!" Nick bellowed, his voice amplified by his gifting, and the entire room shook. The floating orbs flickered and then died.

Mara's lips curled as if this was all hilarious to her. "Oh, Nicholas, you fool."

"I am no fool!" he roared, the ground quaking with its strength. Blue lightning sizzled over his entire body. He raised his arms, and with closed fists, he pounded the ground. An electric blue river snaked its way to Mara and wrapped around her, carrying her back to her throne. "You have always underestimated me," he finished, his eyes pure blue fire. "Always taken me for granted."

The wretched room was once again cast in shadow. The doors flung themselves open with ease, the warriors who'd been working on them diving out of the way. Charlie ran into the room, grabbed my hand, and led me toward the previously hidden door that I could no longer unsee.

"I tried to play nice. You will help us and the princess is no longer part of this deal."

"I knew it. You are just like him!" Mara cried, the flames in her hair smoldering.

Nick shook his head and took a step toward her throne, seemingly confident in his abilities to keep her magic muted. "I am not, and you know it." With a flick of his hand, he snuffed out the inferno that was Mara's hair.

The witch huffed, blowing a strand of hair off of her face that slipped out of its elaborate updo. "Whatever. Just tell me what you want."

"We need you to defeat the Black Roses," Shai chimed in.

There were no niceties now. Just blunt answers.

Mara considered him. She swung her gaze to Nick, then back to Shai, her eyes wide. And then she busted out laughing. Her laughter echoed around the walls and up the seemingly endless ceilings. Her body shook as tears streamed down her sculpted face.

Nick crossed his arms over his chest. "Are you done?"

"You can't be serious," she gasped. "They are still around?"

"They are, and they have been beating on Cristes looking for you," Lana responded.

"For me?" She blinked. "Now I know, beyond a doubt, you all have gone crazy."

"I do not think Melchior would think us crazy," Nick growled.

Mara exhaled forcefully.

Nick clenched his hands into fists. "You weren't so flippant about him once. And I think he still believes you are betrothed to him."

Mara gagged and physically jerked as if she were throwing up.

"Regardless, Cristes has been under attack since you broke her atmospheric dome, with Melchior at the helm of the rebellion," Lana barked.

Mara wiped the tears from her eyes. "Why? They would need the black rose, and we all know I destroyed it."

Charlie, who just yesterday paled at the thought of being in the witch's presence again, walked up to Mara with all the air of a confident king. Mara's eyes tracked him and shone with affection as he approached.

Slowly, Charlie reached out to touch one of Mara's sleeves and gingerly pushed it up. Mossy green veins climbed her skin, intertwining and forging a path directly to her heart.

Mara's eyes widened. "Traitor! After all I did for you," she spat at him.

Charlie carefully tugged her sleeve back down and looked at her apologetically for a split second before returning to my side.

"Thank you," Nick said curtly, nodding at Charlie. "Clearly, the magic of the black rose still resides in you, Mara," he observed. "Melchior believes we have it, but he is confusing the actual artifact with its essence in the capitol's park, where..." Nick swallowed hard. "Where everything came crashing down. Melchior wants Cristes under his control."

"That makes two of us," Mara sneered. "If he thinks—"

"All the more reason to take him out. He is serious competition," Lana reasoned.

But Mara ignored her, keeping her eyes on Nick. "If I were to defeat Melchior, how can you be sure I won't stay in Cristes and rule it myself?"

Nick quirked his brow. "Well, it is because of you that I became well versed in using elements to enhance my giftings."

Mara pursed her lips. "Meaning..."

"Meaning that we would have an ironclad agreement that if broken, the consequences would be fatal," Nick explained.

Mara pressed her tongue against the inside of her cheek.

"Hmmm, that sounds awfully boring. We are in need of some merriment, don't you think?"

Charlie squeezed my elbow and began pulling me toward the door.

As if Nick's power were a mere ribbon encircling her, Mara took the nail of her pointer finger and sliced through the blue lightning. Her eyes glowed orange; she bit her bottom lip and waved. Then she clapped her hands and once again, we were thrown into pitch blackness.

Charlie had me halfway to the door before Ohanna and her team were lit up brighter than the Christmas tree at Rockefeller Center.

"Lydiaaa..." Mara's voice echoed over and over again, ringing throughout the entire throne room. Whimpering sounds sprang from all around as the temperature in the room plummeted.

"Mara, stop this!" Nick shouted.

A blood-orange spot lit up the center of the room.

"Ohanna! Grab as many children as you can and retreat, now!" Lana yelled. As Charlie led me across the room, I turned to find Lana donning the hooded green cloak she wore in my dreams. With her face now hidden in shadows, her eyes were like twin fireflies. She was in a fighting stance, a glowing sword in her hands, ready to strike.

"Not until Lydia is out of here!" Ohanna screamed back.

The glowing ember in the center of the room started to move as if it were a living, breathing entity, expanding on the inhale and shrinking slightly on the exhale.

Charlie abruptly stopped in his tracks. He turned his frantic eyes to me, pleading with me to understand. I gripped his forearm and nodded. I knew going into this that Charlie would choose me if I let him. I couldn't do that to him. I would not let him sacrifice all of these kids for me...again.

"It's OK, Charlie. I want you to choose them."

Tears filled his beautiful blue eyes, and he grabbed my hand and started leading me again to the exit. I yanked my hand away.

The blood-orange swirling hole grew larger and out stepped Mara, her hair smoldering as if it'd been dipped in fire. She twisted her neck to and fro, popping noises accompanying it.

Charlie desperately tried to move me, but I planted my heels and shook my head.

Liddy, what the heck is going on? Will asked from somewhere far away.

I clamped down on that part of our communication. I needed to focus my full attention on Mara. But I sent a quick *I love you* down our bond that I'd hoped he received.

"You fools. You cannot tell an apparition from the real thing?" Mara sneered.

She threw her hands out and everyone in her path nearly froze, many of the warriors with their arrows already nocked and trained on her. One arrow had managed to be set loose, but it moved at a pace so slow it was as if time itself had stopped. I trembled remembering how many nightmares I'd had where I couldn't run fast enough to get away from the witch chasing me.

Charlie grabbed me around the waist, but I thrashed violently out of his arms and screamed at the top of my lungs. "I'm right here, you witch!"

I Won't Let You Choose Me

MARA WHIPPED AROUND, her eyes hungrily searching for me. Charlie scrambled in front of me to block me from her view. But it was too late; she'd seen me.

Charlie spun around to face me. "Run, Liddy!" He jabbed his finger toward the door a few feet away. "I'll distract her as long as I can."

I shook my head. "I won't let you choose me, not again. Go, help those kids."

"No! I made a promise. I will not go back on my word." Sweat beads blossomed on his forehead.

"And I cannot let you hurt again. Not if I can help it." I sighed heavily. "You sacrificed too much for me already."

"And you think letting you die would hurt any less?"

I hadn't realized until Pree started so much pandemonium that she, Nolan, and Justin were so close to me. Pree's eyes were shining with tears that streamed down her face. Under Mara's spell, she was still unable to speak, so loud muffled noises and the shaking of her head were the only ways she could communicate.

Mara was almost to me now, her movements calm and composed, no longer resembling the insect she once reminded me of but that of a queen, albeit an evil one.

"I see you have wisened up over the past year." Mara paused about five feet from me.

Instead of answering her, I reached inside and called on my husband. Instead of violet igniting the veins of my body, white light, pure and brilliant, exploded from my hands, crackling energy ready to be released.

Mara hissed, shielding her eyes. "No! It can't be! You and William had the joining ceremony?"

I stood my ground, ignoring her question. "You refused Nick's deal, but I don't think you can refuse mine."

"Are you negotiating with me, *Princessss*?" she hissed.

"Yes."

"Very well, but could you dim your obnoxious light first? It's hard to have a chat when you're blinding me."

"That's too bad. Maybe you need to get your eyes checked. I think it's the perfect amount of light."

Still crouched and shielding her eyes, Mara spoke, frustration lacing her words. "You have sixty seconds to talk, or things are going to go downhill for him." She gestured toward Justin, who squirmed under her pointed stare.

It took all my inner strength to avert my gaze from my

old friend. The guilt of what he'd endured on my behalf was already too big a burden to bear, let alone acknowledge in this moment.

I focused my fury on Mara. "I will state it in simple terms so you can understand."

"Watch your tone, *Princessss*. Fifty *secondsss*."

Forgive me, I transmitted to Will and Nick simultaneously, then swiftly put my wall up, not giving them the chance to respond and talk me out of my decision.

"You will come to Cristes, as our prisoner, and help us defeat the Black Roses. You will release the children and my friends. After Melchior and his army are defeated, you will scurry back to this nightmare of an existence."

Mara opened her mouth to protest, but I flashed my gifting in warning. She shrank back.

"In exchange, when you have upheld your end of the bargain, you can take me back with you." Collective gasps echoed throughout the room.

"Critosi! No, Liddy!" Nick bellowed.

No one had noticed during the commotion that my swift blast of power unbound the people I loved in the room from Mara's spell that had them nearly frozen. No one had seen her approach, but suddenly Lana had one hand in Mara's hair, pulling her head back, exposing her jugular, and a sword at her neck. "Move, and I will not hesitate to kill you where you stand, witch."

Mara sucked air through her teeth, but I noticed her hand slowly moving toward the inside of her sleeve.

"Don't move or I'll blast you," I cautioned.

Mara rolled her eyes as if she were more annoyed than

frightened. "Fine. You win...for now. But I want collateral."

"You will have none," I snapped.

"Be prepared for a bloodbath." Her voice dropped and her orange eyes deepened to black. I had no desire to see the wicked monster she could transform into.

"Enough with the dramatics. What do you want?" I asked.

"Nolan and your friends stay behind, along with sixty percent of the children."

"No deal," Shai said, coming to stand next to me.

"I've got this," I told him before turning back to Mara. "Nick will create a binding agreement," I said to her. "I will be bound to you. That is enough assurance."

She scoffed. "*Pssh*, he's clever. He'll probably write in some loophole or figure out a way out of it. No, I need to know without a doubt that you will return to Beldam with me after we defeat the Black Roses."

Nick, I reached back out to him telepathically.

I told you not to speak! he growled. *Your husband is going to lose his ever-loving mind and probably kill a few of us.*

Just tell me what to do, I begged.

Put a time stipulation in there. When I create the bond, there will be a loophole, and we will have a plan 'b'.

"Well?" Mara narrowed her gaze at me.

I shook my head, then straightened. "I get a month after we defeat the Black Roses before I return with you, but you return to Beldam, immediately."

Nick continued through our mind link. *Good. Now tell her you will take sixty percent of the children and Pree. Nolan will take care of Justin.*

But I didn't like that. She always went after Justin first to toy with me. "And, we take sixty percent of the children with us now, as well as Justin. Everyone else I came in here with today leaves today...unharmed."

"Nicholas, you have trained this little pet well." She flicked her finger at Justin, and the glaze over his eyes vanished. "Now, if I could move without being decapitated, we could begin the contract."

Nick gave a curt nod. With a few swishes and flicks of his hands, the golden sand that glittered in the light of our combined power scattered, flittering round and round. The particles danced as more and more grains joined them until they formed into a shimmering piece of parchment and golden quill. Nick plucked them from the air, turned Justin around, and used his back to start scrolling.

"You can lower your sword, Lana. I'm not going anywhere." Mara spoke as if she and Lana were friends who'd only had a little squabble.

"Not a chance," Lana replied coolly.

"No funny business," Mara called out to Nick. "I haven't forgotten what you did, attempting to thwart my magic all those years ago."

Nick lifted his gaze to hers. "And I have not forgotten how you chose this path and forced my hand. I did what I had to do." He lowered his eyes back to the parchment. "Now if you'd stop talking for a second, I could get this finished."

Aw, snap! I thought to myself. Nick wasn't pulling any punches.

Minutes passed, the only sounds came from the quill scratching across the parchment and Mara's whines of impatience.

All the warriors had been released from Mara's control, but their bodies stood poised, ready for a fight in case negotiations went south.

I hadn't noticed Charlie slip out of the room, so I was shocked when I caught him as he returned to the throne room. An army of nearly one hundred children swarmed behind him, eyes full of uncertainty.

"Done," Nick said at last. "Liddy, Mara, you will each sign it now."

Mara held up a hand. "Not so fast. I need to read it before I sign it. Which I clearly cannot do, for if I move an inch, I shall clearly bleed to death."

Nick rolled his eyes.

"Don't roll your eyes at me, old man," Mara huffed.

"I have only a few years on you, though you are the reason I have aged more quickly than most of my kind," Nick quipped.

"I rather think that was your fault. You didn't have to meddle," she sneered.

"You forced—"

"Enough, the both of you! Can we please get on with it?" Lana said, frustration roiling from her.

Nick grunted his annoyance and beckoned me closer. We positioned ourselves in front of Mara, Lana's knife still very much still poised for attack. Nick raised his brows at Lana, and she released Mara's hair while moving the blade a few inches away from the witch's artery.

"I will show this to Liddy first so that she may read it, then Mara." Nick gestured to each of us as he said our names. "If you both agree, you will sign at your designated 'x'.

Understood?"

I nodded while Mara purred, "Oh, I like it when you use your prince voice."

Nick ran a hand down his face in response before looking to the ceiling as if Eira himself would rescue him. Nick straightened, unrolled the parchment, and held it in front of me. I began to read:

> I, Nicholas, master of the pact
> Declare a truce, this seal intact,
> This treaty signed, all worries cease
> Let our warring sides find their peace
>
> Mara Hellebore, friend or our foe
> Will stand with us and face the woe
> Defend Cristes against the might
> And join us in the final fight
>
> The Black Roses can no longer stay
> Their desires led them astray
> End their terror in ash and pyre
> And may their futile quest expire
>
> Against my charge thus you will be fused
> No spells cast, no elements used
> No magic or tricks shall prevail
> Lest this end in a tragic tale

For your love and support unwavering
To Beldam no hesitating
All of the children homeward bound
Our friends set free, all safe and sound

After thirty days of victory
and no seed planted in cavity
In Beldam the Princess must wait
In this new land, she'll face her fate

My eyes scanned his riddle, trying to decipher where the loophole was, but I also didn't want to linger too long and arouse suspicion. I gave Nick a stern nod when I'd finished my swift second scan of the document.

Keeping the scroll open, Nick turned on his heel and presented the parchment to Mara. She pursed her lips, her one brow dipping down as she scrutinized his face.

"Pen, please." Mara flicked her wrist and presented her open palm to Nick.

"Are you not going to take a moment to read through this carefully?" Nick asked, clearly curious as to why she was so quick to accept the agreement.

"Oh, I did," she jeered.

"Your mouth and hands will be bound during the signing. No last-minute additions here," Nick warned.

Mara bit her lip. "*Finnne.* I'll read it through once more."

Minutes passed agonizingly slow as Mara's head moved ever so slightly with each line she read on the parchment.

She flicked open her hand again. "Pen."

Nick handed her the golden quill. With a swish and a

flourish, Mara scrawled her name onto the contract. Nick plucked the quill out of her hand before the ink even dried and turned to present it to me. I grabbed the lightweight quill and scribbled my name next to Mara's.

As soon as I lifted the quill's tip from the page, it dissolved back into golden flecks, half of the dust cloud breaking off and surging toward Mara, the other half toward me. The sparkling dust churned around and around each of our right wrists. A cold hug settled over my bones, and I blinked.

Tiny particles of Nick's magic settled into my skin, leaving me with a golden tattoo that resembled a bangle. Mara and I were bound to each other. Just as Ariel was bound to Ursula, I was now bound to the witch of Cristes.

And I wanted to throw up. Hopefully, I didn't screw things up too badly. I shook my wrist out, and the cooling sensation of the magic jewelry adorning my wrist filled me with dread. A force, strong and insisting, pressed upon the boundaries of the wall I'd set in my mind, the one I'd erected to block out Will.

Did he know what I'd done just now? Because he'd been silent for a while, but now...now, it felt as if he were standing next to me, the electric pull of him invading every cell of my body, and they vibrated with persuasion—*Talk to me, please. Talk to me. I need to know you are alright.*

I cracked open the window I'd left within the brick wall guarding my mind.

Everything is OK, Will. We are coming home now. Can't wait to see you.

My chest heaved up and down slowly as if my entire body sighed in relief, but I knew it didn't come from me. I smiled in understanding.

I love you, Liddy. Please never leave me again.

Never. I could only hope to keep that promise after all was said and done.

"Time to go!" Ohanna yelled into the room.

Mara ran her hands down her dress, smoothing out creases that did not exist. "Will I be allowed to pack my things?"

"Nope," Nick said, grabbing Mara by the elbow. With a swish of his hand, a glowing envelope hovered in the air.

Keep Your Enemies Closer

S PARKS OF AQUA AND LILAC FLARED AND POPPED, forming a tight spiral. The same tinkling of shattering glass we heard on our arrival once again splintered throughout the air. I was only given the briefest moment to lock eyes with Pree. Fear gripped me as I feared I may never see my friend again. I mouthed, *Stay safe.* And then, I was looking onto the broad expanse of a familiar land covered in ice and snow.

A few soldiers thwarted Charlie's plans and entered first. They looked left, then right, and a signal glimmered off their armor. They nodded to Charlie, and he stepped through. Sunshine glinted off his golden hair as he assessed his surroundings before signaling to the children that it was safe to come through.

More warriors stepped through and disappeared behind

the edges of the portal. I wasn't sure why I was so darn nervous. I should be happy that I'd be seeing Will soon! Nick must have sensed my unease. He reached for my hand and laced my arm through his, shoring and guiding me into the portal with him.

I'd forgotten just how cold it was outside the wall, where the winds whipped freely, not caged by the wall of coquina and gifting. My hair blew back, my neck stinging from the strands that thrashed against it.

In the not-too-far distance, Charlie and the group of children had already begun their short trek to the sleds. Tia and Tannon were at the helm, along with Jack and a few other mushers bringing up the rear. Tia and Tannon waved enthusiastically at me, and I couldn't help but grin and wave back.

The sun shone brightly, the sky clear. All along the top of the wall, archers stood still as statues, the sun glinting off their armor, casting green specks in the sky and on the ground. Charlie reached the sleds, and his safety bolstered my hope.

We did it. We actually did it.

Nick and I faced the portal. Watching. Waiting. Any second now, Mara would enter with Ohanna and Lana. New guards arrived, handing off the reins of white steeds to the guards that still flanked us.

The second Mara stepped foot on Cristes, soil ignited a series of events I'd later learn were initiated due to the black magic that had lain dormant deep within the lands. The portal closed. A ripple pulsed from the ethers and into her body, her chin tilted up and back arched toward the sky as she inhaled deeply.

"I'm back," Mara cooed. She began to cackle, the same laugh that haunted me every time I closed my eyes. Every time, I had to desperately fight against the accompanying image—a mostly dead Will at the base of Arbolias Sang.

My body tensed so hard that I cried out in pain while a Charley horse, make that lots of Charley horses, drove a hammer into every single muscle. The pain crippled me, and I fell.

Nick caught me before I could crash into the ice. "Are you alright? What is happening?"

Simultaneously, warriors were on their horses looking for the perceived threat, while others had their arrows nocked and aimed at Mara. In fact, the entire wall of warriors had their giftings pointed at Mara now, slicing the air with green light. It looked like we were in a laser tag minefield.

"What?" Mara rolled her eyes. "I don't know what her problem is." She jutted her chin at me. "I can't hurt her without being killed. Besides, I literally just got here. Can't a lady stretch?"

Beads of sweat trickled against my forehead, and the salt stung my skin where my hair had superficially cut my neck. Nick placed his palms on either side of my face. "Liddy, what is—"

Drums. Louder than the first time I'd heard them, they rang out into the air, a battle cry full of terrible promise. Everyone's head snapped to the landscape dotted with ice castles.

Mara clutched her ears. "What in the name of Eira is that racket?"

Ohanna and Lana each grabbed Mara under her arms

and hauled her toward the sleds.

"Unhand me, you brutes," Mara complained. "I'm fully capable of walking on my—"

BOOM!

We all wobbled, trying to remain standing. The horses stomped their feet, growing anxious.

A black cloud rose from the hills of ice and drifted into shape from just behind the last of the ice castles.

BOOM! Solid chunks of Earth flung up from the ground within ten feet of me.

"Not again," I moaned.

LIDDY! Will screamed, and I thought my head would explode.

BOOM! This one came even faster and someone dove into me, covering my body with theirs.

"I got the princess!" the man's voice yelled out to his commander.

Liddy! What the hell is happening? Forget this, I'm coming to you!

No! I tried to respond to Will, but he'd cut off my link to him. Well, that was annoying. But then I'd remembered I'd done it to him practically the entire time I was in Beldam.

The feeling of a warm hug caressed my body. The agony I was in left me as quickly as it came, and I wiggled my way free of the warrior who had me pinned. I stood, alert and pain-free as if I hadn't been crippled by it seconds ago.

Nick scrunched his brows, looking me up and down. "Liddy—"

"I'm fine! We have to go!" A bright flash nearly blinded me. All I could see were spots as I tried to run in what I hoped was the direction of the sleds.

After a terrifying moment, my vision cleared. Warriors were again paired up on the horses. The steeds backed up toward the great wall as one soldier guided the horse while the other faced the battle head on.

A loud buzzing, like a thousand angry bees, whizzed behind us. I whipped around as arrows from Cristes zipped through the sky. Once again, they formed a net, shielding us from the oncoming slaughter.

Charlie and the kids were already at the gate, and Mara, Lana, and Ohanna raced not too far behind them. Nick and I ran after them, and Tia screamed at us, though I couldn't hear her words over the commotion.

She flailed, then slapped her hands down to her sides in frustration, hopped onto the back of her sed, and came barreling toward us. Her sled kicked up snow and it flew wildly, like a giant snow plow racing down snow-filled streets. But no. It was Tia, the best musher in Cristes, doing a U-turn at much too high a speed, though she remained in control the entire time.

"Jump in!" she screamed when she was close.

I sprinted, my legs moving faster than they ever had, so fast I thought they'd dislocate themselves from their hip sockets. I'd only have one chance to get into this sled. Nick kept pace with me, though I knew he could run even faster.

"Ready? Wait...wait... Now!" Tia ordered.

I jumped up and to the side, landing hard on my hip.

"Critosi!" I screamed.

Nick landed with a thud on his feet, his eyes crinkling with laughter. "Language, Princess."

"I learned it from the best," I wheezed, wincing as I sat up.

The battle raged, but it was behind us now. The warriors we'd come with and the ones that met us in the great void of space between the ice castles and the wall were all beating back any straggling magic that attempted to break the protective shield the soldiers on the wall continued to reinforce.

I groaned and lay back on the sled. "How'd they know we would be there?" I asked Nick.

"I am not sure they did. Maybe they have been camping out there since your return."

"Wouldn't we have noticed?"

He shook his head. "Not necessarily. True that would be a long time to wait at the border." He stroked his beard along his jaw. "But not impossible. We will investigate."

At last, we slid through the gates, and they slammed shut, clinking and clanking as giftings sealed them up tight.

The sled glided to a stop and Tia hopped off the back, rushing to my side. "Liddy, that was so awesome! You totally jumped like ten feet!"

I shook my head at how quickly she had picked up lingo from Mortalia. "I don't think so. The real wow moment goes to you, my friend! Did you see the way you manhandled that turn?"

She giggled and swatted my shoulder.

I opened my mouth to speak, but my heart sped up impossibly fast, and I clutched my chest. His presence was a balm to my soul, and my eyes searched eagerly for my husband. He came sprinting around the corner, his eyes glowing a dark green, his veins ignited in white.

I took off toward him. He skidded to a halt and opened his arms wide. I jumped and my chest smashed against his. I was now the koala prize clung to a pencil, though there was nothing skinny about Will. My legs wrapped tight around his waist, my arms wrapped around his neck.

Our lips crashed together, our teeth clanking briefly, but I didn't care.

"Eww, gross," Mara sneered.

Will stiffened, his muscles flexing, and a sudden desire to punch Mara coursed through my veins. I slid down Will and he crossed his arms, sidestepping in front of me to block me from the woman of my nightmares.

"Hello, handsome, so glad to finally meet you," Mara cooed a little too warmly as she exaggerated a curtsy.

A shadowed figure stepped into my line of sight, and they didn't go unnoticed by Mara.

That sickly sweet smile slid off her face. She slowly dropped her chin as she snaked her way into an attack position low to the ground. With nostrils flaring and eyes flaming orange, she hissed.

"Hello, Mara," the man's voice answered. "It has been a long time."

I Forgive You

WHAT WAS *HE* DOING HERE?

"You dare *ssspeak*...to...me?" Mara's voice was pure menace.

"Gavin, wait until we are inside," Nick warned.

But Gavin continued to walk toward her, his palms held out in front of him.

Someone stop him! I begged Nick and Will.

Mara cracked her neck, a movement that sent shivers racing through me. Will reached an arm back and moved me a few feet away.

"Not too close," Shai warned from off to the side, a green flame ready to strike.

"No, come closer, *loverrr*. It's been too long. Let me gaze into those beautiful eyes," Mara taunted.

Gavin took a few steps toward her and she lunged, her red claws aimed at his throat. But they weren't even close to reaching him. Both Shai and Nick held her back with their gifting.

"Let me go!" she screeched. "The bastard deserves to die!"

"And you would die right along with him," Lana reminded her.

"Gavin, maybe we should go somewhere private." Shai tried again to persuade his friend.

Gavin shook his head. "Mara, I need to tell you. And everyone should hear. I am sorry. I am so sorry for how things ended with us. I could offer a million excuses. I was young and distracted and selfish. I am truly sorry. I fully comprehend that is not enough. But it is all I have."

Mara fought against her invisible bonds, and when she couldn't break free, she spat at him. He wiped his cheek with the hem at his cuff.

Gavin continued as if Mara hadn't just disrespected his position. "I also need to say I forgive you. For killing my father, for our child, Ni—"

"Don't you dare say her name!" Mara shrieked. "You defile her memory!"

Gavin continued as if she hadn't spoken. "I forgive you for taking my fiancée from me and robbing me of a future with my fated match."

Mara straightened. Her gaze pierced him through to the bone. If looks could kill, Gavin would be dead...twice. "I didn't ask for your forgiveness," she growled.

"Nonetheless, I am offering it anyway."

"Don't you dare look at me like that," Mara snarled.

"Like what?" Gavin asked, his brows knit together in confusion.

"With pity. There is nothing to pity me for. I am stronger than I've ever been. And I'm so close to getting what I want," she added haughtily.

"No, there is no pity here. I...never mind. Just get better, Mara." With that, Gavin turned and headed toward the castle. I hadn't realized how quiet it was until Gavin's feet crunching through the snow seemed almost too loud.

Mara stood there, visibly shaking but attempting to conceal it by crossing her arms. "Whatever." She scoffed. "Where are you going to keep me?" she asked no one in particular as her eyes stayed trained on Gavin's back.

I can't say for sure if anyone else observed it, but her claws were no longer out, and the orange of her eyes faded from a roaring forest fire down to a simmering ember.

Loophole

I
N SILENCE, TWO BY TWO, we all walked into the castle except for Lana and Ohanna, who still flanked Mara on either side. Nick and Shai led us to the council room.

"What's this?" Will asked, bringing my hand up to eye level, our fingers woven together. He twisted our hands this way and that, the gold on my wrist glinting off the candlelight flickering in the halls.

I wondered if I could play dumb?

"Do not even try to lie to me right now," Will said, dropping our hands but keeping his fingers in mine. I opened my mouth to protest, but he cut me off. "Seriously. I could feel the excuses firing at me."

Mara giggled. "Yes, why don't you tell him, Lydia."

Nick stopped abruptly and massaged the back of his neck

before turning to face us. "Shai and I can take Mara from here. Why don't the two of you return to your rooms to discuss things? You can meet us when you are finished."

Will let go of my hand and crossed his arms over his chest, surveying my face. When I pressed my mouth shut, his gaze moved to Nick's, who mimicked Will's resolute stance, as if daring him to try and get it out of him.

Will looked to Shai, who merely shrugged. "You need to speak with your wife."

I grabbed Will's elbow, leading him past Mara, past a wall of glass with a view of the atrium, and finally, to our rooms.

Will held our door open and locked it behind us. I'd already taken a seat on our living room couch by the time he'd joined me.

He rubbed his hands up and down his thighs over and over again.

"Liddy, I am thoroughly freaking out. Tear off the band-aid. Whatever you have to say, say it quickly."

Closing my eyes, I took a deep breath in through my nose and slowly let it out. I looked directly into his eyes and told him everything from the moment we got into Beldam down to the gold tattoo embedded on my wrist.

Will sat there, taking it all in. He shifted his position slightly, resting his elbows on his knees and cradling his head in his hands. He remained utterly motionless for what seemed like an eternity, and my own worry started to creep in. I had expected him to question my sanity and motives, perhaps even to erupt in a burst out of loud exclamations born of fear at the thought of how being bound to Mara might end. But, no. He simply sat there, so still, it was as if I'd 'Medusa-ed' him.

I touched his shoulder. "Will? What are you thinking?" But I felt nothing from him, nothing down our bond, either, except numbness.

A ripple of emotion tried to break through, and a few tears slipped down Will's cheeks. He closed his eyes and mortared a few more bricks in his wall for good measure.

When thirty minutes passed and Will still hadn't moved, panic seized me. *Did I break my husband?*

"Will, I'm sorry," I said again for the hundredth time. "Be mad at me, hate me, something, anything but this. Please do not shut me out." And still, Will sat there, unmoving. "Please." My voice quivered, and my throat ached with the imprisonment of the tears hammering on the walls to break free.

I moved Will's hands, and he let me, but he wouldn't look at me as I climbed into his lap. With a knee on either side of his hips, I wrapped my arms around his neck, resting my head on his shoulder, and sobbed. I don't know how long I cried for but eventually, Will responded.

He squeezed me lightly at first, but when I sobbed harder in response, he tightened his embrace. "Why are you crying?" he asked, slightly rocking me now.

"I—" I sniffed. "I broke you."

Will laughed, though it wasn't completely devoid of sorrow. "I'm not broken. I was in the middle of a heated discussion with Nick."

"For over thirty minutes?" *Sniff, sniff.*

He wiped my tears away with the pads of his thumbs. "I didn't realize it'd been that long, but... Consarn it! How was I supposed to react to the fact that I have to get you pregnant, and soon, if I'm to help save you from Mara's clutches?"

I froze. My ovaries may have done a little happy dance, but they would need to simmer the heck down right now.

I laughed, then paused to think about it again, and then I laughed some more. So hard, in fact, my body shook with it. Will did not join in, eyeing me as if I'd finally lost it. When I could finally speak again, I asked, "Why on earth would you think I need to get pregnant? Literally, nothing implied—"

"It's either pregnancy, or I have to willingly let Mara take you when this is all said and done." A crease appeared on his forehead as he tried to process his limited options. "And you know I would never let that happen."

"I'm still not following," I said, wiping the tears of laughter from my eyes with the cuff of my red sweater.

Will's strong grip on my elbows stilled me, urging me to grasp the significance of what he was trying to help me understand.

"Post victory of thirty days, if no seed plants...it's the loophole, Liddy."

First Comes Love, Then Comes Marriage

I SHOOK MY HEAD AND CONTINUED SHAKING IT, my movements picking up speed and vigor until Will's strong hands landed on either side of my face, holding it still. My cheeks squished under their pressure, causing my lips to pucker like a fish.

"You didn't know?" His brow furrowed.

"*DoesitlooklikeIknew*?" My words came out smushed together.

"Sorry." He released his hands, resting them on the sides of my hips.

"I'm sure you are wrong. How did you make the connection anyway?"

"Well, seed...planted." Will's cheeks pinked under the words and their implication. "I convinced myself I was wrong.

So, I mind-linked Nick for quick confirmation, and he sent me back an image of you very pregnant. And he may or may not have told me to get to work before blocking me."

My chin dropped, and I swear I could hear it hit the floor.

Will laughed, gently closing my mouth with the back of his hand. "If my body hadn't frozen in shock at the image he sent me, I think my chin would have hit the floor as well."

I swallowed. "Well, I have always wanted kids. I just didn't think it would be so soon."

"You want my babies?" Will waggled his brows at me. Thank goodness one of us was able to joke at a time like this. It eased some of the pressure sitting on my chest.

I smacked his shoulder playfully. "We don't have to do anything. There was a second loophole. Well, not technically a loophole, but we can work on changing Mara's mind."

Will's smile turned down at the corners. "That's a risk I'm not willing to take. I would much rather have a child with you than take any risk of Mara killing you. Besides, babies are a blessing."

"Yeah, and a lot of work," I said. "I'm only eighteen."

"Soon to be nineteen," Will amended as he grabbed my waist, his thumbs caressing my hips. "Listen, this is not ideal. As much as I would love to have a mini Liddy running around, I was looking forward to it just being me and you for a while. You know? Finally get some normalcy when this is all said and done."

"Thank you," I breathed out, my voice laced with gratitude and relief.

"For what?"

"For letting me in, sharing how you feel, and not trying to

convince me that having a kid is no big deal."

"You remember I've never been a fan of doing things because we have to," Will added. "So, just say the word, and I will figure out a way to make us disappear."

I shook my head. "Not this time."

"What do you mean?"

"You mean you caught onto the pregnancy loophole, but you didn't catch that Mara and I are fused...a.k.a. Bonded."

Will swallowed audibly and shot up from the couch. "I'll kill him," he rasped while he stormed off.

Thanks to Harvey, I'd become pretty strong in my upper body over the past year. I dove over the end of the couch and caught him around the ankle. He wobbled a little.

"Let go," Will growled.

"Nope! Don't be mad at Nick. He had to make it look ironclad."

"Fine." Will huffed, bending at the waist and trudging forward as if he were bracing himself through a wind storm, and started dragging me behind him.

"You're being unreasonable!" I yelled.

"I'm being unreasonable?" Will stood and stiffened. Every muscle in his body flexed to the point that his veins popped along his forearms and hands, green embers sizzling to life beneath the surface of his skin. "We're being cornered! All decisions are taken from us."

"What, now you don't want my babies?" I asked, trying my best to sound affronted.

This won me a small quirk on Will's delicious lips.

"Of course I do!" He lowered himself to pry me off his ankle, but I quickly wrapped my arms around his neck.

He squatted fully and wrapped his arms under my knees, swooping me up and bringing me back to the couch.

"We didn't have a choice," I pleaded. "I trust Nick, and this is his fail-safe. Besides, if you remember, I'm the one who had to go and insert myself by speaking. This is his way of protecting me so I wouldn't have to go with Mara."

"It's absurd," Will said, a slight frown tugging at the corners of his mouth.

"Exactly. So absurd, no one...well, no one but you and Nick, apparently, would even think to consider it a possibility."

Will gave me a tight squeeze. "I want you to have the life you deserve, one where we choose when we are ready for a family."

I grabbed his chin and gently turned his face to force eye contact. "Newsflash. Life is a lot of things, but fair is rarely, if ever, one of them. As I said earlier, we're already in agreement about wanting children. A blessing a few years earlier than anticipated is still a blessing. Besides, we are beyond privileged. Just think about how much joy a baby would bring to our family and all the help they will offer."

"Only a few years earlier?" Will cocked his brow.

I giggled. "OK, give or take five years on top of the few years."

We were silent for a long moment, but soon I felt a smile enter Will's face before I saw it.

"What?" I laughed, picking my head up from where it'd been resting on his shoulder.

"So, ummm, do you think we have to go meet Nick right now, or do we have a little bit?" he asked.

I stood from his lap and extended my hand to help him up. "We have time."

Pree: Stop Calling Me Old Man

"**W**HAT AREN'T YOU TELLING ME, OLD MAN?" I asked Nolan, thrusting my hands on my hips.

Nolan stood behind the black marble island in the small kitchen, prepping food for the week for us and the army of children. Previously, the children all took turns doing this, but Nolan had successfully kicked everyone out of his domain. Mara sure loved to put on a show in the throne room, but for the most part, we were left alone in our own quarters.

Nolan peered up at me from behind his glasses. "What do you mean, Ms. Pree?" he asked, acting like he had no idea what I was alluding to, but he couldn't fool me.

I pursed my lips and squinted at him. "Yesterday, when Nick and Liddy showed up here. I thought I heard you tell

Nick you had to tell him something."

Nolan's brow cocked. "Did I?"

"Yes, you did. In fact, you tried to tell him before Liddy opened her stupid mouth and got herself into a stupid contract, thus tying herself to that stupid witch."

"Please, tell me what you really think." The corner of Nolan's mouth twitched, revealing a hint of a smile.

"Seriously, I saw the panic in your eyes. You didn't want Liddy making that deal any more than anyone else did. You were trying to stop it, and you had information which could have."

Nolan shook his head and put down the knife he'd been using to peel and chop potatoes. He came to sit next to me on a high-back barstool. "I might as well share with you what I know. After all, Nicholas trusts you." When I gestured for him to continue and crossed my arms over my chest, he nodded.

"Right," he said, his gaze darting around the kitchen. With a quick swipe, he scrubbed his hands on the dishtowel draped over his shoulder. "I certainly do have information. It is possible this knowledge may or may not change everything." He hesitated, his fingers fretting his bottom lip. "Unfortunately, I could not have prevented Nicholas from crafting the bargain between Lydia and Mara, even if I had tried." He sighed. "Regardless, Nicholas has full control over his abilities and giftings, and I am certain he made provisions for the princess's safety."

I hugged myself. "Mara is sly, and she likes to make people feel and see things that aren't necessarily there. She messes with the mind, making you question reality. I wouldn't put it past her to figure out a way to make sure she gets to take

Liddy with her when she is sent back down here."

Nolan stood and headed into the walk-in refrigerator. He came out with his arms full of carrots, mushrooms, and onions. "Agreed," he said, placing the vegetables on the counter, preparing to chop. "She is very cunning. But Nicholas has always been one step ahead of her."

"Not always," I grumbled.

Nolan slammed the pot lid shut, and the sharp noise jolted me. "He could not have known she would take Charlie by accident," he said, returning to slicing the onions. "I stick to my previous assessment. Furthermore, everything Nicholas has done has been to protect those he loves."

Now that, I believed. When Nick showed me, Liddy, and Will his memories, his love for Mara rang loud and clear... crystal. I truly believed that he still loved her. His motivations were to stop her from harming others—especially herself.

"Gosh, you don't have to cry to make your point," I teased.

He grabbed the hem of his makeshift apron and blotted his eyes. "It's the onions!"

"Uh-huh." I chuckled.

Nolan began to wash the carrots and mushrooms in the sink. "What I am about to share with you, only one other person is aware," he said, avoiding eye contact as he spoke. With the precision of a master chef, he started to slice the mushrooms, the knife gliding through without any resistance.

"Mara's daughter, Nicole. She is still alive."

I stared at Nolan, my eyes wide and slow-blinking. My silence was enough to stun him. Everyone knows I always have something to say. But this? I was not expecting this. When I didn't respond, Nolan stopped his slicing and dicing to look at me.

"Ms. Pree, did you hear what I said?"

I blinked at him a few more times and forced myself to swallow. "Come again, old man?"

"The baby. She is still alive. At least..." His voice trailed off and his brows pinched together. "The last communication I was able to receive confirmed as much."

"How?" It was a loaded question, but Nolan seemed to understand what I was asking.

"As Nicholas showed you, everything was extremely chaotic in Mara's final moments before the protective dome over Cristes was shattered." He went over to the large kettle and stoked the fire underneath it.

"You saw baby Nicole die, but did you really?"

I opened my mouth to protest, but what came out was a little squawk as I was immediately cut off by Nolan lifting his hand to give me pause.

"The babe was mostly dead by the time I got to her. The black lines you saw following her veins were the dark magic of the black rose. By placing a sleeping spell on her, I was able to stop the poison from entering her little heart."

A flashback began to etch itself before my eyes. Will, passed out at the base of the colorful tree trunk. A faint rust-colored glow crept through his veins. Liddy screamed. I inhaled sharply through my nose, remembering the sickly sweet scent that permeated the air.

"So, it's clear you definitely had a hand in helping Nick. Together you designed the fail-safe mechanism in the magical tree room of his hobbit hole, ensuring everyone's safety by putting them to sleep."

Nolan scrunched his face, clearly not understanding my *Lord of the Rings* reference.

"To answer your question, yes, I helped Nicholas create the sleeping spell for anyone who tried to touch one of Mara's envelopes. And yes, the spell is similar to what I did for the baby. You see, she is in a sort of stasis, her growth and development completely frozen."

"Where is she? How come no one else realized she was still alive?" I asked, my words sounding more accusatory than I intended.

"I sprang to action and smuggled her out undetected to one the most gifted of healers in Cristes. Her name is Ruth." Nolan zoned out for a second as if he were remembering the day. "I have no knowledge as to where she placed the baby, only that she would do everything in her power to keep her alive while deciphering how to extract the poison."

"Why didn't you tell anyone? Even after all this time?" I screeched. "This whole time, Mara has been after my best friend and the love of her life, and you could have stopped it?!"

Nick gathered up the veggies in a towel and carried them over to the large pot, dumping them into the boiling water with a quick snap of the towel. He shook his head at me as he flung the white hand towel over his shoulder. "There are many reasons. For one, communication between Mortalia and Cristes was always difficult. Time passes differently in each plane, thus someone could send me an update and by the time it reaches me, the information is already out of date," he explained.

"Eh, not a good enough reason to keep it to yourself," I

grumbled. "Try again."

"There were many who would have allowed for the baby to die without aid." He grimaced, then wiped the emotion from his face. "She was, after all, the product of a woman who helped destroy Cristes as we once knew it. Telling anyone the baby survived was a risk—not only to the baby but to those harboring her."

I covered my mouth. The idea that someone would harm an innocent baby was too shocking to dignify with words.

Nolan seemed to understand my distress. "We did not have much time—infinitesimally less time than needed because Nicholas and Mara disappeared shortly after. It didn't seem pertinent to let anyone know what happened to the baby while Ruth and I attempted to treat her. However, an opportunity came my way to join Shai, Lana, and Brantley on their journey to Mortalia. We were tasked with helping Nicholas save Cristes."

"Yes, I gathered that part," I replied, tapping my foot in impatience.

"I made arrangements with Ruth to keep baby Nicole safe. Nicholas agreed to make the perilous journey once a year to deliver Christmas roses, and Ruth had a clever way of sending updates through Nicholas, who served as a vessel for us."

Nolan turned from the stove to the oven, opening it a crack. The scent of warm, yeasty bread wafted in the air.

"Are you going to ask me yet again why I did not tell anyone about the baby?" Nolan asked.

"I mean, I really want to, but your face is a little smug right now."

A laugh burst from him, and I pressed my lips into a hard

line to prevent myself from laughing with him.

"I told no one because there has never been a guarantee we could fully save Nicole. What would be the point in telling everyone, putting them and baby Nicole at risk, when I was unconfident anything positive would result? Also, Mara was volatile."

"*Psshh, was?*" I replied snarkily.

Nolan tilted his head in understanding but continued. "If she realized her daughter was still in Cristes, there was a substantial chance she would react in a way that would not only harm Cristes further but could also kill her child. This kept Cristes out of the line of fire and allowed me to help Nicholas and Shai whilst protecting William and Lydia."

"I see." I chewed on my lower lip. "Well, you get what this means?"

Nolan took the bread loaves out of the oven and placed them on the cooling rack, then slid off the oven mitts. He took the stool next to me and folded his hands in front of him.

"It means, old man..." I leaned in close to him, speaking in a low, conspiratorial tone. "We can't just sit here and wait for Mara to possibly free us at the end of some agreement that you and I both recognize is going to end with my best friend being Mara's lunch. It's time we need to return to Cristes, like I wanted to days ago. We need to tell everyone that Mara's daughter is alive."

Liddy: Strategy

"**W**HY ARE YOU BOTH ALWAYS LATE?" Mara taunted Will and me from her seat at the council table.

A few weeks had passed since we returned from Beldam, and still Mara seized any opportunity to try to ruffle our feathers. I opened my mouth to protest how we were told to meet when we were ready, but Will whispered in my ear, "Don't let her rile you up."

Nick nodded to us. "Glad you made it. Duncan, please alert the rest of our party. We are ready to begin."

Duncan nodded and hustled out of the room.

Mara sat there, her pointer finger's nail extended, the red talon scraping into the table's wooden surface.

"Could you please not deface the table?" Shai scolded. "It was a gift to their Majesties."

The nail returned to normal and Mara stuck her tongue out at him. "So is this what you all do all day? Sit in meetings behind the big bad wall and not take any real action?"

"Do not answer that." Nick eyed him.

Long minutes passed, during which my eye twitched every time Mara's nails rapped impatiently on the table. *Click-clack, click-click, clack... Click-clack, click-click, clack.*

Finally, Queen Nicole and King Klaus entered the room, Lana and Brantley on their heels. All wore dark cloaks concealing their faces. Upon entering the room, they stood by their seats and pulled their hoods back. Well, all except one. Though her face was covered, I recognized this last person as the queen, her purple sapphire stone glinting off her pinky finger.

I watched Mara from my seat as she stared at the one remaining figure whose hood continued to conceal their face. I braced myself. Mara had been here for a week now, and though we met just about every day, Queen Nicole had not joined us yet.

Nick had shared his memories in movie form to me, and I recalled how much the queen had cared for Mara. My muscles tightened in anticipation of them seeing each other for the first time in decades. Would Mara be indifferent? Or would she actually show honest emotion? Did she ever really care for the queen? She must have, naming her daughter after her.

Queen Nicole brought her hands up and with a gentle push, her hood slipped back, pooling onto her shoulders. I studied Mara, who didn't move an inch. Could she seriously not show any—there!

Try as she might to not react upon seeing the queen for

the first time, her pupils dilated, opening wide. This little involuntary movement provided the only hint she had any feelings at all upon seeing the woman who had taken her under her wing and provided her with every opportunity.

I expected anger to mar the queen's face when she laid eyes on Mara. I mean, the witch was responsible for her kingdom's desperate predicament. I would be beyond angry if I was in her position. But what I both saw and felt from the queen came as a surprise to me. Sorrow. Pity. Regret.

"Is everyone here?" Lana asked.

The king cleared his throat. "Those of us here in this room will decide how we proceed from here."

Queen Nicole noticeably swallowed. "Over the past week, since Mara has been with us, the attacks from the Black Roses have been increasing in both frequency and rigor. Mainly we have stayed patient, guarding our borders as usual. But they are not letting up and my people grow weary."

"What is driving them so hard?" I asked aloud. At first, no one spoke. Nick had previously shared the theory that they were attracted to the black rose's magic, which settled into the lands where Mara had her baby. But what caused the more recent, incessant attacks?

Mara bit her lip and turned to look out the window. "Me," she replied simply. Everyone was silent, waiting for her to continue. She turned to face us and sighed. "Well, it's no secret Melchior believed I was to be his...*pfft*—" She blew a strand of hair from her face. "As if he could ever own me."

"This is true," Nick growled, "but it doesn't explain their renewed strength and drive to get into our gates."

"Does it not?" she asked innocently.

"No, it does not," Shai interjected. "What are you not telling us?"

Mara fixed the hair at the nape of her neck. "Melchior used elemental magic to know where the black rose was at all times. He created a spell so he could always find it, and me."

"And since you ingested it, you basically *are* the black rose now, and Melchior will stop at nothing to have you."

Mara's eyes flashed at Will's words. "How do you—"

"Interesting theory," Nick cut in, clearing his throat. Clearly, he didn't want Mara knowing he'd shared her memories with us.

"Yes, yes...we are all familiar with what he wants. The reason for today's meeting is to decide how we want to proceed," King Klaus said. "We cannot continue to keep our warriors at the wall. They will be down and out by the end of the week. And then where will we be?"

A small giggle snuck its way from Mara. Everyone's eyes bore into her. *The nerve of her!*

"What?" She blinked. "The answer is obvious. If you fall back, the Black Roses will breach your barriers."

"This is not a laughing matter," Nick said sharply. "This is your mess. You are here, under contract, unless you have forgotten, to help protect Cristes from Melchior. A chance to atone." Nick slammed his hand down on the table and, though I wasn't sure if Mara faked it or not, she jumped at the sound. "I suggest you start treating this seriously."

"Or else?" Mara pressed.

"Or else we may need to offer you as a gift to Melchior and be done with this," Ohanna sneered, springing to her feet.

"And just hand them the greatest weapon?" Brantley asked.

Queen Nicole held her hands up. "Now, now, please. Though it may be chaotic just outside our walls, there is no need to invite the chaos in here."

"No, wait. That's not a bad idea," Mara said. She stood, and everyone immediately postured in defense, ready to engage in whatever magic or combat she would throw at us.

"What are you playing at?" the king asked her as Nick's eyes hunted her every move.

She squared her shoulders. "Offer me to the Black Roses."

"You want us to hand you over to Melchior?" Lana asked, relaxing from her crouched position.

"We can do no such thing, Mara," Nick growled.

"You wouldn't actually be handing me over. I would be—"

"The bait," I finished for her.

The corners of her lips curled, but she quickly flattened them. "Sure, if that is what you want to call me. Don't leaders have peaceful negotiations in the middle of combat sometimes? You should invite Melchior to meet with you to discuss my release into his custody."

Lana's eyes sparkled, something new glinting behind the surface. "Your Majesty, this is a solid start of a plan. If we can convince Melchior we have the black rose, something he wants very badly, and make him believe we would be willing to give it to him in exchange for peace, we may be successful."

"He may get angry when he sees we do not have the black rose and can only offer Mara instead," Ohanna said.

Nick and Mara scoffed at the same time, their eyes connecting for a brief moment before dropping their gazes.

"Actually, when Melchior discovers the black rose is Mara, he will be getting two birds with one stone," Nick explained.

"Or so he believes."

"What exactly would the terms be?" the queen asked, her face suddenly pale.

"Well, that is for you to decide. I'm just the bait, remember?" Mara said snarkily, though her tone lacked its usual bite.

"We have our terms." Lana crossed her arms. "We want the fighting to cease and for the Black Roses to give up trying to conquer Cristes."

"You have nothing else to offer them?" Will asked. "I mean, we are not technically giving them Mara, so what happens when Melchior discovers this? What then will we use for a ceasefire?"

King Klaus stroked his beard from his jaw to his chin. "The opportunity to see reason." His eyes flashed with a threat that sent shivers deep within my bones.

Nick: Baiting the Hook

MELCHIOR'S ARMY HAD BEEN BATTLING HARD against our forces in the void between the ice crystals and the wall for nearly seven hours now. The sun would be rising, and soon we would be leaving these gates, offering Mara in a farce of a negotiation.

I understood what my father implied when he said he would give Melchior a chance to see reason. Madness, complete annihilation, is what Father would unleash on the Black Roses if they did not cease in their attacks.

What my father nor my mother realized was how Melchior would be unable to resist the allure of Mara once he knew she was here. Unbeknownst to them, and with the help of Lana, Shai, and Brantley, I had worked to successfully diminish some of the protective wards around the wall. Not enough to jeopardize anyone's safety, especially with much of the city's inhabitants residing in the country, but enough for Melchior to better detect the projection of the black rose's power he so desperately craved.

We needed Melchior desperate—desperate enough to meet with us on the field in a brief moment of peace. So desperate, he'd willingly give anything for just a taste of the black rose's power.

I stood there, Lana on my left, Shai on my right, staring at the barricaded doors, waiting for a signal that seemed to never come. The wind was still blocked by the fortress around us, but I knew as soon as the doors opened, the gale would assault every ounce of my being.

My hand reached deep within the inside pockets of my jacket, gripping and then releasing each of the small glass bottles tucked securely away. The energy of the magic laced within the soil in those bottles set my nerves alight, and I forcibly tamped down on my gifting so as not to respond to it. These would be the first bargaining chips—pieces of the soil embedded with black rose magic in exchange for peace.

None of us spoke. Mara stood several feet away, guarded by Ohanna and a few others. Though she was magically obligated to follow through with the contract, no one dared risk not having her under lock and key.

But few realized—except for maybe Shai and Lana—that Mara's guards were all for show. If she truly wanted to, Mara would strike them down in the blink of an eye. In fact, when we came to Beldam, I was not entirely convinced she didn't just let us take her.

I turned my head when I felt the prickle of a stare at the

base of my neck through the high collar of my jacket. I turned to look at her, and her soft eyes bore into mine, luminescent behind the heavy hood of her cloak. Static skidded over my skin. I bit the inside of my cheek, forcing myself to resist moving toward her. *Thundernation! This woman will be the death of me!*

The sky lightened to cotton candy pink and yellow with a hint of orange, and I nearly lost my breath remembering how soft and innocent Mara's pastel-colored eyes were when I'd first met her, their multiple hues one of a kind and mesmerizing.

"Are you ready, Nick?" Shai asked, pulling me to my senses. Mara's eyes returned to their new, darker hue, and my jaw twitched. I nodded.

Lana raised her forearm, and a flare signal of pale green floated to the top of the wall. Within seconds, dashes and dots of light floated down in return.

"They are ready," Lana said.

Clink, clink, clink. The sound of metal clicking against metal tinkled in succession, grating my already frazzled nerves.

We braced ourselves. But the doors did not open just yet.

All at once, the sky brightened as if it were high noon. Sparkles of light shot out from all directions, raining down into the vast field between the wall and the ice castles.

Flicker by flicker, the giftings knit together and fell from view. Then our door opened, and we walked out into the frigid morning, our eyes set on the clear dome barrier at the halfway point.

Lana and Shai each held a flag. Lana's pennant waved

white, the color of peace and desire for cease fire. Shai's fluttered blue, indicating a formal request for negotiations.

Horses with Cristes warriors atop them would be trailing us, providing a quick escape should we need it. I was prepared to use my gifting to escape Melchior again, just as I did on the night he tried to steal Mara from me.

I shook my head, willing the memory to flee, and focused on the ice castles ahead of us.

The Black Roses stopped firing at us as soon as the doors to the wall opened and they spotted the flags. The only sounds as we trekked across the wide field were the ice creaking beneath our feet and the wind as it tunneled in our ears.

We reached the dome barrier and stood, waiting for Melchior to make his move. I turned my head ever so slightly to glimpse Mara. She was well hidden, her deep purple cloak enchanted to dampen the magic poisoning her veins. We would need to keep her body and face concealed until it was absolutely necessary. With Eira on our side, hopefully Melchior would stay ignorant of her presence for the meeting's entirety.

I turned to fully face the border of the ice castles and adjusted my stance, tilting my neck on each side to release the building tension. *Crack. Pop.*

Lana grabbed my hand in hers and gave it a little squeeze.

Without any pomp and circumstance, Melchior's entire army appeared from behind the castles. In a straight line stretching about two kilometers, all his soldiers took one step toward us at the same time. The ground vibrated with the impact of their boots.

In the middle of the line, soldiers marched forward, then

split, a well-synchronized machine. They fanned out, creating a short aisle exposing a tall figure in the center. The man moved toward us with paranormal speed. Within two minutes, the small group that encircled this masked figurehead was at the newly-erected barrier.

As if they'd choreographed this for months, they executed a series of movements with such precision and skill that I was transported back to the martial arts film Will had shown me a few years ago called *Mortal Kombat*. When the silence grew long and thick with dark and untrusting thoughts, the man removed his mask with a sharp metallic clasp.

I snapped my fingers, and my warriors flung the tent pieces they'd been holding into the air. The meeting tent plopped open as one full piece just as the protective dome came down. A coldness seeped into my jacket, having nothing to do with the temperature outside. Melchior's black eyes were cunning as he narrowed his gaze on me.

"May we have a word?" I asked. "It is about time, do you not think?"

I gestured to the tent, and we all filed in away from the cold.

I took my seat at the immediate head of the table. On my right sat all of those in my party, save for Mara and her guards, who stood off to the side. Melchior swaggered down the full length of the table to its matching head position on the opposite end and took a seat, his henchmen to his left.

"Hello, Prince. You called for this meeting. Now talk before I lose my patience," Melchior drawled.

I cleared my throat. "Yes. We want to negotiate a peace treaty."

A corner of Melchior's lip twitched. "I hope the façade of 'peace' is not why we are here today. You must realize I have no interest in pursuing peace."

I took out the bottles from my pockets and set them on the table, flicking my wrist over them. Their lids twisted off and fell to the table in a ripple effect. Melchior's eyes darkened, if that was even possible, and his nostrils flared as the black rose's essence danced in the air and over his nose. I smiled. "On the contrary. I think you will be very interested in discussing peace."

Pree: Plot Twist

"**O**VER HERE, OLD MAN... NOOO, RIGHT HERE!" I grabbed hold of Nolan's wrist, his appendage acting as my flashlight, and yanked further under the bed I was searching.

We'd been searching all over Mara's little gothic castle for more of those portal envelopes for the better part of a week now, coming up empty. Although we did stumble into some weird common room with these weird boxes resembling TVs from the '50s. Every time we saw a kid using one of them, they'd get this weird zoned-outlook on their faces, their bodies unresponsive.

Nolan and I'd since banned the room from use. The kids protested, scared that if they didn't keep to their scheduled hours, there would be consequences. But so far, they'd obeyed us. Now, their demeanor was much more playful and happy, their skin pinking up from the previous sallowness.

"Don't make me chop off your arm and do it myself," I said, overwhelmed with a sense of urgency to find an envelope.

Nolan snatched his arm back from me, and I was left in pitch blackness.

"What the heck?" I asked as I wiggled out from under Mara's four-poster bed.

"I am sorry, Miss Pree, but I am in charge here. I do not wish to be yanked about any longer nor threatened to lose body parts."

"Excuse me?" I asked, wiping my hands on my jeans. "But if it wasn't for me, we'd still be twiddling our thumbs, bored out of our minds. And you'd be driving me nuts with your incessant worrying about Liddy. You know, we wouldn't even be in this room right now," I argued.

Nolan rolled his eyes. "Are you quite finished?"

"Don't roll your eyes at me, Old Man."

"Nolan. My name is Nolan! Thundernation, woman. And, by the way, I only look older than my years because my stay in Mortalia has sped up my aging."

"Really? So, like, how old are you on the Mortalia scale?" I asked, genuinely curious.

"One hundred and twenty-two," he answered.

Oh, how I wanted to point out how my little nickname for him wasn't so far-fetched. But I reeled myself in. "And in Cristes?"

"Well, I believe our discoveries have shown that Watchers aged on average three and a half times more slowly than humans. Though our age increases the same as you."

"Huh?"

"What I mean is, every year we get older, just like you. We celebrate the day of our birth, just as you do. The only difference is that our life expectancy is around two-hundred and fifty years. So, my age in Cristes is thirty-five."

"But didn't Mortalia speed up your aging?"

"Yes."

"So are you one hundred and twenty-two taking that into consideration? Or—"

He flailed his hands. "What does any of that matter?"

"Fine, I didn't think you'd be so touchy. In any case, we need to case every inch of this bedroom again. An envelope has to be here, I can feel it."

"Alright. You can use my light gifting again, but remember your manners."

"Will do, Old... I mean, Nolan. Now, can you please shine the light under her bed one more time?"

My fingertips traced all along the frame of the bed, but once again, I got nothing but a scratch from a screw. I slid my body halfway under and swallowed thickly when claustrophobia started to rear its head. But I pushed through. I needed to get us to Cristes.

I felt along the center slats of the frame as well. Nothing.

I threw my hands up and yelled, "Help me out!"

"Ahem." Nolan cleared his throat.

I rolled my eyes at him, annoyed by his insistence of manners.

He raised a quizzical brow. "I saw that."

"No, you didn't. Will you please help me out?" I asked Nolan again.

"Look who found her manners." Nolan gripped me firmly around each ankle, and I slid out from underneath the bed on my belly with ease. Nolan proffered his hand and I took it. We both sat on the edge of the bed.

"Are you ready to hear where I think she keeps her prized possessions hidden?" Nolan asked, apparently not perturbed at all by the fact that we'd come up empty yet again, nor that dinner time was fast approaching and he'd be pulled for kitchen duty.

"Whatever." I scoffed and crossed my arms.

"Think about it. She chooses a form of correspondence as her portal, a correspondence that holds significant meaning in her life," he said.

"Yeah, so? We all saw how Gavin supposedly broke her heart with a 'Dear John' letter. Which—plot twist—was written by his dad."

"Well, where does one generally sit when writing a letter?" he asked with an eyebrow raised.

"I mean, if I was Sabrina the Teenage Witch? I'd definitely be writing in my bed next to my witchy cat, Salem," I said.

Nolan's brows pinched together. "I am not familiar with a teenager named Sabrina. But, either way, you are incorrect."

"Then Nolan, oh wise one, please share with me where you think Mara might write her letters."

Nolan's eyes shifted over to the shadowed corner. I followed his gaze and my eyes landed on a small makeup vanity, all smooth black with gold hardware. It provided the perfect amount of counter space to be able to write. I walked over to it and, upon closer inspection, I noticed a seam on the side of the mirror.

My fingers deftly traced the outline until they came upon a button on the mirror's edge. I pressed it and with a satisfying click, the mirror divided in two. I grabbed one side and pulled it open, just like my medicine cabinet at home. Inside was all one could possibly need to write and send a letter—a black feathered quill, a glass pot of black ink, red wax, a black candle in a gold holder, some matches, parchment, and white envelopes.

But I found no envelopes that were enchanted to portal us.

"Consarn it... I truly believed we would find some in there," Nolan said, peering over my shoulder.

"Consarn it?" I quirked my brow at him. "Since when do you use such filthy language?"

A loud rumbling came from within Mara's castle. Alarm bells blared for several seconds, then stopped. Nolan and I rushed out of the bedroom, sprinting to the rec room to help the kids. It only took us a few moments to reach it, but the room was empty.

"Throne room," I huffed out, my breathing heavy and stilted. My stomach soured as it pinched in dread. If Mara had returned, that could only mean—"No!"

I took off in a mad dash to the throne room, Nolan passing me and getting to the door first. He held it open for me, and my heart sank when the room came into view. The kids stood warily in their assigned positions around the room. I wanted to demand that they all go back to the rec room before Mara showed up, but understood why they wouldn't listen to me; the imminent threat of the witch was far more terrifying, and I couldn't blame them. Heck, even I was shaking.

A silence full of nightmares haunted the room. Two male voices echoed down one of the tunnels, arguing and getting louder.

Nolan grabbed my hand and gave it a reassuring squeeze. "I've got you, Preethi." Then his gifting lit him up.

I gave him a sad smile, knowing he was a healer and not a fighter. But I appreciated the man willing to stand up to this newest threat for me.

Nolan and I walked to the center of the throne room, poised to expect the worst. The heat of adrenaline pumping through my body centered on my neck, and it became unbearably hot. My eyes stalked the tunnel entrance to this room.

Two shadows approached.

"Come off it, Charlie. You can't be the only hero. You're just going to have to accept the fact that I jumped into the portal with you. Let me help, man."

I recognized the boy's voice, and I whispered his name a split second before he stepped from the shadows and into the throne room.

"Alex?"

Nolan's light immediately popped off like a blown light bulb. With quick strides, he was over to Alex and Charlie in a flash, and he flung his arms around Will's brother, lifting him off the floor with the force of his hug.

Charlie laughed. "It's good to see you too, Nolan."

I made my way to Alex, hands on my hips. His face triggered the not-so-distant memory of why I was even trapped in Beldam to begin with. You know how the taste of sour Lemonheads can cause an uncomfortable tingle in your jaw, right below your ear? Well, that's what this arrogant boy was. An uncomfortable, bitter thing in a sugared coating.

"What are you doing here?"

Alex's cheeks blazed red and he dropped his gaze, taking a step back from me.

Charlie broke from Nolan's hold and stood before me. He began to rub his arms.

"Are you cold?" I asked him. Nolan had worked his gifting to warm up the place.

He shook his head and dropped his arms to his side. "Hi, Pree, I'm Charlie. I've heard a lot about you."

"Likewise." I grinned. His return smile nearly had me dropping to my knees in front of him, bowed by his beauty. He was glowing, completely different from the boy encased in shadow the night I glimpsed him as he fell out of the portal and into the park.

Alex scoffed. "Same ol' Pree."

"Shut up, you jerk," I spat. "You don't get to speak to me like we're still friends." Anger demanded I turn my back on him, but I held my ground and continued, my voice cold and steady. "You broke my trust that night at the park."

Alex's head drooped in defeat, his hands balled into fists at his sides. A stark pallor overtook his face, a wave of shame draining him of all color.

Charlie placed his hand on Alex's shoulder. "Hey man, she doesn't know—" But Alex jerked away and stormed off through the door.

I crossed my arms over my chest. "What don't I know?" I may have been curious, but I wouldn't allow myself to succumb to an ounce of guilt over Alex's betrayal.

Charlie ran a hand through his blond hair and bit his lower lip. "Alex regrets what he did, but please know his time with Mara was not good. He fought her at first...a lot. It only gave her more motivation to crack him. Do you recall your experience here versus Justin's?"

I nodded, and my brain immediately conjured images of Justin huddled in a fetal position. His agonizing cries made me shiver as I recalled Mara forcing awful images and ideas into his head. He'd recite the details of beating Liddy and a future where he was never loved or wanted with a detachment that was heartbreaking.

Charlie nodded in understanding. "Some of us are better than others at staying quiet. Others are better at standing up for what is right. Those are the ones she digs at harder," he said, tapping his temple with his pointer finger.

Nolan pressed a hand to my back, and I suddenly no longer wanted to puke.

"Thanks," I whispered over my shoulder.

Charlie sighed. "Mara made lots of threats against him and his family. I get that you haven't seen him in over a year, so you can't possibly know how he's been trying to make amends. It's why he hijacked my portal here. He wants to help."

I dropped my arms. "Well, forgive me if I can't just change my opinion of Alex based on your words alone."

"I understand," Charlie said. There was an awkward silence as he peered around, hands in his pockets.

"Master Charlie, what are you doing here?" Nolan chimed in.

Charlie's smile was dazzling. "I am taking you all home to Cristes."

Nick: No Deal

"THERE IS MORE WHERE THESE CAME FROM," I informed Melchior as he snatched the bottles and lined them up in front of him.

He carefully took each one in hand, brought it to his nose, and sniffed. When he finished, he turned his gaze to me.

"You think I would offer you peace for some dirt?"

Some of my companions bristled and twitched, signs that they were about to react to Melchior's taunts. I immediately held my hand up to stop them, keeping my eyes locked on our adversary.

"You and I both recognize that those bottles hold more than mere dirt. I am positive you can feel their strong magic. You are practically salivating."

"Excuse me, bu—"

"Please do not interrupt. Many years ago, the essence of the black rose exploded over an entire area of land within Cristes. An area you have been drawn to, considering you have mistaken it as the actual rose all these years."

Melchior's nostrils flared, and his eyes narrowed to slits. "I have mistaken nothing. I know the black rose still lives. Your point?"

"The point is, we are prepared to excavate as much of that soil as we can, which may be limited due to the frozen ground. Nonetheless, the soil would be yours."

He smirked. "And what does 'Daddy Dearest' want from me in exchange?"

My fingers cramped from the desire to ball my hand into a fist and pummel his face, but I resisted.

"In exchange, you need to cease your attacks on Cristes... forever."

"How can I trust this will be done?" Melchior asked, leaning back in his chair and crossing his arms.

"I propose we make a binding agreement," I said.

Melchior thought for a moment, rubbing the cleanly-trimmed hair on his chin. "I think we're done here." His unexpected response caught me off guard.

"But we have not reached a consensus," I argued.

"You think me so foolish as to immediately agree to your terms?" Melchior snapped his fingers once as he stood, and his soldiers filed in line around and behind him.

I held my breath. He'd chosen to walk out on the opposite side he'd come in on. His new path would cross directly in front of Mara.

Three steps, two, one... I sighed with relief when he

passed her.

He came to an abrupt stop, his head arching back as he pulled air in through his nose in one long, deep inhale. He paused, shook his head, and took another step forward. Then, fast as a cheetah, he shot around and was standing in front of Mara, so close I am certain she suffered his breath on her lips.

"Take off your hood," Melchior demanded, a threat lacing each word.

Lana shot up from the table. We were prepared for this, but we had all hoped it would not play out this way.

"Excuse me," she barked, striding over to him. "You do not get to command my troops." But she was effectively blocked by Melchior's minions, who now encircled Mara and Melchior.

"Take it off now, or I shall take it off for you," Melchior sneered.

I hadn't expected to ever again appreciate the bond I once had with Mara, but there it was. Just a subtle whisper deep within our lost connection. The shivering of a young woman wrought with fear.

But steady hands reached up, red talons on full display, as she slowly gripped the edge of her hood.

"Back. The. Hell. Up." Her voice bit through every soul in the tent.

Melchior didn't move an inch, apart from the slowly spreading grin on his face like he'd just won a prize. It was enough to send me into a frenzy. In a flash, I flicked two Black Rose guards out of my way as if they were nothing more than annoying flies and was at Mara's side.

"You heard her. Back. Up." My words came out slow and

controlled, the 'p' popping on the last syllable.

Melchior raised his hands in mock surrender and took one step back. Mara promptly dropped her hood.

Audible gasps from the mercenaries of the Black Roses echoed throughout the tent.

"Hello, wife." His mouth twisted into a malevolent grin. "I would say I have missed you, but this new version of you is even more appealing…" He scanned her from head to toe. "I didn't think that was possible, but I have never been so happy to be so wrong before."

She gazed coolly at him. "I am not your wife."

"Ah, a little technicality we never got to remedy. But seeing as you are here now, I will gladly take what is mine." Melchior snatched Mara's forearm, pulling her close. In a flash, a blue flame licked from my palm, but Mara gave a little flick of her wrist, a signal for me to stop.

Melchior didn't seem to notice. His nose trailed the side of her neck, lingering at the pulse point, and I thought I'd be sick. His eyes widened, and then his lids dipped, heavy with pleasure.

It all happened so fast I did not have time to react. Mara slashed one hand down, cutting into Melchior's face, and he screamed, clutching the bleeding wound.

"I said, step back," Mara hissed, her hand raised, blood dripping from the tips of her talons.

Melchior and his team advanced, but Lana and Ohanna had a shield up in seconds.

"You Bi—"

"I'd be careful how you address me," Mara warned him. "And I am no one's property."

Still holding his cheek, blood seeping through his fingers, Melchior stood straight and turned to address me. "I want a new deal on the table."

"I will not discuss terms with you until you call your men off," I quipped.

Melchior held up a fist, and his troops relaxed. He returned to his chair and sat down, his cronies doing the same. He pulled a handkerchief from his pocket and held it to his cheek.

I returned to my seat and motioned to Mara to come and sit next to me. Thankfully, she obliged, keeping my authority intact, at least in Melchior's eyes.

"How did you know it was me?" she asked Melchior once she sat down.

His eyes were ablaze in black fire. "You already have the answer."

"Humor me," she drawled.

"We were connected once, you and me." He leered at her, tracing his lips with his wet tongue. "Though faint, my body still knows when a piece of me is near. I could smell and taste you all at once."

I know their connection was only surface level due to the dark elemental magic coupled with his gifting he'd used on her without her consent. But his insinuation... I bristled, and Melchior laughed.

"What do you want?" I asked through gritted teeth.

Melchior's gaze seared into Mara. She stared right back at him.

"I think you can discern what I want, Princeling," he said without looking at me. Instead, he licked the corner of his lips using just the tip of his pointy tongue, like a serpent too anxious to wait for death to taste its trapped prey.

"Since we are negotiating something so major, I do not wish to make any assumptions," I said.

He turned his head to face me and dropped the handkerchief from his cheek. Angry red gashes marred his chiseled face. "You can keep your weak soil. I want her, or no deal." He turned his gaze back to Mara and hungrily licked his lips.

"We are not in the habit of using Watchers as bargaining chips," I said, hoping to deter him.

"Good thing she isn't a Watcher, then," he quipped back.

Shai leaned down to my ear. "Nick, whatever trick you have up your sleeve, now is the time to use it. The air is becoming thick with his dark magic, and I am ready to pull you and Mara out of here."

I placed my elbow on the table, resting my chin against my fist. "No deal."

Melchior slowly dropped his chin, a wicked smile curling the ends of his lips, a little too high and wide. "Is that your final answer?"

"Mara is not for sale. Should you find yourself not agreeable to the infused soil I have presented, things will become a lot more difficult for you. You see, we have merely done the bare minimum in defending our borders."

Melchior scoffed. "I do not believe you."

"It is true. And as you are aware, we have never attacked without provocation. If you should refuse peace, my father will command his troops very differently once we leave this tent."

"Is that a threat, Princeling?"

"No...it is a promise."

Melchior stood slowly, his warriors following his lead. But I stayed seated.

"One more thing as you exit." I leaned forward, pressing my fingertips together. "You should have all the facts as to why you are probably so engrossed with Mara." Melchior raised his chin, and I quickly added, "Beyond your inappropriate carnal desires. Mara, if you would, please."

She looked at me, uncertain at first. But then, her eyes widened ever so slightly in understanding. She stood and wrapped her wrist around the cuff of her robes, sliding the fabric up to reveal veins blackened by Melchior's precious poisonous rose.

Melchior was drawn in like a moth to a flame. Bringing his nose mere inches from her skin, he asked, "What am I looking at?" Although he probably suspected.

"Do you wonder why your attacks have increased three-fold in the past two weeks?" Lana asked him.

Melchior wrenched his head up to look Mara in the eye. "What did you do?" he growled at her.

"I got rid of the black rose," she answered, her voice dripping with feigned innocence.

I tilted my head, giving Melchior a half smile as I gestured to him. "You have been attacking my country for all these years for no reason. You've been chasing a rose that doesn't exist." I leaned back in my chair. "Only its essence is scattered amongst the soil, but even more lives in Mara."

Melchior whipped around, and I refused to respond in a way that matched his anger. He pounded his fist on the table, a small crack slicing through a third of its surface. My entire entourage of soldiers were on their feet, ready to strike at my command.

I stood, forcing calm over my demeanor. "Here is my final proposition. You can have the soil and the black rose's magic from Mara once we extract it. In exchange, we *will* have peace, and the king and queen of Cristes will not destroy you."

Melchior screamed like a toddler raging because he didn't get the right colored balloon. The tent shook with its volatility. "Critosi!"

"This meeting is over. I expect your decision in the next forty-eight hours. Peace during this waiting period is non-negotiable."

I walked over to Mara and offered her my hand, which she accepted. Placing it in the crook of my arm, we exited the tent, followed by my guards. The moment we were outside of the tent, it disappeared. Melchior and his troops stood glaring at us, but we were already safely behind the shield, heading back to the castle.

Mara quickly slipped out of my grasp and hurried away until she'd gained quite some distance from me.

"This is good news! You've figured out how to extract the black magic from Mara!" Shai exclaimed, clapping me on the shoulder when we were about fifty paces from where we'd just vacated.

"No," I said, frowning deeply.

Shai looked around and then leaned in to whisper. "But you said—"

"I know what I said. But it changes nothing if I can extract it from her or not." I ran a hand down over my face. "Melchior won't stop until he gets Mara, with or without the black rose's magic in her. You heard him...he won't stop until he possesses her body, mind, and soul."

Mara: Why?

"WHY'D YOU DO THAT?" I barked at Nicholas as I threw myself onto the cream-colored tufted chair in my small quarters. I ran my fingers over the tattooed golden band traveling around my wrist, pretending to be enthralled with it. In reality, I was avoiding eye contact with him.

"Why did I do what?" Nicholas asked, sitting in the chair next to me.

Ugh, why must he sit so close? I hated how his very presence affected me. I hated the pure light he radiated, an uninvited guest knocking on the walls of my icy heart. I know he wasn't using his gifting on me. That was just who he was.

I steeled myself, fortifying my resolve, before looking into his eyes. Those little lines around his eyes threatened to make me feel something, but I wouldn't let guilt plague me. Sucking him into the portal to Mortalia was an accident. My magic was unstable; not my fault. I would not feel bad about how his life was stolen from him.

"Why didn't you just hand me to Melchior?" I asked.

Nicholas pinched the bridge of his nose and sighed heavily.

I matched his sigh, mocking him. "Do *not* act like I'm putting you out by asking such a question. We both know your life and role here in Cristes would have been easier if you let him take me," I pressed.

Dark eyes stared back at me. His pupils were so large they ate up all the beautiful blue—a blue so light and full of joy. Now, they threatened to give me frostbite. I leaned against the back of my chair, crossing my arms over my chest. If I wanted to, I could leave this place right this very minute, but I needed to be careful in how I expended my abilities.

After all, I no longer had the children to help me keep up my strength; it was a ticking time bomb. Most of my energy was spent keeping the black rose's poison from reaching my heart.

Nicholas's jaw twitched, and he dropped his gaze. Then he stood and went to the one small window that peered out on an abyss of empty, snowy fields. He braced his hands on either side of the window frame.

"Why couldn't you let me love you?" he rasped.

I froze. Of all the things I expected him to say, that was not it. I anticipated reminders of the bargain he'd conjured between me and Lydia. Probably a chastisement about how Melchior would use my power for his gains and demolish

Cristes. But I did not like this turn of events.

I shifted uncomfortably in my chair, and it betrayed me as it squeaked. Nicholas glanced over his shoulder, considered me for a moment, and returned his gaze to the window. For the longest time, he just stood there, not moving. Not uttering a single word, waiting for me to respond.

I hugged my knees to my chest. Resting my chin atop them, I finally found my voice, although I barely recognized its meekness as I spoke. "I've already told you."

He whipped around. "I know what you said."

Before I could process his actions, his fingers cradled my face. My vision swirled and when it righted itself, I was back in my apartment at university, a time I would give anything to forget, sharing my heart with Nicholas while I suffered in a pit of my own despair.

I should have let myself choose you. When I first met you, there was no question you were good. I also knew that you liked me and it scared me. I liked you, too. A lot. But you were special. That was obvious. Someone as special as you deserves the best. You were and always have been too good for me.

I moved my hands to cover Nicholas's, attempting to remove them. I didn't want to revisit my past, but he increased the pressure of his hands—not in a painful way, but enough to let me know he was not finished. He fast-forwarded to a few moments later in the scene he just showed me.

I was not fully into the relationship with Gavin when I found out you were heir to the throne. At that moment, it was clear that you were made for greatness, so I made the decision to go all in with Gavin.

I squeezed his hands and removed them from my face with more force than I meant. A shallow cut on his palm pebbled with drops of blood.

"Enough!" I panted. My body shook, recoiling at the weak creature I was in the moment. How could I let him get this close?

"Were your words true?" he practically growled at me.

"Are you accusing me of being a liar?" I leaned forward in my chair, my eyes growing hot with fire, my nails begging to rip open to talons and hurt him—hurt him like he was hurting me.

Nicholas was on his knees in front of me before I could blink. He grabbed my wrists and gripped them so hard, the force so unorthodox coming from him, I gasped.

"I have had many years to reflect on your words, Mara. Did you ever love me, or was everything you said just tinsel and berry excuses because you were afraid of what we had? Or was it because you were broken?"

I snarled at him, trying to wrangle my hands free, but he refused to let go.

"No, I forbid you to turn into a monster in my presence! You cannot run from me this time. You cannot use my status as an excuse, either, as you know I plan on forfeiting my title to William."

I snapped my eyes down, glowering at my hands now entrapped in his golden gifting; iron-like gloves refusing to let me change into the witch's claws. I studied his hands as they cradled mine, watching them bring mine up and over his head, my forearms resting on the tops of his shoulders.

His face was mere inches from mine, his peppermint

breath tickling my nose. My heart wanted to feel something. It reached out toward Nicholas, light tapping on the cement walls imprisoning it. But I could never trust my heart again. So, I did what I do best. I shut down all of it.

His eyes darted back and forth as he searched my face, but I gave him nothing.

"I promised my love to you, and you scorned me for another." He chuckled to himself, that deep rumble making my insides tingle. "I am probably the biggest fopdoodle in all the realms. You did to me what Gavin did to you. Yet here I am, completely exposing my heart to you again, knowing you could tear it to shreds."

I recoiled as if he had slapped me. "You dare compare me to Gavin? What he did...he broke me!"

He wrapped his arms around my waist, his head fitting between mine and the crook of my neck. His words caressed my ears as his deep baritone voice tried again to reach me.

"You broke me too, Mara." His whisper was a cool breeze on my neck, though his words somehow made me hotter. "I loved you, and for whatever reason, you chose another. Time and again, no matter how much love I showed you, you went back to another. Do you not see the similarities? How badly you hurt me?"

He pulled back, just far enough so we were forced to meet each other's gaze again. A single, crystal-blue tear slipped down his cheek. But he made no attempt to hide the evidence of pain from his face. I shook with the desire to take his hurts, but I couldn't even handle my own.

"By the look on your face, I have my answer. No, you have never regarded my heart. But you have spent the greater part of your life thinking only of yourself."

He slipped out from under my arms and cradled my hands once again. I peeked down, and his gifting no longer encased them.

Nicholas stood and walked to the door. Then he stopped and asked a final question over his shoulder, his expression pensive. "What has fear and revenge done for you? Will you continue to only think of yourself, or will you finally let real love in?" His eyes bore into mine for a long moment, searching for any sign of understanding. Then, he left.

I sat there, stunned, long after he left my chambers. Long after his gifting locked me in my tower of regret. Long after day turned to night. His words tormented me, haunting my thoughts without mercy. Was I truly as guilty as Gavin? And, did Nicholas really just say, after all I had done, after all I had destroyed, after all this time...he still loved me?

What in Eira's name did he expect from me? I was a horrid witch. I was never meant to be loved that way, and I sure as Beldam was no longer capable of love.

Nick: 24 Hours Later

"**C**OME IN," I YELLED DOWN FROM THE LOFT of my living quarters. When I heard the door shut behind the interrupter, I yelled again. "I'm in the library, Shai."

"How do you always know it's me?" he asked when he made it up the stairs and to the table where I was sitting.

I cocked my brown, my gaze barely lifting from the book I'd been studying. "Are you pulling my leg?"

Shai rolled his eyes. He knew my giftings extended beyond most Watchers'. Discerning the presence of the most important people in my life from a moderate distance was easy for me.

"You are a mess," he commented as he came to sit next to me. His movements were lively, as if he hadn't nearly died and spent the better part of the year in intense physical therapy.

I'd been up all night desperately looking for ways to cure Mara of the black rose's poison. But every few words I managed to read were eclipsed by the recent memory of her arms around me, her breath coming in tantalizing wisps across my lips.

I spent half the night raking my hands through my hair, tugging hard to pull myself back to the present. Of course, I was a disheveled mess. My hair probably stood on end. I am sure dark circles plagued my under-eyes. Why? Why was I incapable of letting her go? She did not deserve my love, but would it even be true love if she could earn or lose it?

"What do you want, Abishai?"

"Abishai?" He leaned forward in his chair, hands braced on his thighs. "Oh, Eira, are you alright? You only ever call me 'Abishai' when you are in a foul mood."

"Clearly I am exhausted. Nearly twenty-four hours have passed since we met with Melchior, and I am no closer to knowing how to extract the poison from Mara."

Shai scrunched his eyes and pursed his lips at me. "That is only part of what is eating at you, but I will not press you regarding your inner turmoil." He placed his fist to his heart. "You can tell me anything, cousin, when you are ready."

I nodded curtly and he dropped his hand inside the flannel button-down he wore. Tucked in his waist was a piece of parchment, which he retrieved and held out to me.

"In the meantime, your mother asked me to give this to you. Your father has called a meeting in the council room in one hour." Abishai leaned back in his chair, his hands tucked behind his head, his legs crossed at the ankle.

I took the blackened scroll from him and untied the silver

ribbon, setting a book on the corner of one end to keep the paper from rolling back in on itself. In silver writing that shimmered in the streams of sunlight through my window, I read the words of my enemy.

I, Melchior Bazin, agree to your terms of the peace treaty. I shall visit the wall, with a small contingent of soldiers, of course, tomorrow at four in the afternoon sharp. Any delays will be viewed as an act of war. Furthermore, I expect to be invited in for civilized discourse regarding the negotiations and formalities. Do not make plans to deceive me regarding what was offered, for that too shall be an act of war.

Sincerely,
Melchior Bazin
King of the Black Rose Faction

Post Script: I shall be utterly affronted if my accompanying gift to this letter is not accepted and displayed upon my arrival for the citizens of Cristes to enjoy. My greatest artisans worked their hands to the bone to sculpt her to perfection.

I peered up at Abishai. "What is this gift?"

He grimaced. "A huge sculpture of a Christmas rose bush growing between the pages of a torn letter, with one single black rose blooming from the center, taller than the rest."

"How could he possibly know about Mara and—"

"We cannot be certain." Shai shook his head and leaned back in his chair. "What happened between Mara and Gavin—

his breakup letter, her abuse of the black rose—it all unfolded at university. But there were many ears and eyes at the park on the day you were flung into Mortalia. His spies have always been everywhere."

Forty-five minutes later, Abishai and I made our way to the council room, but not before we took a detour. I needed to inspect this gift from Melchior myself.

I stood in front of the sculpture, my legs in a wide stance, arms crossed, my thumb and pointer finger massaging my chin as I assessed the details.

The marble statue was a monstrosity. The guards had the piece situated in the center of town square, directly in front of the fountain that no longer worked. The climate was far too cold to keep water flowing, thus a shower of frozen water became a piece of art all on its own.

Both the black and white stone of Melchior's gift sparkled delicately in the sunlight.

"What do you think?" Shai came to stand next to me after taking a lap around the sculpture.

"She is beautiful. Too beautiful, as if it's meant to be a distraction. Well crafted...and egregiously oversized." I removed the glove from my right hand, closed my eyes, and pressed my palm on the thick stem of the black rose. I immediately snatched it back.

"And?" Shai's face was scrunched in scrutiny. "What do you make of its aura?"

I stuffed my hand back into the glove, adjusting my fingers into their correct slots, and strode fervently away, back to the castle.

Shai ran to catch up with me. I grabbed him by the elbow

and, when I was sure no one spotted us, dipped into one of the hallway's alcoves.

"There is a great evil permeating the stone," I whispered. "My gifting cannot differentiate if what I am sensing is the stone itself or what lies hidden within the sculpture. But, I do know, as soon as the peace treaty is signed, we must destroy it."

Duncan greeted us at the door to the council room, taking our coats and gloves. "Your Majesties will be here momentarily, as well as the rest of the invited guests. Please take a seat," he said.

I stopped dead in my tracks at the sight of her. Mara was the first one there, with Cobani guarding her. As if she felt my eyes upon her, she looked up from her clasped hands. But the expression she wore was blank. Subconsciously, I reached for her, down the bond we once shared, but stumbled back from the sheer force of her slamming our connection shut.

Her champagne lips pressed into a hard line. I shook my head and continued to walk to my seat, taking the slightly longer route to avoid her.

Shai sat to my right, his eyes flicking between me and Mara. He leaned in to speak to me, but I stopped him. "Do not ask," I whispered through clenched teeth.

Seconds later, Will and Liddy entered the room. Despite all they had been through, their love shone brighter than the sun. Not literally this time, as they had been learning to control their giftings. But one could not help but look at them and know beyond a shadow of a doubt they truly loved each other.

I never regretted, not for one second, bringing them

back together when I did. However, I sympathized with how difficult their journey was and the immense pressure they had to ensure. And now? The pressure handle was cranked up as far as it could go now that they needed to start a family.

Time was a commodity I did not have back in that cavernous space Mara called her throne room. A baby was the only thought I could conjure in the spur of the moment. The best chance I had at saving Liddy was making her a mother-to-be; it was the only thing I believed that could reach inside Mara's stone heart and break it just enough to allow a sliver of compassion through. Perhaps enough to spare Liddy's life. I prayed to Eira they would not begrudge me for too long.

Nick, is everything OK? Liddy's voice echoed through my head, obliterating my thoughts.

I smiled up at her as she handed her coat to Duncan. But I knew she didn't miss how it did not reach my eyes. I stood to greet them and replied to her in my mind. *I am fine. Just tired from staying up late researching.*

Will and I bowed to one another in greeting, but as soon as I righted myself, Liddy wrapped me in a hug. She held me tight until I relaxed a little in her arms. Her gifting flowed through her, seemingly much stronger than I remembered, but with a flavoring I couldn't quite place.

She pulled away before I could investigate further. Looking me squarely in the eyes, she gave me a single kiss on each cheek, then released me to sit in the chair Will held for her. She shook her head imperceptibly, and I knew Will had spoken to her via their gifted communication.

Shai leaned in again. "What am I missing?"

"Not here," I responded. I felt the tingle of Mara's gaze

upon me, but I ignored her. I had been playing both sides for too long. I needed to start doing everything and anything in my power to save Liddy and Cristes. No longer would I continue to attempt to protect a woman who never asked for, nor wanted, my help. And, quite frankly, she didn't deserve it.

But Mara would not be ignored. The tingle turned into spikes and needles battering my skin from the inside out. I clenched my fists, my jaw, every muscle taut with barely restrained agitation, and faced her. She flinched and quickly looked away. Good. I did not care if the burn of my pain, the sting of my decision to let her go, pierced her straight through. At least...at least she felt *something*.

"I apologize for our tardiness," Mother said to the small group of us as she glided in after Ohanna.

"Is this all..." I trailed off as Lana and Brantley came in on my father's heels.

Mother greeted me with a warm hug on the way to her seat. Duncan helped her into her chair first and then my father into his.

"We will cut straight to the chase," Father said, leaning his elbows on the table and steepling his fingers.

A soft knock on the door interrupted him, and his brow quirked in surprise. Duncan opened the door and when Gavin stepped through, my stomach dropped.

"I am sorry for my tardiness. I only returned to my home but a few minutes ago and glanced this invitation." He held it up for us to see.

Mother stood. "Oh, Gavin, I am so glad you agreed to join us. Come, sit between me and Nicholas."

He hustled to his seat, avoiding Mara's scrutiny. I peered

over at her and found she stared blankly straight ahead as if Melchior had his artists turn her into stone. But what did not go unnoticed was the claw marks that marred the table in front of her, her hands now hidden underneath.

Father nodded in respect to Gavin. "Right. As I was saying, Melchior's courier delivered both a letter and a gift to us today. We can infer from these gestures that my son was successful in getting the thorn in our side to agree to a peace treaty."

Mother stood with the parchment I'd returned to her this morning after I'd finished with it. She read its contents out loud for all of our benefits.

When Mother finished, I held my hand up.

"Go ahead, son," Father said, reclining slightly in his chair.

"We may have a slight problem."

Mother sucked in her cheeks, steadying herself by gripping the arms of her chair. "A big problem or a small obstacle we can easily overcome? We've already had the land gifters tearing apart the park to get as much of the topsoil as possible."

"Well, Melchior discovered in our meeting yesterday how Mara essentially is the black rose. He agreed to this peace treaty on the condition we would extract its magic from her."

"Why would he think we're capable of that?" Will asked.

"Because Nick said he knew how," Lana said, eying me suspiciously.

There was a gasp from somewhere in the room, and my mother slumped down into her seat, her regal bearing momentarily faltering.

"Why? What possessed you to offer such a promise?" Father asked.

I stared directly at Mara. "Because, even if I figured out how to extract the poison from her, which I cannot, it would not matter. Melchior wants her, with or without the power of the black rose in her veins."

The room went quiet, and I was the first to break my gaze.

"Does this mean we should prepare for war, Your Majesties?" Ohanna stepped up to the table.

Mother still had not opened her eyes, and Father stared off into the distance, his knuckles turning white as he fisted his hands.

Mara stood to speak, but I launched myself up to stand so quickly that my heavy chair fell back.

"Don't you dare!" I yelled at her.

"How do you even know what I'm going to—"

"You forget that I *know* you!" My eyes flashed and my fists clenched. "Do not pretend for one microsecond that you would sacrifice yourself for the sake of my people and me. You are more dangerous to us with them than you are here. He will use your power against us." I trailed my eyes over her body. "Amongst other things of yours he will use."

Mother's hands covered her mouth, but I continued, driving home my point. "Melchior is cunning. He understands that if we truly go to war, he will lose. But with Mara, he has a very good chance of wiping every Watcher from the face of Cristes. Or enslaving us when he usurps the throne."

"My son, you never had the intention of handing Mara over to them, nor the black magic within her," Father assessed, quiet as he processed all of this.

"Correct on both accounts," I responded.

"Then you have chosen war," Mother said, exhaustion creeping into her words. She inspected me, but for the first time, I do not think she saw her son but the king she wished I would agree to be.

I slammed a fist against the table. "I did not choose any of this!" I took a deep breath to calm myself and hung my head. "For most of my adult life, I have been cornered into making decisions others forced me into. Well, not anymore. Melchior has chosen war, and he started with delivering that monstrosity sitting in the square."

"What monstrosity?" Mara asked at the same time Ohanna asked, "What of it?"

"That is his contingency plan, his insurance he will secure the full power of the black rose. Once he has it, his power would be beyond measure."

Many brows around the table pinched in confusion.

"But I thought—"

I interrupted Liddy. "Yes, you and Will together are impressive, but we have no way to measure your power against another. We have to err on the side of caution and assume Melchior would defeat us if we gave him the most powerful weapon next to white lighter gifting."

"What of the sculpture?" Lana asked, trying to garner my attention.

I turned my attention to her. "I sensed pure evil emanating from the marble. The statue should be heavily guarded at all times. I would sooner destroy the thing but do not want to preemptively start a war upon Melchior's immediate arrival." I pinched the bridge of my nose. "As such, the monstrosity mocks us and should be destroyed as soon as tomorrow's meeting is over or the war begins. Whichever comes first."

Shai tugged on my elbow. "Excuse us for one second." He leaned in close. "If you had no intention of extracting the poison from Mara, why were you up all night trying to figure out how to extract it?"

I blew out a long deep breath.

"Abishai, there are no secrets at the council's table," Mother admonished.

Shai flicked his eyes back to me and arched a single eyebrow. "Nick had intentions of extracting the poison," he said, still staring at me, as if challenging me to deny his words.

"Nicholas, is this true?" Father asked.

"Yes. I briefly had intentions to do so because I wanted to destroy it completely, forever removing the threat it lords over our people. But I quickly realized..." I turned to glower at Mara. "...that I was wasting my time."

Her gaze was fixed on the table's surface, tracing the gashes her nails left. I thought I might feel sorry for how she flinched slightly at my words. But now, I only felt numb. I laid my whole heart out for her yesterday, and she still chose revenge.

Ohanna stepped forward. "Your Majesties, thankfully most of our citizens are still out far enough in the country. We should host the meeting tomorrow as if we are none the wiser of Melchior's intentions. However, in light of this information..." She trailed off as my father stood.

His face paled. "Well, it appears all hope and intentions for a smooth transfer of peace is lost. Tomorrow, we go to war."

Liddy: Welcome Back

I COULDN'T GET COMFORTABLE.

"Are you alright?" Will asked as he snuggled up against my back in the wee hours of the morning.

"Not really. A war is starting today. I may not understand yet how wars are fought here in Cristes, but the history classes you and I have both taken in Mortalia paint a devastating picture."

Will squeezed me harder, his body a soothing heating pad, and I sighed. The past few days, I couldn't stand to be away from him, my very essence so enthralled with him, climbing into his skin wouldn't be close enough. Tia said that was normal for fated pairings and that the bond would calm soon.

"We came up with a solid plan yesterday," Will said,

smoothing his hand over my hair again and again. "I think we'll succeed in stopping Melchior before he can raise his army. When we have him as our prisoner, there will be no war."

"We do have a good plan," I said, worrying my bottom lip.

"Correction, an excellent plan."

I reached behind me and swatted him. "Same thing. I just can't seem to stop these intrusive thoughts that something bad is going to happen to someone I love, especially you."

Will's emotions turned overprotective, and I stiffened. "What? What's wrong?"

He struggled to calm his breathing. I tried to turn and face him, but he held me tighter against him, one of his hands splayed over my abdomen, his nose buried in my neck. I calmed my own racing heart, closed my eyes, and poured calm energy into our bond.

When I could no longer feel his heart beating against my back, I asked, "Are you OK?"

"Sorry. I have no idea what came over me. I think the reality of you being in harm's way finally hit. The plan usually involves at least one or both of us being forced to stay away from the danger, and..."

I turned to face him and placed my palm against his warm cheek. "And this time, if trouble comes, we are tasked with facing it," I said.

"Don't misunderstand me, I do not fear facing an enemy." Will's hand slid over mine. "In fact, I would love to wipe any threat to my bride off the face of the earth. But knowing that you will be in the throes of war has awakened a side of me I never knew existed."

The green of his eyes turned so dark it was as if they were black pits. I shuddered, both with pleasure and fear, seeing the fierce warrior within come to the surface. I closed my eyes and nestled closer to him, my lips tracing their way from his jaw to his mouth. I planted a soft kiss and he readily accepted it.

I pulled away and his eyes lightened significantly.

"Will, we were born for this, we trained for this. Cristes needs us. We need to change our thinking. We are going to play our role of keeping Melchior distracted in the council room so well that this war will be over before you know it."

The corner of his lip quirked. "My, how the tables have turned." But his face fell almost immediately. Creases formed between his brows, and I rubbed my thumb up and down over them to smooth them out.

"What has you so freaked out all of a sudden?" I asked. "We were doing so well with talking through the Melchior situation."

"Yeah, but then you said it would all be over before you know it."

"Isn't that a positive thing?"

"No," he replied, his voice humorless.

"You lost me."

"Mara," he whispered. "We haven't had enough time to make good on Nick's loophole." The color in his face began to drain.

"I don't have to go with her right away. We have a little time." I tried to sound encouraging, but his fears were amplifying my own.

"I cannot lose you, Liddy." He leaned in for a kiss, but I

pushed gently against his chest and searched his eyes.

"You won't lose me, ever. I refuse to even acknowledge the thought. Because if you lose me, that means I lose you."

Will smiled warmly as he rolled over onto me, his weight resting on his arms, though I still sensed the protective beast that loomed below the surface.

He leveled me with his stare. "I love you so dang much." And then, he kissed me into oblivion.

"Wake up sleepy head," Will whispered in my ear. Steam billowed from the bathroom, and a few drops of water from Will's hair dripped on my face. He quickly wiped them away.

I groaned and stretched. "What time is it?"

"Five after eleven. You need to eat before we leave."

Will ambled around the room in his towel before disappearing into his closet.

I swung my legs over the edge of the bed but promptly laid back down. *Ugh, I need a little more sleep.*

Will came out of the closet wearing pants so dark I thought they were black. Until he walked past the window and the fabric hit the light, and an emerald green hue surfaced. He wore a white tank top and placed his dress shirt, jacket, and tie on a hook on the door.

"I need five more minutes," I whined.

"Duncan will be here in thirty minutes, and you said you wanted to shower."

I whined into my pillow, then forced myself to sit up once more. Will was right there, offering his hands to help me stand.

"You've been tired a lot," Will commented, and I sensed the worry creeping up in him. "Is she messing with your dreams again?" A flash of a nightmare entered my mind, and his body went taut, the veins in his forearms and hands swelling to attention.

"No. I haven't been dreaming at all. It must be all this stress." I smiled weakly. "I should just skip breakfast so we can hurry up and get today over with."

"No, ma'am." He shook his head. Haven't you ever heard that breakfast...wait, it's closer to lunch now. Ah, whatever, haven't you ever heard that brunch is the most important meal of the day?"

Right on schedule, Duncan arrived with my food. Will sat across from me at our breakfast nook, filling the silence by going over the day's game plan once again while I played with the food on my plate.

"Are you sure you're feeling alright? Maybe we should call a healer to come to do a quick scan," Will said, biting into a crispy piece of bacon.

"I'll be OK. I think it's just nerves."

"I'm not getting that vibe from you." Will scrutinized my face and looked me up and down.

"Well, maybe the nausea is made worse by the nerves. Either way, there is a lot riding on today."

Will reached over and grabbed my hand. "I'll be right here every step of the way. We are in this together, forever and always."

"Thank you," I said with a smile.

"You're welcome, beautiful." Will bit his lip.

I forced myself to take a bite of my scrambled eggs.

Will watched me carefully as he bit into his sandwich. "Oh, I almost forgot. We received a message early this morning that Queen Nicole would like us in the council room an hour early."

I nodded. "I expected as much. She probably only wants to make extra sure we have ample time to prep, especially if Melchior were to arrive early."

Will and I left our quarters dressed in winter gear. On our way to the council room, we stopped by Melchior's gifted sculpture. At least thirty guards surrounded it. They parted, allowing us to get closer to the monstrous structure.

"Your Majesties," the guard in charge, Cobani, said, bowing the Cristes salute. We took another step forward, but his hand shot out. "That is quite close enough. We are under specific orders not to let anyone within six feet of it."

I nodded in understanding and turned to look at the sculpture. Immediately my stomach clenched, and I clung to Will, wrapping my arms around his waist and pressing my face to his chest.

Will swiftly guided me away and back into the corridor of the castle.

I sighed in relief when the sinister coils of a threatening evil left my body.

"Did you feel that?" I asked him.

"No, but I felt enough from you to get us the heck away from that thing." Will's jaw clenched.

We were almost to the council room when I stopped abruptly.

"What is it?" he asked me.

"You don't think that gift is like a Trojan horse, do you?"

The idea terrified me.

Will appeared deep in thought as we continued on until a female voice stopped us in our tracks. "That is precisely what that is, most likely. I mean, come on, it's *sooo* obvious."

Will and I both stilled. I would recognize that girl's voice anywhere. But there was no way that was possible. Slowly, we turned to face who was behind us.

There, in the middle of the hall, stood Pree, with Nolan at her side.

"*Hellooo*? If you move any slower, your new nickname will be Mr. and Mrs. Sloth."

As if I were struck by lightning, I bolted toward her and nearly barreled into her, Will doing the same with Nolan. We switched, and I hugged Nolan while Will and Pree gave each other an awkward side hug.

"When did you...how did you..." With my emotions roiling, I couldn't form a complete sentence, and I was nearly shouting.

Will walked over to my side and entwined our fingers, offering me his strength.

"Shhh!" Pree pressed her finger to her lips. "We don't want to alert everyone that we're here."

"Maybe we should move this somewhere more private?" Will suggested.

Nolan nodded. "Excellent idea, Master William. There is a secret chamber. It is the last door on your left before you reach the council room."

When he'd only just passed me, he stopped mid-stride. As he turned to face us, his eyes glowed a soft pink. Tears of happiness filled them to the brim, and a single tear slipped down his cheek. But he didn't wipe it away, too distracted by whatever brought him to this moment.

"What the heck, old—I mean, Nolan? We don't have a lot of time here," Pree chastised.

He ignored her and walked up to me and held his hand out toward my lower abdomen. "May I?" He asked with all the joy of a child on Christmas morning.

I shrugged my shoulders, not understanding, but nodded anyway. After everything he'd been through, he brought Pree back to me. I would have given him the moon if I could have.

What happened next was not something I expected. He kneeled before me and, ever so gently, placed his palm against the lower part of my abdomen, his head bowed near my navel in concentration.

After a moment of silence, he peered up at Will and me, wearing a grin that lit up his entire face. "It seems congratulations are in order."

"No-freaking-way," Pree guffawed. "You've *got* to be kidding me."

Liddy: Salutations

TIME SLOWED DOWN, everyone talking and moving in slow motion. Pree practically shoved me through a nearby side door and into a little red room. Nolan made sure the door clicked shut, and then he helped guide Will onto a red chaise.

"I'm... I'm pregnant?" I asked, dumbstruck. But Will and I had scarcely begun trying. There was no way—

"Yes. You are about eight weeks along," Nolan said, beaming.

Pree slammed her hands on her hips, her head bobbing on her neck. "Well, Will. You apparently waited like no time at all before knocking up my bestie."

He'd been silent, still, unmoving in his shock. With no warning, he stood, picked me up off the floor, and spun me around, laughing in delight. His joy, mixed with relief, radiated through him, and I couldn't help but join in his happiness.

Pree curled her lips in disgust. "Am I watching a telenovela right now? One minute you both look horrified and now, you're, what... overjoyed? *Hellooo*, you both remember you're only like nineteen, right?"

Will set me down and knelt before me, placing his cheek against my lower abdomen. "The way you have been feeling recently makes so much more sense now."

"The loophole. All that pressure on us..." I trailed off, feeling its burden lift from my shoulders.

"So unnecessary." Will laughed as he gazed lovingly at me. "It happened on its own. Though how, I'm not sure. We were pretty careful up until a week ago."

"What! You planned this?" Pree yelled her outrage.

"Eira must have ordained this for you both. Salutations," Nolan said, bowing.

"Just goes to show you nothing is one-hundred percent effective." I giggled.

Pree balled her hands into fists and screamed at the top of her lungs. I clapped my hands over my ears. Will froze, his eyes wide with fear, and Nolan? Well, Nolan crossed his arms over his chest and rolled his eyes at her. I never thought I'd see the day.

"Well, now that I have your attention, will one of you please answer me?" Pree asked breathlessly.

"Pree, give us a break. The fact that we're pregnant has barely registered," Will said, looking a little miffed by her tantrum.

"Congrats on the baby, which we will definitely be talking

about in a minute. But I have been stuck in that hellhole for far too long and..." She trailed off, her eyes slipping over my face.

Guilt washed over me, and I could no longer hold her gaze.

"*Stahhhp*. I'm the one who told you to take Justin instead of me because we all knew I'd find a way out of there." Pree winked at me. "By the way, where is Justin?"

Will entwined his fingers in mine. "Until we have a portal that works safely, he is here in our countryside estate. The healers have attended to him, but he prefers to stay out of all of this and keep to himself."

"Yeah, poor guy might need Nick to take his memories before he returns to normal life," Pree said. "Mara certainly enjoyed messing with his head, making him see you die over and over again by his hands."

It was suddenly way too hot in the room. Nausea kicked into high gear, and I nearly tossed what little food I'd eaten.

Will took me in his arms and I nuzzled against his shoulder. Invisible, healing waves washed over me.

"That was already offered. He wants to keep his memories," Will informed Pree.

"Well, good for him," Pree deadpanned. "Now—"

"Pree!" I admonished.

Nolan sighed loudly. "You must excuse, Pree. She is quite impatient because—"

"Because we obviously risked our lives to travel here for a very important reason," Pree cut him off, grabbing my hands and leading me away from my husband to the red Chesterfield sofa.

I frowned at her as we sat down. "How did you get here, anyway?"

Nolan answered for her. "Master Charlie and Alex. They used an envelope portal to retrieve us. They are currently helping the children see that they receive food, shelter, and healer attention. Although, for the most part, their physical health is satisfactory."

"Only because Nolan took it upon himself to care for all of us, not letting anyone else help, the stubborn old man. Do you know he almost worked himself to death?" Though Pree sounded annoyed, her face was soft, holding a glow of admiration for the butler.

Will came to sit next to me. "Yep, that sounds like Nolan. So, what is this news that you broke out of Beldam to share with us?"

Pree locked eyes with Nolan. "I think you should tell them."

Nolan's eyes widened. He clearly didn't expect Pree to let him tell us the story. He leveled his gaze at Will and me. "We need to find Abishai, Nicholas, and their Majesties at once. They will all want to hear this."

Will shook his head. "I'm sorry, but today is just not possible. They are in the council room waiting on us...to start a war with Melchior." He checked the watch charm in his leather cuff. "And he will be here very shortly. We must be in position when he shows up."

Nolan cleared his throat, tugging at his collar, and I'd never seen him so fidgety before. "I believe I shall come right out with it, then," he said. "Mara's baby, according to my last correspondence, is still alive."

Melchior: Sneaky McSneakertons

THESE INFIDELS TOLD ME I was to be received in the council room. I didn't much care where we met as long as I got what I was promised. As I was led down the long corridor, all my senses tingled with the anticipation of what I would gain.

If all went according to plan, I could finagle an acceptable deal in my favor and avoid war. Not that I wasn't prepared to win, should it come to that. My troops would willingly give their lives for my greater purpose, as unyielding loyalty was a requirement to join the Black Roses. But I would hate to decimate the citizens of Cristes, as it would leave me with a much smaller workforce. Not to mention, far fewer of them to rule over and bend to my will.

Half of the best of my personal guard surrounded me,

the other half waiting for my signal within the rose sculpture. Should I not need them, they knew they'd have to escape detection on their own or kill themselves lest the enemy catch them. My armies were at the ready, strategically placed for battle, and I relished in the anticipation of it all.

I couldn't help the smile that slid into place when the council room doors came into view, armed by more Cristes filth. I was so close.

My senses detected the sweet smell of my precious rose that lived inside the woman I claimed as mine. Together, their alluring pull tempted me to break all my carefully-laid plans. But I would remain strong and patient. I was too close to having everything I wanted.

The Cristes guardians who led me through the halls and corridors aplenty, as if to confuse my sense of direction, at last brought me to the council room doors. The warriors stationed to guard our rear remained several paces away. I smirked. They were scared of me. Good. They shouldn't come too close.

I considered toying with them, slowing my final steps, but I was eager to get this over with.

I was about to pick up my pace when I overheard a muffled scream coming from somewhere near me. I stopped, my guard immediately halting.

"Keep it moving!" One of their soldiers dared try and order me. My lip curled in distaste, but I immediately schooled my features.

"Apologies, I need to tie my shoe," I said, my voice saccharine. Yule stepped forward, but I shook my head at him. "Roisin, dearest, if you wouldn't mind."

My faithful servant moved toward me, and I crooked my

finger at her to come in closer. I leaned down to speak into her ear. "Be slow about it."

She nodded and, with her front pressed against mine, glided down my body and dropped to her knees. The guards averted their gazes like good little soldiers, obeying my desires without me having to voice them.

I peered down at Roisin as she began the process of carefully unlacing my tall, black boots. She took her time guiding the leather laces, loosening the straps at the base, as if we weren't on our way to a world-upending meeting. When she could stall no longer, she began to lace them back up.

Before entering the castle, I had the foresight to sprinkle a little of the dirt Prince Nicholas had given me in the tent yesterday into my pocket. I took a pinch and rubbed those same fingers together, reciting an incantation. Immediately, my hearing was that of an alpha wolf, and I caught the words of a man from inside the council room.

"I believe I shall come right out with it then. Mara's baby, Nicole, according to my last correspondence, is still alive."

A new male voice cut through. He seemed angry. "Where is she, and why are we just finding out about this now?"

The first man answered. "That's complicated, but she is with a healer named Ruth. Are you familiar with her?"

Roisin finished, looking up at me for permission to stand. I caressed her cheek, my hands nearly vibrating with joy at what I'd presently overheard. "Well done. You may stand."

She returned to her post on my left, and I turned my attention to Yule. "I've changed my mind. Before we depart this afternoon, we'll be paying respects to the special gift I had delivered."

Yule nodded in understanding. And then we crossed the few feet to the council room's doors.

Liddy: Time's Up

THE BOMB NOLAN HAD JUST DROPPED stunned us all into a brief silence. When Will spoke, I could feel his skepticism warring with another emotion—anger. "Where is she, and why are we just finding out about this now?"

Nolan answered him, his demeanor calm, either unfazed by Will's emotions or expecting his response. "That's complicated, but she is with a healer named Ruth. Are you familiar with her?"

Will and I shared a knowing glance. "Yes, we know her," I said.

"Why did you keep this a secret?" Will asked again as he rose from his seat, helping me up.

"I promise he has exceptional reasoning," Pree piped up.

"Like I totally questioned him better than Columbo, I swear."
She flicked her ponytail off her shoulder. "But we really need
to get to this Ruth chick without being seen ASAP. If Mara
sees us, she might be angry that we didn't uphold the treaty
you made with her. Speaking of stupid bargains, Liddy, I
could—"

"Why?" Will cut Pree off, his face pinched.

"Why, what?" Pree countered.

"Why do you need to see Ruth right now? We're so close
to blowing Nick's plans and starting a war unintentionally, all
because we show up late to the meeting that's happening next
door. Can't it wait?"

"What meeting again?" Pree crinkled her nose.

I flicked my gaze to Will and back to Pree. "We're
supposed to be negotiating with Melchior. He's agreed to sign
a peace treaty in exchange for the soil that the black rose's
magic dissipated into when Cristes fell."

Pree's eyes bulged. "Melchior, the creepy dude we met in
Nick's memories. He's here?"

"Yes," I said.

"Well, when in the heck was anyone going to say
something?" Pree cried out.

Will guffawed. "We literally did when you first got here."

Nolan ignored Pree's dramatics. "And he agreed to peace
with so little to gain?" His lips pursed as he tilted his head,
looking skeptical.

"No," I said. "Nick may or may not have told him that he
was able to figure out how to extract the black rose's magic
from Mara. Nick inadvertently promised him that."

Nolan took off his glasses and rubbed his eyes with the

heels of his hands. "That parley" —he pointed to the wall that was shared with the council room— "is a ruse? I feel it will not end well. Have you considered the possibility that he will try to take Mara?" He put his glasses back on.

"Good riddance," Pree scoffed.

"No, Pree," Will spoke through clenched teeth. "If Mara goes with him, it would mean the end of Cristes."

"First of all, you don't know that," Pree said, but she couldn't hide the uncertainty in her expression. "As to the second thing—"

"But I do," Will interrupted her. "We all do. If Melchior gets a hold of Mara, he will be powerful enough to defeat us."

"But I thought that when you and Liddy got together..." Her cheeks tinted pink. "That you'd be, like, supercharged enough to stop anything in the universe, let alone Mara." She spread her palms. "So, hypothetically, you should be able to defeat Melchior."

Will scowled. "'Hypothetically' isn't enough assurance for me when it comes to Liddy."

"And if Mara decided to work with Melchior on her own, who knows the dark power those two could conjure," I added. "Luckily, Nick made a fail-safe in our agreement."

We all stood in uncomfortable silence for a moment when nausea hit me like a ton of bricks.

Will placed his hand on the small of my back, and a refreshing sensation with tiny little bubbles flooded through me, alleviating the sick feeling as they popped. "We have to get to that meeting," he urged.

"And we need to get to the baby," Nolan said, looking directly at me. "If everything goes south, she may be the only thing that keeps Mara from joining forces with Melchior and killing you."

"Nolan, you grew up here. I trust you remember how to get to the healing sanctum?"

He nodded. "Of course, but on foot, it will take us a while. Not to mention, we are not properly dressed for the weather."

"No, you're not. But we can help." I quickly shared the location of Will's and my quarters, where they could grab gear.

"Do you remember where the barn is?" I asked.

Nolan gave me a quizzical look. "May I ask why?"

"Well, it now mainly houses dogs. Go there and ask for Tia. Tell her I sent you and request she takes you to Ruth."

"Tia?" Pree inquired.

"My friend and the fastest musher we have in Cristes," I explained.

"We will leave first and distract the sentry long enough for you to slip down the corridor toward our quarters," Will stated. "I don't know how long negotiations will take, and assuming all goes well, we'll meet you both there as soon as we can."

Nolan bent his left arm up, covering his heart, his right arm crossing over it, and bowed. "Please be careful. I do not trust Melchior nor Mara at this time. Listen to your instincts to flee should the innate warning arise."

Will responded with a curt nod. He opened the door a crack, peering up and down the hallway.

He stood straight and opened the door halfway, ushering me to join him at his side. He stepped out and I did the same, hooking my arm in his. The door creaked behind us, but Will jolted his hand behind him to stop Pree and Nolan.

"Your Highnesses! We have been eagerly waiting for you." The soldier, Cobani, walked toward us, his face relaxing with relief. The other guard remained stationed at the door.

"Oh dear, I apologize," I said, forcing heat to my cheeks so I appeared flush. Will caught the hint and gave Cobani an impish grin.

Will reached his arm around my shoulder and squeezed me a little into him, giving him a wink. "Sorry, I took my new wife on a little detour. We aren't late, are we?"

Cobani suppressed a grin and cleared his throat. "No, you have a few minutes before the session commences. Let's get you in there."

We rushed a few paces, and the other guard held the door open. I bumped into him, feigning a slip of my heel, hoping it was enough to allow Nolan and Pree to slip away undetected.

We walked into the council room, and the silence was deafening.

Nick's eyes flashed at us as the guards ushered us to our seats. As soon as we sat, he spoke into our minds.

You both better have an excellent explanation for cutting it this close. You could have foiled our plans with repercussions far beyond your wildest of nightmares.

Though I so did not appreciate the lecture and wanted to make some salty retort, I also knew it wasn't the time, especially since he was just stressed like the rest of us. Plus, he didn't know what I knew. I responded quickly, *Nolan and Pree are here. They intercepted us.*

Nick's brow ticked up, but he immediately schooled his features.

Will added, *They are on their way to the healing sanctum.*

To visit Nicole.

Nick's eyes jutted over to his mother, his brows crinkled in confusion.

No. Mara's Nicole, I clarified.

Nick coughed, the sound loud and intense, echoing over the silence. Duncan brought him a glass of water, which he greedily gulped down.

I'd been so preoccupied with Nick I almost missed the prickle of someone's eyes on me. I searched the table, and my gaze landed on Melchior, his mercenaries dressed in all-black gear with silver hoods crowding behind him. Their backs faced their master so they could intercept possible threats. As soon as my gaze caught his, he tilted his head, his eyes darkening.

Goosebumps crawled up my arms, but I couldn't look away. And when he mouthed, *Hello, white-lighter,* the corner of his mouth quirked up, and my world momentarily tilted.

I forced myself to break eye contact, allowing myself to calm and take in the rest of the room. Almost every inch of wall space was secured by a warrior of Cristes.

A clock chimed, signaling the start of the new hour, and the start of our meeting.

Liddy: 1, 2, 3... War

THE KING AND QUEEN STOOD, holding hands, their eyes partly aglow with their white-lighter power. They spoke in unison. "We welcome you, Melchior, King of the Black Roses—"

"Thank you," he cut them off. "I'm not interested in formalities. I would very much like to cut to the chase. I don't want to be here any more than you want me here."

"And what is it you would like us to cut to?" the king asked, his voice pinched.

Melchior inclined his head and narrowed his eyes. "For one, Mara, my flower, needs to come much closer to me. She might as well be a thousand kilometers away, and I have no choice but to wonder...why?"

Nick stood, his chair screeching and nearly toppling with

the suddenness. But one look from Mara, and he sat back down. She gave Melchior a smile like that of a cat ready to devour the meal it had just toyed with. Without a word, she sashayed over to her enemy but stopped just out of arm's reach.

Melchior leaned toward her and inhaled deeply, then pursed his lips and scrunched his eyes in suspicion. Mara performed a mocking curtsy and turned, her hair fanning out around her.

"Halt!" Melchior whirled around.

The fake smile Mara wore dropped into a deep scowl. "You've checked out my assets. May I please return—"

Melchior stood swiftly and Mara flinched. "I am going to stop you right there. What was offered was not procured. The black rose's magic still lives in you. I have been deceived."

His hands dipped into his pockets, and my stomach dropped. I clutched tighter to Will's hand. My gut screamed at me.

Nick's gaze whipped to mine and Will's. *RUN!*

Neither of us batted an eye at the intrusion of his words. Careful not to look at me, Will used our mind link. *We need to drop to the floor and get out of here, NOW.*

Queen Nicole stepped forward. "I am sorry, but how dare you make such an accusation." Her eyes sparked as she clutched a fist over her heart.

Melchior gestured to the room, his troops fanning out on his side of the table as if they were one unit. "Oh, really? How do you explain Mara, then? The power of the rose still thrives in her veins when I was promised it would be extracted."

King Klaus straightened, his expression a practiced mask

of stoicism. "Is that not what you wanted? Mara and the black rose's essence?"

Melchior threw his head back and laughed.

Now! I yelled down to Will through our bond. We dropped to the floor and quickly crawled behind a partition, looking for a way out.

I peeked around the corner as Melchior righted himself.

"You must find me a fool!" He tossed the contents of his pockets, flinging black dust into the air. It suspended itself before darting in swirling patterns around the room. Everywhere it touched, the person jolted, then froze.

I paused, my mouth hanging open as I watched some of it land on Nick, and he froze. Will swung back around, grabbed my arm, and shoved me hard. I slid through the secret exit just before the black dust reached me.

Nick: Over My Dead Body

HALF OF MY LEGIONS WERE SPELLED, frozen against the wall before I could even stand.

Black dust speckled the air but stilled under Melchior's authority. He smirked at me before puckering his lips. Then he blew out a short breath in my direction, and the black sand raced through the air and over anyone else previously unscathed.

Though my physical body was frozen by his sorcery, I still felt my gifting just beneath the surface, lively and steady. I reached for it and succeeded in igniting it. My chest glowed brilliantly in its haste to protect my people, but my light only made it halfway down my arms before it was stopped.

My eyes were still capable of tracking, and I followed the movements of my parents as they jumped into action together. They threw up a shield around themselves and their immediate guards, Lana and Ohanna, and—

I panicked when I detected Will and Liddy's chairs empty. But then a shadow of a purple gown flitted from behind the screen, and I sighed with relief.

"This is an act of war!" Father shouted from behind his ward.

"Then war we shall have." Melchior held his hand up and snapped his fingers.

One of his henchmen procured a horn made of bone from inside his armored vest and blew one long, deep note that reverberated throughout the room and rumbled in my chest.

"Yule, Roisin, grab her...now!" Melchior barked, pointing his long, slender finger at Mara, who'd been one of the first spelled by the black sand.

My parents watched, helpless. The black sand pummeled against their gifting. If they were to drop it to keep Mara from his clutches, they'd be frozen too, leaving Melchior in complete control of Cristes.

As the guards that once tormented her advanced, she bolted in the direction Will and Liddy had gone. The enchantment did not work on her. She...she'd been faking it.

Mara made it out the door, but Roisin and Yule were close on her heels. I fought against the spell that restrained me, the portion of my veins where my gifting had ignited bulging and glowing a hot blue. But I remained a prisoner. I searched the room until my gaze landed on Shai. A subtle flexion of the neck and a slightly pinched expression, and I knew he was working his invisible restraints.

Luckily, Melchior had fixed his glare at his mercenaries.

"To your positions." He slinked my way from his end of the table, his swagger just begging me to punch him in the kisser. Melchior stopped in front of me and brazenly dismantled my personal space, invading every inch as he got right in my face. Shai was mostly free of the sorcery that encased him, his skin glowing a faint pink as he attempted to heal himself. The cords of his neck popped with the strain of effort.

"You may have kept her from me for many years, but she was never and will *never* be yours," he said, his breath sickly sweet on my cheek. A knife flicked out from behind his back so fast I would have missed it had I not felt its pressure against my stomach.

"What do you think—"

"Shhh. No need to cause a scene." Slowly, Melchior let the tip sink in a half inch. My eyes bulged as pain lashed my abdomen. My body jerked, the cold blade slicing a little wider, and my parents nearly dropped their shield.

NO! I screamed at them telepathically. Besides Will and Liddy, they were the only ones who knew of my gifting. Father was unable to speak to me in this manner, but Mother could.

Son, I cannot let him kill you! she cried.

I would have keeled over from the grief in her voice if I wasn't frozen in place.

"Now, I'm going to ask you a question, and you are going to answer it," Melchior said, his voice deadly.

He sprinkled some pink dust near my face, melting just enough of the ice-cold magic to allow me to speak.

I worked my jaw for a brief moment. "And if I don't?" I growled at him.

The blade sunk in another half inch. Blinding white

sparks danced in my vision, and I bit down the scream that lodged in my throat. "Where can I find Healer Ruth?"

I stared at him, not understanding how he could possibly know her or why he would want her.

The blade eased in another half inch. This time, I grunted against the pain, and black filled the edges of my vision.

Thwack! "Oh, no, you don't." Melchior chuckled darkly, the sting of his slap smiting my cheek. "You'll have nothing but time to sleep when I am done with you."

You have three seconds to stop this or I am ending him! Mother's scream echoed within the confines of my mind. Meanwhile, Ohanna slammed herself against the ward over and over, her oath-bound duties to protect the royal family flooding her system, but my parents would not let her through. She screamed at them, pleading, but her sounds were muffled against the shield's power.

"I will ask one last time," Melchior bellowed. "Where can I find Ruth, the healer?"

"If I tell you, you will just kill me."

He shrugged. "Maybe, maybe not." He ticked his chin, and an assassin appeared directly behind Shai, a knife poised at his throat. It was Lana's turn to panic behind the protection of my parents' shield as she could do nothing but watch her brother's life be threatened.

She glowed a green so dark it nearly snuffed out her light. *Mother, tell Lana I need her to keep her head.*

Mother stood by my cousin and forcibly put a hand on her shoulder. Lana stilled, and Mother bent to her ear and relayed my message. When Lana's eyes cut to mine, I imparted another message.

Tell her that no matter what happens, Cristes needs her, her warrior giftings, and motherly nature—a deadly combination—to avenge us.

I watched as Mother communicated this for me, and Lana acknowledged me with a curt nod. Then she sat, closed her eyes, and began to breathe. In and out, her abdomen filling and contracting, and I swiftly realized what she was doing.

Melchior continued, oblivious to the exchange that'd just occurred. "But if you don't tell me, I will make you watch as I kill your cousin right in front of you, leaving you with the knowledge that you could have saved him. Of course, you would cease to exist immediately after, but you'd spend eternity in Eira in regret."

The knife in my side was hard to ignore, nausea threatening to bring me to my knees. I feared any moment Lana's warrior ghost form would appear and catch notice. I cleared my throat loudly to keep the attention on me. "Do you give your word that you will not harm Shai if I tell you?"

Melchior nodded, the corner of his lips ticking up like he'd just won.

Words quickly spilled from my lips in an effort to protect my cousin, my friend. "Then say you promise to seal the contract."

"I promise," Melchior sneered. He called his guard off, but they were already watching our exchange intently, solely focused on me now, not noticing that Lana's second form— the darker warrior within her—had escaped the shield and come to play.

"Ruth is at the healing sanctum," I said.

Melchior tilted his head at me. "And where is that?"

"About five miles north of the castle's center."

He took a step into me, his hand still on the hilt of his knife, using his free hand to pat me on the head. "Good job. Now, I can't have you following me." He shoved the knife all the way in, twisted it, and tore it out. "Good boy."

I couldn't crane my neck to see if I was bleeding, but I could feel the blood soaking my clothing. I expected pain to ravage me, but numbness seemed to spread from the wound and I couldn't even move my hands to try and staunch it.

The world lost all color, everything before me painted in differing shades of gray. Melchior faded from my sight as he raced behind the partition in the direction Mara fled, Yule and Roisin trailing behind.

Nick: All At Once

As soon as Melchior vanished from the room, the black sand that had been moving around in the air as if riding a current paused in mid-air and then promptly fell, some bouncing off the ground before going totally still.

Then everything happened all at once. Lana's ghost warrior zipped through the room and engaged in battle, first with the soldier that held his knife to Shai's throat. Like a blur, she moved from mercenary to mercenary. My parents dropped their shield at the same time a blast of their combined gifting struck every frozen watcher straight in the heart.

A cacophony of swords and knives clashed in my ears, but my own heartbeat drowned them out. I surveyed my abdomen and dropped to my knees as blood seeped out and stained my shirt, the crimson flow spreading in concentric circles on my white shirt. My eyes snapped to Shai, praying he was safe, just as Lana's ghost slayed the man holding a knife to his throat. Shai broke free from Melchior's spell, jumped onto the table, and ran across it to reach me.

Shai laid me on my back. He ripped my shirt open, the buttons flying. The sight of an oozing hole in my abdomen threatened to pull me under. I turned my head away, watching the chaos unfold in front of me.

My parents' gifting was strong, and they decimated the soldiers of Melchior's armies that started to swarm into the council room. But then the light dimmed, and I realized Mother was alone in her battle.

"Son!" Father yelled to me, grabbing my hand. Sparks of gifting flew past my vision from every possible direction, exploding objects around us. "Stay awake. Stay with us." He whirled around to face Shai. "How bad is it?"

Shai peered at my father. His mouth moved. I could tell he was yelling by the popped veins of his neck, but his words did not register.

Abruptly, Shai and Father slid me under the large table and out of the chaos.

Bells tolled throughout the city, the warning Cristes used when we were under attack, though they sounded far away. I had no idea who'd been able to slip out and alert the city.

A hot, searing pain, followed by fierce pressure, invaded every nerve ending in my body. I ground my teeth against the pain. Beads of sweat trickled across my forehead and streamed down my back.

"Do not move. This is going to hurt," Shai cautioned as

Father knelt by my head and held me down at my shoulders.

I gave a pathetic chuckle as if I had not already endured—

White hot pain, a thousand times worse than before, stabbed my gaping wound. The pressure and tugging that followed felt as if I were simultaneously being crushed and stitched together.

I could not bear the torment any longer. I managed to eke out, "You have to get to Ruth. Mara's child, Nicole—she's alive."

And then there was nothing.

Liddy: Oh Baby

ANNON BROUGHT THE SLED to a sudden halt in front of the pink building, causing a spray of snow to fly up around us.

I had already spotted Tia's sled tied up at the side of the sanctum and hoped she'd returned back to the barn. I hopped out of the sled and turned to Tannon. "Hurry, you must return to the castle in case the others..." I trailed off, remembering the chaos Will and I had avoided by the skin of our teeth.

"On it!" Tannon bowed.

Will nodded at him. "Thank you." Tannon played a short melody on his wooden whistle and was off. Together, Will and I rushed into the doors of the sanctum.

It was the first time I'd entered the sanctum since my year of intense physical therapy. It was the first time Will had been back since we worked to heal Shai, the merging of our gifting too intense not to be noticed, even by those in other realms, and we were separated.

We pushed through the door and the halls were eerily deserted. It was quiet, too quiet. I comprehended how part of that was due to the fact that most citizens had been evacuated to the country and northern borders as a precaution. But the energy of the healing center was eerie.

"Where to?" Will asked.

"I'm not sure," I responded. I scanned the halls to my right and left, blinking, hoping my gifting would guide me.

Will grabbed my hand and faced me. "I have an idea." He leaned his forehead against mine and closed his eyes. I did the same.

His gifting sparked, then ignited. The healer portion came to the surface, its warmth blanketing me. Bright pink light illuminated behind my eyelids, and I wished I could see how Will glowed fully with this new color now that we were bonded and his gifting fully awake. My giftings reached out to his, wanting to combine with it. And when they did, an explosion of colors sprang forth. I was certain our powers lit the entire entryway and then some.

"Found her," Will breathed. I opened my eyes and met his gaze. He kissed me on the nose, took my hand, then took off down the hallway leading to the room that he and I had shared over a year ago.

"How do you know?" I asked him.

He didn't stop running but called over his shoulder. "I sensed her need— the baby. She's close."

We passed our room and came to a fork in the hall.

Though no sounds echoed throughout the halls, the air was thick with emotion. Will followed the curve on the left, past all of the exotic plants in every possible shade of green. That familiar fragrance still filled the air. Will stopped so suddenly I plowed into his back and nearly bent my wrist to breaking.

"Ow," I whimpered, dropping his hold.

"Sorry," he whispered back, his brow furrowed as he surveyed the wall of plants.

"What is it?" I asked.

"She's behind here. But how do we get in? There's no entrance."

I bit my lower lip and searched for a hidden symbol like Shai had in his house. White petals caught my attention. Like last time, they were tucked behind some leaves. I brushed the leaves back and the flower sprang, its petals uncurling, showing its magnificence.

"Are we supposed to smell it?" Will asked.

"No," I responded immediately, recalling how it made me lightheaded. "But I do think getting into this room has something to do with it."

Will leaned down and brought his hand up to the base of the flower, placing its stem in the padding of his thumb and forefinger. His hand glowed, and the outline of a door appeared at once.

The frame slid back, creating a gap. Will and I stepped through it, and the door slid back into place. The area we came to was bare, save for the plants lining three walls, illuminated by the lights strung from the ceiling.

Muffled voices sounded from down the long corridor, and as we followed them, they grew louder and more distinct.

A few doors greeted us. I opened one and was met with a large open space containing at least twenty mini-greenhouses, just like Nolan had in his apothecary room.

"Not in here," I yelled.

Will was closing another door. "Not in here either."

Straight ahead, a shadow moved across the floor of the double doors. Will and I didn't hesitate as we barreled through them.

Pree, Nolan, and Ruth all stood in a small circle.

"Good grief, Liddy!" Pree clutched her chest, panting. "You didn't have to come in here like a bat out of hell, scaring us all half to death."

"The only one scared is you," Ruth said matter-of-factly, and Nolan hid his smile behind his hand. But then he saw the urgency on our faces.

"Your meeting is over so quickly," Nolan said, raising a questioning brow, though there was no question in his statement.

"You could say that." Will ran a hand through his hair. The room went still, all eyes on me and Will.

I sighed. "I trust that the most powerful Watchers were all in that room ready to defend Cristes, but I followed my instincts, as you instructed."

I finally took in the scene before me. By all accounts, this appeared to be a normal patient's room, much like the one that Will and I spent a lot of time in. But there was one major difference.

Instead of a fully grown patient's bed against the wall, an enclosed bassinet stood tall with a tiny newborn baby in it. The clear walls allowed us to see Gavin sitting on the other side of the glass, peering in at the tiny, still body.

I let go of Will's hand and came to stand next to Gavin and the isolette. The baby's coloring seemed better than I'd recalled from Nick's memories, but dark veins still crawled over most of her body. I stumbled when I placed my hand on Gavin's shoulder. The regret, the grief, the utter despair this broken man carried plunged me into a black hole I couldn't climb out of.

Will was at my side in a flash, prying my hand off Gavin's shoulder. My husband brought me into his chest, cradling the back of my head, and I sobbed into his shirt, shedding the tears Gavin had been too paralyzed to release.

Will's arms relaxed and I immediately missed them when they disappeared. But then Pree's arm was over my shoulder, and she led me to a chaise in the corner. She sat next to me, laying her head on my shoulder, keeping her arm wrapped around the other.

When I finally calmed, I stared back at Nicole in awe. "All this time, she's been here alone," I whispered, my chin wobbling with the effort to keep my emotions in check.

"Not alone," said Pree. "Ruth is with her a lot. And someone named Leo? I guess he grew too curious one day and caught on to Ruth's secret."

"Oh, has he been in here today yet?" I asked, scanning the room for him.

"No. Apparently, he's at the temporary shelter seeing after all the kids we brought back with us," Pree answered.

I didn't know how to respond.

Pree wrapped her arm around my shoulders. "This is all pretty heavy, isn't it?"

Memories of black-speckled dust entered my mind, and I shook my head. I didn't want to worry about what was happening in the council room.

"Has Ruth let him hold her yet?" I nodded my head in Gavin's direction. His face was now plastered against the crib's side.

"No, Nicole hasn't left that isolette since the day she was born," Gavin answered, lifting his head off the isolette to look at us.

A neon blue light flickered on in the bassinet, and Gavin flinched from the sudden intrusion. He blinked his eyes several times and continued to marvel at his baby girl.

Ruth and Will came to join our little huddle.

"I am sure you are all wondering if I have gotten anywhere in curing her." Ruth set her clipboard down at her side and leveled her gaze at us. "The answer is, not nearly as far as I would like. The UV light is something that I created about two decades ago, and it keeps her internal organs and cells strong. It is why her skin looks so much healthier; the poison has been contained, maybe even receded slightly."

"But you haven't found a way to take the poison completely from her?" Pree asked.

Ruth shook her head, her lips pressed into a hard line.

"If she stays hooked up to your machines, can her dad hold her?" I asked. "In Mortalia, where I was raised, they say that skin-to-skin contact can really help a baby to heal."

Ruth's eyes flickered to Nolan's, a question in them. He placed his hands in his pockets, the gesture so casual for him, it momentarily distracted me. And then he said, "What do we have to lose at this point?"

Mara: Sweet Talker

OGS, LOTS OF BIG, FURRY DOGS, CHARGED ME. My breath quickened and my heart hammered in my chest. My mind couldn't decide if I should panic or flee, so it just screamed incoherently. I slammed my fist into the ground, channeling my gifting into the earth, silencing my thoughts.

The dogs came to an abrupt stop, some whining, some crying, and a sled I'd just noticed nearly toppled to the side.

I came upon him and peered over the side of the sled. A young man lay stunned, his eyes wide and unblinking, even though he clearly tracked me.

"Tannon, right?" I stood and bushed my hands off.

He nodded his head.

"Right, where are you coming from?" I asked.

But this silly boy continued to only stare. My patience wore thin, and I nearly laughed when he flinched as I took a step around the sled to his side.

"You know who I am, yes?"

Another nod.

"Then you don't wish to anger me, do you?"

He shook his head.

"Good." I stopped directly in front of him and bent low, my face intruding on his personal bubble. "I will ask this once more. Where are you coming from?"

"I..." He cleared his throat. "The Healing Sanctum." He hitched his thumb over his shoulder.

Drums sounded, and goosebumps spread across my skin like a festered rash.

I turned my head. Melchior was drawing near. His lust for my magic, for the magically enforced bond I never agreed upon with him, tugged at me. I whipped my head back around.

"Did you take William and Lydia there?"

Tannon nodded. I hopped into the sled. "Good. Take me there now." I kept my voice low so as to not attract Melchior, but I infused it with enough malice that I almost smiled when the sleigh vibrated with Tannon's fear.

He blew a little chippy tune into his flute whistle, and the dogs took off at a sprint faster than a lightning bolt striking the ground.

The sled turned and picked up speed, but not before Melchior's body crested the hill, his guards in line with him. He puffed his chest and let out a roar to Eira.

"Faster!" I yelled, spinning around to face the direction the dogs ran.

Another tune came from Tannon, and the dogs indeed raced faster.

The building came into view and as we approached, the sled slowed. I did not wait for it to stop completely before jumping out. After landing on my feet in a crouched position, I stood and strode to the door.

The boy watching me nagged at my conscience for some reason. Nicholas would tell me the boy deserved some gratitude. He'd tell me the boy probably saved my life, not knowing the risk he took.

I stopped with my hand on the door, ready to pull it open, and called over my shoulder. "If I were you, I'd leave immediately and take a route where you won't be seen."

"But my sister's in there," he said, biting his lip. "I cannot just leave her."

"Suit yourself." I shrugged. "Find her and flee."

The boy took a few steps toward me as if he were coming with me.

I held my hand up to stop him. "You are not entering through these doors. Now be gone. You have wasted enough of my time."

The entrance doors shut behind me with a loud click and I looked for a way to lock them. Melchior would be here soon. He'd find me. He always found me.

I slid the metal locks in place, one at the top and one at the bottom of the door, and stood there, not knowing what I was doing nor which direction to move in.

After a few moments of hesitation, I took a step, but a knock came at the door.

"Go away, boy! I *said*, not through here!"

"Open up, my little flower. You cannot hide from me."

Melchior. He was fast...too fast.

My stomach wanted to spew what little contents remained from yesterday's dinner. I frantically scanned my surroundings, searching for anything to use to barricade the door. Spotting a bench and some chairs a few feet away, I snatched them and began stacking them in front of the door.

"I thought you might be here because you, too, uncovered the secret these royal filth have been keeping from you."

What is he going on about? I bit my tongue, not wanting to let him know I didn't know what he was talking about.

As if he had read my mind, he continued. "I'm fully aware you do not have this information yet. No. You have always had a knack for survival, for self-preservation. You came here because you saw that princeling and princess run out, and your instincts kicked in. Or maybe it was the perfect opportunity to exact your revenge on them."

I straightened after stacking another chair against the door. I wasn't even sure I was breathing. His life would be so easy to end, and I believed I could do it. But then why did I still fear him so?

"My flower, I can help you with your revenge." As if he had placed a spell on his words, they passed through the door like it didn't exist. I winced at their clarity and closeness. "You must realize by now that I care about you. I have never stopped wanting you. And not because of what you could offer me in regards to your abilities, but because of *you*. I have always seen you." Melchior's voice dripped with insincerities, but there was a misting of truth drizzled into his words.

"What secret are you privy to?" I finally found my voice

and asked through the door.

"It has to do with your baby."

Stone-cold anger, as bitter as the ice choking these lands, coursed through my entire body.

I blinked a few times. "*Excussse* me?"

"Your baby, Mara. Now please open up so I can tell you about how we are going to rescue her."

I would kill him if he were lying. Wrap my hands around his slithering neck and squeeze. And I would enjoy it, too. I'd enjoy watching the life drain from his perfect almond eyes. My hands shook as I tried to unlatch the doors. *Damfino!* My control slipped, my claws came out to play, my heart raced, and my hair started to ash. I flung my hands forward, and my magic pummeled the doors open in a big gush of anger-fueled power.

Melchior's guards all had their weapons at the ready and were about to charge me, but he held his arm up, his fist clenched, stopping them.

"Hello, my beautiful, fierce flower."

I wanted to smack the smirk right off his too-perfect face.

I held my hand up, talons out, ready to strike. "What do you mean, rescue my daughter?" I snarled, the monster that lived within me on full display.

He cocked his head at me, taking in my metamorphosis. I couldn't tell if it pleased him or threatened him or both, but I did not care. "Exactly that. Your daughter is here, alive, and in this building. Just think, all this time, they have kept her from you. *Tsk, tsk, tsk.*" He clicked his tongue.

"You're lying," I growled, ready to tear his head off.

He held his hands up, a sign of peace. I let out an

exasperated laugh. Peace and Melchior did not belong in the same sentence.

He reached his hand out like he was going to touch me, but dropped it, seeming to think better of it. "I have no reason to lie to you. I simply want to save your daughter, and together, we can raise her. You remember, right? That having you as my wife, with a family of our own, is all I've ever wanted?"

With my hands on my hips, I spat, "Liar."

But he did not rise to match or surpass my anger. He wore a look I'd never seen before and when he spoke, I could no longer detect any insincerity.

"Is that so hard to believe?" He smiled, but it didn't reach his eyes. "She's part of you, my powerful flower. That is enough for me." His eyes scanned my body, and a strange sensation crept over me. "And when you are ready, we will try for another baby. I'll give you as many babies as you wish. Because the day you disappeared from me, I nearly died." He extended a hand to me once again. "Your leaving taught me a great lesson in that anything from you is a precious gift to cherish."

Liddy: Liar, Liar

"**S**OMEONE'S HERE." Will whipped his head to the door.

"No, not someone." I swallowed the hard lump that formed in my throat. "Mara." This knowledge seemed to pull Gavin from his pit of despair.

Nolan had been chatting in the corner with Ruth but interrupted her mid-sentence and ran over to us.

"You told her?" Nolan asked, his voice full of concern.

"No!" Will answered at once.

"This is not good," Pree said, wringing her hands. "We need to get Nicole and ourselves out of here, now." She shot up and started pacing.

"They will not be able to enter here," Ruth assured us. "The wall is enchanted and the entrance hidden."

"But we found it," I said, looking at my husband.

Ruth smiled, seemingly unfazed. "That is because you are very powerful."

"So is Mara," Nolan said pointedly.

Pree's cheeks were flushed with panic. "Listen, we cannot stay here. She will likely kill us all. Do you know how mama bears get when anything comes near their cubs? Things are about to get crazy, and I don't want to be here when they do. Y'all have powers. I'm literally a sitting duck, defenseless."

"Pree is right. Mara's anger, knowing this was kept from her, is of far more immediate concern," Nolan said. "Ruth, is there another place we can go?"

Ruth nodded. "Yes, we have an escape tunnel. But we cannot access it through here. We need to go back into the hallway and through the mini greenhouse."

"What about my baby?" Gavin's voice was rough, as if he had swallowed gravel.

"Do not worry," Ruth reassured him. "We have plenty of us to move her safely. Once we unplug the isolette, the battery will kick in. I will roll the bassinet, and each of you can carry a machine that feeds it."

We all sprang into action, unplugging the machines and eagerly waiting for Ruth's signal to move. But our progress was cut short when the door flung open, and Leo stumbled in, collapsing onto his side in the archway.

I jumped back and gasped.

"Leo!" Ruth's voice rang out as she sprinted toward him, grabbing his arm and dragging him to safety. She dropped to her knees and cradled his head in her lap.

Mara, rather the monster that haunted my dreams, stalked in. She would have stepped on Leo had Ruth not flung herself into action, whisking him out of harm's way and securing his body with her own.

Mara stomped to the side, and the room grew darker. Melchior sauntered in with a smug smile, and his personal guard fanned out to secure the perimeter. Will squeezed my waist, pulling me closer as his body turned viridescent. The protective beast inside him assessed each weapon drawn, ready to fight to keep me and our baby safe.

"Get-away-from-my-baby," Mara gritted out, each word slow, punctuated with fierce promises of sudden death if we didn't obey.

We all took a few steps away from the bassinet. Everyone except Gavin. Her eyes flashed at him, and he was pushed away from the covered crib by an unseen force. He tried to fight against Mara's power, but she cocked her head at him in that insect-like manner as she assessed him.

"She's my baby too!" Gavin screamed, the veins in his neck popping with the strain of his body as he struggled against the invisible power, clawing his way back to Nicole.

Melchior cocked his brow and stood next to Mara, carefully entwining his fingers with hers so as not to lose one by her crimson blades. She looked down at his hand in hers, then back to Gavin.

Gavin's eyes followed their hands, his face hardening. "Intimidate me all you want," he spat at them. "I don't care. It will never change the truth you refuse to see. I *never* lied about my feelings regarding our baby. I wanted her just as much as you did." His face softened, his voice breaking. "And I could not wait to be her father. Part of me died the day my father told me you had lost the baby. But we both know he lied to me, straight to my—"

"Enough!" Mara screamed. We all clapped our hands over our ears as a tiny crack broke into the side of the bassinet. Melchior gave his head a little shake, a sinister smile spreading across his face.

"Stop!" Nolan yelled, running his hand protectively over the glass as if his touch could mend it. "You will kill her. She has to stay isolated until we figure out how to save her from the poison."

Mara retreated back a step, her hand pressing over her mouth, clearly horrified that she just compromised her daughter. With his hand still clasping one of hers, Melchior walked Mara over to stand directly in front of the bassinet. Mara's eyes transformed from black pits to bright orange, and black tears trickled down her cheeks.

"Shhh, my flower. Do not stress. I'm here now." Melchior took some of the special soil from his pocket, whispered softly to it so only the soil could hear, and blew it at the isolette.

Mara tried to slap his hand away. "What are you doing?" she shrieked, fear radiating off of her in crippling waves.

But Melchior stood unwavering and unphased by Mara's despair. "Just watch, my rose."

I realized everyone in the room had pressed in toward the baby, and we all held bated breaths.

As if someone had poured a liquid-clear glue over the isolette, the crack filled in slowly, starting at each fractured end, melding through the middle. Mara gasped as Melchior lovingly cupped her cheek with one hand.

"I told you, I will always take care of you and her." Then he dropped his hand and faced Ruth. "What happens if we were to remove the covering of the bassinet?" Melchior's eyes never left the baby, but he clearly directed his question to Ruth.

"She dies, you jerk fac—"

"Pree!" I hissed, gripping her elbow and yanking her back to me.

"Are you sure you know what you are talking about, human?" Melchior looked down his nose at her.

We knew the history of the Black Roses and their opinions of humans. Pree took a step back from him but maintained her scowl.

Ruth looked to Leo. His eyes remained closed, but his pained face told me he was still alive and breathing. She cleared her throat. "We do not have hard data on this as the risk was too great," she answered. "Thus, we cannot be sure."

Melchior stroked his smooth jaw. "Explain what the machines are for," he commanded her.

Ruth stood, her face hardened, showing more emotion than I'd ever seen from her. "Some offer vitamins and minerals. Others are ready to do the work of her organs should any fail. And that..." She pointed to the smallest device in Nolan's hands with the faintly glowing bag attached to its pole. "...is the only thing keeping the poison from entering her heart and killing her."

"Well, if I may..." Before anyone could stop him, Melchior detached his hand from Mara's, sustaining a deep cut across one finger. Blood smeared the glass as he popped the lid off the bassinet and it crashed to the ground.

"No!" Pree and I screamed at the same time. Gavin's face paled so quickly I thought he'd pass right out. As if he had the same thought, Nolan gripped Gavin around the waist, holding him up.

Mara whirled on Melchior. "Put it back, right now!" Her eyes swirled back to black, her hair floating in small tendrils of flame.

"Easy, my flower. All her needs are met. She is strong, like us, to survive all these years. See?" Everyone's gazes followed to where Melchior pointed. Nicole was still hooked up to her wires, their leads still perfectly attached to the machines and devices we still held. "I am simply helping you to hold your daughter. Do you not want that?"

The flames of Mara's hair immediately extinguished, the remnants of ash transforming her strands back to platinum. Melchior snapped his fingers, and Yule scuttled over with a chair. "Here. Have a seat. I will get Nicole and place her in your arms." Mara bristled at that. "Calm, my little rose," Melchior cooed. "I will be gentle and make sure no wires get cut." He gestured to her hands, still like razor-sharp claws.

Gavin made to protest, but Nolan silenced him with a hand on his shoulder and a curt shake of his head.

Will started leading Pree and me toward Nolan, inch by inch. If the guards noticed, they did nothing to stop us.

Mara looked down at her hands before closing her eyes. "Alright. You bring me Nicole, and I will calm down."

Melchior turned to face the baby, and warning bells within my gifting began blaring. I sent the warning to Will in case his gifting hadn't picked up on it.

I feel it too, Will spoke to my mind.

With smooth and gentle movements, Melchior cradled Nicole in his arms, the wires slung over his forearm. Ruth handed him a blanket and retreated quickly to her spot by Leo, who was now sitting up.

Gavin's body rebelled at seeing a monster get to hold his precious baby before him. He charged them. Mara held her hand out toward him, and his movements turned jerky, as if she had tied him up. He strained and yelled out, pleading. Tears poured down his face.

I so badly wanted to fix this for him, for everyone. The injustice of it all. A feeling of intense sorrow and guilt wrecked me so that I could barely stand.

Mara looked at Gavin. "Did you know she was alive?"

Gavin swallowed down a shuddering whimper. "I already answered you."

"Answer again!"

"No. Not until just before the meeting started today. As soon as I overheard, I raced straight here."

Mara studied him. "If you can settle down, I will remove my magic from you and let you hold her. But you do not get to hold her first. If you ruin this for me in any way, I will kill you."

My jaw dropped. Was Mara actually being somewhat reasonable?

Gavin nodded, then he lurched forward as soon as the resistance he'd been fighting disappeared. He scrambled to his feet and bounded toward the bassinet. But when Mara's eyes flashed in warning, he halted his steps and waited.

Will had gotten us to Nolan. We were inching our way toward Ruth and Leo, who were off to the side by the door. Gavin, Mara, and Melchior were so distracted we'd reached the healers in under a minute. From there, we could see Mara's profile with a clear view of Melchior. The bassinet obstructed some of our view of Gavin, but we could still see his face.

Melchior took a small step forward, still cradling the baby.

"My flower, she looks so much like you. I cannot wait to raise this beautiful girl as my own, with her beautiful mother."

Gavin growled as he postured toward his enemy.

"Final warning," Mara spat at her ex.

Melchior continued his taunts. "This royal filth is a liar." He inclined his head toward Gavin. "He never wanted her. Don't you remember? He threw you in the trash...for another woman."

Gavin barred his teeth. "Mara, he is trying to bait me. Out past is painful, but—"

Mara's eyes flashed at Gavin and his mouth shut immediately, though I wasn't sure if it was of his own volition or if she made it so.

"He wouldn't be able to take care of her as we can. He doesn't love you. How could he love a product of something that came from you?" He stroked Nicole's cheek. "No, she will come with us, because I love you and she is of you. I guarantee we can extract the rose's magic from her. Nicole will live a full and happy life with us."

Melchior chuckled as he stood over Mara. She reached her hands out for her baby, and I wasn't sure if she'd even heard a word Melchior said, but at least the claws were gone. Melchior took another step forward with nothing else to do but hand the baby to her mother. His eyes remained laser-focused on Nicole. And then Melchior bent to lay the infant in Mara's arms.

I reached out with my gifting toward Gavin. His pain was so great my heart nearly cleaved in two. Too many things happened at once. The baby fell into Mara's hands, and a small flash of silver appeared at Melchior's side. Then Gavin was in the air, flying at Melchior. Mara cradled the baby to her chest as the men crashed, hard, onto the floor.

Liddy: Chaos

"**H**ELP HIM!" I SCREAMED, not sure who I was yelling at, but Melchior's guards were advancing, and in seconds it would be one versus ten.

"Stay here!" Will ordered. Without hesitation, he used his green warrior skills and giftings to fight the guards closest to us, starting with Roisin and Yule.

Gavin was losing steam far too quickly, which didn't make sense as he, too, was part green.

"*Ahhhhh!*" Pree screamed as she charged at a soldier and jumped on his back. The soldier whipped this way and that, trying to shake her off. He got a few punches in Pree's side, and I swore I heard a cracking sound, like twigs breaking on a forest floor, but she remained fastened to his back, choking him out.

I ran over to Will, thrusting the heel of my hand into a guard's nose. Will was busy with Yule and couldn't see Roisin getting back up from the blow he'd given her. Her sword was drawn, and she was about to stab my husband in the back.

I summoned my gifting and blasted her. She hit the wall with a sickening crunch and slid down it, landing in an awkward heap. Her eyes remained open and would never blink again, a sight that would haunt my dreams for a long time.

The door flung open again, and I nearly cried out in relief. Shai and Lana burst in with Ohanna, Brita, and a few more Cristes guards.

Shai barely had time to take in the scene before a guard closed in on him. Ruth and Leo escaped from the room, and Will backed me into the corner they'd just vacated, shielding me with his body. Nolan had an unconscious Pree draped over his shoulder.

I peeked out from behind Will's body. Mara seemed oblivious to what was happening all around her. I watched her body begin its transformation back into the girl she used to be, her hair growing long and golden. Her eyes were no longer black nor orange, and I imagined they were that beautiful pastel mosaic I got to see in Nick's memories.

I heard the agonizing scream of a man, and my head whipped to where Gavin had been fighting Melchior.

Gavin lay in the fetal position, clutching his side. Melchior was crawling away, blood trickling from the corner of his lower lip. With an effort he stood, a knife still in his hand, Gavin's blood dripping onto the pale wood floor.

Melchior stalked toward Mara, and she stiffened as if his

very presence repulsed her. Gavin screamed again, "NO! He's going to kill her!"

Shai reached his friend, his hands trailing all over him, looking for the source of the blood. There was *so much* blood.

Mara's gaze jerked from her baby to Melchior's face. He smiled at her, blood staining his teeth, as he tried to hide the knife at his side.

"He is a liar," Melchior said. "He tried to steal the baby, so I took care of it. He was the one who wanted Nicole dead."

Lana was by Mara's side in a flash, her arms outstretched for the baby. Mara didn't even hesitate. She stood and transferred her baby to my mother-in-law, who then placed the baby back in the isolette and wheeled it toward me and Will.

Mara turned to face the man that had haunted her for too long.

"Is that so? And what are you concealing against your leg?" Her voice was seething, collected, and definitely misplaced amidst the chaos in the room.

"Nothing slips your notice." Melchior grinned and presented the knife. "I had to do it. He was going to kill her."

Mara's gaze flickered over to where Gavin sat with his back pressed into Shai as Nolan held his hand over a seeping wound. He was far too pale, and I bit back a scream at the unfairness of it all, my heart hammering. Mara's facade slipped a little when she saw the man who, yes, broke her heart once upon a time, but also the man whom she once loved fiercely and had a child with.

"He's lying!" Blood gargled Gavin's words. "If I hadn't tackled him, his knife would have pierced the very heart of our souls... Nicole."

Mara rose and cocked her head at Melchior. I stood, transfixed, as she started to morph once again into the witch. Melchior looked wildly around him, but his guards were either subdued or dead.

"You may not have ever been fond of me, but I've always been truthful." He plastered on a pleading look and lifted his chin. "Why would I hurt her? I told you I wanted to start a family with you and her."

When Lana saw that Mara was actually considering his words, she chimed in from across the room. "Nicholas is at the castle, fighting for his life, because of him. And..." Lana's chin wobbled, a glimpse of unexpected vulnerability.

Mara righted her head, her transformation complete, and she hissed at Melchior. "You lying, bastard. Tell me the truth, or I shall kill you."

"I am speaking—"

Mara slashed her hand down and across Melchior's face in one fell swoop. A gash re-opened the newly healed scars on his cheek, this time clear to the bone.

"The truth!" she screamed.

He clutched his cheek and stood as if pride were the only thing keeping him upright. "Nicholas had to go. I knew as long as he lived, he would hold you in his clutches, and you'd never fully be mine."

She cocked a perfectly arched brow at him. "And my daughter?"

"My flower, surely you've realized after studying her that nothing can save her. I simply wanted to put you out of your misery and move on quickly."

"I can smell the lie rolling off your tongue like the rot of a thousand *sewerssss*," she hissed, raising her hand. "Say it... the real reason. By now you realize I've figured it out."

Melchior flinched. "Alright, alright. I wasn't lying when I said it was impossible to save her. But we also needed the black rose's magic within her to save you. That magic is dangerously close to your heart, and you are days away from death. Killing the child is a necessary sacrifice in order to save you. I can give you another baby, but I cannot make another you."

Mara smiled sweetly, and I clutched Will tightly, my instincts screaming at me to look away, but I couldn't. Mara's next words confused me.

"Thank you," she said to the horrible monster in front of her. She took a step toward him and opened her arms, her claws retracting. "For your honesty, for your offering of family and protection."

I hadn't realized that Pree had come to and was now standing next to me, a huge bruised bump forming on her forehead. "She can't possibly believe that player!" she whispered to me. I couldn't believe Mara would fall for Melchior's games, either.

Melchior's stern face softened. "I'm so glad you can see clearly. I offer you great power and a second chance at a family."

Mara beckoned him closer and wrapped her arms around his thin waist.

No! I screamed inwardly. Mara could not join him. Together they would destroy Cristes and everyone I loved, starting with my unborn child.

With a protective hand over my abdomen, I moved

out from behind Will, a plan solidifying. First I would kill Melchior and hope that someone could handle Mara before she ended me. But as I took my first step, Mara jerked back, taking Melchior in fully.

"Thank you for telling me what was in your heart..." Her grip intensified on Melchior's forearms, and he fell to his knees as we all heard the sickening crunch of bone breaking over his shrieks. "For a heart as black as *yoursssss* isn't capable of love."

Mara's arm drew back, claws springing to attention. Before I could blink, she punched through Melchior's armored chest and drew back, holding his still-beating heart in her hand.

Liddy: True Love's Sacrifice

Melchior dropped to the floor like an anchor hitting the bottom of the ocean.

I gagged and buried my face in Will's back.

"That was some serious Temple of Doom vibes right there," Pree breathed next to me.

I turned my head and gawked at her, thinking she was trying to be funny. But a green tinge colored her skin. She looked as sick as I felt, but still, she stared at Mara watching Melchior's heart beat its final rhythm. *Lub-dub.*

Gavin tried to move and howled in pain. Shai steadied him. "Do not move, Gav! Someone, get Ruth or Leo in here! Now!" he shouted. A few of our guards bolted out the door.

Gavin kept swatting his arms away. "No, can I..." He took in a shuddering breath. "Can I hold my daughter?"

Lana walked up to Gavin but kept her eyes on Mara, who still stood frozen, though she'd dropped the heart by then. When Mara didn't move to protest, Lana continued on to Gavin.

"Wait!" I cried, and everyone stared at me.

We can heal him, I spoke to Will's mind. He dropped his watery gaze to me and entwined his fingers in mine. Together we walked over to our group of friends huddled on the floor.

"We can heal him," I spoke to Shai, who still had Gavin's back pressed against his chest.

"Yes, please," Shai croaked out, the helplessness in his voice bringing tears to my eyes.

"No...not yet," Gavin rasped between words.

"Please, you do not have much time," Nolan pleaded, his eyes shiny with tears.

"I just want to hold my daughter first."

Lana pushed through us and knelt next to Gavin. She placed Nicole in her daddy's arms. His body visibly relaxed some, and he finally rested against Shai instead of straining against him. As Gavin held his daughter, Nolan continued to attempt to heal the gaping wound under Gavin's shirt. Lana sat next to Shai, wrapping him in a hug as best she could, letting him cry into her shoulder.

Nolan's shoulders fell when the flow of blood finally stopped. He stood and left the room, Pree hot on his tail. Will and I stood there, looking down on Gavin, who was finally holding his daughter after all these years. And I sobbed, loud and ugly. No one seemed to mind. Will just held me tighter to him.

"Hi, baby girl. I am your daddy," he cooed with tears in

his eyes. "I am so sorry it has taken us so long to meet, but holy Eira, you are the most beautiful thing I have ever seen."

I suddenly felt as though I were intruding on a private moment. I turned around to offer some privacy and flinched as Mara— the real Mara, not the witch— was mere inches from me, torment scrawled across her face.

Will immediately held his hand out, white light burning from his palm. "Do not get any closer," he growled.

She merely looked from him to me and back to him unfazed, stepping around us to get to Gavin.

"There were so many things I was going to teach you. I am a very good dancer, and I also wanted to make sure you knew how to swim." He looked up at Mara when he said that, giving her a weak smile, and returned his gaze to Nicole.

I didn't like how he kept talking in the past tense. Mara's hand covered her mouth and real tears, crystal clear, ran down her face.

"Your determination to live inspires me. So, I want to share a few things I have learned over the years. One, there is no shame in recognizing that you need help and asking for it. Pride is not something to lose everything you care about over. Two, no one is perfect. But, still, you were made to shine, so shine bright. And third, always choose love."

Nolan returned along with Pree. She held a few Christmas roses while Nolan had a few tincture bottles in his hands. He said nothing as he slid back to Gavin's side. He unstoppered a bottle and held it to Gavin's mouth.

At first, Gavin refused, but Shai held his head back while Nolan held his chin, pouring the concoction down his throat, then holding his mouth shut until he swallowed. Nolan held his hand out to Pree, who handed him a rose. Nolan opened another bottle with his mouth and sprinkled the contents over some of the petals.

Gavin continued to stroke his daughter's cheeks, her nose, her lips, her chin. Nolan lifted Gavin's shirt, and I nearly passed out at the sight of the exposed intestine. But Nolan calmly broke off some petals and placed them in Gavin's wounds.

Surprisingly, Gavin's color improved some, and I clung to Will's arm, hope blossoming in my chest.

"Nicole, you would have easily been the best part of my day. And now that you are here again, I can't imagine life without you." Gavin sniffled as he placed a gentle kiss on the babe's forehead.

I watched as a tear trickled down his cheek. His happiness turned my own happy tears on full blast. Gavin's eyes widened as if an idea just came to him.

"I have faith that you will make a full recovery and live a long and happy life," he said. He leaned down and cooed some more in her ear.

What happened next would shock all of us to our very core. Gavin took a needle out of one of the bags hooked to Nicole and shoved it into his vein. He held his hand over the connection, and within seconds, the dark veins scattered over Nicole's body began to lighten, the black liquid oozing straight into Gavin.

"Gavin, no! You are not strong enough!" Shai cried.

He smiled, his face smooth and serene. "No, my friend... I have never been stronger."

His arms started to drop and when Nolan reached to help

him, Mara inserted herself, offering her hands to hold him up.

Gavin's eyes found Mara's, but he seemed to be having difficulty focusing. "We could have done this together. We would have been great at co-parenting—"

"Shhh, none of that matters right now," Mara responded, then recoiled slightly as if her words surprised her.

"Oh, but it does. I hope you know how truly sorry I am for how I hurt you. I never..." Gavin gasped, trying to suck in enough oxygen. The poison had raced up his arm, disappearing beneath his shirt. "I never wanted that. But sometimes life surprises us in unexpected ways. For example, it brought me Ellasyn, and it gave you another opportunity to choose Nick."

"What are you—"

"Come on, Mar. He was and has always been your fated match. I was just too selfish to realize it." Gavin shuddered and grimaced, panting through the poison's newest assault. Black vines peeked out of the collar of his neck.

Mara sat back on her heels.

Gavin grit his teeth. "Nolan, do me a favor?"

"Anything, Master Gavin."

"Please tell Nick I am so sorry. Tell him I love him and I'll see him again in Elysium." His skin ashen, Gavin's chest rose and fell rapidly. "Tell him I could think of no other man I'd want raising my child but him. He is everything a child could hope for and more...so much more."

"No, buddy. You are going to tell him yourself," Shai said through tears.

Gavin's voice was barely a whisper. "Thank you all for loving me even when I didn't deserve it. Have peace knowing I'll be living my best life, happy and reunited with Ellasyn in

Eira. We will meet again."

Gavin's head lulled to the side as he lovingly peered down at his baby. His breaths grew more ragged and labored with each inhale. "I'll love you forever," he whispered and kissed Nicole's cheek. At last, he sighed with relief and closed his eyes for the last time.

Liddy: Mother Knows Best

"No," Shai breathed out. He shook his friend's shoulders. "No, no, no, wake up, brother." But Gavin didn't respond.

Lana was silently sobbing when Ruth rushed in moments later. She raced over, and despite his bloodied body marred with black streaks, she used her gifting to assess his limp body. She dropped her gaze and shook her head.

"Will, Liddy...please." Shai looked at us. Those were the only words he could choke out, but we knew what he meant. Will and I came to kneel by Gavin's chest, placing one hand on his body and entwining our fingers with the other. I focused as much energy as I could into Will, who in turn channeled his healing gift into Gavin.

When we opened our eyes sometime later, everyone had

shielded their eyes, but Gavin still lay there, lifeless.

Mara cradled her baby to her chest, but even she seemed to be watching us with keen interest. Her eyes were rimmed with red, her under-eyes a myriad of blues and purples.

A long time passed in silence. All the bodies had been cleared from the room except Gavin, who lay covered with a sheet, Shai still kneeling by his side. Nolan was in a corner speaking quietly with Ruth while the healer attended to Pree's head wound.

When Mara finally spoke, it jerked us all back to the present. "If the rose's poison is gone, why is Nicole not waking? Does she need to return to her bassinet? Has it been too long without the aid of the machines?"

Mara's eyes traveled over each of us, landing on me and Will. I took a step back and she bit her lower lip, cradling her baby closer to her.

I think she wants us to heal Nicole but doesn't want to ask us, or maybe she doesn't think we would, Will spoke through our link.

Well, yeah, she wanted to kill me and take you as her king to rule Cristes, I replied, careful not to give anyone any reason to suspect the unique way we communicated.

Pree effectively broke the silence when she stepped forward and actually spoke with kindness. "Ruth said Nicole was under a sleeping spell."

Mara looked at Pree like she had two heads. "What does that mean?"

Pree rolled her eyes.

"Pree," I scolded. Understandably, we'd all just been through something traumatic, but did she want to bring out the witch?

Pree sighed heavily but reined in her frustration. "It means true love's kiss might wake her, duh."

I elbowed Pree and she gestured wide to me mouthing, *what?*

But Mara didn't appear bothered by the slight. She bit her lower lip, contemplating her next move.

"But Gavin kissed her, and..." Will trailed off.

"Maybe there is more to it than just true love's kiss," Lana offered. "Have a little faith in the bond between mother and daughter."

Ever so gently, Mara lowered her head and gave her daughter a brief, gentle kiss.

Pree caught Will's and my eyes, and we all collectively held our breath before turning our gaze back to the baby. I nearly gave up hope, but when Nicole yawned and blinked her eyes against the light, we all broke down in tears of joy and relief.

Once the coast was deemed clear, Lana stayed in the healing sanctum with Nolan while Shai rushed Will and me out. We'd thought Tannon and Tia had driven their sleds to safety, but they had stayed put, hiding behind a tall snowdrift just in case they were needed. Tannon continued to wait for the others while Tia raced the three of us to the castle.

Once there, we sprinted to the council room and were met with a nearly dead Nick. Will and I worked quickly, not even having to exchange words, our giftings knowing exactly what to do. Healing Nick was difficult. Apparently, Melchior had dipped his blade in poison before stabbing him. But our ministrations held, and he was able to make significant strides in his recovery.

The war ended swiftly. Once the Black Roses had learned their king was dead, most of them surrendered. A few fled, but our scouts would eventually find them.

Now, we were all preparing for tomorrow's funeral service for Gavin. Mara stayed in her quarters with her baby, both Lana and Queen Nicole tending to her as if she were no longer a threat. Without her ability to siphon power from kids, her body continued to weaken against the black rose's poison within her. Each day brought her closer to death, as we could see by the black veins extending past the mark Ruth drew on her skin to measure its progression.

Gavin had been able to figure out what no one else had. He used his gifting to pull the magic from Nicole's veins. But the essence of the rose had to go somewhere, and it would only go to a living host, self-preservation and all. What the magic wasn't able to discern was that Gavin was gravely injured and his body couldn't fight against the strength of the rose's poison.

A knock at the door stirred Will and me from the couch, where my feet rested comfortably in his lap. I groaned and Will smiled, patting my knee.

"I'll get it." He gently lifted my ankles, scooted out from under me, and set my feet back down on the throw pillows.

At first, I didn't pay attention to the muffled voices, but then they began to rise before abruptly cutting off. I used my connection to Will and immediately knew he was not in danger, though he was miffed.

I cocked my brow and tilted my head at him as he entered the room, and he tried to give me a smile that didn't quite reach his eyes. Nick strode in behind him, walking a little more carefully than normal.

"Nick!" I perked up and launched out of my seat. "I'm so glad to see you healthy again." I greeted him with a hug. He hugged me back, released me after a long moment, and I helped him into a cozy armchair.

He laid his elbows on his knees and steepled his fingers. Will's warm body snuggled close to my side as he wrapped his arm across my shoulders.

"You're freaking me out. Will you just spill it already?" I gripped the arm of the couch, not sure if I could handle any more drama for a while. I was still recovering from all the gifting we'd used last week, not to mention, growing a baby.

He stalled for a long moment, shooting me a sidelong glance. "Congratulations on the pregnancy."

I rolled my eyes and smiled. "Oh stop, that is old news, as I am sure Lana and your mother have told everyone at this point."

"I... I only now just sensed it," Nick said, his cheeks turning pink. "I am sorry. In retrospect, it probably wasn't necessary, as I don't believe Mara will follow through on her threats to you. There has been enough bloodshed..." He trailed off, his eyes filling with tears that he refused to shed, blinking them away. "Listen, I realize a baby is probably not what you wanted or needed right now, but it was the only loophole at the time—"

I held up my hand to stop him, grinning. "We understand

the pressure you were under, and we are so thankful for your quick thinking. We don't have a crystal ball when we make our decisions. Sometimes all hindsight does is torment us with the 'what ifs'."

"Turns out..." Will sprawled his palm over my still-flat-for-now lower belly. "We had already beat you to the punch. We were pregnant before you made the bargain."

Nick cocked a brow and shook his head, chuckling in disbelief. "Well, my gifting must have sensed your little bundle and provided me with the idea on the spur of the moment." His smile faded after a few moments as he appeared to drift off somewhere. I leaned forward and placed my hand on his knee, drawing his attention back to the room.

"Please tell me why you really came," I said. Will squeezed my shoulder; whether it was to comfort himself or me, I wasn't sure.

Nick cleared his throat. "I recognize how outrageous of an ask this is, and it makes me the biggest jobbernowl that I am here, asking anyway. I promise not to take offense if you offer all the worst tinsel and berry excuses in all the realms. *Pssssh!* You do not even need to offer excuses. You can just say no—"

"Spit it out, man!" I'd never seen him ramble on like this, and his nervous energy was creeping into me, making me feel all sorts of jittery.

He ran a hand down his face and peered at me through his fingers, like he couldn't bear to face me, the look in his eye desperate and pleading. "Will you heal Mara?"

I sat there. Minutes ticked by, and though Nick dropped his hands, he let the silence linger, patiently waiting for a response from us. The silence grew awkward. Heck, I'm sure he would have liked a reaction— any reaction, no matter what it was.

I swallowed. My words came as a tiny whisper. "Does she even want that?"

Nick nodded. "Her daughter is alive. She does not want to miss out on raising her. She has a second chance at motherhood, no longer burdened with the thought that she killed Nicole. But, if she does not receive help, she will perish...and soon. It does not seem fair—"

"Fair? Nothing about this has been fair, and most of our troubles have been thanks to her," Will growled.

Nick nodded in sympathy. "I completely understand. I truly do not expect you to say yes. I just..."

"You love her." I smiled weakly at him. "You love both of them," I amended. It didn't sound right to leave Nicole out of the scope of his love.

Nick dropped his gaze from me as he nodded, using the back of his hand to quickly swipe away the tear that finally escaped. "I did not come here to guilt you into doing me any favors. Eira knows she probably would not do this for you."

"I understand that she would want to live for her child," Will said, "but I believe what Liddy was asking was whether or not she'd want the two of us to be the ones to heal her."

Nick played with his silver beard. "If you had asked me that question a week ago, I would be able to answer you with a resounding no. Now? I am not sure."

My brows knit together. "Are Will and I even capable of healing her? I mean, Gavin discovered that the very essence of the black rose will try to survive and will only leave willingly if going into a living host."

Will tensed at my question, his eyes going wide. "You're not suggesting that Liddy and I become the hosts, are you? Because that is a hard 'no'."

Nick shifted in his seat as he waved his hands. "No, no, no. Not at all. Ruth and Leo have been working on something, actually. Once we extract the poison from Mara, it will filter into an enchanted Christmas rose that is still planted."

I leaned forward, tenting my hands. "But doesn't that create another black rose essentially? What if one of the Black Rose fugitives hears about it and all of this starts over again?"

Nick smiled. "Ruth, with Nolan's help, has inferred from the data they were able to collect, thanks to Gavin's sacrifice, that the Christmas rose is strong enough to nullify the poison. Basically, it would cease to exist."

"Like an antidote?" I asked.

"Exactly." Nick smiled.

"Why can't she just eat one of those, then?" Will asked.

Nick heaved a heavy sigh. "Because then it would no longer be a living host for the poison."

"So, if the Christmas rose is doing all of the work, what do you need us for?" Will pressed.

"That poison has lived in Mara for a very long time. You will be there to ensure that the poison does not try to retreat back into Mara once it figures out the Christmas rose is killing it. Eira knows what damage it has done internally to her. As a result, you would need to heal any damage to Mara's body as the poison is extracted, strengthening her."

I turned to Will. "I know, I know she doesn't deserve our help." I grabbed his hands with mine and brought them to my heart. "But—"

Will closed his eyes. "You make it really difficult to contradict you when you look at me like that."

I giggled. "Will, look at me...she does not deserve our help. But she experienced an unfathomable pain. Does it excuse her choices and actions? Absolutely not. Not to mention, if we help her, what justice will be served?"

I could feel the anger warring within him, an emotion he had every right to feel.

"Justice will be served," Nick whispered, but he kept his head down. "We, along with many other people, have a right to be angry and seek justice. However, would we be any better than her if we let her die? If we let her child grow up without her mother or father?"

Will looked to Nick, whose head was still down, waiting to see if he'd interject. The only move Nick made was to begin massaging his forehead.

Will dropped his head back onto the couch. "Awww, man. Using the orphan card! For your information, most Disney characters are missing at least one parent and they go on to save the world."

"It is not a card." I smacked him on the shoulder.

He caught my hand in his. "I guess it's not our job to dole out a punishment."

"And I wouldn't want that responsibility," I added.

Will nodded. "So, go ahead, ask me."

"Would you help me save a dying woman and give her a second chance at life?"

"As you wish."

Liddy: Grace and Acceptance

NICK LEFT IMMEDIATELY TO MAKE ARRANGEMENTS. As we waited for Nolan to come and lead us to Mara's chambers, my heart trilled in my chest, threatening to break free of its cage and fly away.

Will came behind me as I stared out our window off the family room. He ran his hands up and down my bare arms. I watched the cuffs of his black sweater as they moved, relaxing waves of energy sedating my heart back into a normal rhythm.

"Please, do not be nervous. I'm confident that we can do what Nick asked of us. We can heal her and make sure the poison continues to flow into the Christmas rose," he reassured me.

"That's not what I'm worried about," I said, although he was partly correct. There was something else that plagued my mind even more.

"OK, so what's on your mind?" he asked, continuing to stroke my arms.

"Don't lower my heart rate too much, or you may find me passing out here in a minute," I cautioned.

Will lowered his head to my neck and found the little hollow spot between my collarbone and shoulder, giving it a kiss.

"Yep, that definitely got it pumping again." He chuckled, and I laughed with him for a moment before turning serious again. "What if she says no to our offer of help?"

Will turned me to face him, the bottom of my long black dress twirling out a little and hitting his shins.

"Then that is her choice."

"But what about Nicole?"

Will's expression softened as he rubbed the spot between my brows, smoothing my worry lines. "Look, if she says no, there is nothing we can do about it. Not a single minute of worrying about that now will change it later. And I'm sure Nick and the queen would take care of the baby. But I believe she has changed. Do you think the Mara we knew only a week ago would have come to Gavin's funeral?"

Gavin's funeral service was held at sunrise. Brilliant shades of red and yellow pierced through the windows set high in the towering walls, casting scattered rays across the casket.

Mara refused to miss it, though she was very weak and put herself at risk to do so. Nolan procured her a wheelchair and helped her down to the sanctuary. She was the last to arrive, but with a practiced air of indifference, she paid no attention to the harsh stares, the surprised gasps, or the Watchers who cowered in her presence.

She had Nolan bring her up front, on the section of pews opposite Gavin's mother. A black veil covered her face, but she held Nicole in a way that made it seem as if Mara was helping her baby girl not to miss a minute of seeing her daddy.

I had to hand it to her. She was strong as heck, on her deathbed yet paying homage to the man who both loved and broke her. But I guess, in a way, he also saved her, sacrificing himself for their daughter, the one thing Mara loved more than anything.

"Hello, Earth to Liddy?" Will murmured. I blinked at him as he cupped my cheek. "Where'd you go?"

"You know what? You're right. I too believe she's changed for the better. But also, I need to accept the fact that the outcome of all this is out of my control."

"Exactly." Will placed a kiss on the top of my head. Then he splayed his hands over my uterus. "All this stress isn't good for the babies."

I giggled. Just last night, Nolan had paid us a visit to check on our growing miracle and jovially told us the babies were doing fine. That's right—twins. I think I was more surprised than Will. In fact, he seemed quite pleased with himself.

I teased him just this morning. *"What are you so smug about? You took health class with me. It was merely a happy little coincidence that my body made it possible for twins."*

With a downturned mouth, he said, "I don't believe in coincidences."

I sighed, sliding my arms around Will's waist and snuggling in close.

"I need to change." I sighed again. The fatigue stage of pregnancy had decided it was the perfect time to kick in. Will released the hug first, but I lingered. "Just one more minute, *pleeease*?"

"How about you go get dressed right now, and then you can have five more minutes with me?" Will asked, waggling his brows at me.

"OK!" I stepped away from him and shimmied out of my long skirt. It hit the floor, and I used my foot to flick it toward our bedroom.

My black yoga pants had been hiding underneath the entire time. It was cold here, so there was no way I wasn't going to layer. I went into my closet and plucked a thick, red sweater to go over my black tank top.

I ran back into the room and jumped into Will's arms, wrapping my legs around his waist and hugging his neck. He walked us to the couch, and I burrowed into him.

Right on time, Nolan knocked on our door. "Prince William, Princess Lydia, are you ready?"

Nolan's eyes were pinker than usual— they were also puffy. Though he didn't shed a tear at the funeral, it was apparent he'd done so in private.

We followed him through many hallways and finally arrived at a narrow passageway. I wasn't expecting a small crowd to be waiting outside Mara's door. The queen, king, Lana, and Brantley stood off to the side in a tiny alcove, not talking but simply standing as if their minds were elsewhere. Nick sat in a chair next to the door, and Shai sat on a small bench across from him.

Everyone's face expressed a pain that cut deep, with red-rimmed eyes and dark circles underneath. Their skin had paled, losing most of its color and luminosity.

Feeling the pain of others was something I wasn't immune to, and tears began to build in my eyes once again. I'd barely known Gavin, yet the pain of losing him was so hard. I couldn't imagine what it would be like to lose someone who was your best friend or a close member of your family.

Will slipped his hand onto my lower back and held me to him. He didn't try to stop my emotions nor try to persuade them in a different direction. Not today. Today we would feel everything we needed to. To hide or ignore our grief would dishonor Gavin.

Nick glanced up at me and Will, doing a double-take when he finally registered our presence. He sniffed hard and short, then stood.

He cleared his throat, once...twice. "I will take you in."

Will stepped close to him and whispered, "Why is everyone here?"

Nick answered without missing a beat, like he'd been expecting the question. "For moral support."

Nick knocked on the door once before pressing the latch and opening it. He ushered us in and swiftly closed it behind him.

Mara lay asleep in bed, her golden hair spread out perfectly around her head, a true sleeping beauty. Every trace of the witch was long gone. Now, she looked more like the young woman in Nick's memories from before the fall.

Pree paced back and forth as she bounced a swaddled baby in her arms. "It's about time you two got here."

I quirked my brow at her, gesturing to the baby.

"I know, I'm just as confused as you are, but somehow Nolan convinced me to help her." Pree tipped her chin at Mara. "And, well, I do love babies." She smiled down at the sleeping infant in her hands.

I attempted to peak into the little bundle, but Pree edged out of the way. "Don't you dare. I just got her to sleep."

"I was only going to look!" I pouted.

"Uh huh. And if your breath tickled her cheek or nose?"

"Well, if the volume of your voice hasn't woken her yet..."

Will scratched the back of his neck. "I don't think now is really the time, ladies."

If Pree had any Watcher giftings in her, I'm pretty sure she would have zapped my husband with her laser eyes.

Mara coughed, drawing our attention to her, and her eyes fluttered a little. "Nicholas?" she rasped.

"I am right here." He came to her bedside, kneeled, and collected her small hand in both of his.

She smiled but winced with the effort.

Nick frowned. "There are some people here who would like to see you."

Mara opened her eyes halfway and blinked slowly. "No." She closed her eyes.

"No?" Nick asked, confused.

"I cannot ask them." Mara forced the words out, her voice weak and barely audible.

Nick's face was stricken, pinched in pain.

I studied her. What I felt was not pride. It was as if she had made up her mind that we would say no and take away any hope she had.

"You can and you will." I stepped toward the foot of the

bed, emboldened.

"Why?" she croaked. "So you can have the pleasure of saying no to me and watching me suffer in my final hours?" She grimaced. "I would deserve it, but if you don't mind, I don't feel like hearing it."

"Yes. You do deserve that, and you will hear it whether you like it or not. But in terms of taking pleasure from your pain? Don't you dare confuse me with Melchior, and I am not your mother. And I sure as heck am not you."

Pree gasped and Will grabbed my elbow.

Mara's eyes snapped open at my words, but I continued.

"You messed up, big time. You tortured me for over a decade, tried to kill me multiple times, and broke a lot of families when you stole their children."

Mara winced. "Go on...seems like you have a lot to say. I'm *dying* to hear it."

Pree let out a snort of laughter but quickly composed herself and pressed her lips together when I turned to look at her.

"I do have a lot to say," I began, my voice firm. "You don't deserve Will and me to be here to help heal you. But...your daughter does. The people who clearly love you do too, or you would have been dead a long time ago." I gave Nick a pointed look, and he smirked but avoided my gaze. "And since I love the people who love you, I don't want to see them hurt more than they already are."

Mara's eyes widened, and she turned her head to Nick, her movement appearing more like a flop of the head. "Is she saying what I think she's saying?"

Nick reached out and cradled her cheek. Unable to speak,

he nodded instead.

Will straightened and crossed his arms, leveling her with a glare. "Liddy and I offer our healing services. In exchange, you will never threaten my wife, our children, or my family again. In fact, never again will you hurt another living being."

Mara closed her eyes, and a tear trickled down her cheek. "I never wanted to harm anyone. I haven't been in control of myself for the longest time. And then, the times I was in control, the guilt became too much. It's been easier to ignore it and make excuses."

I, for one, was not expecting her candor. No one said anything. What could we even say? We couldn't possibly comprehend what it was like to have the essence of a powerful object stuck in us for decades.

"Right. Shall we get started?" I asked.

Nick popped up from his chair and knocked three times on the door. Nolan and Shai promptly entered the room while Pree walked the baby into the hall. But before she could close the door entirely, it opened again.

"Charlie!" Will pulled his brother into a bear hug.

Charlie smiled and patted Will's back. "I wanted to be here for this. Mind if I lend a hand?" He glanced at Nolan, who was about to inject a needle into Mara's arm.

Nolan nodded and held out the device as Charlie made his way to the side of the bed.

"Hi, Mara." He smiled at her.

"Hi, Jai... I mean, Charlie." She smiled back weakly at him.

His smile turned into a knowing smirk. "I have always believed that an incredibly sweet woman was trapped under a curse, and I wanted to be here to help her defeat the monster."

Well, shoot. The waterworks were flowing throughout the room.

"I don't deserve your kindness." Mara hiccupped through tears.

"Ah, but who in this world deserves anything?" Charlie winked at her, found the spot he'd injected her so many times before, and inserted the needle.

Nick leveled us with his stare. "Will, Liddy...be diligent. Do not hesitate."

We nodded our understanding.

Nolan held the brilliant white Christmas rose that sparkled without any visible light source. With a swift move, he slid the needle on the opposite end of the tube into the base of its stem. Shai unstoppered the vial, held it over the rose, and tapped it a few times with his index finger. The dust sprinkled over its soft petals, and at first nothing happened. Then, the rose began to move, almost like it was breathing. Its petals expanded and retracted repeatedly, creating a mesmerizing effect.

I watched in fascination as thick, black sludge traveled down the tube toward the rose.

"It's time," Will whispered into my ear before turning me to face him. He leaned down and pressed his lips to mine. I relished the warmth that spread through me, all of me igniting at once. Breaking away from the kiss, I wrapped my arms around my husband, savoring the moment.

Channeling all of my giftings into him, he directed our light to Mara, and she gasped at the contact.

"Amazing," she breathed. But we weren't finished.

We used our hands to trace the paths of the poison that had vacated milliseconds prior, mending the damaged parts and shoring up those that were weakened.

The process took longer than expected, but eventually, every last drop of poison was drawn out and absorbed by the Christmas rose. As we watched, its petals swirled from white to black and back to white again, now with marble-like black streaks throughout. We held our breaths, hoping our theory was right.

The Christmas rose began to wilt and shrivel, its tips drying and turning brown before breaking off and floating away on a tiny dust cloud. Nolan yanked it out of the soil and placed it in a glass container, where it crumbled to ash.

Turns out, we were correct. For darkness cannot survive in the light.

Mara: Oh Snap

IT HAD BEEN A FEW DAYS since the poisonous magic was extracted from my body, and due to the unsuitable weather, I decided to take Nicole for a walk in the arboretum. I couldn't help but feel a tinge of guilt, knowing that I was the reason for this and so many other repugnant things that happened to Cristes.

I longed for the green, lush landscape that had once defined Cristes. I yearned for the sun and thick humid air that I could practically swim in. For too long, darkness had surrounded me, hiding in the deep caverns of a horrid place that I had unintentionally created with my magic.

I will fix this before I leave, I thought to myself, the idea both thrilling and a little depressing.

"What troubles you?" Nicholas asked as he approached

me. It struck me how handsome he looked, nearly stealing my breath.

I surveyed my surroundings, hyper-aware of the many eyes fixated on me. The soldiers that trailed my every move tried to remain hidden, yet their presence loomed over me. The citizens of Cristes still harbored a deep fear of me, and I could feel the weight of it with every passing moment. As for others, the acrid bitterness of their animosity permeated the air as they crossed my path.

I snapped my fingers, and everyone around me besides Nicholas and Nicole froze in place. They wouldn't remember what happened and it wouldn't hurt them.

I glanced at Nick. "I am sad because I cannot stay here."

Nicholas's face fell. "Sure you can," he pleaded, his voice laced with sadness. The depth of his heartbreak was tangible, and I couldn't bear to see him in such agony.

I cupped his cheek with my palm, shaking my head in resignation. "While your family and friends may have offered me grace, too many others would still seek to see me burn at the stake for my crimes against this beautiful country."

Nicholas made to protest, but I placed a finger over his mouth to shush him.

"You cannot argue that po—"

He tried to talk again, but I shook my head with a sad smile.

"No, you cannot simply say that, as their king, they have to 'get over it'."

Nick moved my hand from his mouth but did not let go of me. "I am no king."

"I have no desire to live the rest of my days as an outcast, forever walking on eggshells around people who may or may not have forgiven me. I've lived too many of my years feeling unwanted and used by those around me. I refuse to live that way again." I needed to forge a new path for myself.

"I don't want to lose you. Not when I've only *just* gotten you back," he whispered, nearly choking on a sob.

"I don't want to lose you either," I confessed, standing so close to Nicholas that I could feel the warmth of his breath on my forehead. "But we both know the people deserve justice and that I must face the consequences for the harm I've caused."

"But it wasn't you who did those things," Nick urged. "It was the poison."

"Does it matter?" I blinked at him. "Nicholas, it's the only way to move forward."

Nick stayed quiet, but his hands fidgeted with the chains of his vest, his nervous energy nearly rubbing off on me and silencing the hard truth I needed to share.

I lowered my gaze. "I can't look at you when I confess this next part, because I don't know how you will react. But a long time ago, you were brave enough to confide in me, and I must be courageous enough to do the same with you."

I breathed in the familiar scent of him, pine and snow and cinnamon, and the heavenly blend nearly melted me. "A long time ago, I was a young girl who was lost and hurting with no self-worth. I truly didn't believe I was good enough for you. It was my first mistake, which prompted so many bad decisions in its wake."

Nicholas stood strong, his muscles taut, but I knew he was listening, for his arms came around me and secured me in their strength.

"Despite all the bad decisions I've made, they led me on this outrageous journey and taught me so much," I said, my voice trembling. "I now know how precious love and life are. And Nicholas, you once told me you would always choose love. Well, from now on, I'm going to be brave enough to do the same."

I took a deep breath, gathering my courage. "So, here goes. I'm in love with you, Nicholas. I have been since the moment you pulled me out of that cave and breathed life into me. And ever since, you've never ceased fighting for me, rescuing me from danger. I am sorry it took me so long to both admit it to myself and confess it to you. But the truth is, I have always loved you."

Nicholas was silent and unmoving for so long I began to question myself, fearing that I'd unintentionally frozen him. Was I going to have to repeat myself, feeling the same fear and vulnerability all over again?

"Nicholas... Nick!" I lightly tugged on his arm.

A slow smile crept onto his face, and his eyes twinkled. "You love me?"

I heaved a heavy sigh and rolled my eyes at him. Then I drew up close, rose to my tippy toes, and lightly pressed my lips to his.

Epilogue: About 5 Years Later
Christmas at Nick and Mara's

"**K**ING WILLIAM, QUEEN LYDIA, please come in!" Nolan greeted us at the base of the new Arbolias tree. Now when we portaled in for a visit to Mortalia, instead of entering at Nick's hobbit hole—as Pree used to say—we entered the basement of Shai's former mansion.

As we stepped out from the tree, I was struck by its beauty. "Nolan, it's incredible!" I exclaimed, marveling at the countless glowing ornaments that floated all around its foliage like stars. It was a sight that filled my heart with joy, a reminder of the magic of Christmas and what it meant to Cristes.

"Thank you, Your Maj—"

"Nolan! My man!" Will cut in, forgoing formalities and

giving Nolan such a big hug, the man's feet lifted off the floor.

As soon as Will released him, he was assaulted. "Unkie Nolan!" The twins cried out in unison as they charged at him, each attaching themselves to one of his legs.

"Can I take your coat, my queen?" Nolan asked, grunting against the tiny attack yet still bowing to me in Cristes tradition.

I shrugged out of my coat, my newest baby bump on full display, and draped it over the coat rack myself.

"You know you don't need to use our titles when addressing us. You're family." I smiled.

"Old habits." Nolan chuckled as he walked in big strides, giving the twins a ride.

"Ella Rose... Charles John, please get off of Nolan."

"Uh oh," Will said. "Mommy middle-named you. You better do as you are told."

"But Mooom!" Ella whined.

Nolan bent his head to look at them. "You two have grown so much. Guess what? Everyone is waiting for you upstairs, and I even baked your favorite Christmas cookies."

The twins nearly collided with each other as they ran for the elevator.

"Wait for me!" Will raced after them.

"How are you feeling?" Nolan asked me.

I rubbed my swollen belly. "This one has been a little easier on me than the twins. Only a few months left to go. We'll get to meet this little princess before we know it."

Nolan and I walked to the elevator. Will had somehow miraculously held it open while keeping the impatient kiddos from pressing all the buttons.

After Mara fixed the break in the dome that protected Cristes, it took a little over a year for the land to fully thaw. Nick and Mara had already left for Mortalia permanently and took up residence in Shai's mansion, which was now their permanent home.

Years later, Cristes was the landscape I experienced years ago via Nick's memories. The home my heart always longed for when I knew this world wasn't meant for me.

Nick gave up his crown, as he always said he would, and chose love. His parents spent years training Will and me to ascend the throne. And a few months ago, they retired from their positions of leadership.

So how did Nick and Mara wind up in Shai's former mansion? After Mara confessed her love for him, they married in a private ceremony and left Cristes with Nicole to live a mortal life. Well, more mortal than in Cristes. Nolan, with Ruth's help, had perfected libations that kept them from aging too quickly. Eventually, when the humans would start to notice, they had plans to move into Lana and Brantley's Florida home.

Me, Will, and the twins have been coming to visit them every Christmas since they left Cristes.

While taking the short ride up, I asked Nolan, "So, how is Ruth?" To say I was shocked that Ruth and Nolan were married was an understatement. They both took their jobs very seriously, but Ruth didn't want to be without Nolan any longer and knew he desired to stay with Nick in Mortalia.

The elevator doors *dinged* and slid open.

"Ella, Charles! Get over here and give your titi a hug!" Pree yelled from the family room. Charlie stood next to her, his arm wrapped around her waist, his nose nuzzled into her neck. They had gotten married a little over a year ago, twice. Once in Mortalia, and once in Cristes.

"Ewww, Unkie Charlie, no one wants to see all that kissing," Ella admonished her uncle. My children ran to Pree, nearly knocking over the robust, beautifully decorated Christmas tree they stood near.

Charlie crinkled his nose and smiled at her. "So don't look, Miss Sassy."

Ella stuck her tongue out at him. He dramatically sucked in a breath, "That's it! I'm gonna get you!" Ella ran, squealing as Charlie chased her.

Little Charles was already playing with the train under the tree.

"How is the children's home doing?" I asked my friend. She and Charlie had become liaisons for Cristes, spending half their time in Mortalia and the other half back home in Cristes. Charlie and Pree had worked closely together the entire first year after the war, ensuring that every child Mara had kidnapped had been fully restored to their home.

We'd discovered that Mara had chosen children with bloodline ties to Cristes. Each human child had the opportunity to return home or stay in Cristes. It was a lot of work, wiping memories and creating false memories to reintegrate the children back into their normal lives, but Charlie and Pree worked tirelessly to make it a reality.

Pree and Charlie also acted as liaisons between Cristes and Mortalia. They helped oversee all Watchers who were once again tasked with traveling between realms to collect Christmas roses and study the realm. Christmas Eve was always a busy time. Alex was actually their full-time employee in Mortalia, and he would try to stop by later that night once all Watchers were accounted for and on their way back to Cristes.

"It's wonderful! Our fundraiser last month provided more than enough to keep the facilities going strong for at least three years."

Nolan handed each of us a full champagne glass.

"That is wonderful news!" I celebrated with her, clinking my glass of sparkling grape juice against hers. "Will you be staying in Cristes again before the baby is born?"

"Of course! I wouldn't miss meeting my new niece," Pree answered.

"How are Dani and Sara?" I asked, taking a sip of the fizzy drink. Dani and Sara didn't know about Watchers; Pree and I felt it best to keep them in the dark about it all. To their knowledge, I was living out a real Princess Diaries experience. They believed that Will had traveled here undercover and that he was actually a prince of a small, unknown country, and I was now his queen.

Pree flicked her curled locks over her shoulder. "They're doing great. Sara and Matt completed renovations on their home in time for Thanksgiving, and I think family planning is on the horizon. Dani's salon had a soft opening last week. She had a great turnout. Plus, I think her beau is going to pop the question soon."

The entire Jameson family, in addition to Nick and his parents, were all pivotal in helping to restore me and Pree back to human society. That meant that no one remembered we'd vanished. Instead, they believed in a new memory.

It went something like this: I graduated early, and it was super top-secret because I was becoming a princess. Pree came with me because I could only bring one person, and she insisted. No one seemed to have any trouble believing *that*.

The doorbell rang and a few moments later, Justin, my parents, and my not-so-little brother, Mickey, entered the family room, escorted by Nolan. Ruth was stunning on Nolan's arm, wearing a formal red dress, though I was still getting used to seeing her without her white coat.

"Mom, Dad!" I exclaimed as I greeted them both with a warm hug. My parents were fully in the know about everything. They took it reasonably well and only asked like a million questions. We also had to keep reassuring them to not feel guilty about dismissing my nightmares.

"Liddy, my beautiful daughter. You are positively glowing," Mom gushed.

Dad kissed my cheek. "Now, where are those gorgeous grandbabies of mine?" He walked off with Mom in search of the twins.

"Hey, Mickey. You ready to graduate high school?" Will asked, coming up behind me and rubbing my shoulders.

"Totally. Sitting still, being talked at all day long is so boring," he complained.

"How is baseball going?" Will inquired. "You training hard?"

"Yes! Justin has been a huge help. I can't believe he lets me train with the Cubs sometimes!"

Justin no longer suffered from PTSD. Though Nick offered to alter his memories, he didn't want that. But he did accept our help in clearing his name. He regained his baseball scholarship, graduated college in three years, and was picked in the first-round draft by the Chicago Cubs. Sports enthusiasts believed he would help lead them to the world series, a feat that had not been accomplished in the past century.

Nolan came into the family room and rang a little gold bell. "Dinner is now served. Please follow me to the dining room."

We walked down the spacious hallway and I smiled, remembering my reaction to this place when I'd first stepped foot here. Will squeezed my hand and leaned in. "Maybe we can sneak away to my old room after dinner and have our dessert up there." His devious smirk that highlighted his dimple still set my cheeks to flaming hot after all this time.

A loud commotion behind us had us all whipping around. Uncle Shai was draped with children. Nicole was on his back with Ella and Charles hanging off his arms and Gauge, Mara and Nick's son, was upside-down, clinging to his leg. His gorgeous redheaded fiancée, **Noeleen,** giggled by his side.

As soon as I was first introduced to her last year, I remembered Noeleen from my time spent in Nick's memories. She was the girl at the dance club who wrote her number across Shai's chest. Apparently, she waited for him after all this time, for they were a fated match. They were getting married in the spring.

We arrived in the dining room and I marveled at its beauty. I recalled Nolan making Valentine's Day extra special for me and my friends.

"Nolan, you really outdid yourself this year!"

"Actually, my queen, it was Mara who decorated this year."

As if she heard her name, Mara sauntered into the dining room with Nick, Lana, and Brantley on her heels. They all wore aprons and carried sizable serving dishes.

I kept expecting to see Queen Nicole and King William, but they spent every Christmas in Cristes. The main reason was to ensure that someone in power watched over our people. Also, they hated the cold, and so they always visited Nick and Mara for an extended time in the early summer.

We all took our seats at the dining table that seated eighteen, and all the kiddos wedged between their parents.

Nick spoke first. "We wanted to thank you all for continuing our tradition and spending another Christmas with us. May Eira bless each and every one of you in this season of harvest and in the new year to come." He held up his glass, and we each reached for our own. "To our friends and family who mean the world to us, we love you. Merry Christmas."

"Merry Christmas," we all responded in unison.

Everyone sat except for Mara. "I know I say this every year, but in case you all have forgotten since last time, thank you, from the bottom of my heart, thank you for saving me..." She eyed her husband and then me and Will. "And for giving me a second chance. I am forever, eternally, grateful. To love and grace!" She lifted her glass.

"Saludic!" we all cheered.

After dinner and presents, we lounged around in the grand family room, swapping stories and happy memories. The kids were all passed out, one in a box, two on the couch, and one in Mara's lap.

As I gazed about the room taking it all in, I started to glow with happiness. I laid back against Will's chest, my belly satisfied and my mind content.

"What are you glowing for?" he murmured as he played with my hair, though he knew exactly why. He could feel it.

"This." I gestured around the room. "All of this. We are so rich...rich in friends, in health, in family, and in love. We are truly blessed. I don't think I'll ever stop glowing."

"Good, because you were made to shine." He placed a kiss on my temple.

"Mommy?" Charles croaked, his little voice gruff with sleep. "Will you sing for us?"

"Did Daddy tell you to ask that?" I quirked a brow.

Little Charles closed his eyes and smiled sleepily, snuggling his head against one of the throw pillows. I shot a bemused glance at Will, who suddenly found the ceiling very interesting.

Soon, a chorus of song requests echoed throughout the room.

"Fine!" I sighed dramatically. "But only if you all sing along with me, because I'm pregnant and tired." Everyone laughed and agreed, though Pree insisted I start things off.

Nervous? Will's voice popped into my head.

I smiled and reached for his hand, giving it a little squeeze. *No,* I assured him. *Not any more.*

My time in Cristes had helped me overcome much of my performance anxiety, reminding me it was a gift meant to be shared. So this time, I didn't delay opening my mouth to bless the others. I lifted my voice, loud and clear, my gifting tugging on the heartstrings of every person in the room. One by one, they all joined in, our voices ringing in harmony.

And for those of us who could, we glowed brighter than the ten thousand lights on the fourteen-foot Christmas tree.

Life certainly can be unfair and unjust. But it can also be beautiful and amazing. One thing is for certain; you cannot have light without the dark. And I would travel through the darkest of shadows all over again to be here, at this moment, having found the gift of light within the people surrounding me.

The End

Acknowledgments

My readers - Thank you for sticking with me through the TWITE trilogy. Your unwavering support and patience in waiting for its conclusion have been such a gift. I have been deeply touched by your excitement, private messages, reviews, social media posts, and comments. They have encouraged me to keep pushing through the challenges of writing and publishing, especially with my health being a huge obstacle.

Special thanks to Erin - We made it! I had English spellings instead of US, wonky sentence structure, incorrect word usage, too much detail, too little detail... the list goes on. Thank you for helping make this a story my readers can actually read while preserving my voice! Your turn!

Julia - You may think that all those writing sprints I encouraged you to do were only for your benefit. Let me tell you... I wouldn't have finished book 3 without them! I am grateful for your patience in listening to my indecisive ramblings and providing helpful feedback and support.

My dear friends - For the random telegram messages where I poll you with questions. Thanks for answering without hesitation and for your support.

My Family - For years I have been trying to balance the demands of my chronic illness while homeschooling, being a mom, friend, and wife, and running a podcast that is trying to change the literary world. I get told often, I don't know how you do it! To be honest, it's because of all of you! You are my support and my cheerleaders.

After this release, I plan to take a little break to really invest back into my family the way they have invested in me. I also need to focus on my health. Don't worry, I have plenty more stories which I will definitely write, but part of a balancing act is knowing when to sprint ahead and when to pull back. Now is a season for pulling back. Visit www.lauradetering.com to get my newsletter or visit my socials @authorlauradetering so we can stay in touch.